Everything Happens for a Reason

PRAISE FOR *EVERYTHING HAPPENS FOR A REASON*

'Emotionally engaging, witty, clever and wonderfully satisfying'
Daily Express

'A stunning debut ... a wise, moving, and thought-provoking novel'
Susan Elliot Wright, author of *The Flight of Cornelia Blackwood*

'Very few authors can be funny and break your heart at the same
time, but Katie Allen is one. *Everything Happens for a Reason* is a
beautiful novel, bursting with raw, emotional honesty and
authenticity. It's a book that will take you on a compelling journey
through grief and survival, then haunt you long after you turn the
last page' Gill Paul, author of *The Secret Wife*

'So affecting. Profoundly sad. Funny. I just loved it'
Louise Beech, author of *This Is How We Are Human*

'Darkly funny, yet poignant and moving, this is one of those books
that gets under your skin. A brutally honest portrayal of grief,
Rachel's quest to find out if everything happens for a reason is both
heartbreaking and heartwarming. Full of memorable characters
and written in a clever way, I couldn't put it down'
Anna Bell, author of *In Case You Missed It*

'Some books teach you, others touch your soul ... then there are
books like this one that bury deep and create a home in your heart.
A touching, moving and emotional debut'
Emma-Claire Wilson, *Glass House Magazine*

'You'll laugh, you'll cry … you'll finish this book, set it aside and wonder at the honesty, and empathy of this writer. *Everything Happens for a Reason* deserves a massive audience'
Michael J Malone, author of *A Song of Isolation*

'Quirky yet insightful, bright yet wistful, amusing yet emotional … full of contradictions that fuse into the most surprising, moving, and beautiful novel' Liz Robinson, LoveReading

'Allen masterfully balances tragedy and humour in this vital story about making sense of the profoundly nonsensical – the death of a baby. This is also a book about human – and animal – connections and how they can shape us and make us, as well as misshape and break us. I'm so glad she wrote this, and hope it throws light on a grief that is still relegated to the shadows'
Julia Bueno author of *The Brink of Being*

'A captivating insight into life after loss. Providing a different, yet incredibly honest, perspective of a mother's journey. Insightful, witty and humbling'
Jenny Mison, Midwife and Founder of @thebirthingbible

'Heart-rending, honest and humorous; I've never read anything like it before. So thought-provoking and poignant, it's a completely wonderful debut and highly recommended reading'
The Book Magnet

'*Everything Happens for a Reason* is the bittersweet story of a grieving but courageous woman trying to make sense of the cards she's been dealt. Funny, sad, thought-provoking, I had an absolutely brilliant time with Rachel'
From Belgium with Booklove

'Katie has woven a beautiful story of loss and hope, in such a constructive and sublime way ... absolutely life-affirming'
The Reading Closet

'Heartbreaking and emotional ... Katie Allen has written a portrait of a woman in the midst of profound grief that is raw, truthful and immensely powerful but which makes you laugh even as you cry and which ultimately leaves you with hope. I really liked Rachel and I loved this book' Live & Deadly

'Witty, heartbreaking, charming, disruptive and human ... it stays with you long after you close the cover' Live Many Lives

'When you realise who the emails are addressed to, it hits like a hammer blow ... At times, it's very funny indeed – there's a thread of quite perfect observational humour, driven by the strength of the book's characters. I was quite blown away by this wonderful debut. It's very different, incredibly powerful, intense and emotional – but also a sheer joy to read, and entirely unforgettable'
Being Anne

'Honest, uncompromising ... both witty and emotional. It illustrates moments of hope and moments of despair. It is a book that lingers in the mind, and one which many will be able to empathise with' Jen Med's Book Reviews

'*Everything Happens for a Reason* is a raw, honest portrayal of coping with loss ... A unique, darkly witty read that, despite the subject matter, will make you feel warm and uplifted' Karen's Reads

'One of the best books I've read for a while ... well thought out, believable, sad, funny and shocking' Helen the Bassist

'A heartbreaking story packed with emotion, but let us not forget the humour that is in the storyline as well ... an incredible debut novel that I will not forget' The Last Word Book Reviews

WHAT THE READERS ARE SAYING...

★ ★ ★ ★ ★

'Wonderfully written, darkly funny and will keep you engrossed'

'A wonderful cast of characters, and told with heart and more than a spark of humour. I really enjoyed it'

'Raw, truthful and immensely powerful'

'Felt like an emotional rollercoaster reading this. So well written and everything explained and described beautifully'

'A gem of a book that tackles a tough subject with real skill and will touch you in unexpected ways'

'There are some interesting twists and turns as the novel reaches its conclusion and a few moments of tension that surprised me. I will remember this novel and these characters for some time'

'Few people can deliver a beautiful story portraying something as sad and hurtful as the loss of a child, and yet that's what the author does here'

'This is a very touching, wonderfully written book'

'The characters are so well written you feel as though you are there with them'

'A very sensitive subject ... totally heartbreaking but so beautifully written'

'Sensitively addresses the subject of still birth'

'This was a truly heart-warming tear-jerker ... it touched my heart'

'What a beautiful book ... the novel way this was written – through emails from Rachel to her stillborn baby boy – brought a personal and insightful view to the story. Quirky, thought-provoking, heartbreaking, but fantastic'

'Beautiful. Thought-provoking. Sad. Eye-opening. I finished this book and genuinely wasn't sure what to do with myself. A beautifully written book about such a sensitive topic'

'What a heartfelt book ... my first from this author, but not my last'

ABOUT THE AUTHOR

Everything Happens for a Reason is Katie's first novel. She used to be a journalist and columnist at the *Guardian* and *Observer*, and started her career as a Reuters correspondent in Berlin and London. The events in *Everything Happens for a Reason* are fiction, but the premise is loosely autobiographical. Katie's son, Finn, was stillborn in 2010, and her character's experience of grief and being on maternity leave without a baby is based on her own. And yes, someone did say to her 'everything happens for a reason'.

Katie grew up in Warwickshire and now lives in South London with her husband, children, dog, cat and stick insects. When she's not writing or walking children and dogs, Katie loves baking, playing the piano, reading news and wishing she had written other people's brilliant novels.

Follow Katie on Twitter @KtAllenWriting and on her website: katieallenauthor.com.

Everything Happens

for a Reason

KATIE ALLEN

Orenda Books
16 Carson Road
West Dulwich
London SE21 8HU
www.orendabooks.co.uk

First published in the United Kingdom by Orenda Books, 2021
Copyright © Katie Allen, 2021

A catalogue record for this book is available from the British Library.

ISBN 978-1-913193-61-4
eISBN 978-1-913193-62-1

Typeset in Garamond by www.typesetter.org.uk

Printed and bound by CPI Group (UK) Ltd, Croydon CR0 4YY

For sales and distribution, please contact info@orendabooks.co.uk

Everything Happens for a Reason

For Finn and all my family

To: LRS_17@outlook.com
Fri 17/2, 09:15
SUBJECT: *What now?*

I know what's going to happen. You see it too. I'm colouring in too
hard, over and over the same patch, and the paper's falling apart.

I go round and round that day, the night, and the morning. I reach
the end, go back to the start, do it four times, five, more. It takes
hours, and sometimes minutes, depends what you include. I take
different starting points – here, the taxi, the room – but I always go
to the end. Sometimes a detail emerges, like that toddler pressing all
the buttons in the lift and how we went down before we went up. It
doesn't help. I can't make myself believe it, I don't want to believe it.
It doesn't make sense.

They get that too. Everyone – well, not everyone. Most of them.
They call (I don't pick up), they text to say how bad they feel for me,
how sorry, how awful it must be. You know, telling me what I should
feel but at the same time careful to say they can't imagine how I feel.
All that energy poured into imagining something that they don't
want to be able to imagine or don't want to tell me they can imagine
or at least they imagine I don't want them to imagine or to imagine
them imagining. See? I'm going fucking mad here.

Sorry, inappropriate.

Hang on, the door's about to go. Van's stopping on the double
yellows, it'll be for me.

To: LRS_17@outlook.com
Mon 20/2, 18:38
SUBJECT: *Invasion*

Sorry, gone longer than I meant.

If you're reading these, you'll be wondering what I've been up to.

I have that effect on people. Will from Continuity called last week, asked, 'What do you do all day?' I told him laundry – which is true. No one tells you how helpful sadness is for staying on top of housework. I have a system: socks in one load, hang them in their pairs; T-shirts in another, iron while damp. It's bad for the polar bears, but they'd understand. Two hours too late, I came up with a better line for Will. I'll have it to hand next time: 'All those little jobs I've been meaning to do for years.' If pressed, I'll say, 'Gutters, the loft, sorting photos.' They'll know I'm busy and productive and everyone will be happy.

But because it's you, I can tell you I haven't started on the gutters (too wet). The loft is not something I can do on my own and the photos would set me back months – there are 10,543 and each photo costs me an average of four minutes' preoccupation. ('That row about that driver'; 'Never again dungarees'; 'Did we know that's the happiest we'd ever be?')

What do I do? The last few days have just gone. But I can't say what with, apart from a socks and pants cycle.

I can tell you how it started though. With an invasion.

I was right, the florist van was for me. Jean and Tim, my mother's friends. You don't know them.

I was still behind the front door, picking out bits of rosemary added by some hipster florist, when the letterbox clattered open. He's a light-footed creep, that postman.

To be fair, the post's helpful. It gives the day shape. Washing machine on, coffee, post, empty machine, hang, iron. Routine's important.

If you were into that kind of thing, you could use the post to measure how much time has passed. At the start, it was almost all cards. Now, nearly three weeks on – two weeks and five days – the cards are thinning out. We're back to bills and bank statements. Except today, along with an insurance renewal for Lester and something from the taxman, sorry, tax person, there was a card. That's what it looked like at least. I won't bore you with what a Trojan horse is, but that's what it was. Innocuous magnolia envelope, murderous contents.

I pieced together the Bristol postmark and the handwriting – biro, bulges on the a's, b's and d's, like an elephant had sat on them. Liz.

Liz is on the you've-left-it-far-too-long list, along with cousin Jools, two women in Outreach and Vic from primary school.

I'm not unreasonable. I know some people were on holiday, or out of stamps. Some late arrivals managed to make it off the left-it-far-too-long list. But the deadline's passed for the rest. Each day they stayed silent, they made you smaller.

I stare at Liz's magnolia-clad appeal for clemency lying on the table. The kitchen table. I stopped to make coffee.

I should have known. Why expect maturity from someone who dots her i's with a daisy.

You can tell I'm stalling. I might as well tell you. Explains the three-day silence. And like I said, no one likes a long silence.

I tear the envelope – easily, it's cheap paper. Inside is a single postcard.

And this is the stupid bit, I pull it out without thinking. I drop it. It lands face up on the table, and it's too late to look away. Its glassy little eyes stare up at me.

Who the fuck sends a picture of a newborn baby to a grieving mother?

To: LRS_17@outlook.com
Mon 20/2, 19:20
SUBJECT: Plan

Didn't mean to leave you with that. He came in, with daffodils, and he doesn't know about this. You know who. But I'm not going to give him that name. There's no value in spelling this out – you of all people should see that. Let's just call him E.

I've put him a chicken tikka in. I ate earlier. Routine.

People underestimate the power of structure. You watch them making up dinner on the fly or setting off without checking the trains, packing the day of a flight. Take Callum in Creativity, aka Mr Sorry-it's-all-I've-got-in. Started with him serving up Bolognese with rice, then he's eating cereal with apple juice and Sally walks out when he brings her a coffee with yoghurt stirred in. Next comes the mental breakdown and they think you need a Harley Street head doctor to work it out.

I've made a plan for us. It's a simple one – two strands: I tell you what I've been up to, and I give you some pointers on what you should be up to. It's amazing how many charts there are, targets, timelines, all sorts. Like now, for instance, you should be able to recognise me.

To: LRS_17@outlook.com
Mon 20/2, 21:47
SUBJECT: Unsure

E's gone to bed early. I'm waiting to take biscuits out of the oven, ginger and vanilla. No, not together. Two trays, one vanilla, one ginger, because I'm becoming someone who doesn't know what they think or want.

The daffodils started it. 'But they're your favourites,' says E.
'Were.'

The ones outside our hospital window were early, mixed in with snowdrops. My mother says the same thing every year when they appear – 'Start of new starts' – and she brings out her three daffodil tea towels, puts away the primrose ones. Bluebells come next.

They'll be gone by the time we go back for the post-mortem.

To: LRS_17@outlook.com
Tues 21/2, 11:54
SUBJECT: *Before-and-after markers*

E called and said I have to remember to eat, so I went to the deli on the edge of the common, the one with rocky road.

It's when I see the sign – the way they've made the U in Lou's Beans look like a cup – that I feel it. Like being lighter, a sort of ease. If you want an image, there's this advert for incontinence pads (nappies for grown-ups). A sixty-something woman running along a beach behind a Dalmatian like neither of them will ever tire.

For a minute, that's what it was like. Because the last time I walked up that road, waited at that crossing and walked in to order a decaf skinny latte, you were with me. I knew where I was going and I would never tire.

I queued for a minute then left without ordering. The lightness had worn off. I can't be there anymore, because nothing's the same, is it? I could do that walk again and again, I could use that same non-biological washing powder and put on the same playlist – a mix of Mozart and Miles Davis compiled for your benefit – but any illusion of before will be just that. The walk's all different anyway, the trees are full of white blossom. Can you see them?

Everything's segmented by these moments that I'll call before-and-after markers. The hospital is one. The markers fall, splay themselves out on your timeline like a body across a train track, and nothing is the same. There's no crossing back over a marker. Or the only going back is the cruel kind, like this morning, a glimpse of before on a walk to a coffee shop.

And the markers bring on physical symptoms. Not just the avoidance tactics you'd expect: the deli, medical dramas, E. But symptoms inside me.

Take this one: I call it phrasal retentiveness. It's like someone built a library in my head and I now store away every trite phrase, every text message, every ad slogan. (The incontinence one, by the way, is 'laugh like everyone's watching.' Which comes from 'dance like nobody's watching', which in my brain has turned into 'load the dishwasher like nobody's watching', because there are upsides to being alone.)

It's all exacerbated by the fact that in the after, everyone only ever speaks to me in old borrowed phrases, scared to improvise. It's all 'deepest sympathy', 'thoughts and prayers' and 'anything you need'.

I hear them once and they are there forever, stuck on repeat and word perfect. Sounds useful, doesn't it? No doubt a career in the intelligence services beckons. But for now, the phrases are all I have for company and they're crap at it.

You need examples, don't you?

We'll start with Bristol Liz. Yes, the glassy-eyed little creature on the card was hers. Did she even tell me she was pregnant?

Once I was breathing again, I turned his face away. On the other side, she and Tom were delighted to announce the arrival of their predictably named little boy, Max. Italics proclaimed 'our little family has gotten [sic] eight pounds heavier'. She'd had them sent from home.

At the foot of the card, the elated new mother had managed to scrawl *Hey, Hope you're well, Liz xxx.*

Hope you're well. Really? How do you think I am? Never better, so well I'm running a marathon in memory of basic fucking manners.

To be fair, Liz almost certainly does hope I'm well. Everyone does. Not because they particularly care, they just want life to resume, or never to be disrupted in the first place. In the world of baby showers and families putting on eight pounds, there's no place for our story.

Stupid phrasal retentiveness. 'Hey, hope you're well' is unstoppable. Sometimes I hear it in her transatlantic squawk, sometimes in my voice and sometimes in the Bristol accent of a gentrified cider farmer drawing out the you'rrre.

This is how it will be now. Haunted by other people's clumsy words. Liz's 'hey, hope you're well' and the likes of 'when will you try again?' and 'at least he didn't suffer.' Sorry, you didn't need to hear that one.

To: LRS_17@outlook.com
Tues 21/2, 15:57
SUBJECT: Weakness

E's going to be late, 'lots to catch up on'. Catch up from what? He never stopped working. Bad timing, big campaign, he said. Shouty Americans keep calling in the middle of our night. He puts them on speakerphone to make me laugh. It's all 'sunset the old branding', 'hit kids hard with this', 'those drones won't launch themselves'.

He'll stay late, go on for a quick drink, then another. 'Come and join us,' he said on the phone.

'They don't want me in the way,' I said.

'They'd love to see you.'

'Another time,' I said. 'Don't rush back. It'll do you good.'

Don't blame yourself, he was like this before, says it's part of the job, 'the industry'. You're the excuse to take it to extremes. The excuse he can't talk about. And if he were here, what would I say to him? After what I did to us.

I was left with the consolation of ironed pyjamas and toast without crusts in front of the TV (sound mostly off for fear of the phrases). That was the plan. But because she always senses these moments, my mother calls.

I ignore her first two attempts and give in on the third.

'Napping? It's Tuesday. Come to prayer night,' she says.

She deploys her usual lines: 'It's just what you need, Pebble', 'a place to reflect', 'friendly faces'.

I picture the friendly faces as medical students gathering round a bed to gawp at me, their worst car-crash victim yet. Their heads tip to one side, they try to smile but can't mask their inner 'Oh, shit! You're a mess.'

But it's intriguing – more so than *The One Show*, which let itself down last night by dedicating a full ten minutes to the prospect of snow disrupting Pancake Day. Plus, it's a chance to meet Emma and Graham – the prayer-group leaders described as 'like family' by my mother – and all the other names that have come to dominate her Sunday lunchtime ramblings. The hotchpotch of lonely Londoners who took her in after my father's latest affair.

I have the urge to refer to her as Grandma. Hope that's OK.

Well, your grandma can't believe it when I say, 'You're right. I'll come.'

She's overflowing with travel information and directions, as if her prayer group is an Al Qaeda cell that meets in a disused sewer works. As it turns out, they use a primary school in Elephant and Castle. It's reachable by no fewer than seven different bus routes, an Overground station and the Northern Line, raves Grandma. 'Emma and Graham are all about equal accession,' she says. I let it go. Maybe it was intentional.

What do people wear to prayer nights?

To: LRS_17@outlook.com
Tues 21/2, 22:40
SUBJECT: *Worst one yet*

Should never have left the house. Never have taken the Tube. New phrase: 'Everything happens for a reason.'

To: LRS_17@outlook.com
Tues 21/2, 23:05
SUBJECT: *Does it?*

Why say that? E's still out. I'm taking something. Will explain in morning, if I can.

To: LRS_17@outlook.com
Wed 22/2, 10:46
SUBJECT: *Prayer night, or Some People Are Always Waiting to Pounce*

I suppose Elephant and Castle sounds magical to you. It's not. No elephants, no castles. But Grandma was right about the transport links.

She'd wanted to meet outside for a 'quick pre-chat' and go in together. I declined by reminding her of the local crime rate – helpful thing about Grandma is she scares easily.

Instead, I arrive late and find them singing in a circle, about fifteen of them. The man with the guitar has to be Graham but he looks nothing like his name. You're picturing a silver-haired school bus driver, bit of a belly, aren't you? Not this Graham. He's in his thirties, slim, neat beard and a voice wasted on hallelujahs. Next to him is a tall Asian woman, singing louder than the rest, hands raised to the low classroom ceiling. Emma, no doubt. She's wearing a green wrap-over cardigan, obscuring a baby bump. Thanks for the heads-up, Grandma.

The door's closing behind me and I reach back for the handle but it bangs shut. Sodding fire doors. Graham's blue eyes look over and your darling Grandma gives Emma a broad smile, like a fox cub presenting its first kill. Sorry, unintended ginger joke.

Emma makes a big show of welcoming me and tells the group that

'Moira's daughter' is going through 'dark times'. I'm glad I dressed in black. I'm commended for 'reaching out', like we're in sodding Motown. She'd get on well with Liz.

At least Emma speaks with big arm gestures, allowing me to establish that the cardigan is simply an unflattering cut. Bought online, probably.

In keeping with our classroom surroundings – papier mâché volcanoes, a solar system arranged with no regard for scale – Emma divides us into three smaller groups. Our task: to discuss 'healing love'. I am with Graham, a skinny woman with a gold necklace that says Deb, and an older man.

Grandma's group join hands in a corner and mumble a prayer that no one seems to know with any confidence. As they stand, I notice she's wearing trousers. They're old-people trousers (loose, cream, folds down the front) but young for her – young to fit in with her new friends.

Our group keep their hands to themselves but sit far too close together on low desks. Because there was a Tesco Express on the way and they were on offer, I have a pack of ginger biscuits in my bag. As I pull them out, a woman in the next group looks over. Graham makes things worse. 'How sweet. Are they vegan?' he asks.

'Of course,' I reply, hoping they're made with kitten milk and the eggs of trafficked chickens.

But he's moved on and is telling us to go round the group and talk about how 'God's love' has guided us out of some valley or other. As you'd expect, we say nothing and stare at the unopened biscuits on my lap. Their eyes wander to my clammy hands, then my you-know-what.

'I can start us off,' says Graham. 'Some of you know about my old life.'

Don't get your hopes up. He goes on to describe what any normal person would call casual drinking but, in Graham's mind – with Emma's help – has morphed into full-blown alcoholism. To Graham,

God appeared not in a crack house, nor in a jail cell, but at the champagne bar of a Michelin-starred restaurant, in the form of Emma, a City lawyer. Or something like that. I spent half his account wondering when and how to open the biscuits.

The older man, Ian, has a more interesting problem: gambling. Slots mainly. Sometimes horses. And yes, God's set him straight. Or so he claims.

When it's Deb's turn, we wait as she reuses the same tissue over and over, stopping and starting her story. 'What I want to say, is that God was there, never left me,' she blubs. I don't know if this is the best or worst moment to open the biscuits.

'I mean, after I lost Rupert,' Deb carries on.

I reach for her hand. It has to be her child. Deb's too young to lose a husband. Rupert was Deb's baby. That's why Grandma brought me here.

'His face was the first thing I saw in the morning, the last at night,' Deb goes on. No night-time visits? Not a newborn. I take back my hand. 'At the end I moved him into my room, put him right by my bed, where I could reach through the wires, stroke his ears. He liked that.' A rabbit. A fucking rabbit.

Don't worry. When it came to my turn, I knew exactly what to say.

'My baby died. My human baby. Three weeks ago. Luke.'

Deb and Ian try to smile, it's all they can think to do. Graham's face doesn't move, he's been pre-briefed by Grandma. 'He's safe now,' Graham says. 'God has a special place for him.'

'Like Rupert,' says Deb.

Graham squeezes Deb's arm. 'Like Rupert.'

'Actually, the Bible's not clear on that,' says Ian. 'It says nothing about heaven for animals.'

I offer Deb a clean tissue.

'Like you say, Ian, it's not clear,' says Graham. 'But it doesn't say there isn't a heaven for animals.'

Ian leafs through the Bible on his lap, stops to read something out. 'And children—'

Graham cuts him off. 'He's safe now. They both are.'

Before I can ask if you hadn't been safe before, the big, happy circle reforms. More songs, hands in the air and closed eyes. You see what I'm surrounded with here? I tell them and they're singing. Singing and dancing like children. Your own grandmother.

They're all doing the same smile. It's like a yoga class. All so sure of themselves and the way they've decided to live their lives.

I bet you're smiling too, at all this chaos over here. You should be trying to by now, anyway.

Emma's still getting her breath back when she closes the evening with a prayer. She's asking God to help us accept 'His plan'. She's piling phrase upon phrase, and I don't need to tell you what that means for me. The words seep into the cracks in my brain like when I spilled honey on the wicker lounger. And her prayer has chapters, patience for politicians, comfort for refugees, thanks for the spring. My chair scrapes the floor, Grandma grabs my wrist like I'm a toddler. I shake it free and whisper loud enough for all of them, 'This was a stupid idea.' Only Graham opens his eyes.

On the Tube home, 'he's safe now' and 'all in God's plan' play on a loop in my head. Trust the sodding God phrases to be all-powerful.

'I'm sorry?' says the man next to me. Older, tweed hat.

'Ignore me,' I say, and he does. There's nothing unusual about chanting 'all in God's plan' on the Northern Line.

The train stops and I realise my second mistake of the night. Going via Oval.

Of course our driver chooses to linger there. And while he's going nowhere, I'm dragged nine months backwards, to the day I saved him. The same day it all started – depending on your view of things. I was on my way to lunch with E. I know it's not the most hygienic of things to admit to, but I had the test with me, in my handbag. Every time I looked in, the two little stripes were a deeper pink. Like

GCSE, A-level and uni results rolled into one. We'd aced it. You'd have my blonde hair, his blue eyes, but you wouldn't need glasses. His height, my patience, his confidence. I knew you were a boy.

I have a cycle like a panda. We'd done the April test too early, tried another one in May. This time we'd promised each other we'd wait, but I knew that was the day to do it. I could always buy another if it was too soon. I had this plan to hide it under his napkin at the restaurant, surprise him.

I wasn't supposed to be there. I'd taken the Bank train by mistake, realised in time, got off at Oval to wait for the next Charing Cross one. He was at the end of the platform, pacing in squeaky trainers. You've heard the story a hundred times since, it's one of my best. People asked me to tell it at dinner parties and in the office (they won't do that with our story). But what I really remember is a jumble, pieces missing.

It lasted two minutes, three at most.

He steps on the yellow line, back, over the line, back, to the edge, back. His coat flaps, the kind that catches in doors. Wrong for the weather.

He's touching his face, mumbling. No one else has seen him, or at least that's what they pretend. Train lights on the walls, the sound, the shaking, he's about to go, I throw my arms around him, fall back. I cushion our landing, but his elbow smacks into the ground and he shouts something like 'no' or 'ow'. It's his only sound. He's shivering, so am I, my arms around him. He smells of sweat, and something wet, mud. I loosen my arms as he sits up. His one hand clasps the bad elbow, the other hand covers his face, and whatever it looked like a minute ago, it's gone from my mind. A man asks, 'You alright, love?' The doors close and the train leaves, without me and with him still here.

And there I am, at Oval again, and 'God's plan' is chanting itself hoarse in my head.

When I surface at Clapham Common, I have a voicemail from

Grandma, for whom God's plan has yet to include learning to text. It begins with the usual admonishments. 'Storming out! Those are my friends,' she says.

'He was my baby,' I say over her message.

Her voice slows, I'm Pebble again, and she asks if I'll give the group another try. Francis is howling in the background, a cry of solidarity for his human sibling. She shushes him and rambles on at me, 'And think about what Emma said – God's plan for you.'

I didn't listen to the rest. I called back. 'All planned? This? Taken away from me?'

That got her. 'All I'm saying, Pebble...' She pauses. 'All Emma and Graham are saying, is everything happens for a reason.'

To: LRS_17@outlook.com
Wed 22/2, 17:34
SUBJECT: *Besieged*

My mother keeps calling. I've switched off my phone, disconnected the landline. Turned the lights off for when she drives over.

Where to begin?

You could go big and ask about tsunamis, earthquakes, hurricanes. Or go medical: cancer, kids' cancer, eczema. Or political: wars, child soldiers, Brexit.

I should set Graham and Emma an essay:

The Indian Ocean tsunami killed a quarter of a million people; more than one child an hour has died since the war in Syria began; my baby was taken before he could live. Using examples, explain how and why Everything Happens for a Reason.

And yet.

And yet.

Let's say for a minute they were right. When it comes to you, to us. It would be worse if there were no reason.

To: LRS_17@outlook.com
Thu 23/2, 00:52
SUBJECT: *Early-onset old age*

Slept an hour, up again. You get these guests – like E's mother – who bring too much luggage, unpack into every available space and tell you what to buy in for their breakfasts (plural). That's Everything Happens for a Reason. It's on an open-ended stay and things will only resolve when one of us kills the other.

And the man from Oval's here too. He'd been gone for months, there was no room for him. When I half close my eyes, he's rolled up in a ball at the end of our bed, giant hands covering his face.

To: LRS_17@outlook.com
Thu 23/2, 12:16
SUBJECT: *Lie in*

Everything Happens for a Reason and I stayed up into the small hours, like the first evening that any houseguest arrives, when the enthusiasm is still genuine and there are easy things to say.

We thrashed things out over the ginger biscuits, washed down with raspberry leaf tea left over from your last week here – an effective show of courage from my side.

EHFAR, as it shall be known from now on, turns out to be a foreign visitor. If pushed, I would say Germano-French: brutally direct, yet exasperatingly philosophical. No time for 'the flight was fine, thank you', instead it's straight in with, 'why do you act like I don't exist?', 'you can't resist me', 'you know what you did.'

It's a sign of a weak mind, writing down your problems to 'work them through' – kind of thing Tina in Coaching recommends. But making a list was the only way to keep EHFAR from delivering all its blows at once. You don't need to see it all but it was something like this:

The reason?

- Glass of wine at lunch
- Blue cheese in salad dressing
- E
- Dangerous mother
- Impending nuclear holocaust
- Disabled

And yes, when we get the post-mortem we can definitively cross off the first, maybe the second and probably the last one. (For the record, I'd have kept you.) But even the edited menu is like that choice between a sheep's foot and a kangaroo's doo-dah. (Seriously, who books a honeymoon in the Australian Outback?)

I tried Googling Bible verses, philosophers, the words 'any such thing as unexplained death'. Even worse, I put it to E as he was getting up.

'Bollocks,' he said, doing that thing where he reaches up to touch the ceiling. 'Don't listen to her. It's just shit, that's what it is.' He offered to work from home.

'I'm fine,' I said. 'I'll get some sleep.'

To: LRS_17@outlook.com
Thu 23/2, 23:12
SUBJECT: Only way out

They dropped EHFAR on me, they will have to disarm it.

I called my mother (sorry, the whole Grandma thing isn't working for me) and got Graham's number. I woke her, but she likes to feel needed.

When Graham texts straight back, I picture him as a religious meerkat, always on alert, miniature guitar on his back. He'd love to come over for coffee, he says. Is eight too early? (Happy people. Bet he jogs, too.)

To: LRS_17@outlook.com
Fri 24/2, 13:05
SUBJECT: *Connections*

Graham's visit is messy.

The newsagent only stocks biscuits containing eggs and/or other animal parts. So I peel and chop some carrots, arranging them as a crucifix, then a sun. In the end, I manage to create a random pattern. Thank God we said eleven.

I move the more sweary of E's 'artworks' and rearrange the contents of the recycling bin so the beer bottles are obscured by a copy of the *Guardian* – Graham seems like someone who helps clear the table.

What people wear shouldn't matter, but it does. I lift down the box from the top of the wardrobe and find the pre-you jeans. The widest ones do up easily and the first top I try – dark green, high neck – works well with them. I brush my hair and I'm back to how I was, in the before. The last traces of your short life are leaving my body. The bleeding has slowed to a trickle.

It's wrong. We can't do this yet, or ever. I climb into bed and wrap myself around that long pillow we bought for you. I feel for your kicks.

But he'll be here any minute. I pick myself up, wash my face and put the jeans back in their box. I stick with the maternity cords. At least that's the plan. It's only when I'm in the doorway, staring at Graham's dog collar, and his eyes wander down to my bare thighs that I realise I missed a step.

'Sorry, mishap,' I say. 'In the kitchen.'

I run upstairs while he parks his bike on the hall carpet.

When I return, he's let himself into the lounge, Bible on his lap.

He gestures to the carrot sticks. 'I didn't realise you had an older one.'

'I don't.'

We pray for you while the kettle boils. He says that you're in God's care now. He's part vicar, part child-protection services. You're safe, nothing can harm you.

'I saved someone's life,' I interrupt.

He mumbles, 'Amen.'

'Last summer. Oval Tube. He was jumping, I grabbed him.'

His palm is sticky, I slide my hand free.

'What happened to him?' he says.

'The Tube staff took over.'

'What about you? Was there someone for you to talk to?'

'They pushed me out the way. I couldn't see him, his face. But it's nothing really. You would have done the same.' I retreat to the kitchen, asking, 'Do you think everything happens for a reason? Someone said that to me.' I linger by the sink, giving him time to get his answer right. When I return with the coffee, he has his Bible open.

'Not what it says in there. I want to know what you think,' I say.

He closes it before I can see the page. He pulls off his dog collar – it's plastic and springy. 'You can touch it if you want,' he says.

I flex it, turn it over in my hands. I want to hold it up to my neck and look in the mirror.

'Yes,' he says. 'Yes, I do think so. Everything happens for a reason.'

'Then it's a shitty system.' I hand the dog collar back. 'How do you explain that to Syrians? Or the tsunami people, abused children? What reason do you give them?'

He's ready with an answer. 'There are connections you cannot see. You're being too earthly.'

In other words, it's still my fault.

To: LRS_17@outlook.com
Fri 24/2, 17:19
SUBJECT: *Visiting day*

I attached some photos for you, but removed them again.

Helen, the midwife, brought them round. They were on a memory stick, 'so you only look at them when you're ready,' she said.

I tried changing them to black and white, to help with your fingernails and your lips, hide it a bit, you know, the blood. (One day, I'll Google how that happened.) But black and white makes your lips black and that's worse. It says on your charts that you should be looking at pictures now, three weeks. Black-and-white ones with lots of clear shapes work best. I bought you that *Art for Baby* book from the Louvre, on the babymoon – that's what they call your last holiday without a baby, where you talk about how you won't change and how things will be hard, but that because you know they will be hard it won't matter, and that really, everything will be perfect.

The ones of your feet came out well. I've printed one, put it in my wallet. I keep looking at it, like that's all I've lost, your feet. I saw someone posted that you can commission an artist to do a painting or a sketch, without the bruises and marks. Is that offensive? I'll print another copy of your feet in black and white, and stick it in the back of the art book for you.

To: LRS_17@outlook.com
Mon 27/2, 10:18
SUBJECT: *What about work?*

I've run away. I'm on a damp bench. I can't go home – for the next three hours, at least.

Anca is there. It's her day. Monday used to suit us. We'd tidy and clean on Sunday before we paid her to tidy and clean the next morning.

Last week and the one before, I convinced E to tell her not to come, and to tell her why, and to pay her anyway. She dropped a card through the door. Then I gave in and told him she could come back today.

I should have planned to go somewhere, get out before she came. But the truth is I haven't left the house since prayer night. Who would? Well, I'm out now.

And she was early. She rang the bell and let herself in before I could answer. I was halfway down the stairs when I heard her key, bashed my shin fleeing back to the bedroom. She started on the kitchen, making herself a coffee, phone on loudspeaker to a friend or sister, the cutlery drawer opening and closing, barstools scraping on the tiles.

Of course it occurred to me that I should let her know I was in the house. It was either that or climb out a window – that also occurred to me. But the longer I sat on the edge of the bed, the harder I was stuck there. You can't get away with 'I didn't hear you come in' when the other person's been hoovering your lounge. Instead, I opened a magazine, ready to look up and say, 'oh hi, Anca', and I listened. And do you know what I heard? Your wardrobe door, in YOUR room, with YOUR things. That unstuck me.

She looks round, your little blue hairbrush in one hand, bag of cotton wool in the other.

'You don't need to clean in here,' I say.

Behind her, the other things from your changing table are on the wardrobe shelf. She's putting you away.

I try again: 'You don't need to do this room.'

'You're not at work?' she says.

'Please, just leave this room.'

'It's OK. I'll tidy it for you.' She takes your grey cardigan off its hook on the wall, hangs it inside the wardrobe.

'Please, it's fine like this. I'll do it, later. I've got nothing else to do,' I say.

'What about work?'

'I'm off work.' I need to explain. 'I can stay off. I get the same leave, the same as if it hadn't, you know.'

'Work might be good. Get you out.' She waves towards the window.

'I go out,' I say. It's the longest conversation we've ever had. 'I am out all the time, lots to sort out. And I might change job anyway, find something better for me.'

She closes the wardrobe door, picks up your art book, the black-and-white one, with your feet tucked inside the cover. 'Shall I leave this?'

I grab the book. 'Just leave everything. Don't touch it. I want it like this.'

'Okaaaayy.' She puts her hands up. 'I'll do your room. Don't walk in the kitchen, the floor's wet.'

'I'm going out anyway.' I motion for her to leave your room first and close the door after us.

I can't be in the house with her. I hate this, all these people telling me I'm messed up, too sad, lazy. Her meddling hands. Meddling hands, held up like a hostage, like I'm the dangerous one. Because that's what they really think, all of them. That it's my fault. It's all my fault and I might as well get on and live with it.

I left a note and twenty pounds on top of her handbag in the kitchen. *We don't need you to come any more. Here's some extra. Thanks.*

Don't worry, I'll put your things back tonight. I've got the book safe. I should have told her to leave the key. I should text her. I need to walk. Walk and think only about walking.

To: LRS_17@outlook.com
Mon 27/2, 10:47
SUBJECT: *What if*

Back on my bench. Did I know this all along and hide it from myself, from you?

It was your book, black-and-white concertina people, all holding hands and touching toes, disappearing off the edges of the page. The last picture, called 'All One'. I bet you worked it out ages ago – that's how you see the world at this stage, all of us connected to one another, you and me, everyone. You'd love chains of paper people, I'll make you some. And Graham saw it too – he wanted me to piece it together myself, the whole 'connections you cannot see' thing.

It goes back to then, last June. Your cells were going about their business, happily dividing, he was pacing on Oval platform, seconds from death, and I was the one who stopped him. He got to live and you...

He's the reason, isn't he? The only possible reason. The obvious reason. The EHFAR REASON.

It's freezing. I should go home. But Anca's still there. I can't go home. No, not home. I know where I need to go.

To: LRS_17@outlook.com
Mon 27/2, 14:32
SUBJECT: *On it*

I'm back. Anca left the key.

I need you to trust me when I promise you I'll find him, make it all make sense. Are you in him? Is that too obvious? I've started, in the obvious place. Sorry, keep saying 'obvious', but that's because it is. I'm so slow. This is what they call baby brain. Not blaming you. It is what it is. It all is. And most of it is obvious.

You wouldn't believe how hard it is to find a human working at a Tube station. When the machines rise up, the London Underground will be their headquarters.

I looked around for a few minutes, waved at the CCTV, knocked on the ticket window. I hurt my hand banging on a thick metal door. The man who finally emerged from behind it was resigned to the imminent robot revolution.

'What's this say?' he asks. His tea splashes as he gestures to the sign.

'Staff only,' I reply. 'But I'm looking for someone.'

'I'm busy,' he says.

'Doing what?' I ask it out of genuine curiosity.

'What's it look like?' He steps back. I'm about to lose him behind the sacred door.

'I saved someone's life,' I say. 'Here. Last year.'

That's got him. I tell him I need to find someone who was working that day, 21st June.

'Do I look like a walking logbook?' He likes rhetorical questions.

I look at my shoes, chastised.

'What day of the week was it?' he says.

'A Tuesday. Tuesday morning.'

'Lola usually does Tuesdays,' he says.

'Do you think she'll help me?'

'Doesn't mean she was on Tuesdays last year, does it?' he says. It's impossible to tell if he's playing with me, or thick. 'Try her. Southbound platform.'

He won't let me through the barrier so I have to tap my card and pay again.

She's not what you'd expect, nothing ever is. She's older, short and what my grandma used to call 'plump'. I watch her from a bench for three or four trains. Was she there that day?

The machine instructs people to 'mind the gap' and to 'let customers off the train first', but she adds a human touch, informing them it won't be stopping at Tooting Bec or there'll be another one in four minutes. Her accent is African, I'd say West African if pushed, probably Ghanaian. When there's a lull, I approach. Her badge says 'Omolola'.

'I need to talk to you,' I say. She looks around, like she's checking who else can hear us.

'Next train in six minutes. Driver shortage,' she says.

'It's about something that happened last year, twenty-first of June, a Tuesday, you work Tuesdays.'

'Sometimes.'

'I need your help. Just two minutes.'

'You should ask my manager,' she says.

'It has to be you.'

'There's a train coming, you have to wait.' She waves towards the silent tunnel.

'You said it was six minutes.'

'If you are going to get abusive, I will report you.' She puts her hand up to her radio.

'I should be the one reporting you. You're supposed to be here to help.' It comes out cold; it's the voice E has after a New York trip. He's made me like this. You, it, meddling-hands-Anca. Everything has made me like this.

Omolola looks terrified. 'Come back at twelve. My break.' She walks away to a machine in the wall.

Only twenty minutes to kill. I go to the northbound platform and sit on the same bench as that day. There's a woman in his spot. Is she going to try too? Is this where they all go? That happens with suicide, favourite places. She's blocking my view of the edge. I move over to her and stand too close. She walks along the platform and I go back to my bench.

There was a murder case I read about once where they took the witness and the whole jury on a field trip to an industrial estate. They asked the witness, a woman who'd been jogging, to stand in the very same spot where she'd watched the murderer and the victim fighting, an alleyway between two factories, one made tyres, the other made ice-cream.

'I need you to picture the scene,' the prosecutor says to the witness. She closes her eyes and sucks in air thick with the scent of rubber. After three breaths, she opens her eyes and tells them how he ran towards a hedgerow, tripped on a kerb and went back on himself to drop the knife down a drain. They search the sewers and pull out the knife, still covered in DNA and fingerprints. He got twenty years, she got a new identity.

The smells on Oval northbound platform are nothing distinctive. That same canned Underground smell of metal grinding on metal, fried chicken and sweat. Still, I gulp it in, try to picture him. I focus on that spot, where we trembled together. I imagine peeling his hands away from his face, feeling the shape of his cheeks with my fingers.

Back on the southbound platform, Omolola is being very punctual about her break time and I have to run to catch her on the escalator. She stands on the left, but it's quiet.

'Last summer, in June, do you remember the man who tried to jump?' I ask.

'We get them a lot,' she says.

'But I saved this one. Grabbed him, pulled him back.' We're at the top of the escalator, she accelerates towards the staff-only door. 'I need to find him,' I say.

She shakes her arm free and taps her card to open the barriers. 'I can't help you,' she says.

'But everything happens for a reason.'

'Not today,' she replies.

I'll try her again tomorrow.

One of those artists emailed back, they charge £650 and up. E's good at drawing.

To: LRS_17@outlook.com
Tues 28/2, 14:44
SUBJECT: *Something we can do together*

Didn't work out. E's fault.

It may surprise you to learn that he of all people is taking packed lunches to work. Don't worry, not an economy drive. He's on a Neanderthal diet. Nothing packaged, nothing processed. He says we need to look after ourselves. He wants to run home from work three times a week and he's ordered a new bike for weekends. There's a note stuck to the fridge asking me, *COULD A CAVEMAN EAT IT?*

It's in a book he bought from a life coach at the office. 'It's something we can do together,' he says, pointing at 'recipes' for raw broccoli with raisins. How am I supposed to have room for anything new?

'And tell Anca we need to switch to bleach-free cleaning products,' he says. 'I'll send you the link to order these organic ones. Tanya uses them.'

'Who's Tanya?'

'You know her, Belgian, she was at the dinner at the Korean place. One of the grads. She's on Sam's team.'

'Who's Sam?'

He's left the conversation, back to his phone, emailing Tanya about bamboo toilet brushes and edamame beans. My mother was right, handsome men make exhausting husbands. When I was little I thought she meant because of all the weightlifting and jousting they would have to do. Her choice of storybooks, and words, are responsible for all sorts of mess.

I haven't told him about Anca. That I let her go.

E left me a lunchbox. Grilled chicken, boiled egg, lettuce leaves and seven walnuts. Either he wants to starve me back to a size ten or he thought supplying a meal would secure my help – he also left a shopping list. Presumably the cavemen were able to fly in their strawberries and avocados out of season, and their womenfolk spent their days making almond butter.

It was late morning by the time I'd tracked down all his items, filled the fridge and added my own note to the door in reply (*YOU TELL ME*). I left my lunchbox for him to eat at dinnertime. Repetition was doubtless the main characteristic of the cave people's diets.

When I get to Oval, it's Omolola's break time so I have to bang on the steel door. The same man appears, a sandwich in one hand, free newspaper in the other. Name badge says 'Vernon'.

'You still can't read?' says Vernon.

'I need to see Omolola.'

His mouth hangs open, there's unchewed bread in his back teeth.

I try again: 'Lola. Can you get her?'

'Left early, hasn't she?'

'Of course,' I say. 'You should try the caveman diet.'

To: LRS_17@outlook.com
Tues 28/2, 22:49
SUBJECT: New York

Tanya with the permanent tan was supposed to have moved to New York. But her Facebook says she came back to London at Christmas. Farcical caption under a selfie on that famous ice rink: 'Back soon for another bite of the Big Red Apple.' Red? It was never red. Now it's circling in my head. Big Red Apple. She's wearing a red beret. Her page is all selfies, taken from above to hide her double chin and eye bags. E will see that. She won't age well.

To: LRS_17@outlook.com
Wed 1/3, 00:05
SUBJECT: Stop time

March now. Our last month together is gone.

To: LRS_17@outlook.com
Wed 1/3, 16:52
SUBJECT: *Her name is Lola*

Didn't I tell you to trust me? Lola – that's what she prefers to be
called – is brilliant. Got her on a bad day before. Here's a piece of
pound-shop wisdom for you: no one ever knows what's truly going
on in someone else's life.

I have to go out again in a minute, but this is where we are.

I braved the end of the morning rush and caught her before any
break times. It was that point in the morning when the suits were
gone and it was all hairy men in suede trainers and thick-rimmed
glasses, and women in long skirts with fluorescent ankle socks. I
struggled through their rucksacks to Lola's platform. She recognised
me but seemed to think we were meeting by chance.

'You still looking for the man?' she asks.

'I feel awful about before,' I say. 'I shouldn't have asked you.'

'Why you need to find him?' Her voice is efficient, strong.

A train pulls in, and she speaks into her radio and waves a plastic
paddle about. She's not wearing a wedding ring – guessing it's a
health-and-safety thing. But then why would she be allowed hoop
earrings? Why is anyone?

The train leaves, the platform clears.

'It's silly. You won't get it,' I say. 'I'll let you carry on.'

'I remember him ... and you,' she says.

'You all took over. I had him, on the ground, you pulled me off,
pushed me away.'

'You did a good thing,' she says.

'I need to find him.'

She strokes out the creases in her jumper. She needs the next size
up.

'But I know you're not allowed to help me,' I carry on. 'It was silly, I
shouldn't have asked.' The next train rumbles closer and I turn to leave.

'You been looking for him this whole time?' she asks.

'I just started. I need to find him.'

'Why?'

I wait while she does whatever it is she does. As the train leaves, I follow her eyes up to a CCTV camera.

'I wasn't supposed to be there,' I say, and because her eyes are telling me she wants more, I tell her about you. How I was on my way to surprise E with the news. Her face shows she understands. But it's not like with other mothers; I don't resent her for it. Anyway, hers must be grown up. I'd guess she's at least forty-five, had them young.

'What did you have?' she asks.

'A boy. Luke.'

'He's at nursery?' She's looking at my empty arms.

I listen for a train, anything. You'd love nursery. You're on a waiting list for one where they speak Mandarin.

There's a bench along the platform. Lola sits next to me, asks, 'What happened?'

'He just stopped kicking.'

She squeezes my hand, leans closer. Her shoulder's pillowy.

Your chart says your hearing is fully developed now. I wish you could hear Lola's voice. It's in my head. 'You did a good thing. You did a good thing...' It's a cross between an airline pilot and a nurse, authority and comfort. She gets it. All those singing Christians, Bristol Liz and the time-will-healers have been belittling you, and don't even start me on the 'I had a miscarriage too' walrus at the hairdressers. But Lola's different.

I left her to her paddle waving and radioing, and waited by the barriers for her next break. After one of her colleagues asked if I was lost, I moved to the bus stop outside, glad of my new habit of wearing two jumpers under my coat (padding). I went back inside a few minutes before twelve.

Lola smiled, she looked relieved that I hadn't fled.

'I thought I could buy you lunch,' I said.

She had thirty minutes but knew somewhere quick, she said. It was a kebab shop where she gets a discount. She ordered wraps with chips for both of us and I paid.

She's different above ground. Her voice is louder and she laughs her words rather than speaking them. Her tight black curls bounce around when she talks.

It turns out she also has phrasal retentiveness.

'You said everything happens for a reason,' she says, as we find a table at the back.

'I thought you weren't listening,' I say.

She gives me a teacher look.

'He took Luke's place. I need to know why,' I say.

'What would it change?'

'I thought you got it. He's out there living. What's he doing with it?'

She checks her watch, tries to catch the kebab man's eye. 'What would make you feel better?' she asks me.

It's a stupid question, hurtful. My answer's out before I can stop it. 'I want my baby back.'

A plate clunks down in front of me, chips fall onto the tabletop. He's slow to retreat.

'I mean, say you find him, what would make you feel better?' asks Lola. She pulls her phone from her pocket, checks the time on that and calls across to the waiter, 'Put it in a takeaway box.'

'I haven't had a chance to think it through,' I say. 'But say it's something like this.' I find a pen and an old envelope in my bag. 'Say he was a brain surgeon and since last June, he's saved two people a week. That's, roughly, seventy-eight lives. And what if half of those people he saved were social workers, police officers or fire fighters, and each of them has so far saved three more people. Now we're up to one hundred and ninety-five lives. Or if you go back to the start, count him as well, you're looking at one hundred and ninety-six lives saved. All because I was on that platform. All because of Luke and because everything happens for a reason.'

Her face concentrates hard as she adds it up with me. I finish out of breath, like the underdog in a courtroom drama. It's unclear whether it's my delivery or the sheer numbers, but she says she'll help, she'll get me the records for that day. She's going to log in when the office is empty. We're meeting at six. I said I'd buy her dinner.

To: LRS_17@outlook.com
Wed 1/3, 18:27
SUBJECT: Stupid

How could I have been so stupid? And I pulled you along with me. I waited outside the station, where Lola said, for twenty minutes, and now I've retreated into the relative warmth of Sainsbury's to watch for her through the window. (Writing this on my phone.)

It's all stupid. Me, Lola, my plan, meeting here. Why would she help me? She just wanted me to go away. Should have worked it out from the meeting place – no one would ever ask anyone to try to find them outside Brixton Tube. The body smells are medieval. And there's so much anger. I'm watching them now, two tides colliding. The commuters trudge out with headphones and hungry faces, and in barge the socialisers on their way into town – porn-star make-up, two drinks away from a fight. In the midst of it all, there's a man gesticulating and shouting into a microphone about an indiscernible god. He's so angry, it's making a shield around him.

The security guard in here keeps looking at me – like I'm the type who'd nick their three-day-old carnations. At least I'm fitting in. Hang on, he's saying something.

To: LRS_17@outlook.com
Wed 1/3, 21:28
SUBJECT: High-five

We have a name. A first name AND a surname. Can you believe it?
Ben Palmer. Ben Palmer of Kennington. Early Googling shows
nothing obvious, but it's so much to work with.

It's all down to Lola, who continues to be full of surprises. She did
make me panic for a bit there but turned up in the end, right after I
was thrown out of Sainsbury's. (Quite proud about that. I was
'loitering', apparently. And he called me 'miss', not 'madam'.)

Thirty-five minutes past six and you know what she says? 'Sorry
I'm a bit late.'

I throw my arms around her – put it down to relief and cold
combined, and she seems like a hugger.

'You find him?' I ask her, shaking the blood back into my
fingers.

'We need to go somewhere first.' She's walking.

I jog to catch up as she heads down the street. The pavement is
one long bus stop, and she weaves between walking sticks and
pushchairs. Where was her sense of urgency half an hour ago?

We turn into a quieter road. She's faster than you'd expect. She
stops at a metal gate and presses the buzzer on an intercom. There's
a click, and I follow her through the gate and then a door, propped
ajar with a Dr Pepper can. We climb to the third floor, where a
woman the same build as Lola is waiting in a doorway. Instead of
curls she has long braids, but her face is just like Lola's.

Lola doesn't introduce me. The woman shouts back over her
shoulder, 'Josephine. Josephine!'

She and Lola speak in another language. It's fast and loud. It seems
the woman is also upset by Lola's timekeeping. Behind her, a little
girl appears. She's in a maroon school sweatshirt. There are beads in
her hair, and yellow paint. She sits on the floor and pulls her boots

on. When she's finished, she looks up with a proud smile, she has a dimple on one side, her eyes are deep brown and bright. She's beautiful.

Lola says something to her.

The girl looks up to the woman, says, 'Thank you for having me.' Her voice is loud and happy.

As Lola turns to leave, I smile at the woman. Were they talking about me?

Outside, I say to the little girl, 'You must be Lola's daughter.'

She nods. Her mother nudges her arm. 'Yes,' she says, without making eye contact. She feels as awkward as I do about me being there.

'I'm Mummy's friend, Rachel,' I say. 'We were supposed to go for dinner. Are you hungry?'

She nods again but instead of nudging her this time, Lola laughs. 'She's always hungry. Best you don't ask.'

'Where would you like to go?' I ask Josephine.

'McDonald's,' she says, shuffling from one foot to the other.

'I told you not to ask,' says Lola.

Josephine grins and we high-five – it's the first time I've done that in twenty years. I put my hand back up and we do it again, high and low. It should be cringey but it's not.

McDonald's has changed. You order from a touch screen and they bring the food to your table.

This is Josephine's domain. She orders apple slices instead of chips for herself and for me, a burger without tomato and a Diet Coke without ice. 'Customised,' she says.

At the table, she asks, 'You know why I ordered orange juice?'

'Vitamin C?'

'It's my name. Backwards. O-J. J-O.'

'What can go backwards and forwards at the same time?' I ask.

She looks around for clues and when her eyes settle on Lola, I say,

'That's right: Mum.' I find a pen from my bag and write on a napkin, *OJ – MUM – JO*.

She takes the pen and adds pictures. The Tropicana bottle, the mum and the daughter hold hands. I wonder what Josephine's dad looks like.

She slides the napkin back to me. I turn it over and write, *BAD MUM DAB*. She takes it back and gets to work on a portrait of Lola dancing. It's my second portion of chips of the day.

Lola swallows and hands me her phone. It's fuzzy but she's photographed her computer screen, a log for 21st June.

There it is. Ben Palmer. At least the screen says, 'NAME GIVEN: BEN PALMER'. Under address it just says, 'Kennington'. Guess he had a change of heart mid-debrief. Makes sense – you wouldn't want someone like Vernon calling to check on you. He also refused medical help and they had to guess his age as late twenties. The way Lola has framed the picture, it isn't clear if there was more.

'No mention of me?' I ask.

'It's a busy station,' she says.

Josephine gives me her last chicken nugget, but I feel obliged to offer it to Lola.

'Kennington's something,' I say. 'We'll start with the online phone book.'

That's her chance to say this is where we part ways. When she doesn't take it, I surprise myself and hold both my hands up to Josephine and we double high-five. I put the napkin into my bag as we leave (picture attached). We've swapped numbers, might meet tomorrow.

To: LRS_17@outlook.com
Wed 1/3, 22:15
SUBJECT: *True*

Just texted Lola: *I can't believe you did this for me.*
    Everything happens for a reason, she replied.
    With anyone else, I'd say they were mocking me.

To: LRS_17@outlook.com
Thu 2/3, 03:12
SUBJECT: *Hospitals*

How can you tell the difference between insomnia and staying up to get stuff done? I'll admit I'm not the happiest sleeper, but in this case, it's quite handy. I've been going through staff lists on hospital websites.

Ben Palmer could be a fake name. But the way it looks, he started telling them the truth then clammed up, why else give a first name and a surname but be all coy about your age, especially at his age? Hard for you to understand, but anything in the twenties is young, something people show off about.

No luck with brain surgeons or any other kind of surgeon so far. Guess that was just a silly feeling I had. You do have to wonder what would push a brain surgeon to do it. Saving lives all day but not a care for your own.

To: LRS_17@outlook.com
Thu 2/3, 16:17
SUBJECT: *Abi*

I was meant to find Lola.

We went back to the same kebab place. We were waiting for our food when Lola said, 'It happened to my sister, Grace, back home in Lagos.'

'What happened?'

'She lost a child.'

'Really? I mean, sorry, I mean that's awful. Sorry.'

I felt stupid. And arrogant. Lola would think I couldn't imagine it happening to anyone else. Which I can't, but I know it does.

But this is worse. I can't stop crying. Is it OK to tell you it's worse?

She was six. A little girl, Abi. A brain tumour. It went away and came back. She was six, like Josephine now. It was two years ago.

'I should have been there. I should have gone,' Lola kept saying. 'She was getting better. They told us she was better, treated, they could cure it.' Her sister had a little boy, too. He was three at the time. 'I should have gone, cared for William,' said Lola. 'Grace is the baby of the family. I should have gone to her.'

'You couldn't have known. And you had Josephine,' I said, and then chanced it: 'You were on your own.'

'I should have gone.' No tears but I couldn't see her eyes, she stared down at her hands tight together on the table, nails digging into her skin.

'How is she now?' I asked.

'Not good. She says no one will ever understand. God will get her through it.'

You know you were loved, don't you? Did you know as you went? You always will be.

To: LRS_17@outlook.com
Thu 2/3, 16:33
SUBJECT: Idiot

Stupid me with my stupid brain surgeon.

To: LRS_17@outlook.com
Fri 3/3, 09:46
SUBJECT: *God*

I texted Lola:

Your sister knows you love her. You were there in so many ways.

She replied ten minutes later:

God bless you, Rachel

To: LRS_17@outlook.com
Mon 6/3, 20:07
SUBJECT: *Bad name*

I know I'm not one to talk, but Ben Palmer's parents couldn't have chosen a more common name if they'd tried. Do you think it was wrong for us to pick your name when we did? Before, I mean. Add that to the list of potential reasons – hubris. There's this Yiddish saying: 'Man plans, God laughs.' But if we hadn't done it then, you and I wouldn't have had that time. Time together as named people. And it stopped E's family giving you some idiotic title like 'bumpy bean' or 'knickknack'. Luke Summers is a great name, everyone said so.

E left for New York last night. He offered to cancel it, I said I'm fine, will start on the garden. He'll be back on Wednesday. He asked me to fire Anca while he's gone. 'You can't even tell she's been,' he said, and used his monkey toes to pick up a clump of dust. It's good you got my feet.

Back to Ben Palmer, of which there are many but none the right one. We've branched out into all Palmers, in case Ben is a nickname.

There are fifty in the phone book and many more on Facebook and Twitter, at least half of them are unpleasant. That could just be a London thing. I checked, and the national wellbeing statistics show below-average life satisfaction and higher anxiety in most parts of London. Did you know they actually ask people 'do you feel what you do in life is worthwhile?' What score would you give me? It's out of ten.

I also looked up the origins of Palmer. It started out as the name given to a person returning from the Holy Land, bearing palm leaves as proof, and it came to mean 'missionary'. That appealed to Lola, who goes to a church one hour away by bus.

Lola and I met in her lunch break on Saturday (one of her sisters had Josephine, E was visiting his mother) and again today. I took a list, and between us we've called all the Palmer numbers I could find and messaged the rest on Facebook. (We don't mention you, just say we need help finding Ben Palmer, that I have an important connection with him, that he's probably been looking for me too.) Phone calls are harder, more than once we've descended into giggles, like schoolgirls making prank calls. To the kebab man it must look like we're falling in love.

Lola spoke to one Palmer who claimed he was a 'Ben', but she said he sounded far too old. 'Ready to die,' she said.

'That'll be him then,' I said.

She gasped and swiped at my arm, but she was laughing. Her giggles pour out at the slightest thing. She makes me feel I could make it as a comedian. She hasn't mentioned Abi again. Should I ask more? And when can I ask about Josephine's dad?

This afternoon, I went to Ben Palmer Senior's address in Brockley to be thorough. He invited me in for a cup of tea and I was halfway through telling him our story when a carer arrived and asked me to leave so she could change him. He told me to call again, to bring a Battenberg. I've always wanted to make a Battenberg, fairy-tale colours, you'd love them.

To: LRS_17@outlook.com
Tues 7/3, 09:22
SUBJECT: *Expectant*

'Where are you? We're expecting you.'

Expecting.

A phone call when I'm still in bed.

Her voice is angry, or panicked. She asks if it's me and says it again, 'We're expecting you. Now.'

'Who are you?'

'The surgery. Your baby has his check. We sent you a letter.'

I hang up.

The landline rings again.

'Are you depressed?' she asks. 'If you come in, we can help you.'

I want to believe her, about all of it. I roll over, pretend it was a dream.

To: LRS_17@outlook.com
Tues 7/3, 15:40
SUBJECT: *Faith*

What is it they say in detective shows? The scent has run dry?

'Have faith,' is all Lola says.

It sounds right in her voice. Not in my mother's, who phones every morning to read out Graham and Emma's 'Daily Bread' email.

Today's call comes as I'm in Waitrose with E's hunter-gatherer list. My phone's wedged in my pocket and I drop a box of eggs trying to answer it.

'You have to learn to text,' I shout.

'I could just give them your email,' my mother says.

'Sorry. Carry on.'

To: LRS_17@outlook.com
Wed 8/3, 02:24
SUBJECT: *Sleep*

Where you are they're very much into the truth and what it means –
says so in the leaflet Graham left on the coffee table. But this is what
you need to know: truth comes in layers. Here's a way you'll
understand it: the earth is a ball but if you cut it down the middle,
you would see it's made of different layers. At the top, there's layer
one, grass in the garden. Right at the bottom of the layers, or in the
very middle of the ball, is what they call the core. No one's been there;
you'd have to go through burning-hot melted rocks to reach it.

For truth, layer one is the grass where we spend most of our time,
five is the core. Like this:

LAYER ONE: Truth you tell people that isn't a lie. (Example: 'I'm
planning to come back after Easter.')

LAYER TWO: Truths you share with a few people because you
trust them – or you want them to trust you. (Example: 'We'd been
trying for a year.')

LAYER THREE: The things you hardly ever tell anyone.
(Example: *Convinced myself it would be a girl.* That was in a text
message from E to his sister after our twenty-week scan.)

LAYER FOUR: Things you tell no one. (Example: At the back
of my underwear drawer is an airtight sandwich bag with the
knickers I was wearing when your waters broke.)

LAYER FIVE: Stuff that's true but you don't even let yourself see
it. (Example: What actually happened that day.)

But I see it.

They still don't understand what starts labour off, how the body knows what to do. You knew. You went by the calendar, and I woke to twinges on your due date. We had a good breakfast – muesli and yoghurt – and the twinges grew stronger, pushing your feet up into my lungs. I cradled your heel through my skin as it poked out. You'd had an early start and seemed in no rush. The bag was packed. E was on his way home, he said. Sleeping seemed the best thing to do.

When I woke, your foot was still up high, still moved with every contraction. But what happened to the rest of you? Your little breaststrokes? Your karate kicks? When did I know?

Sure, Everything Happens for a Reason. I went to sleep and left you.

To: LRS_17@outlook.com
Wed 8/3, 20:06
SUBJECT: Some secrets are OK

Awkward moment with E. He found one of my Ben Palmer doodles.

He doesn't think like us, he wouldn't get it. I had to say Ben was a character in a new TV series.

'What's it called?' he asks.

'*Feet*,' I say.

'Can we watch it together?' he asks.

I tell him it's released on YouTube, twenty-minute instalment each day, citizen filmmaking, Jodie in Diversity put me on to it. 'It's not for you,' I say.

To: LRS_17@outlook.com
Fri 10/3, 09:03
SUBJECT: *Too much*

First time I've been sick since those early days. It was for something then – in theory. Now the only upside is weight loss, but the sagginess remains. Our antenatal teacher said some women like the changes, they 'feel more like a mum'.

I'm sleeping in your room. E washes his hands every time I look at him. 'The deal's closing next week,' he says. I don't ask what deal. He said he'll make soup tonight.

This morning I kept a rich tea biscuit down. That gave me the strength to take a shower (it really has been that bad). I had three missed calls when I came out. And a WhatsApp message. Lola:

> *Can you babysit JoJo today?*

> *What? I don't understand*

> *She's sick. School won't have her.*

> *I've got the same big*

> *I mean bug*

> *That works well.*

'Look after yourself,' they all say. No one bloody means it. The last thing I need is new germs. I had plans. I'm going to the council to ask about death records. And there's a drop-in session at Ben Palmer's local Samaritans. If he tried again, I might as well find out now.

If you don't hear from me, assume Josephine had a different and more aggressive strain and it was too much for my already frail body.

To: LRS_17@outlook.com
Fri 10/3, 19:18
SUBJECT: *Breakthrough*

I survived, and even better, I have a new path of enquiry. Credit goes to Josephine. She reminds me of those risky young hires we have sometimes. The ones with degrees in physics who may well drive away the rest of the team but you hope they'll invent new ways of doing things and pull you out of a rut. I tried to coin the term skunks for them (ingenious but dangerous – as in skunks are, not my invention of the term).

Skunk Josephine showed me a world of people online that Lola and I had missed. It could be something. But I don't want to raise your hopes before I know more. You've had enough of that in your short life – sorry, phrasal retentiveness. A social worker said that on a TV show about foster care. Made me think of you.

You're wondering how it went with Josephine. Well, she's at a difficult age. And whatever this bug is, it's made her regress to an even worse age.

She was watching cartoons when I arrived. Pink onesie, duvet round her shoulders – an oversized baby scooping handfuls of Frosties out of the box.

'On the mend already,' I say to Lola.

'Lazy, lazy teachers,' she replies and shouts to Josephine, 'Why you have to tell them you were sick?' They'd made it as far as the playground before Josephine described to a teacher how she'd been sick in her mother's bed. Wisely, the school has a forty-eight-hour quarantine rule.

'How are you feeling?' I ask Josephine.

She doesn't hear me over the TV. Wet crumbs fly from her mouth onto the rug as she laughs at her cartoon. I've brought alcohol gel.

'We'll have fun,' I say.

'Josephine,' Lola says, louder. 'Rachel will stay with you now.'

We go into the kitchen, where the walls and every cupboard are covered with Josephine's pictures of people with oversized heads, and with certificates, all with precise praise, as advocated by your parenting books. One says, 'For using full stops and finger spaces', another, 'For a vivid poster on carnivores and food chains'. Lola talks me through the antihistamine medicine and the EpiPen and hands me a laminated list of banned foods – nuts and sesame are the problem. She shows me a Tupperware of tomato soup in the fridge, a loaf and a bottle of Calpol. 'If she gets a fever,' she says.

'How do I know?'

'You touch her.'

She should eat if she's hungry but not if she's sickly, Lola adds. 'She likes apples.'

Lola says goodbye, Josephine grunts back and we're alone. I must have been the tenth person she called. She has sisters with kids, neighbours.

On a cupboard there's a photo of a little girl in school uniform, but it's not Josephine. It must be Abi. She looks well, happy. Nothing makes sense.

I sit in the armchair. I'm studying the EpiPen instructions when the cereal box lands by my feet, spreading Frosties across the carpet. Josephine's choking. Oh God, nuts in the cereal. Hidden nuts. Lola wouldn't. She was tired. Josephine can't breathe. No, she's coughing. Laughing?

'Cover your mouth!' I kneel, scoop up the mess, put some back in the box, tip them back out, there could be sesame traces on the floor. I shouldn't be left alone with her.

Josephine sniffs, gags, coughs. She's going to be sick. I open kitchen cupboards, the airing cupboard, knock over the drying rack with Lola's bedsheets. No buckets, no bowls.

'Get to the toilet.'

Her eyes are fixed on the screen. I move in front of the TV. 'Be sick in the toilet.'

She stamps on the floor. 'I'm not sick. More *Danger Mouse*.'

'Enough.' I switch it off.

She makes a whining sound. I can't switch it back on, there's that whole chapter in one of your books, 'consistency, always'.

'Shush. Please stop.' I join her on the sofa. 'How about a story?'

That works. She jumps up and returns with three thick books, cardboard pages. She presses against me as she sits down.

'These aren't stories,' I say, looking at a picture of a shoe and a rubber duck, the words 'BLUE' and 'YELLOW' beneath them. 'Where are your proper books? Roald Dahl?' Nothing. '*BFG*? Stories?'

'I like these ones.'

She leans her head on my arm, leaves it there. I make up a story about the duck living in a shoe, eating pink ice-cream and swimming in black paint. She wraps her arms around my arm, says she's Duck Three in the school show next week.

'Your duck is Donald,' she says, pointing at the book.

'He's Dylan,' I say.

'He's Donald.'

Dylan becomes more adventurous. He wanders through the green forest, eats a red toadstool, swells to twice his normal size and ends up in a white ambulance. Josephine whimpers. At the hospital – no obvious colour – Doctor Black Cat says the toadstool was deadly poison. Josephine's full-on crying.

'It's only a story,' I say, both flattered and alarmed. I make my hand into a dog shape, like a shadow puppet. 'Doctor Brown Dog says, "Don't be silly. Calpol will fix it." And Dylan Duck flew all the way home.'

'Again,' she says. 'No toast soil.'

'Toadstool.'

'Donald marries Daisy,' she says.

'Story's finished.'

'I'm hungry,' she says. It's ten past ten.

I make her a Marmite sandwich and coax her over to the table. 'I like jam,' she says but eats it. 'Mummy puts orange squash in my water.'

'She'll rot … it'll rot your teeth.'

'Can we play?' she asks. 'I'm the baby.'

'I'm too old,' I say.

'You're like Mummy,' she says.

'I'm younger. And I mean I'm too old to play.' So is Josephine.

'Pleeeeease.'

Half ten. Four more hours.

Josephine puts the duvet around her head, grips it under her chin. 'Hold me like a baby.' She sits on the floor, tugs at my trouser leg. My sickness is coming back.

'I need a cup of tea,' I say.

'Baby sick,' she says.

'Stop! You're not a baby.' My head is pounding.

'Baby sick. Make Baby better.'

'I can't. Get off!'

'Help me. Help me. Help me.' She's chanting, holds my leg. 'Help me. Help me.'

'I can't,' I shout. 'Some babies just die.'

She made me say it. And the midwife said it first. Josephine slumps back.

'It's OK,' I say. 'Please stop. Don't cry.' I kneel, stroke her hair.

'I die. You said.'

'No one's dying.'

'I don't want to go forever. Kayla's cat goed forever.'

Does she know about her cousin? We stay on the floor. My cuff is damp. We'll go over irregular verbs later.

'You ever tried warm orange water?' I ask. 'Makes you better.'

That's what she'll remember from this day. I'll be the woman with the warm orange squash.

She drinks two mugs, still on the floor. We're exhausted and empty. She asks for my phone. 'Just this once,' I say, like we both know there'll be more times together, a chance to do this better.

I show her pictures of our cat, Lester: curled up on E's lap; a selfie with all three of us in bed, stretched out with his tummy in the air. 'Look at his matching grey beanbag and his posh collar,' I say. 'He's spoilt.'

'Spoiled? What happened to him?' she asks.

'Don't ask me. My husband made him like that. And his ex.'

Josephine shows no recognition of the word ex. If I ask about her dad, will she tell Lola?

'Oko,' she says and we veer off in another direction. If only everyone was like Josephine. 'Oko, oko, oko.'

'It's only a palindrome if it's actually a word,' I explain.

'Oko,' she says again. 'Yoruba for husband.' She writes it down for me, there are dots under the O's.

She picks up my phone, asks me to go on Gumtree and shows me how she looks for kittens.

'I didn't know you're getting a cat,' I say.

'Not yet.'

E used it once to sell a bike. Why didn't we think of it before? Turns out you can find anything and anyone on Gumtree.

'Do you want *Danger Mouse* back on?' I ask Josephine and take back my phone.

To: LRS_17@outlook.com
Sun 12/3 15:23
SUBJECT: Visitor

I've had to borrow Francis. Gumtree was the gateway, Francis is the key, or something like that. But like I said, no hope-raising yet, just trust me.

'I wish I'd thought of it sooner,' my mother says, handing me a roll of poo bags and a new tennis ball. She goes back out to her car. Francis howls. Lester's on the kitchen counter, back arched, claws digging into the oak.

My mother comes back with a velvet cushion, dog food, a Tupperware and a shoebox full of medicines that is bigger than the dog himself. 'Fresh air, exercise, a morning routine. He'll get you back to normal.' She hands me a bowl inscribed *SAUSAGE'S SAUSAGES*.

Things are getting out of hand. 'I can only take him for two days. Three at most.'

Francis was my replacement when I moved out. She redecorated my room for him. I wonder who'll be his replacement – he can't have much longer, his brown fur is turning to grey around his mouth and on his toes. Then again, E went grey at thirty. Not on his toes.

She produces a set of printed Francis instructions from her handbag as if she always carries them. 'Feeding times are in here. Water always. Maximum one pizzle a day, supervised.'

'Pizzle?'

'His chews.' She rattles the Tupperware. 'And don't forget his safe word.'

'His what?'

'Safe word. To tell him when to go. Do his mess.' She shoos Lester off the kitchen counter, helps herself to my disinfectant spray and paper towels.

'That's not what a safe word is,' I say.

'Makes him feel safe, relaxes things. You say "business".'

'Business,' I repeat back.

'Higher. It's the tone they understand.' She's spraying the counter a second time.

'He has a safe tone?'

'Yes. And the safe word,' she says.

'For when it gets too much? When he's uncomfortable?'

'If that's how you want to put it. And I don't know why it's funny

– we all need to go, Rachel. Don't forget: before the car, after walks, last thing at night.' She tuts as she throws the paper towels in our overfilled bin. It's E's job to empty it, or it used to be.

I try it again, sing-songy: 'Business!'

'Not now!' shouts my mother. 'Francis, Stop!' He lowers his leg. 'Clever boy. Naughty Rachel.' She crouches down to kiss him, 'Don't forget, Mummy loves you.' She gives me a squeeze on the arm – that's new since you. 'Behave yourself,' she says on her way out. He's not listening.

Again, I hesitate to tell you any more for now.

Either way, it'll be nice to take Francis to meet Josephine. I've promised she can walk him. She also asked me to come to her school play tomorrow, Duck Three's big day. 'Watch me, watch me, watch me.'

I said I'd try.

To: LRS_17@outlook.com
Sun 12/3, 22:47
SUBJECT: *Unreasonable*

You'll like this. I've been looking into divorce. Not like that. But reasons people cite, like has anyone ever put 'inside-out socks'? Maybe with an explanatory footnote, like:

*The complainant suffered sustained spousal assault in the form of inappropriately orientated socks, underpants and other garments placed in the familial laundry basket.

Turns out there are only five official reasons to pick from but one of them is unreasonable behaviour, so there you go.

The leaflet from the bereavement midwife said talking to each other will help. Must be written by an idiot. When I see E, I see you not here.

To: LRS_17@outlook.com
Mon 13/3, 12:57
SUBJECT: Dog day

We are never getting a dog. Or perhaps it's just Francis. Poor thing can't help his parenting. But we need him. There's a Ben Palmer waiting to meet him. Dog walker Ben Palmer from Gumtree. I emailed him, set up a meeting. Now you know.

I'm shattered and it's not just the nerves. Francis and I were up at the same time as E, out in the garden in the dark. My mother was right about his 'itty bitty bladder'. I sheltered in the doorway calling 'business' to him while he circled on the spot, crouched, edged one paw off the ground, circled, crouched. His big eyes looked up at me to say, 'My real mummy brings an umbrella.' More than once I tried to step back inside, leaving him to get on with it. Each time, he followed me in, his business unfinished, then barked at the door as soon as I closed it. My mother didn't mention this particular need for accompanied peeing in her notes. Should have known. I was twelve when she stopped following me to the toilet. She'd perch on the edge of the bathtub, asking what I wanted for dinner or what I made of my father's latest receptionist. 'I was that slim before I had you,' she'd say. I remember the day I asked her to stop. 'These things start and you don't want them to end,' she said. 'You'll see.' She had no one else to talk to.

The in and out to the garden goes on so long and annoys E so much, I can't help laughing.

'For God's sake.' He shouts louder than he needs to over the yapping. 'I don't know why your mum couldn't leave him with her neighbours.'

'They're away. Half-term or something.'

At eleven, I phone the number on Ben Palmer's advert to ask if we can meet earlier but get his voicemail. I call three more times and listen to the message. ('It's Ben, bark after the beep.') He sounds happy enough. Cocky.

We'll set off soon. It's Peckham, not Kennington, but close enough, and people move and they lie. His voice sounds the right age. The next email you receive will be the big one (unless you're already the unlucky recipient of erectile dysfunction spam, in which case you get that subject line all the time – I should log into your account). And if you don't hear from me, you have three options to pick from:

1. I've solved it. Everything happens for a reason. Ben Palmer is the Second Messiah and we have run away to form a sect in New Mexico, or hopefully Provence.
2. Ben Palmer is a serial killer, I shall end my days in a flat in Peckham and Francis will take several months to eat my corpse. As the last person to know of my whereabouts, ideally you should send help.
3. It isn't him. I will never find him. Nothing happens for a reason.

To: LRS_17@outlook.com
Mon 13/3, 18:54
SUBJECT: Stumped

However you pictured this, forget it. Abandon your notions of hugs, tears and Radio 4 True Life stories. But it's him, definitely him, our Ben Palmer. Same shoulders, same smell, and the coat. It was hanging on the back of the door in his pathetic little flat with empty walls and bizarre show-home cushions. I don't know how to explain everything. I'm on my third attempt here. What am I supposed to think? God, if you'd seen him. Can you see him? I'm not being clear. He was the right Ben Palmer but the wrong man to save.

The bed was in the lounge; it's all one room, hob and sink in the corner. And no TV. He has nothing. I'm not a snob, just saying he's not a brain surgeon. He's a Gumtree dog walker. Arrogant with nothing to be arrogant about. And if he recognised me he hid it well. Oh God, I hate telling you any of this. Of course he didn't recognise me. I'd done my hair the same as then, a loose plait, my usual bit of eyeliner and blush. I wore a top the same shade of pink as the summer dress. Pointless. He can't even remember last week. He's taking something, probably anything he can get. He had marks on his arms.

Do you know what wound me up the most?

Me. Me and my stupid need for him to like me.

He's not even my kind of good-looking. He has this look-at-me beard and a tight T-shirt. But his eyes look frightened and interested at the same time. Imagine someone who's been abandoned by everyone else in the playground and you come along and ask to play with him. Except in this case his saviour stank of dog vomit because that's another thing my mother failed to mention about Francis.

And we were late, because it's all metered parking where Ben Palmer lives, though quite why is a mystery.

This is how he greets us: 'We said two. I'll struggle to get him a proper walk in.' His voice is low and harsh.

I give him a few seconds. We're there to meet him, I explain, like I said in the email and in my voicemail, to see if my dog likes him, not for dog walking today, I don't have any money on me. I talk and talk, waiting for him to recognise me. But he doesn't look at me. He's down on the floor, fussing over Francis. 'And who is this handsome old gent? What is he, twelve? Thirteen?'

'Francis. He's fourteen.'

'And in such good shape!' He kisses Francis and picks him up. He whispers to him while I'm still speaking, explaining about his medication, that he can't walk far. Neither of them can hear me. Francis is licking Ben's beard with the same mouth that splattered my passenger seat in half-digested tuna. Ben puts him down, looks at me, but still doesn't see it.

'Some people take the piss, you know. Book an hour, leave them two,' he says.

'Hard to trust anyone.'

His hair is like the fur on a water rat – it's not quite dry and goes into hundreds of tiny clumps. I want to break them up. He's a mess. Who thought this loser from Oval was worth the same as you? Nothing makes sense.

It was his fault I made an idiot of myself. He was asking Francis how he likes walkies in the parky-wark, is he allowed biccy-wiccies and what time is beddy-byes. 'And what should Benny-wen call you?'

'Frankie-wank,' I suggest.

Ben doesn't laugh. But I do, at my own joke, at Francis's tuna mouth, at Ben's doggy talk. I'm six years old, being told off, and I can't stop. Ben ruffles Francis's head and then his own, and now he's more hedgehog than rat. We went over a squashed hedgehog on the way.

'I guess Francis-wancis works too,' I say.

That gets a smile and he steps back, lets us in. It's like a show home that's too small for anyone to want. His clothes are on a bookcase, folded into squares like you see in Gap. There's only one radiator but it must be on full. Ben is barefoot.

'Did you always want to be a dog walker?' I ask. 'Is it the only job you've had?'

'Pays the bills,' he says. 'I'll need cash up front for today.'

I want to ask about his short-term memory. I explain again that we didn't come for dog walking today. 'And I just said, I don't have any cash.'

'Seriously? There's a cash machine at the end of the road. You said "sitting" on the phone. It's fifty quid for the night. You can pick him up at ten tomorrow,' he says.

'But I don't need sitting today. I just came to meet you.'

'That's how you made it sound. I booked him in. Had to turn down someone else.'

I take Francis with me to the cash machine, in the rain. On the way, I explain to him that Everything Happens for a Reason, that this is our way to see Ben again, for me to start over in the morning. He understands, he prefers Ben anyway.

As I hand Ben the money, I hold my face up for inspection. 'Don't bother to thank me,' I say.

I drove straight to Brixton for Josephine's show. But thanks to Ben Palmer's upfront cash policy, the school hall was emptying as I arrived.

At their flat, Lola answers the door wearing a dress and holding a mop – the old man upstairs flooded her kitchen again. Josephine rushes up behind her, caked in yellow face paint. Why do people insist ducks are yellow?

'Where's the dog? Where's Francis?' asks Josephine.

'Duck of the hour! Star of the show!' I say. She'll imagine I slipped in late, watched from the back.

'Where's Francis?' she asks.

'He had to stay with his new dog walker. I'll bring him when I pick you up tomorrow.' I look at Lola. 'The dog walker's called Ben. Ben Palmer.'

Lola's forehead creases. She thinks I'm joking. It's the first time I've seen her out of uniform, and with eye shadow. She looks younger and more grown up at the same time. It's a maxi dress, right to the floor, black with bright-pink flowers. Her bare arms look good.

In the kitchen, she refuses my offer to mop and so I sit and watch, hoping her dress is machine washable and searching for words to describe the real Ben Palmer.

'He could have been homeless, on drugs, dead,' says Lola. 'God provides.'

'He probably is on drugs. How could he not remember me?' I say.

'You weren't important to him that day. No one was.'

'I'm not saying I'm important. But I did, you know … if I hadn't, he wouldn't be here. And Luke would.'

She stops mopping. 'You don't know that.'

'The thing is, I do. It's the one thing I know. Someone somewhere wants me to know it. Like they wanted me to find you and find Ben.'

She can't argue with that. She wrings out the mop and waits for me to pick up the other end of the table so she can reach the last puddle.

Josephine shouts from the next room. She's sprawled on the sofa, on the TV a sausage dog is advertising insurance. 'Why does he get Francis? I was supposed to get Francis.'

I go over and she lunges at me. Her hair smells of toffee popcorn and hot tea. It's shea butter – you'd love it.

'Let's draw him,' Josephine says.

'Who?'

'Francis. Then he'll be here.'

Six weeks this week. I know you're a fast developer. If you were here, if you could see Ben Palmer, you would grab on to his scraggly beard, look into his blue eyes and make him explain everything.

To: LRS_17@outlook.com
Mon 13/3, 20:03
SUBJECT: *What am I here for?*

Top three understatements: This is not how I envisioned my spring. Things are tricky with E. Life without you feels like someone has ripped my arms off and I will be looking for them, and for you, forever.

To: LRS_17@outlook.com
Mon 13/3, 23:17
SUBJECT: *Special Agent Sausage*

At this point, my only hope lies in little Francis pinning down Ben
Palmer in his show-home bed, licking his secrets out of him and
developing the ability to report back in the morning.

It wasn't going to be obvious right away. The brain surgeon was
just an example for you and Lola. Now as I sit in the bathroom – I'll
explain in a minute – I am working through it again. This is what we
know: he's not a brain surgeon, nor is there any evidence he runs a
vast philanthropic fund, but he is quite nice to dogs. Or maybe he
does run a fund, a charity, and he gives it all away, lives like a monk
(the throw cushions had a bit of that Tibetan orange in them). The
reason is something we cannot see, as Graham would say. But we're
closer to finding it. And this could sound weird – or not, because
you are closer to those in charge and probably know this already –
there's something in him, as in, I sensed you there, a bit of you.

Why am I in the bathroom? The simple answer is that using my
phone in the bedroom pisses E off. The longer answer is that I am
wise enough to know when I have exhausted his patience.

First sign was the shouting as he came in.

'You haven't brought him into bed, have you?'

I'd climbed under the duvet after *The One Show* – pretending to
lie on a train track and then under a shroud, if you really want to
know.

E called up the stairs. 'You know he'll end up pissing on you. Or
worse.'

I roll to face the window. Behind me, the landing light goes on.
'Oh hi,' I say. 'Did you just come in?'

'You haven't got him under the duvet?'

'What?' I prop myself up on the pillows. If he asks about the
jumper, I'll say I was cold. He can't see the jeans.

'Francis. Where is he?' E grabs a corner of the duvet. I slam my hands down.

'It's freezing.' I make my voice croaky. 'What are you doing?'

'He's not in his bed.'

'He's probably under the sofa.' Maybe I had been asleep. I can't think fast enough.

'He's not anywhere downstairs. Nor in the guest room,' says E.

'Please don't call it that.'

'Where is he?' E's looking under our bed, which is absurd because even my slippers won't fit under there and Francis has been above his target weight for several years.

'He's gone,' I say. 'You seemed so pissed off at having him in the house, I told Mum to come back early. She's collecting the rest of his stuff in the car tomorrow.'

'God. You always do this, you...'

'There's Bolognese in the fridge,' I call down the stairs.

I retreat under the duvet and wonder which of us would make the worse parent. I search for a tune for Everything Happens for a Reason, my constant bedtime companion. Slow and low, like Nick Cave, sounds best, although I can also see it working as a Eurovision song, fast and insincere. Downstairs, E turns on the TV, microwaves spaghetti, opens a beer. So many unexpected elements to the caveman diet.

When and how are we put in these groups? The philosophers like you and me; the depressives like Ben; and the easily pleased Es of the world, skipping through life from one little indulgence to the next, KitKat to quiz show to glass of red. There are those calendars with patronising orders to live by: 'feel a tropical beach between your toes'; 'slurp oysters from the waves'; 'ride on a seahorse'. I'm bringing out an alternative for our austere times: 'stand in a sandpit, have a fish finger sandwich and treat yourself to an Uber to work. (Because if those little things don't cheer you up, nor will a trip to Barbados.)' Some people are born to be happy whatever.

E finishes shouting answers at the TV quiz and clunks his plate into the sink – my cue to hide in the bathroom. 'What are you doing now?' he asks through the door.

'Epilating.'

A philosopher would follow up, E goes to bed.

He'll be asleep by now, but I won't flush. I wonder if Ben Palmer flushes at night or if it starts the dogs off. Do dogs have litter trays? Do you think he has the same ones all the time? Is it enough to live off?

To: LRS_17@outlook.com
Tues 14/3, 19:20
SUBJECT: Dressing gown

Tiny blue dressing gown. Add it to the off-limits items. In a bathroom in Peckham.

There are obvious places I know not to go: the café with the soft-play corner, parks with daffodils, buses 35, 45, 345 (stopping at the hospital). But I'm never safe from random attacks.

It was the same one I bought for you. And they had the matching towel on the radiator, teddy-bear ears on the hood. I know this self-pity is predictable (at least something is), but WHY US? WHY?

I unpacked yours when I came in, it's on my lap. The whole hospital bag smells of your arrival. Non-biological washing powder and the leaking lavender oil.

Your chart says bath time is a big part of your day now. Do you think I can take something, go to sleep and we'll wake up together, put you in that dressing gown? I'd read to you, tell you stories like this one, let's call it 'A Better Day with Ben'.

No more wallowing. Story time.

As you will remember from the last instalment, I let Ben keep Francis overnight, my ticket to a second meeting.

Because everyone says I should be trying new things, I decide to take the Overground – known to my younger colleagues as the Ginger Line.

In preparation, I spend half an hour searching for the Peruvian hat with ear flaps and another twenty minutes emptying the contents of my handbag into one of E's rucksacks. I transfer all the little pieces of you – the pregnancy test, a lip-balm tin holding your hair, the scan pictures – into another handbag with a long strap I can wear across my chest. I can't do rucksacks anymore – remember that one E gave us at eight months, after that fall? It balanced you out but I looked like a pregnant girl scout.

It's too early for the Ginger Line's clientele. The platform is empty. Ben Palmer should have tried here.

When I'm on the train, a message arrives from E:

Sorry you misunderstand me

Then another:

Misunderstood. Bloody autocorrect.

It's the kind of non-apology you hear from philandering politicians. I don't reply and another text arrives a minute later.

Thanks for the Bolognese. Delicious.

Another minute and he sends a spaghetti emoji followed by a smiley face licking its lips. I reply with a face sticking its tongue out but smiling. He replies with two kisses and a potato emoji – for Spud, a silly name I used to call him. (The night we met, people were talking about nicknames. He said his was 'King Edward'. I asked, 'Because you look like a potato?' He said, 'What? No. Because my parents have this thing about me ruling the world.' When he asked me to dinner, I took him a King Edward potato, to prove my point: they're a famous potato.)

I find my notepad and prep for Ben Palmer. I wouldn't say HR was my passion and I'll probably end up doing something else one day, run a café or, with the right support, study law. But I'm good at my job and the skills are transferable.

The trick with interviewing is to start from where you want to end up and work back.

I make a list of the things I must find out about Ben Palmer. Then I number them in order of priority.

4. Was there a specific reason to jump, or a range of factors?
2. How many friends does he have? Where are his parents?
3. Are they glad he's still alive?
5. What has he accomplished since last June? Did he feel different on or after 1st February this year?
6. Where does he see himself in five years' time?
1. What would he like to say to the woman who saved him?

Once you have your list, you think about how to formulate your questions. There are basic rules, like keeping things open to pre-empt yes/no answers (number three above, for example, you'd phrase as 'How glad is everyone that you're still alive?'). You also tailor your questions to what makes the interviewee most comfortable. Try to find a common interest, or invent one. So for Ben Palmer, you might ask, 'What dogs did you have growing up?' 'Do your parents still have dogs?' Finally, in the back of your mind you need one overarching question that you never reveal. That might be, 'Can I be sure this person won't leave/mess up/get arrested (delete as appropriate) like the last one?' Or more specific, like, 'Is this person desperate enough to move to southern Hungary when our powdered-foods division inevitably relocates there in six months' time?'

I'm not saying the overarching question is always easy to find. With Ben Palmer, whichever way I phrase it, the answer would only ever be no. Who could be worth more than you? I crossed out all my attempts and instead wrote, Everything Happens for a Reason. I added a question mark and when I looked up we were at Surrey Quays. I'd missed my stop.

It was some time after ten o'clock when I arrived at Ben Palmer's. I braced for rebukes about 'taking the piss'. No doubt he'd also demand an extra day's money for the twenty-minute overshoot.

He answers the door in an open hoodie and boxer shorts, Francis under his arm.

'We're not quite ready,' he says.

'Ready for what?'

'We're having some breakfast.' Ben kisses Francis, puts him down.

I perch on the end of his bed, there's no sofa. The cushions are plumped up and aligned same as yesterday. Ben takes a jug from the microwave and pours the contents into two bowls. He adds honey to one and dips his finger in the other and places it on the floor for Francis. I watch his stomach muscles as he bends. He's not how you'd imagine a suicidal loner. More like Mr April from a Hot Guys With Sausage Dogs calendar. Though I suppose one can be both.

'Natural bacteria,' he says at last.

I don't know what I'm supposed to answer.

'Yoghurt and porridge,' he adds. 'It's what his gut needs, dog his age. You tried him on sweet potatoes?'

'Once or twice,' I say. 'Fries and mash. But he turned his nose up. Something about the seasoning being off.'

'He's too old for canned food. You know that, right?' The sharp edge is back.

'Have you got many walks booked today? Maybe Francis and I could join you.'

Ben leans down to Francis, lets him lick his spoon. 'You would love walkies with Biscuit the beagle-weagle, wouldn't you?'

'I love beagle-weagles too,' I say, and I mean it. They're proper dogs.

'Alright,' says Ben and we wait while he finishes his porridge, with the same spoon.

The dressing gown is the beagle's fault. He lives down the road from Ben, in a single-fronted Victorian semi. Ben has their alarm code. It's a similar layout to our place. The beagle barks from behind a stairgate to the kitchen and Francis replies from the hall.

'Go here,' says Ben when I ask if there are toilets in the park. 'Door before the kitchen, or top of the stairs.'

I choose upstairs where he won't hear me. It's when I sit down, I see it. On the back of the bathroom door. I start a text to E, that someone's stolen our life. They have the organic chamomile shampoo and body-wash set. The same bath thermometer. I don't send it.

They're using one of the bedrooms as a study, anatomy books. In another there's a cot and a changing table with an open pack of nappies. In the master bedroom, there's a Moses basket by the bed. A white babygro hangs over the side of the basket, ready for bedtime. On the bedside table is a stack of square photos, mock Polaroid style. They've written dates on them. Under a picture of a newborn wrapped in a hospital blanket, it says *4.2.2017*. Two days after your birthday – or whatever I'm supposed to call it. I slip a close-up of a hand into my pocket.

We go to a park called Telegraph Hill. The beagle, Biscuit, can't wait to get away from us humans. When Ben lets them loose, Francis scuttles behind his new friend. Here's a funny thing: when he speeds up, one of his back legs doesn't touch the ground and he's running on three, you'd love it. They stop every twenty yards to sniff each other and whisper about us.

Ben nods hello to some of the other dog walkers and to a woman about his age, late twenties, sunglasses, small dog. He seems happy to walk in silence, apart from the odd remark about Francis, who is apparently 'calm for his breed' and 'clearly well socialised'. I'm silent, too, the dressing gown has derailed me. I meant to review my questions while I was in the bathroom.

At the top of the hill, there's a view across to Big Ben, the London Eye, St Paul's. 'This is amazing,' I say. 'You must feel like you have the best job in the world.'

'Beats working, if I'm honest.'

'Funny name, Telegraph Hill. You're so young, I bet you don't know what a telegraph is.' What's wrong with me? A few hours with Francis and I've turned into my mother. I don't know what a telegraph is either. Same as a telegram? 'Can't decide if I love or hate the Shard,' I say. Ben accelerates to catch up with Biscuit. 'Did you grow up around here?' I ask. He pretends not to hear.

Francis stops to do his business and looks to Ben, not me, for reassurance. 'Clever sausage,' says Ben and bags it.

I stay a few steps back after that. The poo bag isn't airtight and it swings back and forth in Ben's hand like those incense shakers in old churches. Whenever I get too close, I stop and pretend I'm sizing up the Shard. Other dog walkers must think we're a fighting couple. The whole point of this walk was to make him open up. Fresh air, his own turf, chatting side by side. Did you know that's what men prefer? Go in any pub and you'll see it: women facing each other at little tables, men side by side at the bar. I read that when you were growing, in an article about boys and mental health.

I catch up with him after he's dropped the bag in a bin. I feel for the notepad in my bag, I can't see the questions.

'So, do I pass?' Ben's facing me, holding Francis.

'Pass? Pass what?' I shove the notepad deeper into the bag.

'Like, make the grade. Do I get Francis?'

'I'll have to check with my mum … I mean, she likes to walk him too.'

Ben's embarrassed for me. 'I've got a special offer on sausage dogs,' he says.

'Free portion of fries with every order?' I say.

He covers Francis's ears and tuts.

'Yes, you make the grade. I'll bring him back tomorrow,' I say. 'Right now, he has a date with a little girl.'

To: LRS_17@outlook.com
Wed 15/3, 15:35
SUBJECT: *Never wash off*

Oh God, oh God, oh God. Remember Francis's pizzles? A woman in Ben's park told me what they are. Full name Bull Pizzles. No way my mother knew. Ben said, 'It's better they get eaten than go in the bin.' He did that thing animal people do, where they make it seem like you're the one with a hygiene problem.

We walked with him and Biscuit and a spaniel called Meredith, who was mad but seemed to come from a nice home, same road as Biscuit. She rolled as much as she walked and tried to climb on top of Francis. I've looked it up, some girl dogs do that.

Ben was chattier today. He says he tries to fit in at least six dogs a day. I get the impression he hasn't been doing it long. Another dog walker, Pete, seems to have started him off. Ben picks up dogs that Pete doesn't want or can't fit in. Biscuit was one of those, 'bit of a pain, squirrel chaser'.

I can't hear an accent, just neutral southerner, maybe some Essex that he's trying to hide. He's bad at eye contact but smiles at people he seems to know from his walks. He walks faster than normal, but I suppose he's in a rush to pick up the next dogs. I asked him if he wanted to stop for a sandwich at the park café. He didn't say anything, so I said, 'I mean, can I buy you a sandwich? I'm paying.'

More silence. 'I promised I'd get Meredith back, then I've got three Cockapoos.'

I'd scared him. I'll just go for some of the walk tomorrow, meet him at the top of the park, twenty minutes or so, show I care, that he's hired, but I'm not mad, or in love with him. We'll build up from there, for as long as it takes to find the reason – why they swapped you, what makes him so much better. I should hate him. But he's not hate-able. Behind the hard voice and the angry walk, there's something frightened, that needs help.

To: LRS_17@outlook.com
Wed 15/3, 15:49
SUBJECT: Upside down

I'm so slow. But you see it, don't you? We're coming at this the wrong way round. We didn't save him because he was doing great things, we saved him because he has great things yet to do. Wow – I'm JFK, somebody shoot me. Sorry. Point is, Ben needs more saving. Gentle saving, without sandwiches for now. I'll make a list of all the things he's here to do.

To: LRS_17@outlook.com
Thu 16/3, 10:36
SUBJECT: Fwd: Shower for Maggie, 1pm, Sunday 16th April

Now I understand what happened. You lived, I died and I'm in hell.

> Begin forwarded message:
> From: Florence Roach
> Thu 16/3, 10:20
> SUBJECT: Shower for Maggie, 1pm, Sunday 16th April
>
> Dear All,

Six short weeks until Maggie and Damian welcome '**Little Button**' (working title!).

You all received the SHOWER SAVE THE DATE back in January but in case it got lost or you haven't had a chance to **RSVP** yet, please do so as quick as you can for the caterers – still waiting on six of you. ;-)

Maggie has made a special request to use the shower to announce the gender with a **cake** – it will be cut after the sandwiches (and a few little **surprise games** we have prepared). The colour of sponge will reveal if Button is Mini-Mags or Diddi-Damo. Place your bets!!!!

A few reminders:

– If you click through to the shower page you'll see again the **lyrics** for the song ('The Power of Mums') to be performed before the food. Tune is 'Power of Love' (Huey Lewis/Back to Future one, NOT Frankie Goes to H :-)))). Feel free to read lyrics off your phone on the day if you don't have time to learn them.

– As per the SAVE THE DATE, everyone is asked to bring a **short poem** or message to write on the decoupage paper that will cover the **unicorn**. (Mega thanks to Krish for papier-mâché wizardry!!)

– If you haven't yet managed, please upload your **video** – ideally starring your own little buttons* – or email it to me if you're struggling. *Sorry, no kids on the day – we're hoping grandparents are in town for Easter weekend and you can all have a few hours off!

– Please don't leave without a *postcard*!!! Plan is to send Button a card every fortnight for his/her first year. We've put the address and stamps on and date in pencil – all you have to do is fill in your special message and pop it in the post. If your brain's anything like mine these days, you'll want to set a reminder!

– GIFTS: On the shower page, you'll also find the *gift list* with your allocated items (no one wants ten changing bags!!!) and suggested websites (please do check delivery times!). There have been a couple of questions about blue or pink, but as mentioned before, Maggie and Damian will be bringing up Button in a gender-neutral home and preferred colours are *white and grey*. (No yellow, please!)

– FOOD & DRINK: We thought it would be fairest to split the cost (excluding Maggie and her lovely mum, Susan, of course!!!). If everyone contributes, it's just *£20 a head*. Give me a shout if you need my bank details again, or the details for the JustGiving page for Maggie's chosen charities.

– DRESS CODE: *Party dresses!* (But no stilettos, please!)

Phew! Think that's everything.

Looking forward to seeing all of Maggie's special ladies,

Flo
xxx xxx
xxxxxxxx
xxxxxx
xxx
x
@Flofigures

'A life without purpose is like the sky without stars.' – Anon.

To: LRS_17@outlook.com
Thu 16/3, 10:40
SUBJECT: *Astronomical idiot*

The sky always has stars, you just can't always see them. They are suns in other solar systems. I'm attaching a diagram for you.

To: LRS_17@outlook.com
Thu 16/3, 10:43
SUBJECT: *Koumpounophobia*

That's what they call the fear of buttons.

To: LRS_17@outlook.com
Thu 16/3, 10:48
SUBJECT: *Stuck*

Did I tell you the Save the Date was a magnet of their scan picture? I took it off the fridge. E put it back. I need a nap. Ben at two. Bet he hates baby showers. Do you think he got someone pregnant? Was he running away?

To: LRS_17@outlook.com
Mon 20/3, 16:22
SUBJECT: *Natural*

My mother said the baby shower could be 'helpful' and described Maggie as 'close family'.

'A sister-in-law isn't close, she's just a consequence of marrying someone,' I said.

'Being cold is no way to cope,' my mother said.

I asked if she knew what the pizzles were made from.

'They're all natural, if that's what you mean.' She stirs in a second sachet of sweetener. We've stopped for a coffee in her park.

'Natural what?' I ask.

'I don't like to think about these things too much. The vet started me on them. You haven't been talking to those raw-food women on the common, have you?'

Dog food has movements.

'It was a woman with two terriers,' I say. 'She told me about pizzles.'

'They're his favourite, perfect size, why would I fiddle with that?'

'Please don't say "fiddle".'

She lifts Francis onto her lap, does her baby voice to him, 'Your silly sister.'

I know I'm being childish. If you were here, I'd tell you it's just body parts, nothing to giggle about. We were going to bath you in the en-suite sink, safer than the bath tub, perfect size.

To: LRS_17@outlook.com
Sun 26/3, 14:13
SUBJECT: *Mother's Day*

No one has called to check on me. Lola texted. I bought myself a box of chocolates. Not from you, but because I was in Tesco, they were on offer and I didn't fancy anything else for lunch. We can say they're from you, if you like. E is at lunch with Susan and heavily pregnant Maggie, a phrase bomb waiting to detonate. We told them I am taking my mother out.

To: LRS_17@outlook.com
Mon 27/3, 21:10
SUBJECT: *Walkies*

Busy few days, been meaning to write more. I've got myself into a silly situation. As you've guessed, Ben has indeed become Francis's dog walker but that's of limited use – talking to Ben at drop-off and pick-up is insufficient. Wouldn't it be amazing if you could mic up a dog like a mole, the spy kind, I mean, not the cute garden animal? Well you can't, so I am going on the walks with them. Paid walks, as in I pay him fifteen pounds a time but I walk with him. You'd think Ben would make some attempt to decline the money, or give me a couple of walks for free. But he's desperate. He says it's going well but he lives off porridge, he's fallen out with his landlord and he can't afford to text me back. Don't take this personally, but the etiquette is you reply to messages, even when there's no question. Ben doesn't even reply to offers of help, like when I was doing an Ocado order and texted to ask what size bulbs he uses in the kitchen – one corner's in darkness. 'That was for me?' he said, when I asked him about it the next day.

We have the money of course, but the absurdity winds me up. Then again, life doesn't get more absurd than maternity leave without … we have this. E says to see it as a chance to try new things, read more, think about what I want. He knows what I want but he refuses to talk about you, what happens next, how we survive. He needs to go to New York next month, he says. It was a 'quick trip', then 'maybe a week or so' and now it's 'they basically don't know how long they'll need me.' But when he says, 'I can cancel if you need me to', it sounds like he means it.

Won't change my routine, which is both settled and sensible. E leaves, I get up, two dark-chocolate digestives and two coffees, collect Francis from my mother ('You're right, Mum, the fresh air makes everything better'), Ginger Line to Ben's, the walk, drop Francis back ('We're both getting so much out of this'), my mother feeds me sandwiches and crisps ('I'm so relieved you're normal again, Pebble'), stop at the little Tesco, more eating, then sleep. Sometimes Francis stays over, my mother says it makes him, and me, more settled. Sometimes I fit in hoovering or TV and when Lola's needed me, I've picked up Josephine (a whole other email, she's amazing), and most days I make time to bake something for Ben – he acts and looks hungry. He's a savoury type and loves cheese scones, focaccia, goat's-cheese muffins, but without the chives – it's helpful when people are honest. He's vegetarian but eats 'sustainable fish'. He eats anything with banana but not pears (like me!) and is not bothered with chocolate unless it's in cookies. I make enough for E. I taped a note to the green tin: *Don't be a caveman every day.* Quite pleased with my drawing of an unhappy stick man in a leopard skin.

The dressing gown is still there. Usually on the peg, today I found it on the bedroom floor. They've had more pictures printed – he has a mini rugby shirt. Biscuit comes with us Tuesday, Wednesday, Thursday, while the owner is out 'getting her nails, eyebrows and toes done', says Ben.

'She's probably out at baby groups,' I say.

'Groups?'

'Like read and rhyme at the library, baby yoga at the health centre.'

'And what about Biscuit?' he asks.

'You think he'd benefit from reading and yoga?'

'You know what I mean. See it all the time. Baby comes along and dog gets shoved under the bench.'

'Down the bench,' I say.

'Alright, Oxbridge.'

No need to correct him on everything. 'It's nice for Biscuit,' I say.

'Seriously? Can you imagine Francis sharing you with a baby?'

'Hadn't really thought about it.'

He's smarter than he wants me to know. It's as if he's scared to be himself. But that's the most insight I have on Oval, and in case you were wondering, no, he still has no idea it was me.

How do I know? I checked.

'God, we're lucky walking round parks while everyone else is struggling in and out of the city,' I said the other day. 'Know what I don't miss one bit? The Northern Line. Oval was the worst. Like shoving yourself into a cattle truck.'

'Seriously? Cattle trucks?' he says. 'Do you know some of them are just two weeks old, calves taken from their mothers, no light or clean water. Disgusting what humans will do.'

'OK, not cattle trucks. But you know what I mean. I went via Oval every day. Don't miss it one bit.'

He has these clever phrases – I'm hoping they'll drown out my other ones. You'll love this one about London. 'Full of people who insist on paying tuppence for a penny bun,' he says.

'Hang on, you've lost me,' I say.

'People only want stuff if it's expensive. Good news for me. Set your prices high, you've got something they want really bad.'

'I want a refund,' I say.

'You're the one who insisted on paying tuppence.'

'Which makes you a penny bun.'

Another phrase is 'he speaks Ben'. I've asked him why Francis ignores my pleas for him to stop eating Biscuit's p— (I can't even type it.) 'Why does the little weirdo only stop for you?' I asked.

'He speaks Ben,' he answered. 'And don't call him that. Poo has essential bacteria.'

Wish I spoke Ben. I've tried everything we ever did in

development training. He does go along with fun stuff. We did that thing – if you were a biscuit, what would you be.

'A teacake,' he says.

'Soft in the head?'

'Not quite sure what I am.' He laughs. (It's not as clever as it sounds. The whole is-it-a-biscuit-or-cake-for-tax-purposes malarkey has been back in the news.)

I should have made more of the moment. But it only came to me on the way home. I texted him:

You're a fortune cookie. If someone could look inside you, there's a message, the answers xxx

The next day I ask if he liked my message. He pulls out his phone, switches it on – he's supposed to be running a business, for God's sake.

'Why have you saved me as that?' I say.

'What?'

'20Q. On your phone. What's 20Q?'

'It's from a book I like,' he says.

'What book?'

'You wouldn't know it. Fantasy series. She's an astronaut.'

I'm telling you this not because I'm flattered but to show how little Ben knows or enquires about me. He doesn't ask what I do apart from this weird moment when he asked if I was a journalist – guess I have that look. He's never asked about E either (you'd hope he's noticed the wedding ring), or if I have kids. I've Googled 20Q and can't find the astronaut – just this online game.

Anything he does know about me is because I've offered it up in exchange for more of him. I rehearse on the train over, like a randy old man on the way to speed-dating. This was a good one: 'Always thought I'd have left London by the age of thirty-four. Bet you're not even thirty yet.' Nothing. I had to add, 'How old are you actually?'

He says he's twenty-seven.

I told him about my job, said I'm on a sabbatical, all I got back was he's done 'this and that' and 'can't beat dog walking'. We all practise phrases.

'You should put the dogs on Instagram,' I said the other day. 'Drum up more business, digital word of mouth.'

'False economy,' he says. 'It's a bunch of people you can't trust. Any sensible business owner knows you stay off all that.'

'Really? I thought that's what start-ups did, that's all they did.'

'Only the idiots,' he says. 'So most people, I guess.'

He says I'm the second person to come to him via Gumtree, all the others were via his friend Pete and dog owners recommending him to each other. Francis is his 'breakeven dog', he says. 'So I can take the ad down now, no more randoms.'

'I am the opposite of random,' I said. No reaction.

I know nothing about his past. He knows I've been in Clapham three years but when I asked 'what about you?' he dashed to pick up one of Biscuit's deposits – gives new meaning to the avoider's favourite, 'hang on, I have to get this'. But at the end of every walk he says the same: 'See you tomorrow?'

I need to take him away from the dogs, and maybe get him drunk, ask him braver questions, or just tell him about Oval. He'll recognise me, understand, help me work out what it is we need him to do. He's someone in waiting, he's waiting for his life to change but can't make it happen himself. You see that a lot. And there's something in us, what we are when we're together, Graham's connection you cannot see. What is it I cannot see?

I've been so desperate, I thought my mother might be able to help.

'Do you chat to other dog owners?' I ask her over fish-finger sandwiches (Friday).

'Have you and Francis made some little friends?' She's come from the hairdressers and her whole bob moves as one when she speaks.

'Do the other people talk to you? Do you walk together?' I ask.

'There's Rosemary with Rusk – terrier, getting on a bit, she has to carry him; and there's Mindy and Freya – Labs, their owner's the one who helped me that time with those lads; and the girl with a Huskie and a cross – always has a coffee, funny combination, Francis went for the Huskie, it's the ears. If it's early, there's Tinsel with the two women – think they're together; Badger with the older man – uses a stick—'

'You don't know any of their names?'

'The dogs' names.' She reaches over, wipes tartar sauce from the corner of my mouth. 'And Rosemary.'

'And do you and Rosemary talk? Does she know your name? About me? About Luke?'

She peels open her sandwich. 'Goodness. Forgot the vinegar.'

'Why can't—'

She's gone, calls from the kitchen. 'Forgot your apple juice too. What's wrong with me today?'

I haven't told you about Bug, real name: Ben. So we have to call him Bug. He's come out with us a couple of times and stayed over at Ben's. You'd want to roll around on the floor with him, he's what you call a puggle – Mum's a beagle, Dad's a pug. Imagine Biscuit had Francis's baby, it would look something like Bug, but rounder, like it lived off ice-cream and chips. (Sorry, always promised myself I wouldn't dodge this topic with you: Francis and Biscuit couldn't actually have a baby, because you need a man and a woman, or what we call a male and a female, or at least a sperm and an egg, at the very start, to make a baby I mean, not to have one. Two dads can have a baby, Francis and Biscuit would be great dads, actually they wouldn't, but two other boy dogs would, or two mum dogs. Bet you'd like two mum dogs.)

Bug is living proof that it's better for everyone when genes get mixed up. Unlike Francis and Biscuit, he doesn't eat p—, he doesn't roll in p— and he doesn't smear tennis balls in p—. He fetches them. Last couple of times, Ben left Bug and me to ball-throwing while he took the others up and down the hill. Also unlike the others, Bug doesn't go on a lead. Not because he doesn't need to (which he doesn't) but because he has to be able to escape. There's no nice way to put this: Francis and Biscuit bully him. One growls while the other sniffs his bottom and they nip at him. Bug shakes and yelps and his tail curls under his tummy. Bug's owners aren't helping with the novelty collars – today diamanté. I'm ashamed of Francis, but Ben says there's nothing we can do. 'The world's just shit to some of us,' he says.

'Doesn't sound very dog-trainery,' I say (he's doing an online course in canine behaviour – taught Francis to play dead on command).

'First principle of any training is to accept limits,' he says.

Predictable motto for someone who's happy with breakeven. I've done a quick spreadsheet. If he had six more per day and two overnight dogs on two nights a week, it would take him four months to afford a van that massively expands his catchment area (or whatever dogs call it) and he'd be on fifty to sixty thousand a year by Christmas.

There are so many ways he can make himself more attractive. Tell people about his behaviour expertise, trim his beard, wear a belt. I'll help. I've found recipes for homemade peanut-butter treats. I've ordered a bone-shaped cutter, they'll photograph so well. And I rang Mesh from IT, he says there's a good website name available, Peckhamexperts.co.uk – broad in case we want to go beyond dogs. People miss me, he said.

Tomorrow, we're trying a different park, with a stream for them to paddle in and more space for Ben to practise a new manoeuvre with Francis; he calls it an emergency stop. I hope the new park's emptier. The hand signal for stop looks like a Nazi salute. 'STOP!' Is that what he shouted as we fell onto the platform?

To: LRS_17@outlook.com
Tue 28/3, 23:57
SUBJECT: *Found it*

You beautiful little genius. It's you, isn't it? Because I said going beyond dogs? You're helping me, you're making it all make sense. This is what we found him for. We're going to change grief. It's all been for this, everyone's nastiness, carelessness, Liz's card. We'll stop it all. Griefbusters. It all came from Ben. And you. Get some sleep. I'll tell you everything in the morning.

To: LRS_17@outlook.com
Wed 29/3, 10:46
SUBJECT: *It started with tofu tacos*

We ended up at dinner together. Because he said I was being 'offensive' about vegetarian food. All I said was, without meat it was difficult to achieve strong flavours – 'clout', I think I said.

'Because that's what matters to you, flavour?' asked Ben.

'In food, yes.'

He said he'd prove me wrong, he knew a great place near his flat.

'We could go into town,' I said. It's been two months since I crossed the river. 'I read about this Indian vegetarian place in Covent Garden.'

'What's wrong with my place?'

'Nothing, just fun to go somewhere new,' I said.

'Like Covent Garden? Hang out with tourists and theatre people?'

'Fine, your place.' If he'd been in a better mood, I'd have challenged him over the apparent xenophobia and homophobia.

'Eight?' he said.

'I'll have to check.'

Women shouldn't check with men before they go to dinner, but I texted E to be polite:

Did I mention I'm out tonight?

Oh God, not your mum's prayer group again?

They mean well. Defrosting a piece of salmon for you. x

An evening with Ben talking about animal welfare easily matches the prayer group for fanaticism and menacing smiles. Like when he said, 'I love the fact you all hate them being killed, but you'll eat them once they're chopped up.'

It was one of those places where you can bring your own wine, so I packed two bottles of white in my largest handbag. The second was a back-up, in case he drinks a lot. He does.

I wore a T-shirt, jeans and Converse (leather-free) and promised myself I wouldn't sound like my mother. We'd drink tap water, I'd make no comment on the wine getting warmer and I'd ignore the dirt under Ben's nails. Instead, I ended up sounding like my father. It was Ben's face as his eyes went up and down the menu. I felt the same – twelve pounds for cauliflower cheese with pumpkin seeds on top (untoasted, it turned out). 'Order anything you want,' I said. 'I'm paying.'

He didn't argue. But none of that's important.

We were on the main course when it happened. When people ask, and they will one day, I'll tell them he was eating risotto, I was trying tofu in a taco. Both were smothered in cheese in an attempt to make them more appetising – and Ben keeps telling me vegetarianism's good for losing weight.

'Not as good as my mum's,' he said, pushing a mushroom around the bowl. (Everything was served in bowls, so of course I could hear my mother's voice: 'Bowls are for dogs and monks.')

'Risotto's so hard to get right,' I say. 'Bet your mum's an amazing cook.'

'She was.' He puts his fork down, in a way that looks over-practised.

'Oh God, Ben, I'm so sorry. I didn't realise. I—'

'It's OK. It was last May. You know, cancer.'

'What type?' Why do people ask that? Why am I asking that?

'Everywhere by the end. Bowel at the start,' he says.

He'd been waiting to tell me, must be why he ordered the risotto, he didn't know how else to do it.

She was in a hospice at the end, back home in Bedford. Worst thing was, his dad didn't even know what was happening or who had died.

'Alzheimer's,' says Ben, pouring himself more wine. 'Mum used to say, "my fault for marrying an old man", tried to laugh about it. He got worse at the same pace as her cancer, like he was doing it on purpose.'

'You've had so much to cope with.'

'Doesn't everyone? But yeah.'

'Where's your dad now?' I ask.

'We moved him in with my sister, back home. We sold his house to pay for carers. Hardest thing was clearing it. We should have waited but my sister wouldn't, said to get it over with, quick before the summer, you know, before Brexit.'

'Brexit vote,' I interrupt.

'What?'

'It was a vote for Brexit. Not actual Brexit.'

'Whatever. She got these people in and they chucked half of Mum's stuff without asking us. Letters, theatre programmes, all her crosswords and sudokus. Mum used to tear them out of the paper every morning, used a little ruler, they were on a trolley by her chair. I was going to finish them, I'd told her I'd finish them.'

No one wails at gravesides any more, at least not in Bedford and Clapham. But all that grief has to go somewhere. We gather it up and squeeze it into one pot. For Ben it's lost sudokus. For my father and many like him, it's other people's driving. He swears, growls and spits out all his amassed fury inside the safety of his car. For me, I suppose it's baby showers and bragging Liz's. And maybe the phrases, and daffodils, and the left-it-too-long list. Ours is too big for one pot.

'He was called Terry,' says Ben. 'The man who threw it all away. Like this kid we called Smelly Terry at school. Said he'd pay us for anything valuable, charge us to get rid of what was left and we'd be left with a bit of a profit. Called it a "profit" from our mum and dad's stuff.'

'Were you?'

'Hundred and sixty quid. From her cut glass, couple of leather jackets, some paintings and a sideboard.'

'It must have been worth more than that,' I say.

'Course it was.' He picks up his glass, he's shaking. I can't picture him finishing a sudoku. 'But we were rushing, not thinking.'

'There's got to be a better way to do it,' I say. 'Like specialist, more sensitive house clearers when someone's passed away. Same thing happened to my friend. No time to grieve. No time to work out what to keep when her mum died. Lost all her gymnastics trophies and a gold watch that was her granddad's.'

'They're like buzzards.' He does weird claw shapes with his hands.
'Vultures.'

'Same thing,' he says. (I checked, they are not.)

'We should be anti-vultures,' I say.

'We?'

'You and I. We'd do it so much better. We could start a sensitive house-clearance business, for people who are grieving. We should do it! I'm super-organised, you'd know what to do with their pets.'

He laughs. 'Yeah, I suppose I am the expert on dog reallocation.' He sounds it out, posh voice, 're-all-oh-cay-shun' and pours me more wine from up high, it splashes.

'Think about it. We find people who are being forced to clear out their loved one's things – I don't know, look at notices in the paper, undertakers, word of mouth. We'd do a nice Gumtree advert, that would be you. We'd give them extra time, help them sort things into keep, pass on, sell ... no ... reincarnate, help them by giving their loved one's items new roles, new lives.'

He laughs again. It's a nervous laugh; people get scared of what they are supposed to do. 'Expensive way of clearing a house,' he says. 'I can just see you, spending four weeks looking for the perfect owner for a ten-quid Ikea rocking chair. Or like, "Excuse me, madam, this lampshade is looking for a purpose, can you help it?"'

'I'm from London, not the nineteen-fifties,' I say. 'Doesn't have to be expensive. It's about being focussed, knowing our mission. But I suppose we could charge more than normal ones.'

'You'd need a van, and a name,' he says. 'What are you doing?'

'Looking for a pen.' I find a pencil in my bag, write on the back of the menu. 'Van ... Name ... It should be something about new lives, afterlives, caring, calm, grief soothers.'

'Griefbusters!' he says.

'That's brilliant. We're griefbusters. And we can do all sorts of extra grief services too,' I say.

'What, we're undertakers now? Can I wear a top hat?'

'Stop it. I mean we could do memorials, like you have a while after the funeral, less rushed, better staged. Help people pick out poems, songs, flowers, nice quotes. We'd find out everything the person liked, make their favourite foods.'

'But they wouldn't be there,' he says.

'We'd do the work, find out all the little details, were they crusts-on or crusts-off, brown or white bread, mayo, no mayo. What's that grin?' His face looks like he needs the loo.

'My mum would have loved you,' he says. 'Took her ten minutes to ask what sandwich you wanted. "The little things," she'd say. "The little things."'

'"The little things" is a good name. Oh my God, that's what we'd do! Genius. Find out all the little things, everything about them and we could write messages like they came from them, all their little phrases. Special letters to their families, each in the style of Mum, Grandma, Sister.'

'Like they wrote them? Like they've come back to life? Jesus, Rachel.'

'Exactly!'

People like Ben just need examples of how they can succeed before they will try to succeed. He gets it now. He's looking into vans, costs and pricing, I'm working on a list of services. I've texted to say I can't walk with him today, too much to flesh out. He says he's 'super busy' too. My idea is we are there from the start to however long they need us. They turn to us when Liz's card comes, or better still, we head off Liz's card, we work out who it's safe to talk to, where it's safe to go. We know what it's like.

I need to call Lola. She'll love this.

To: LRS_17@outlook.com
Wed 29/3, 15:58
SUBJECT: *Proof*

Look what I found on one of the forums. I was trying to stay off them but now I need them for research. And sometimes they help. Who knows if they're all telling the truth, but I can pretend they're as crushed as us. Some are worse. Some women, and one or two dads (which I'm trying not to find weird), are still going on there years after it happened, retelling their story, everything that happens to them comes back to the baby. Like this one who started a new thread last week. It's like she's willing us to do it. I'm pasting in her post. You won't believe it. And you'll find it reassuring, all these other grown-ups also looking for answers. Will this be me in four years? (With a little more proofreading, 'obvs'. ;-))

Nightmare – mums house
Posted: Fri 24-March-17 20:26
by AngelMiasMummy

Just had the worst day and need your wise words ladies.
For newbies my precious Mia was born asleep 29 march
2013 (so obvs march my worst month) After Mia was taken
everything went bad. Her dad left. Got back with my old
boyfriend then 2 miscarriages and he moved away for work.
Mum got worse the cancer was back and in her spine. Lost
her boxing day. With Mia now. She left the house to me and
my sis. Solicitors doing the will said to sell now spring is the
best time (yeah thanks and he knows about Mia) and don't
leave it empty over winter. The house is full to roof because
she was a big collecter like plates ashtrays dolls. All nice
but not my style. So we called these people to come and
make a price for it all. They come today. The man says the
woman is his wife, family business but we get a bad vibe.
She's older than him. They both too old to be lifting boxes.
My sis put everything we're keeping like special plates and
photos and mums napkin ring in spare room and a note on
door DO NOT TOUCH ALL TO KEEP. We leave them
looking round and my sis and me both get that weird feeling
at the same time. He's in spare room her too they've got
the photos out on the bed and she's holding the shawl
mum made Mia and her nails are disgusting like she's been
digging with her hands. My sis asks what they doing and
he says people are always after old photos. Says he sells
them by weight. Asks if these ones are isle of wight he
knows the light house. Don't touch the shawl I say. She just
holds it and asks is it homemade. So my sis shouts at her
too, just get out. Read the sign this stuff is all off limit. But
they just stand there like it's all theirs and I can feel Mia

getting upset crying. Ahhh Hastings he says and look Rita that's the old chippy at Whitstable. So proud of my sis she shouts Just drop them detective dickhead (LOL!). He says Jesus it's just stuff and asks what's in the loft. NOTHING for you she shouts Just go. He's not even sorry just says call us when your really ready.

Anyone else gone thru this? How long did you wait? Gut says it's too soon after Mia and now we lost Mum it's too much. But also could do with the money and can't look after the house. Wish you could of seem him with his just stuff and her nails on Mia's shawl. Feel sick thinking they doing this to people who lost someone.

To: LRS_17@outlook.com
Wed 29/3, 16:41
SUBJECT: More proof

I broke my rule and wrote on the forum. I didn't mention you. I said she should call trading standards, report them, there are rules about these things. There must be rules. And I remembered what the solicitor told Susan when Roger was in the hospice: move the valuables out of the house. Take the shawl to your house, I told her, your mum would want that. She must be online a lot because she wrote right back, said thank you, good to know there are good people who 'wanna give back'. Then someone wrote underneath: 'For every bad apple there are twenty golden ones'. Golden Apples would be a good name.

Hers is the busiest thread on the site. So far, the general consensus is for her to wait to clear the house, it's too soon. 'It was eight years till I started to feel healed,' said one woman.

I'll be forty-two.

To: LRS_17@outlook.com
Wed 29/3, 23:30
SUBJECT: *Revolution*

It's too soon to tell E. He'd need profit forecasts, growth targets and a logo. I've taken the laptop into your room. He's somehow got the idea I'm helping someone at the prayer group with their CV. The dead rabbit's mum did seem like she could get a good job with a bit of help.

Lola didn't have time to listen properly when I called her. 'When would this be?' she asked. Now, I told her. 'Is now a good time?' she said. I'll explain it in person next time I am there.

Mia's mum's thread is getting longer all the time. The replies are all bereaved mothers and daughters and sisters, all with stories about being swindled and belittled. They need someone who's been through it. Me with my experience and Ben with his mother, whatever led to Oval.

It's like Mia's mum said: this is how we give back. Me for what I did to you, and Ben for what he did to us both. I'll put all those years of logistics experience, all my people skills to good use, and – please, don't take this badly – I'll make something brilliant out of this. House clearance that cares. Ben wouldn't even need to give up the dog walking. He could do both. I'd pay him a salary, keep him on a retainer for when the work comes in. His flat's always impeccable; he has a gift for sorting and tidying, those kind eyes and the Gumtree experience. It's like building and plumbing, we'd only have to be marginally better than the rest to be seen as amazing. But we will be amazing. We will do things so many times better. House clearance is the wrong term for it. We'd sit down with people/victims, talk about the person they've lost. We'd pick out charities they want to help, contact people they want to involve. There'd be 'keep', 'part' and 'donate' piles. We'll use colour-coded bags and boxes. And we'll offer extras, like a keep-pile processing service where we put the photos into albums, create scrapbooks of letters, organise long-term storage for those sensitive items that can only be confronted after a suitable passage of time. (I have most of the wording sorted. I've been a bereavement volcano waiting to blow – diagram attached; you'd love volcanoes.)

We'd start off gently, but expand. Once we've made the connection, there's so much more than house clearance, we'll do full-blown grief services. I've already started making notes of how and how not to treat a bereaved person, language to avoid. WE COULD ERADICATE THE PAIN OF PHRASES.

My best idea is afterlives. To be fair, I think I read it somewhere, but the way we'd do it is more appropriate. We'd collate the dead person's letters, photos, phone messages, stories from their family, and work out the kind of person they were, how they spoke, what they cared about. Once we have that virtual character sketch we'd create messages they'd have sent if they'd been alive. We'll send them on birthdays, anniversaries or at a pre-agreed regular interval or, if the family prefer, at random. You need an example.

Barry Samson dies aged fifty-seven, heart attack. He was a chemical engineer for a big cosmetics company. In his spare time, he built model railways, enjoyed board games and would watch anything with Robert Downey Jr. or Julie Walters. He loved Italian and Chinese food ('Chinese invented pasta,' he'd say every takeaway). At Christmas he pinched pigs in blankets off the turkey plate before he carried it through to the table, where his wife Sarah carved. He hated melon and white chocolate. He leaves behind: Sarah (fifty-six), sons James (thirty-one), William (twenty-eight), granddaughter Bella (two) and tortoise Robert Downey Jr. Jr. (twenty-five – an anniversary gift to Barry from Sarah). Barry was born in Glasgow but the family lived in London (early clients will be local). A video from Bella's last birthday party shows him to be articulate, kind and humorous, but his widow reports that sometimes Barry's jokes go too far. 'He once told my mother they could use her gravy to fix the national pothole crisis,' Sarah tells us at the familiarisation sit-down. 'She moved to granules after that.'

And what do we do with it all?

Firstly, you have the obvious scheduled messages, the birthdays of the above ('Grandpops here...'), wedding anniversary ('Hen, I'm making our linguine tonight. Make yours for seven and we'll sit down together'), Robert's annual vet check-up. ('Outliving everyone! You show 'em, Bobby-bairn! And give that nurse a peck on the cheek from me.')

After-Barry would send recipes, help with the day's crossword, comment on the news ('If that dunderheided Bob Dylan's a Nobel laureate then I'm prima ballerina at the Bolshoi!'). He'd run a Twitter account and appear in the comments sections on news sites (he is anti-Brexit, pro-royal family but anti-Charles, wants more rights for reptiles).

This bespoke messaging would be my area; Ben would be more on the house clearance and pet rehoming side.

To: LRS_17@outlook.com
Thu 30/3, 08:46
SUBJECT: *Talk*

Here are words any counsellor will tell you not to use on your partner: 'never' and 'anymore'.

On his way out, E says, 'We never talk properly anymore.'

'About what?'

'The world. Such mad times, so much going on. It's like you don't see it.'

'God, I have enough to cope with,' I say.

'That's how we got here. We alienate people, disenfranchise them.'

Tanya's lent him a book about rural Americans.

If he knew all the things I'm doing for alienated people. I was up until one. I've fleshed out afterlives, drafted our mission statement and started a task list for Ben. Remember Peckhamexperts.co.uk? Mesh texted last night, asked if we want to go ahead with it, he's offering to take photos of Ben with the dogs, asked for his number. Perfect timing, I wrote back, and asked him to get some pictures without dogs too. I don't know how to ask what he charges.

To: LRS_17@outlook.com
Thu 30/3, 14:46
SUBJECT: *Hysterical*

This will come out wrong however I say it, but no wonder he tried to kill himself. He goes mad over the tiniest things. Things that aren't even his problem. Not meat this time, although that did come up. This was about forums, I think.

He'd started off in a bad mood. When I found him at the park he was yanking at Biscuit's lead and shouting at a Chihuahua named Eleanor. But Francis got the usual kiss and tummy-rub and I got a thank-you for the breakfast muffins – I put a tube of beard conditioner in with them (left over from E's phase).

Eleanor's owners had forgotten to leave cash out, another owner had cancelled an hour before.

'I can lend you some money, if it helps,' I say.

'I have money. God, Rachel. That's not the point. They take the piss, like I'm doing this for a laugh. Like I'd choose to walk a fucking Chihuahua.'

'She's not much different from Francis,' I said.

'Seriously? No offence but it feels like you don't know anything about dachshunds.'

'Dinner was lovely,' I say.

'Enough clout for you?'

'Why are you being like this? Yes there was. But I stand by my view that the flavours are richer with meat.'

'So selfish.' He says it to Biscuit but I hear.

'Whatever you want to think,' I say. 'But I know you feel the same, otherwise you wouldn't eat fish.'

'Fish aren't meat. It's not the same.'

'Why not? We still kill them to eat them,' I say.

'They choose if they want to get caught.'

'What? Like if they feel suicidal they jump into the net?'

His face stays the same, but he changes the subject. 'You said you wanted to show me something.'

I find my phone. 'Look at this, read this bit. It's just like we said. And everyone underneath, it's all people who've been through it, too.'

'What is this?'

'Just read it. Look, this bit here.'

He hands back my phone, walks off.

'It's research,' I say, catching up. 'I went on different grief forums. And look what everyone's complaining about, house clearance, people ripping them off, throwing everything away. Like your mum's sudokus.'

'Oh my God, you're still talking about that?'

'I know it's hard. I'm sorry. But this is a way to make it better. To help other people. I've already—'

'Already what? Please tell me you haven't been writing on there? Talking to these fucking losers?'

'They're not losers. They're bereaved parents. And daughters, sons, different bereaved people,' I say.

'What did you write?'

Eleanor's yapping, she wants to be let off. He drops her lead and she runs towards another dog walker.

'I'll go after her,' I say.

'What did you write?'

'What does it matter to you? I said I was sorry for everything they were going through, gave them some practical tips. Look, she's bothering all those dogs on the lead. I'll go.'

When we return to Ben he's on his phone, leaving a message about the missing cash.

'Feeling better?' I ask when he's finished.

'What do you think? I tell you something about my mum and you blab it all over the Internet.'

'I didn't. That's not what I did. We said we were doing research. You vans, me clients. I'm showing you proof that our idea's genius, and you're screaming at me because you're fifteen quid down.'

'Thirty. And I'm not pissed off about that. I'm pissed off because you're all over the Internet making up bollocks about grief.'

'Oh my God, you sound like an old man. Next thing, you're going to tell me the Internet gives you cancer.'

Shit.

'Wow!' he says.

I run after him. 'I'm sorry. I didn't mean that. It came out wrong. I'm sorry.'

He's a sulking little kid, marching with his arms stiff by his sides, eyes fixed on the ground.

'Come on, Ben. I'm sorry. You know I didn't mean it.'

'And you know I hate the web. I told you a million times. All that Instagram bollocks you're into, you know I hate all that, what it does.'

'I didn't say anything about you. Why would I? I just said it sounded awful and wouldn't it be nice if there were people who cleared houses differently. You're massively over-reacting.'

'God, Rachel. You're so blind. And the funniest thing is people like you think you're the opposite, you know everything. One day you're telling me animals like being killed, now you're some fucking expert on my mum dying and you think making me go on some forum and whine about it with total strangers will make it all better.'

I was the one who stormed off. 'And you're being thick on purpose,' I said as I went. Then I had to double back because he had Francis and I had Eleanor. We swapped leads in silence.

How much did he drink last night? I've texted him, said I need his email, to explain things. Nothing back. I should sulk too, but we don't have time for that.

To: LRS_17@outlook.com
Thu 30/3, 15:23
SUBJECT: *Not good*

I can't get through to Mesh. Only just realised he is calling Ben today, about the website photos. I left a message, said Ben had a personal emergency, couldn't talk today. Then another message: 'If you already left Ben a message or texted or something and he does call back, don't mention the site. It's complicated but he's having some problems. Sorry, should have warned you. Just pretend it's some sort of mix-up. I gave you the number but it's the wrong number, as in, I gave you his number instead of someone else's, you were looking for another Ben, one from work.' Mesh isn't picking up.

To: LRS_17@outlook.com
Thu 30/3, 15:56
SUBJECT: *Dangerous*

Too late. Mesh had already called him. He said Ben went 'catshit crazy' – people swear a lot in our office, sorry. Ben's turned his phone off. Should I go round?

And Mesh is mad at me too. No, it's worse than mad – he thinks I'm damaged and pathetic. No one's going to believe we can set up this business.

He called me from the office canteen, I could hear the coffee machine. 'How do you even know this guy?' Mesh asks.

'Long story, but short version is he walks my dog. My mum's dog. And he's sweet underneath it all.'

'Sweet? He's dangerous,' says Mesh.

'He just has anger issues. Mental health. It's not his fault. Sorry, I should have warned you. Was it bad?'

'He was screaming down the phone. Could only get half of it. First he thought it was a prank, said you were sick, and evil – he said evil, about you. So I tried to laugh along with him, but told him "no, it's for real" and that you were paying for it, it was his lucky day, professional website, boost his business, and he lost it. Web's evil, you're evil, I'm evil, doesn't need any help. "Take it down," he says. "It's not up," I tell him, but he's like, "How do I know that?" And, "What if she puts it up, interfering cow." I told him that was out of line, calling you that, you're my friend and after everything you've been through.'

'What? You mentioned Luke?' I ask.

'I don't know. To be honest, Rachel, I didn't know what to say to him, how to talk to someone like that. I don't do conflict. When people scream at me about the printers, I always make it into a joke, you know, how they keep me in a job and everything. Always works. But he just kept going, ranting, calling you names. I just said it was unfair, talking about you like that, now, with everything that's happened. And he just says, "Yeah, poor, poor Rachel," and puts down the phone.'

'So you didn't say specifically about Luke?'

'I don't think so, I don't know,' says Mesh. 'God, I'm sorry, Rachel but it's like there was something a bit wrong with him, learning difficulties. I know you want to help but not now, you know.'

'You're right. Everyone's right. I'm sorry I got you into this.'

'Stop apologising. It's normal,' he says. 'You're looking for ways to make it all OK.'

'I am.'

To: LRS_17@outlook.com
Fri 31/3, 08:27
SUBJECT: *Silence*

Ben will calm down soon. I've stopped sending texts and voicemail doesn't work, just says this moron's phone is switched off. He'll miss me soon enough. Me and my fifteen-pound dog walk. And Francis. I'll send him a picture of Francis, one of my mother's many puppy ones – she used to email one a day. She stopped when he was ten months old, and I always wondered why. I promised myself I wouldn't do that with you. There'd be pictures every day forever, emailed to her and to Susan, if they behaved.

To: LRS_17@outlook.com
Fri 31/3, 11:15
SUBJECT: *Rude*

If his voicemail was working, here's what I'd say: 'I don't expect you to thank me, you didn't ask me to do it. But I did and you're here. You have no idea what this cost me. Now here we both are and we can make it all make sense. It was your idea. Call me when you've calmed down.'

And maybe another one: 'I have a name for the business. Luke's Touch. If you call me, I'll explain it.'

To: LRS_17@outlook.com
Fri 31/3, 14:21
SUBJECT: *Antidote*

Still nothing. I've promised Lola I'll pick up Josephine and I've promised Josephine I'll bring Francis. It's the last day of term so we're going for ice-cream, which is terrifying on the nuts front, but Lola insists it's safe and I haven't had ice-cream since before you (minor listeria risk).

To: LRS_17@outlook.com
Fri 31/3, 22:16
SUBJECT: *Exposure*

When the bereavement midwife said there would be good, bad and awful days, is this what she meant?

You'd think Lola would see what Josephine's school is for me.

There was a programme on the other night where people with spider phobias went to a workshop at a zoo. They start off with a talk from a spider keeper about how only 0.000001% of deaths are caused by spiders.

'You're more likely to die jumping onto a chair to avoid a spider,' she says.

I'm not a statistician, but isn't that also 'death caused by a spider'? The official deaths data is badly lacking in detail on causes. I'd like to think that when I go, a proper record is kept. But if we suppose 'spider bite' comes under accidental poisoning (3,187 cases) and falling off a chair comes under accidental falls (5,605), spider keeper Natasha is correct for the latest year of available data. But, and this is the kind of thing we would be learning together if you were here, being bitten by a spider is not actually poisoning. Poison is something you eat. If *it* eats *you*, it's venom. Did you know suicide was the leading cause of death for people aged twenty to thirty-four? Actually, it's 'suicide and injury or poisoning of undetermined intent'. So they don't always know if someone meant to kill himself.

Back to Natasha. She showed the phobics spiders in tanks, and they finished their day holding a tarantula – accompanied by unwarranted hugging, weeping and misappropriation of the word 'journey'. It's called exposure therapy.

St Margaret's Junior is my zoo. Today, a woman known to me only as 'Kayla's mum' was my Natasha.

Francis and I were doing well. We'd agreed to stop trying Ben's phone, we had a pre-sliced apple, cash for ice-cream and we were equipped with a large jute bag to contain a whole term of Josephine's artworks and her many items of spare clothing. We arrived five minutes before pick-up time.

Most of us wait on a wide part of the pavement by the gate. A couple of parents have a system in place where their child is handed over to one of the pavement mums by Miss Jones (my age, doing her best) and walked down to their own mothers or fathers in waiting cars, engines running. I don't know if this is a paid-for service, arranged on a rotation basis or done out of charity towards the car-bound.

The pavement mums can be divided into three groups: with baby; pregnant; or with baby and pregnant.

Today, as usual, I station myself nearest the gate. No one minds, they're in no hurry to collect their kids. I keep my back to them, pick up Francis. He twists and whimpers. 'Fine. Hate you too.' As I place him on the ground, a girl runs towards us, she's holding up something red with feathers, a mask or a picture, she shouts, 'Muuuummeeeey!'

'Careful—' Too slow. Her feet hook under Francis, her hands hold the artwork aloft and her chin slams into the pavement. Francis yelps. There's a second's silence and the girl shrieks.

'Kayla! Oh my God!' A mother realises it's her child on the ground. 'Take Kane, will you?' She thrusts him into my arms like he's a bag of shopping.

He can't be more than two months old, he's asleep, weighs nothing. He's too low, I try to get both arms round him, his head is lolling. Francis's lead pulls on my wrist.

The mum is on the pavement, pressing a tissue against Kayla's bleeding chin. Miss Jones has gone for an ice pack. 'That dog shouldn't be on school grounds,' someone says behind me.

'It's disgusting,' says her friend.

The baby's slipping. 'I can't hold him,' I say. 'I don't know how.'

'You're a fucking nanny,' says Kayla's mum.

'I'm just a friend.'

'She's bleeding,' says Kayla's mum. She pulls away the tissue, there's a tiny spot of blood. She presses it back on and Kayla shouts out in pain.

No sign of Josephine, she's always last. Francis tugs. I unhook his lead from my wrist, if he runs into the road, it's no more than he deserves.

'You need to get him under control.' The friend again, behind me. She stamps on the lead as Francis runs past.

'Can you just hold him for a minute?' I ask. 'Or do a swap?' I try to move my arms but the baby's about to drop.

'I can hold him,' says another mum, sunglasses. I shuffle towards her, baby tight to my chest, but she crouches down, she means Francis. Before I can stop her, she approaches from the front. He gets her knuckle, she slaps at his nose. He barks and Kayla howls.

'Feisty,' says Sunglasses.

Miss Jones is back, her arm around Kayla's shoulders while Kayla's mum punches a message into her phone. The baby is still, so still, and heavier. He's in an all-in-one suit, thick layers. Where's his buggy? He must have come from somewhere. His chest was moving up and down before. His lips are different, blue. It wasn't my fault. He just stopped. He just stopped breathing. They do that, so tiny. I'm on my knees, the baby's on his back on the pavement. I rub his chest. 'Wake up! Wake up!'

'What the fuck are you doing?' Kayla's mum, his mum, shouting, pulling me off.

'He stopped breathing.'

She has him up on her shoulder, his arm moves, or it doesn't, it's just her. The suit's so thick, why isn't she pulling it off? He's silent. Miss Jones strokes his cheek, looks at me, she'll be the one who says it. I only had him a minute, a few minutes.

'He's sleeping,' says Miss Jones.

'Sleeping, like asleep sleeping?' I ask.

Kayla's mum turns his little body to face me. 'No, like awake sleeping.' She laughs, they all do. His mouth opens and closes, she slides in a dummy from her pocket.

Josephine's come from somewhere, she's wrapped around my waist and holding Francis's lead.

'Something happened,' I say. It's to the mums. I'll tell them, about how there was no warning, you were healthy and just stopped kicking. They don't hear. 'Something happened,' I try. Josephine pushes her rucksack, coat and a pile of cardboard into my arms. It lands on my feet.

'She's gone without you,' says Kayla's mum as I gather toilet roll tubes into the jute bag.

Obviously, I'm glad Kane was fine. I assume it's Kane, not Cain. OK, I found her on Facebook, she's called Kaytlin and it is Kane. She hasn't posted anything about today.

To: LRS_17@outlook.com

Sat 1/4, 23:20

SUBJECT: Fool

The people opposite have new blinds. Took him two hours to put them up.

Caveman diet is now weekdays only.

Francis is on stronger medication. 'Anxiety drops,' says my mother. I weighed him. Took five.

To: LRS_17@outlook.com
Sun 2/4, 04:06
SUBJECT: *There are no words*

It was in three of the cards, two text messages and five Facebook posts. I don't want you getting the wrong impression that I am massively popular. At my current reckoning there would be twenty-six people at my funeral. People post on your Facebook if they've been in the same school as you, at the same party, or in the same lift. There are no words.

It's not quite true. There are some words. Like the euphemisms in the forums: 'born asleep', 'with angel wings'. And there's the one I hate. From another time, at least that's what I thought: 'stillborn'. Would you believe me if I told you I thought stillbirth didn't happen anymore? That it was for people from long ago, like Anne Boleyn? It's not in any of the books.

That's what I told them. I was on my own. I took a taxi. After the nap. Once E was home. I told him I just wanted to be safe. Would be there and back before the casserole's done. If I'd let him do the potatoes, I'd have gone sooner. When did I know?

Worst case, I told him, you're on your way and he can get there for the delivery, bring the bag. Very worst, it's a C-section, he'll miss it, still have a lifetime.

In the taxi, you moved again. Or was that the speed bumps? You were telling me you were OK, no rush, breathe. So I smiled at the mum when the little boy pressed all the lift buttons, I could wait, just a precaution.

'Due date today?' says the midwife at the desk, she's young and she's overcompensating with a matron voice.

I was due something. Those words are there, loads of them, everyone loves those words. Due, expecting, pregnant – all bursting with promise. Bursting, that's another one and then they 'burst' with pride when their babies smile, walk, go to university, win Oscars.

'And it's your first?' says the midwife. 'Normal to be nervous on the due date. Best thing is rest.'

'He's slowed down.'

'Probably getting ready.' She looks up from her paperwork to give me a go-away smile.

'I mean he's barely moved.'

Pen down. 'Since when?'

'Not long. I can't tell.'

'It's OK.' She walks around the desk. 'Let's have a little listen.'

The radio was on, music, adverts, one for a Valentine's Day pizza deal. She was listening for you but the radio was on. 'Shouldn't you turn that off?' I said. She went over to the windowsill, the music stopped. More gel, more gliding, pausing, gliding.

'I'm just going to call in a colleague,' she said.

This was it, when they'd tell me they had to get you out, emergency caesarean. Needles, cutting, no E. None of that mattered, I was about to hold you.

The midwife came back with a doctor and an ultrasound machine. The doctor's face stayed fixed on the screen, her arm stretched backwards, moving over your silhouette. She held still in one place. She knew. She knew but she was giving me another minute not knowing.

'I'm so sorry, your baby's heart has stopped, Rachel.'

That's the phrase. I wake up to it, go to sleep to it. 'Your baby's heart has stopped, Rachel.'

'Get him out, start it again. Quick, he has me and I'm breathing, get him out.'

'It doesn't work like that,' the doctor said.

'It does, he's been moving all day. He's big, they said at his scan. Find another doctor.'

'There's no heartbeat.' She points to something on the screen. 'He's passed away.'

'That doesn't happen. It doesn't. He's still in me. He's big. Get him out, help him.'

They called E, handed the phone to me.

'OK,' he said. He said OK. 'I'm coming.'

The midwife stayed with me. Her name was Shona. She stayed with me all night and I said sorry, over and over. I'm sorry. And then, in a word, that stupid word, you were stillborn. Around about this time, two months to the minute.

And they told me to stop saying sorry, it wasn't my fault. 'Don't do this to yourself,' said E. 'It's not you.'

I screamed at him, at the midwives, the doctors. I never scream. But they say everyone does in labour. 'Let loose, you might not get another go,' our antenatal teacher had said. 'Practise at home. In bed, if you prefer.' (She meant into a pillow.)

I screamed. 'I'm sorry. Sorry, sorry, sorry!' and 'What have I done?'

And they sent in another doctor, one with numbers, on how it happens every day, no one can change it, you're all so fragile, sometimes nature is cruel, he said. I wanted to believe him.

E told me it happened to a woman at work. The midwife said, 'We had two last week.' It stopped the screaming, that and the epidural and the sickness. You can't throw up and scream at the same time. And maybe it did just happen. 'Like cot death,' the midwife said. 'You wouldn't blame another woman for a cot death.'

I wish I'd wished harder. Every push, I wished they were wrong. I believed they were, it didn't happen anymore, you'd gasp for air, they'd press a button, doctors and nurses would rush in, save you.

They wrapped you in a towel, white, maybe blue. E held you first. Handed you to me, the way we'd said in the birth plan. You were heavy. I whispered to you. Did you hear me? 'Sorry, sorry, sorry.'

And I was right. It was my fault. And his. A whole life lost for Ben and no one ever asked me, no one told me that was the deal. I did what anyone would do. I reached out for him, like you catch a toppling wine glass. I need you to believe that I'd have let him fall, if I'd known. Or someone else could have caught him. Why did it have to be me? Always the good citizen. Picking up everyone's litter, fishing teabags out the recycling bin, stopping dog walkers from jumping off Tube platforms. I can hear my mother: 'Just keep your hands to yourself.'

I should. What does it do for the world? There's a bloke in Peckham making a beagle happy, and occasionally a sausage dog. Here's something I wouldn't tell anyone else: I think about killing him. Any mother would. If it would bring you back, I'd do it. Shove him in front of his train, poison his porridge, pay someone on the dark web. I'd have to buy bitcoin first. But the world doesn't work like that. I can't have you back. I have Ben instead.

To: LRS_17@outlook.com
Sun 2/4, 10:41
SUBJECT: *Queries*

E's cooking a roast. I said I'd get up, make a crumble, but he said have a lie-in, catch up. No sleep after that last email. I kept picturing the birth – can we call it that? I don't like delivery, it conjures images of parcel chutes, vans and the gates of heaven, they're chained shut, no one can remember the twenty-digit code for the padlock, but you're small enough to slip through the gap. The timing confuses me, when you went where. I've texted Dog Collar Graham.

To: LRS_17@outlook.com
Sun 2/4, 16:16
SUBJECT: *Ridiculous*

He's alive. E went for a bike ride so I drove over to Ben's flat. He wouldn't open the door, shouted some words I can't tell you. Similar, I imagine, to the words he said to Mesh.

Maybe it's pride. He wanted to set up his own website. Do you think he's worked out who I am, doesn't know how to thank me, feels ashamed? God knows what Mesh told him about you.

I'm overthinking this. It's probably a pictures thing. Some people hate having their picture taken, often it's the best-looking ones, they can't bear the idea of the camera catching something less than perfect.

He'll get over it and in the meantime, the break is helpful. There's so much planning to do for Luke's Touch. And I've promised E I'll rest more. He says I have all the signs of sleep deprivation. He read out a list from a website.

'I'm not clumsy,' I said.

'What about that vase? But it's OK, I'm not blaming you.'

'Good, because that was Francis.'

The Francis thing needed to stop too, he said. I tried telling him my mother was having her floors done.

'She has a million people she can ask,' he said. 'Why us? Now?' It was a rare and comforting acknowledgement. He claimed Lester was having an allergic reaction to dog hair. They saw the vet yesterday, who charged him seventy quid for the diagnosis, prescribed antihistamines and said Lester would recover as soon as he had his house back.

To: LRS_17@outlook.com
Mon 3/40, 09:17
SUBJECT: Results

Sixty days. Marked with a letter about the post-mortem. A date at last. They say they're sorry, some results went missing, but now it's done.

There are results but I don't have them. Won't for another eight days. A secretary has seen them. I called her.

'We can't talk about it on the phone.'

'Just tell me if you know. Did it happen for a reason?'

'Dr Singh will be able to answer all your questions.'
Who does Dr Singh think she is?

To: LRS_17@outlook.com
Mon 3/4, 17:36
SUBJECT: *No answer*

No one normal sulks for this long.

After his flat, I tried his usual routes. On Biscuit's road a woman came out in her slippers, said she'd seen me a few times.

'Are you looking for someone?' she asks. Her accent's unexpected, a strong G on the end of 'looking', it doesn't match her polyester blouse and joggers.

'My friend, we're meeting out here. You know what it's like, if I ring the bell, it wakes the baby.'

'You must have the wrong day. Jessica's away until Saturday,' she says.

Jessica, that was it. Jessica, Rob, Oliver and Biscuit.

'Oh goodness,' I say. 'I remember now. Cornwall. Baby's first holiday.' That's how they'd written it on the calendar. 'Biscuit will love it down there.'

'They didn't take him, left him with the dog walker.' She nods towards Ben's road.

'Oh, he's with Ben, of course. I'll drop her a text, see if she wants me to check in on him.'

'You won't catch him now, tends to be out until around four.'

'Jess always said everyone knows everything on this road,' I say. 'Such a community feel.'

'It's my job, Neighbourhood Watch.'

When there's more time, I'll tell you about accents, class and trust.

I tried his flat again, she was wrong about four o'clock. I waited half an hour, gave up – just for today. You're thinking I've let you down again, let him go, forgotten about EHFAR. I don't expect you to understand. Your social skills don't start developing until next week. Ben will let us back in.

To: LRS_17@outlook.com
Mon 3/4, 21:36
SUBJECT: *Better this way*

I have Josephine from Wednesday, for the rest of the week. It's Easter holidays and Lola has to work. She tried reasoning with her supervisor, Vernon. No matter that she did Christmas Eve, Boxing Day and half-term. Whenever Lola talks about Vernon, she says 'Godless, godless man.'

'Two days off for me, and he gets five and lives alone,' she said tonight.

When Josephine had left the kitchen, I asked, 'What about her dad? Does he ever help in the holidays?'

'Another godless man.' She laughs. 'He wouldn't even know her. Left when she was tiny.'

'I'm so sorry,' I say.

'Better this way. Tea?'

I feel bad for feeling good. Of course I want her to have a dad, a nice one, even if he would be competition.

The Easter plan is perfect for us. Almost nine weeks. Your chart says it's a good time to arrange playdates, and there's the nagging about 'Mum needs to socialise too'. We'll go to the Science Museum.

To: LRS_17@outlook.com
Tues 4/4, 17:04
SUBJECT: *Of all the places*

E is wrong about sleep. I'm like those ultra-marathon runners you read about, my body is feeding off the emptiness. And I had to do it today, I have Josephine from tomorrow.

Ben clearly wanted me to think he'd fled somewhere, his sister's maybe, but thanks to our sleuthing with the Neighbourhood Watch lady, I knew better. And the lights were on when I drove past last night.

I took the train early this morning, composed Ben's daily text message en route (*sometimes the best days of your life are happening right now*) and got into position by the bins down the side of his building. I'd taken precautions in case he looked out of his window. This sounds a bit extreme, but a) it's actually perfectly normal, and b) I am telling you, so you'll understand the lengths I'll go to for you.

I still have the wig my mother wore during chemo. She wanted to throw it away, but I took it, because you never know. (You can apply EHFAR to most things, if you think about it.) With a beanie, it looks like my real hair. Darker suits me.

Lola and her sisters change their hair all the time. Wigs, weaves, extensions. You give up a Saturday, get a new you.

It was our first proper spring day, I wore my largest sunglasses. I played with my bouncy new hair as I waited and, for the benefit of passers-by, I kept my phone to my ear.

At 10.47, Ben came out, eating a banana, Biscuit pulling on the lead. When he turned a corner, I followed. I made my steps small, hung back, picked up his banana skin.

At Biscuit's house, Ben let himself in and stayed inside longer than he needed to. He was stuffing something into his pocket as he re-emerged with Biscuit and then they turned the wrong way, away from the park. Biscuit put up no resistance.

They stopped at another Victorian terrace and came out with a dark cockapoo I've never met.

Ben talked to them, something like, 'I know it's more fun with Rachel Wachel. But Benny Wen is too proud to say sorry wo-rry.' They walked further from the park. Ben kept his head pointed down. The sunniest day of the year and he was staring at tarmac and dogs' bottoms. We passed under a railway line and the dogs tugged Ben onwards. Then I saw it. He should have called me, I should have made him talk to me. He's going to try again. He's been walking the dogs in a cemetery.

To: LRS_17@outlook.com
Wed 5/4, 22:03
SUBJECT: *Bat-shaped*

Do you know how I imagined life with you? Like this: sprawled out on the bed, head swirling from so many things that you don't know what to think when. Cheeks prickling from the sun and fresh air. Feet hurting. I'm hungry but still full, sick from sugar and chips. A proper school-holidays day, a trip. When we did them – Broadstairs for sand, Southend for the two-pence machines – your grandma would let me sleep in her bed when we got home. 'Keep the day going,' she'd say.

I'll try and put it in order for you. First thing you should know is we needn't have worried about Ben. Second thing is that's all it was, a trip away, the ordinary hasn't changed: you and me apart. Look at how it started.

I got up early to make cookie dough before collecting Josephine. E was messing about with his fresh mint tea and blocking the sink. (I know I go on about it, but diets are dangerous. George Osborne did the five-two, his chum David Cameron gave up bread, and next thing you know they're holding the referendum.)

E was reading my recipe. 'You know I can't have those during the week.'

'Not everything's for you,' I say and eat a chunk of dough. His eyes move to my waist. I break off another chunk. 'We need to talk about the funeral.'

'It's not—' He checks his watch except he's not wearing one. He looks over to the broken clock on the oven.

'It's 7.05. You have twenty minutes.'

He's about to cry. The first tears since the hospital, that I've seen.

'I know it's upsetting,' I say. 'But if we want people to come, we have to tell them. We need readings. Food.'

'We don't,' he says.

'People will expect something, cake, sandwiches. We need more red.'

'We don't,' he says. 'We don't need a funeral.'

My scream comes out as a whimper. I grab his mug and throw it against the bottom of the sink. It stays intact, the mint tea pours out. I should have dropped it from higher up, or hurled it at him, but he's got his laptop.

'Hey!' he says. 'You can't get those anymore, they've gone into administration.'

'You'll mourn a mug?'

'I am mourning. I don't know what to do, what we do, what even happened. But a funeral will make it worse. You heard the bereavement woman, we don't have to do anything, or we can do something private, small. Why would we make things harder? In front of everyone?'

As soon as he's left, I go back downstairs to put the dough in the fridge – never skip the chilling phase, whatever the circumstances. (I'm working on a list for you, Rules To Live By. That's on there, along with: cut flapjacks while they're warm, and don't marry someone in advertising.)

I take the car to collect Josephine. She's waiting for me in a winter coat. She hands me a booster seat and a pink rucksack bulging with another coat. A Barbie pokes out of the side pocket, wearing a vest but no knickers. I repack her.

I'd texted Lola about E and the funeral, to tell her that now the post-mortem was done, the vicar had given us a slot the week after, I'm seeing him on Friday. She didn't text back and now she's rattling her house keys, herding us out the door. She's late for work. Everyone has somewhere to be.

I make her stop and show me the EpiPen one more time.

'It's easy,' says Josephine. 'Backwards gel bats.'

'Gel bats? Gel bats? ... Got it. Stab leg! Stab leg backwards,' I say, and we do our high five. 'You're brilliant ... Ouch!'

Lola's pinching me. 'Not leg. Here, in the thigh,' she says, making a stabbing movement with the other hand. 'And count. Hold and count to three, slowly.'

At the car, Josephine shows me how her booster seat fits in the front. 'I do my own seatbelt now,' she says and tries three times.

'You can do it next time.' I know I'm being what the books call a snowplough parent. Or is it helicopter?

Compared with yours, the charts are somewhat lacking in details for Josephine's age group – I guess parents are supposed to have worked it out by then. I have only vague memories of being six (or 'seven soon'): getting a Gordon the Gopher puppet from my grandma (your great-grandma); letting go of my purple kite at a beach; a Trafalgar Square pigeon pooing on my head and my mother combing it out while the whole of London looked on. I don't remember picking radio stations in the car, requesting drive-thru McDonald's for breakfast or offering tips on parallel parking. But there's something about Josephine that makes you go with her, see where she might take you.

She wanted to make the cookies bat-shaped.

'These are drop cookies, they spread,' I explain.

'Have you tried?' she says.

'It won't work,' I say.

'Have you tried?'

I give her a third of the dough and her own baking sheet. The rest I weigh out into equally sized balls, topping each with a pinch of coarse sea salt.

While the cookies bake, I find Josephine a ping-pong ball with which to torment Lester. She bounces it towards him and he lets it roll past as if it was meant for someone else. She tries again.

'He's too old to play,' I say.

'Like you,' she says, and tips her head on one side because she knows she's funny.

'That's not fair.'

'What does he do?' she asks.

'Sleeps. Eats. Makes my husband feel needed.'

'You should get a new one,' she says.

'That's not how it works.'

'Will you get another—' She stops herself. It must be about you. I'm not ready for this. Lester saves me by climbing out of his cat flap. 'Cooool,' shouts Josephine. She lurches after him, tries her own head in the flap. When it doesn't fit she pushes a handful of her braids through instead. 'Soooo cooool.'

'Don't get your beads caught,' I say. 'Tomorrow we'll borrow Francis off my mum. Take him to the park.'

'Cooool. Does he fit in the cat door?' She lists the tricks she's going to teach him, 'high five, kisses, sausage roll', and sways her hips as she talks, always dancing. I should warn her not to say 'tricks' in front of Ben, he says it's demeaning, prefers 'commands', which means being made to do something.

Her bats come out as ovals but my cookies are perfect circles, ripples of caramel on top, chocolate evenly distributed. I give her a red icing pen and she writes 'STAB' on her ovals.

Traffic to Nunhead is light and the cookies are still warm when we arrive.

'Does it have swings?' asks Josephine as we walk through a gate flanked with upside-down torches. Life turned on its head.

'You already asked that,' I say. 'But there are dogs, remember.'

'Are there toilets?'

We grapple with her tights-and-leggings combo behind a crypt, and she holds on to my leg to balance.

I can't be sure Ben will return, but Biscuit's with him all week and they have to walk somewhere. Josephine points out every squirrel and parakeet. She runs towards a fox lying rigid on a tomb like he's a sphinx. For me, there are the gravestones. Wonderful names like *TEMPERANCE SNELLING* and *PHILANDER CLEMENT*. Intriguing dates like 1943–45, or the mother and son who died three months apart. *TO DIE IS GAIN, SLEEPING NOW, REUNITED.* They're called epitaphs. They can replace the phrases in my head. More thought's gone into them. Most of them. One says *See you*, feels like an inside joke. It's from the nineties.

Josephine tugs my arm. 'Is that your friend?'

His back's to us. The cockapoo's on the lead, Biscuit's up ahead. I edge the lid off the Tupperware, gulp in the cookie smell. He needs me. Grieving people need me. The Temperances and Philanders need afterlives. They all need us, together.

'Ben?' I jog closer, holding Josephine by the hand. 'Wow! And Biscuit.' I crouch down, let Biscuit sniff the Tupperware. He prods his wet nose into my eye. 'I have missed you so much, so, so much, my little Biscuit Boy.' Ben is trying not to smile. 'I made cookies. They're warm.'

'This is harass—' He stops. Josephine has pushed in front of me. She stares up, reaches for his beard.

'Can I touch it?' she whispers to me, like he can't hear. I shake my head.

'This is Josephine,' I say. 'It's Easter holidays. She's doing a project on Victorians.'

'Nunhead is one of the great Victorian cemeteries,' Josephine beams. 'The Magnificent Seven.'

He takes her in, reassesses everything he's ever assumed about me.

'Can I hold the lead?' asks Josephine.

Ben's eyes are fixed on her braids. 'If your mum says so,' he answers at last.

'MUM?' says Josephine. Her eyes are huge. She's flattered.

'I just thought...' starts Ben.

'Have a cookie,' I say. 'Josephine's just mine for this week, her mum's at work.'

Ben is looking at my wedding finger. I took my rings off to make the cookie dough, left them on the kitchen table.

Josephine walks ahead of us, holding the lead for Figaro, the cockapoo. She wanted Biscuit but he pulled her over in pursuit of a squirrel. Now she's telling Figaro how naughty boy dogs are.

'Figaro's a boy too,' I call after Josephine.

'No, she's not,' says Ben. I am so alone.

We pass other dog walkers and some nod hello to Ben. There are joggers too and a group of mothers power walking with prams. When did people start using cemeteries like this?

'Where's Francis?' Ben asks.

A gravestone reads *OUR HEARTS ARE BROKEN*.

'Where's Francis?' he asks again.

'That's why I've been trying to call you. Well, that and—'

'Oh God! He was fine last week. What happened?'

There's another stone with identical black marble and gold letters, the same words: *OUR HEARTS ARE BROKEN*. Picked out of a catalogue.

'I don't understand,' Ben says.

'It's nothing like that. My mum took him. She's been so down, and you know how Francis has a nose for people with ... you know ... I was trying to let you know that I don't need him walked anymore.'

'But he's OK though?'

'Obviously, he's been pining for you, scratching your name into his basket. But he'll get over it.'

Ben rubs his hands over his face, hiding a smile. 'How did you know I was here?'

'Please have a cookie while they're still warm.' I hand him the Tupperware and run after Josephine.

At the cemetery gates, I say to Josephine, 'Tell Ben who we're seeing tomorrow.'

Ben answers for her. 'The Smurfs?'

Josephine looks at me for a translation.

'At the cinema,' Ben says. 'They're on all the buses. Everyone loves Smurfs, don't they?'

Josephine pulls on my arm, jumps up and down like it's Christmas morning.

'Thanks, Ben,' I say. 'Not the Smurfs. Another time. Even cuter, but rarely seen on buses ... We have Francis – for the whole day.'

'Francissssss,' says Josephine and the Smurfs are forgotten.

'We could walk him with you,' I say to Ben. 'Unless you're busy with the Smurfs.'

I overfill the rest of the day with Josephine. We go to Pizza Express and sit among the children enjoying school-holiday treats and too much time on their parents' phones. I tell the waitress about Josephine's allergies and she shrugs, says, 'You can check.' She brings me a folder full of spreadsheets where they have ticked the allergens for every item on the menu. Did you know some people are allergic to onions? I check the dough balls and margherita pizza seven times. It's like taking an exam. As soon as I've handed the folder back, I ask for it again, to check my checking. I feel in the pocket of my coat for the EpiPen, I'll keep my hand on it while she eats.

'Most things are fine,' says Josephine. 'But if I have sesame, I will definitely die.'

Aside from the threat of sudden death, she's a good restaurant partner. She gives me her dough balls in exchange for my pizza crusts (I ask for the folder back first) and lets me finish her ice-cream. She keeps her coat on all meal.

At the playground we have to queue for the swings. She befriends a younger boy in dungarees on the climbing frame. She takes him around by the hand, hugs him, picks him up. His mother gives me a 'you must be so proud' look. I smile back and find a bench far away from them. The mother's carrying a baby in a sling.

I sit on the bench no one else wants, among a jumble of bikes, scooters and skate boards, and think about Ben. Is this how we'll handle every disagreement – pretend it didn't happen? Will there be a four-day shutdown every time? Will he change when I tell him about you, why we're calling it Luke's Touch? Your charts say you can spot patterns now.

He was nicer to Josephine than I'd expected. Then again, it's Josephine, everyone loves her. She'll be a stand-up comedian one day, or a head teacher.

She comes down from the climbing frame to talk to the mum, and demonstrate her cartwheels. The mum crouches down to show Josephine the baby.

'Time to go,' I call, walking over. 'Let's go.'

'Thomas has a baby brother.' Josephine pulls me towards the mum.

'That's lovely.' I tug her the other way. 'We're late.'

'You're hurting,' she shouts.

I give the mum a 'you know what it's like' look. She has both arms tight round her baby, like she can't trust the sling to hold him.

Josephine sniffs as we walk through the common. 'I don't like your cross voice.'

'I'm sorry, OK? Here.' I hand her an apple from my bag.

'You're still doing it.' More tears.

I give her a tissue. 'It's just the toy shop closes soon and I wanted to get you something.'

She stops. Throws her arms round my waist, squeezes tight.

A place on Northcote Road has them in the window. She picks a green scooter and a jungle animal helmet. The man in the shop assembles the scooter, and on the walk home I pull her along, the way I've seen other parents do. She's tired and leans against my arm, we're the perfect height for each other. We pass back through the common but the mum with the sling has gone.

When I drop Josephine home, Lola makes me stay for spicy rice (nice flavours, bit dry). We eat the stab cookies for pudding.

Josephine keeps her new helmet on all dinner. It squashes my shoulder when she leans on me.

'I made her promise to always wear it,' I say to Lola and drum my fingers on its hard shell. 'But I meant when you're scooting, you daft donkey, not always, always.'

'You shouldn't have got it,' says Lola.

Josephine makes an eee-aww sound and cookie crumbs spray across the table. Lola shouts something in Yoruba. 'But I'm a daft donkey,' says Josephine. 'Eee-awwww!'

We didn't get a chance to talk about the funeral. Lola said once that she went to her niece's funeral, but she called it a service. Maybe it wasn't the funeral, more like a memorial. If she had advice about us doing one, I suppose she'd share it. I wish I could tell her more about the business, my plans with Ben. It never seems the right time and there never seems a way to say it.

And now here I am in your room. E is still at work, hiding. This isn't some tiff over bins or an Amex bill.

You were a person. Our person. You need a funeral.

I've left him a note on the fridge.

To: LRS_17@outlook.com
Thu 6/4, 00:37
SUBJECT: *Like this*

I can't sleep. And just as you're starting to go longer stretches.

It starts with the rolling over and checking. Emails, Facebook, Twitter, the news. Same order every time, and sometimes the Gumtree pets section, for Josephine. Then I go round again. Emails, Facebook, Twitter, the news. OK, that's not true. Emails, PeckhamExperts, Facebook, PeckhamExperts, Twitter, PeckhamExperts.

Middle of the night is worst. When I wake, I need to check. Check on something. I wish I could tell you what I hope to find. A different Ben maybe, with smiling pictures and a hire-me website. There's never any change, it's 'under construction'. I called Mesh earlier, told him Ben's calmed down, and that I'd come back to him about photos. 'I want to help, but not like this,' Mesh said. 'Makes no sense, you with someone like that.'

When E came in – after midnight – I was in your bed and on Ben's website.

'You're sleeping in here now?' E asks. 'And when did you get like this?' He held up my note from the fridge.

I'd planned the key messages.

'I haven't changed. Everything else has,' I say.

'How?'

'You need to ask?'

'Yes, what's changed?' He's looking around. Should I have rearranged the furniture?

'Everything,' I reply. 'It's like we were in this big marathon, we knew where we were going, we were rushing there with everyone else, we were promised the same thing at the finish. They all made it. They all have babies.'

'That's not even true. You're looking for ways to make it worse than it is,' he says.

'It can't be worse. It happened. The worst thing happened. He was alive and now he isn't. He needs a funeral. Luke needs a funeral.'

He drops the note, walks out.

'They don't charge for baby funerals,' I call after him.

I pick up the note, trace my finger over where I've written your name. I line my fingertips up with yours on the paper, three of my fingers are wider than your whole hand. Little handprints taken at the hospital, the midwife brought them round with the memory stick of photos and a curl of your hair. A loose sheet of paper. We should frame it. It's your first playgroup artwork – you were the arty kid who picked black ink over yellow finger-paint. Don't worry, I didn't use the original. I scanned it and printed copies. Also made it the background on my phone, my laptop and his computer.

To: LRS_17@outlook.com
Thu 6/4, 08:16
SUBJECT: *Unread*

I need to have my phone checked, things aren't sending. Or they're not arriving. They're probably landing on the wrong phones – some poor crofter in the Scottish Highlands is getting texts for Lola, asking if we should go with John fourteen or Corinthians fifteen. I like to think a Devon widower called Reg is receiving Ben's quotes of the day. Feel sorry for whoever gets E's this week.

To: LRS_17@outlook.com
Thu 6/4, 09:22
SUBJECT: *Fridays*

That sound you just heard from all the way over there was my phone smashing against the wall. Almost. If I had smashed it, my mother would owe me a new one.

She'd love to help out, but it's a Friday. That's what she said. 'Help out', like it's a jumble sale.

'This is my baby's funeral,' I say.

'The vicar will talk you through it. They're very experienced.' Her TV's on in the background, the weather.

'What if he asks about readings, prayers? Don't you want to help choose? This is your specialist subject.'

'That's offensive, Rachel.'

'You're offensive, Moira. I can't go on my own.'

'You have a husband, don't you?'

'Whatever you have on a Friday that's so special, you can cancel,' I say.

'I don't understand why you're only asking me now,' she says.

'I've been busy.' Stupid slip – she wouldn't understand about Ben, or Josephine, or the business. 'I've been busy sorting stuff. Walking your dog. And grieving. For your grandson.' (I'd been waiting to use that.)

'I miss him too. We're all upset. But you have to look forward. And you know I can't do Fridays.'

'Actually, I don't. I did have your hour-by-hour timetable stuck to my fridge but Anca threw it out.'

'How is that lovely Anca?'

'You don't have to say she's lovely just because she's Romanian. What do you do on Fridays?'

'Your father,' she says.

'I can't believe you're still doing that. He just wants a free meal out of you.'

'Sometimes he stays over.'

'Oh God, that's disgusting, that's worse.'

'It's not actually any of your business,' she says, and then tells me how things are better and that it's best I keep Francis until Saturday morning.

At Christmas, she started a scrapbook for your future baptism. Cake pictures, poems, a menu. She asked her friend Jean to knit a shawl.

Your funeral will be planned by me, Francis and a vicar I've never met.

To: LRS_17@outlook.com
Thu 6/4, 09:26
SUBJECT: *Mine*

She doesn't get to miss you.

Off to pick up Francis, then Josephine. Ben at eleven.

To: LRS_17@outlook.com
Thu 6/4, 20:17
SUBJECT: *Bedford*

I'm looking for someone on the Internet who can vet people for drugs. Like, you send in some of their clothing and they check it for traces. It's not a side of HR that I know, but it's big in America.

There's something wrong with Ben. I asked him how his dad's been when we were in the graveyard and he says, 'When did I tell you about my dad?'

'At the veggie place,' I said. 'Your sister's caring for him, back in Bedford.'

'It's not Bedford. More kind of like outside it. A town down the road.'

He said Bedford, the night of the tofu, the night we had the breakthrough. I checked my email to you, it was Bedford. I remember it because it sounds like Ben. Bedford Ben. I meant to say to you how cool it would be if it always worked that way. I'd be Rachel from Rainham, you'd be Luke from Luton (sorry). Lola from Lagos works, except she's really Omolola. E from Edmonton.

People are funny about where they're from, so I left it.

Josephine's approach to Ben is better. It's much like her approach to securing after-school ice-cream: merciless.

'What's your favourite meal? Best Taylor Swift song? Which dog do you like best?' She holds his hand, swings it back and forth as she talks. 'Will you come to my birthday?'

'Can tell why you two get on,' he says.

'What's your wife called? D'you have a baby?'

'Slow down,' I say. 'Give Ben a chance to answer.'

'Tell you what,' Ben says. 'No more questions and you can hold Fizzy all the way home.'

Josephine takes the deal and sings the rest of the walk. I must print her out some lyrics.

As she ran after Francis, Ben said, 'It's so weird how she's a mini you.'

'Except prettier,' I said.

'Yeah, maybe. But you know, a clever boots, smiley, a bit exhausting.'

At the cemetery gates, as soon as Ben hands Fizzy's lead to Josephine, she asks, 'Why don't you like questions?' I want to high-five her but I need both hands to grab on to the lead. Fizzy is a Great Dane.

'Ben, why don't you like questions?' she asks again.

'Who said I don't like questions?'

'Rachel,' she says.

'What? I never said that.' I can feel the red in my cheeks.

'She's kind of right,' says Ben. 'People can find out too much. It's not safe.'

'Bit dark in front of a six-year-old,' I say.

'Almost seven,' says Josephine.

'Just being honest,' says Ben.

'Important to be honest, isn't it?' I say to Josephine. 'One of the golden rules.'

'Wouldn't it be cool if me and Francis could ride on Fizzy,' says Josephine.

To: LRS_17@outlook.com
Fri 7/4, 18:22
SUBJECT: *Pretending*

Know what Josephine said when I picked her up this morning? 'Are we going to be humans *all* day?'

'I'd rather not,' I answered.

She chose kangaroo, I chose penguin. Francis was himself.

Had to tell you before my battery goes. (I'm in the car, waiting to go in and see Paul, the vicar, whose partner must be a banker or celebrity because his house is huge. I'll leave Francis in the car.)

Josephine's been making slo-mo videos on my phone all day, mainly Francis running and his 'new' high-five. (I didn't tell her he already knew that trick, formerly known as 'paw'.) We used time-lapse for my penguin waddle. She kept sending them to Lola, who wrote back, *LOL* every time.

Oh my God (OMG!), just hit me, LOLA, she's Laughing Out Loud Always.

To: LRS_17@outlook.com
Fri 7/4, 21:16
SUBJECT: *Charlotte's coming*

Charlotte called, as I was leaving Paul the vicar's. You don't know Charlotte, but maybe you heard her voice on Skype when you were growing, it's low and makes her sound more serious than she is. We shared a house when we were at university. She lives in America now. She's over next week for work – first long trip since she had Zoe. She wanted to do dinner on Wednesday, I told her about the funeral and she said she'd come, do a reading if I like. (Paul gave me a list to pick from, described them as the 'gentler options'. He said one of the choices I'd brought with me, about a time for everything, was 'too direct'. I'd hoped we'd discuss it, that and EHFAR. Apparently, there is a time to search, but also a time to give up.) But don't worry, we came up with a sort of plan.

Charlotte's staying here on Tuesday, says we can talk properly, she'll sit up with me the night before, she's been wishing she was in London, still can't believe what happened, I could come over to them for a long weekend, there's a cheap direct flight. I didn't tell her about Luke's Touch – I've been having these silly panics that people will think it's too soon, that I'm too ambitious, that I'm OK.

To: LRS_17@outlook.com
Sat 8/4, 19:04
SUBJECT: *Three days…*

…to your post-mortem. Horrible words and I won't try to imagine what they mean, what they've been doing. It's not you though. You're in your new place. I must lack imagination, because I see it as a garden, with slides and swings (no queue), the grass is dry, good for picnics, no wasps, you have access to a laptop.

I don't understand E. I left the hospital letter on the island for him.

'I've booked the day off,' he says this morning, running his finger over where I highlighted the date. 'We'll get a cab there together.'

'Oh. I thought I'd be going on my own.'

'Why would you say that? Of course I'm coming,' he says.

'Why?'

'For you. And for me. Both of us. We need to know what they found. What it means.'

'What it means?' I ask.

'For next time.'

After his run, we went into town together. I bought a dress but didn't tell him it was for the funeral. 'You could wear it to Maggie's baby shower,' he said. 'If you go. She loves purple.'

'It's mauve,' I said. How can he imagine me going to a baby shower?

He bought a new travel bag but didn't mention New York.

I found a giant Dairy Milk bar and a tub of Mini Eggs for Charlotte – she can't get them over there.

As we came out of Selfridges, I took E's hand but my words came out weird. 'Let's treat ourselves. I'll show you what I've been up to.'

It had more screens than the Brixton one. I showed him how to order sides, a drink with no ice, barbecue sauce. It was our first meal out since the Valentine's disaster (we made it to starters, table next to us turned up with a newborn).

'Interesting choice,' he says as we take our trays from the collection point.

'The chicken wrap? Healthier.'

'McDonald's,' he says.

'I love it. Don't have to talk to anyone, chips with everything and over in ten minutes.'

'Very you,' he says.

To: LRS_17@outlook.com
Sun 9/4, 08:36
SUBJECT: *Real life*

Someone should warn grievers about targeted adverts. Luke's Touch will have a tool to block them. I guess mine are from looking at your charts. I get wet wipes, baby-friendly hotels, teething gels. All with smiley pictures, all still here. One just now – for a terrifying Super Suction breast pump – made me think about that day at John Lewis with my mother. You remember, buying the basket, bedding and buggy, £950 in one go. And we had that tiff over sterilisers.

'I won't have anything to sterilise,' I said. 'I keep telling you, I'm going to breastfeed.'

'When you were born, we just went with the advice, they told us formula was better,' she said.

'Like they told you smoking was safe?'

'You're fine, aren't you? If you buy the steriliser and bottles now, you'll have them just in case.' She took a starter set off the shelf, tried to hand it to me, but I folded my arms. 'You know, Pebble, you're going to have to grow up when you're a mum. Realise things don't always go to plan. You're all breast milk and water births now but—'

'How about I have my baby the way I want?' I said. A woman looking at nursing bras overheard me, smiled in support.

'You could,' said my mother. 'Or you could listen to someone who's done it before.'

'I always knew you'd be this kind of grandparent. At antenatal they said we have to set rules of engagement. They said older generations mean well, but their ways belong in the past for a reason.'

She walked off, took the box with her. Do you remember how much you kicked? I found her in the café.

Anyway, hate to say it but she was right about kids: you don't know what it's going to be like. Take mobile phones. I always swore you wouldn't have one until you were at least sixteen. Josephine's asking Lola for one for her seventh birthday next week. I know. But when you think about the practicalities it does make some sense. At the moment she has to use Lola's to message me. Like the text she just sent:

This is JoJo.
Hi Lehcar,
Look kool:
?Was it a car or a cat I saw?

Or yesterday, I woke up to a photo of her alarm clock:

05:20

My reply was genius. Waited for seven past seven and rotated it:

LO:L

To: LRS_17@outlook.com
Mon 10/4, 10:16
SUBJECT: *Limbo*

This time tomorrow I'll know. I called the secretary again, left a voicemail.

'I know you can't tell me the full results over the phone, but a little sneak peak, you know, a previewette. It would really help, with my mental health, you know, my anxiety. Prepare me. Was there a reason? In case you don't have it, my number—'

A long beep stops me.

'It's Rachel Summers, I just left a message, about the post-mortem, but we got cut off, machine ran out, I think. I do know I shouldn't ask, but it would really, really help, and I am his mum. Just a nudge, a nod, something. I'm on 07—'

Beeeeeep, longer this time, the machine feels embarrassed for me.

I'm late. I still have to collect Francis and get to the park for eleven.

To: LRS_17@outlook.com
Mon 10/4, 16:04
SUBJECT: *Monkey*

I told Ben I can't see him tomorrow, 'hospital appointment'. He didn't respond. 'But I'm OK,' I said. 'Nothing serious.'

'That's good,' he says.

'It's not women problems, if that's what you're thinking.'

'It's none of my business.'

'If it was something serious, I'd tell you.'

'Why?' he says.

'Because we're setting up a business together. And I'd want you to know.'

'Do you want me to have Francis?' he asks.

'That's not why I'm telling you. My mum's having him.'

'So why are you telling me?'

This time it's me who runs after Biscuit. He's weeing in a puddle that Bug the Puggle is drinking from.

Ben loved the penguin video I made with Francis and Josephine. It was his idea to make another one. If you could have seen him today, you'd never believe Oval happened.

To: LRS_17@outlook.com
Mon 10/4, 23:37
SUBJECT: Reasons

What if the police are waiting with the consultant? And they take me away before I can see her report? The one that says how I killed you. The secretary looking on, shaking her head.

'You can't do this to yourself,' says E. 'They told you before, it's nothing you did.'

'Then why are you coming with me? You want to know, too. Was it me?'

'That's not what I said. We need to know if one of us carries something, if it could happen again.'

It's called foeticide, or child destruction, and you can go to prison for life. Never appears to have happened in a stillbirth, more like people being stabbed while pregnant or late self-administered abortions. But until I get there tomorrow and no one arrests me, I won't know I'm safe.

Do you already know what they will say – you and the secretary and Dr Singh, all in on it? And what about EHFAR? This is the ultimate test, isn't it? Except we've been warned not to put our hopes (their word) on anything conclusive. You'd grown well, you were a good weight, nothing in my blood tests.

In summary, my options are as follows:

A – It was the nap. Prosecutors call it aggravated neglect. I get twenty-five years.

B – It was the blue cheese. They call it aggravated poisoning. I get twenty years, and cheese producers are forced to change their labelling. It becomes known as Luke's Law.

C – There's something babies die from. You had that. It happened for a reason.

D – There's something babies die from. You had that. It happened for a reason. It could happen again. E leaves me and procreates with Tanya.

E – There was no medical cause. Ben took your place. He needs to know.

To: LRS_17@outlook.com
Tues 11/4, 10:22
SUBJECT: *Perfectly healthy*

That's what she called you.

No prison. But what instead?

To: LRS_17@outlook.com
Tues 11/4, 11:46
SUBJECT: Fwd: Study: Most stillbirths unexplained

This is how communication works. You wait for someone else to say what you couldn't be bothered to formulate yourself and you hit a little 'share' button. Sometimes you add an explanatory comment. For example, I sent your grandmother an article about the tastes of certain politicians, adding, 'This is what everybody else calls a safe word.' To communicate with a wide audience, you do this via networks like Twitter and Facebook, where other people can indicate their agreement or otherwise, also with a single button. For moments when you crave a deeper connection, you can email an individual. For example, this is from E:

> Begin forwarded message:
> From: ERSum
> Tues 11/4, 11:14
> Subject: Study: Most stillbirths unexplained
>
> *ERSum saw this and thought you would like it too:*
>
> **International study finds majority of stillbirths have no identifiable cause. Scientists say answers 'decades away'. Monitor movements, expectant mothers told.**
>
> It's every parent's worst nightmare but baby loss continues to strike daily, and in most cases the heartache remains…

To: LRS_17@outlook.com
Tues 11/4, 17:53
SUBJECT: *Epic fail*

You'll like this, it was on a list, Top Ten Epic Fails of All Time. A family bakery in Texas received an order for the most expensive wedding cake in the state's history – daughter of an oil baron marrying son of a hotel magnate and tastes to match. Cost thirty thousand dollars and took twelve weeks to design and make. It was eight tiers of alternating red velvet and vanilla sponge, decorated with sugar flowers, a mix of calla lilies, roses and bluebonnets (the badly chosen Texas state flower), and topped with two marzipan lovebirds in a sugar-work cage, gilded.

The oil daughter was a minor socialite, so a local news channel took the opportunity to film a 'behind-the-scenes' report on the cake – ended up becoming one of the most viewed things on the web (well, the meme of the key bit), there's a link to it in the Epic Fails. I've watched it seven times. The report starts with the finishing touches to the cake. The mother, father and son baking team – Janie, Tyler and Tyler Junior – are there with their matching aprons, prominent logos, talking about how it changed their lives (the challenge, not the thirty thousand dollars). The reporter reels off cake data: 2,600 flowers; 792 eggs ('That's a whopping sixty-six dozen!'), the bride's weight in butter and enough fondant icing to cover a king-size bed.

Tense music plays like someone's docking a spacecraft as six people load the cake into a van. Janie 'Mother Baker' Johnson wipes away farewell tears. At the other end – father-in-law's flagship hotel and golf course – the bride-to-be waits in pre-wedding cashmere casuals. There is pacing.

Tyler Junior has travelled with the cake to oversee its enthronement (his word). He's first out of the van, hugs the bride as if they know each other and opens the back. More weeping. 'It's perfect', she says, 'So perfect'.

'You like?' says Tyler Junior. 'Whole lotta love went into this.' (He has hopes of his own baking show.)

Five hotel employees file out in mint-green polo shirts and tight tan trousers, a man in a chef's hat wheels a trolley towards the van, the camera catches Tyler Junior giving a nod to his culinary rival. More space-docking music as they slide the cake out. They've put the next bit in slow motion and I've replayed it over and over, but it's just not clear what happens. Tyler Junior's on one corner, his back to the camera, giving directions to the rest of them, when something grazes his shoulder and lodges itself in the third tier. Someone – maybe Tyler Junior, maybe the man next to him – lets go and the whole cake tips, the others can't hold it. All eight tiers smash into the ground. The camera zooms in on the shattered sugar cage and the crushed wing of a lovebird. The bride screams, she shouts 'Holy Foot!' over and over. You can watch that bit in slow motion too, or there's a version where they've made it into a song. Tyler Junior slumps to the tarmac, rolls onto his side and stays there, he's forgotten about the cameras. There's a long beep sound as his mouth lets out a cry.

The groom and his father come running from the golf course, they heard screaming.

'Oh my God, Honey, what happened?'

Through the weeping she tells them, 'Golf ball. Wrecked. Totally wrecked.'

That was four months ago. So far, neither father nor son has divulged who hit the offending ball. My follow-up reading also reveals Johnson's Bakery was never paid the thirty thousand dollars, and lawyers are still wrangling over fault and domain (the cake was partly in the bakery's van, partly on the hotel-owned trolley when the ball struck). The wedding was cancelled. The bride's the new face of an insurance company (slogan: 'For all those Holy Foot Moments') and has been spotted with another man, identity so far unconfirmed. I'll keep you updated.

The perfect cake, months in the making, destroyed at the eleventh hour. Ben's right, the world's just shit to some people.

Wouldn't it be lovely if the bride ended up with Tyler Junior?

To: LRS_17@outlook.com
Tues 11/4, 18:17
SUBJECT: *Normal*

'It's normal to feel lonely, especially after your first baby.' That was on a poster in the hospital waiting room.

To: LRS_17@outlook.com
Wed 12/4, 13:47
SUBJECT: *High steaks*

It was a mistake to try telling my mother in person, what little there was to tell.

'You're early,' she said as she opened her door. 'Dad'll be here in a minute. I bought sirloins. You could share mine or I'll put you some fish fingers in.'

I had said I'd come over in the afternoon – for tea, because she always needs to know the refreshment in advance. But it made more sense to get it done early, get back to work.

'I don't need any lunch. I won't stay long,' I say. 'I wanted to talk to you about yesterday and the—'

The front door opens. He used to ring the doorbell. I always ring the doorbell. It's not our house.

'Pebble! This is a lovely surprise.' It's unconvincing, he would have seen my car parked outside.

'Bit early for shorts, isn't it?' I say. Some people shouldn't be allowed to retire.

'How's Ed?' he asks.

'We're OK, good days and bad days. Glad the post-mortem is over.'
I stumble backwards as my mother fusses by our feet, repositioning
her sausage-dog draft excluder.

When she comes up, my father kisses her on the lips, and I change
my plans.

'Mum thought it would be nice if we had lunch together,' I say.
'Rock, paper, scissors for the second sirloin?'

'Ooh, so much at ... stake.' He laughs. (It's what you call a pun,
you'd love them. I've written myself a text-message reminder to tell
it to Josephine. Did I mention I've started texting myself? Nice to
wake up to messages.)

'Stop being so silly,' my mother says. 'I'll go to the butcher's. Or
you can have something from the freezer.' She means me. 'Or share
mine. Or I've got some of those microwave rice pouches you like.'

'Spinning juggling balls,' my father whispers to me. It's this silly
thing we say, whenever she starts babbling. She said it once at a
dinner party: 'Being a mum is all spinning juggling balls.'

'Or eggs on toast? I've got lots of eggs,' she carries on.

We go round in circles for a while: there's no need to go out, it's
no trouble, or there's plenty in the freezer, or she can jump in the
car, be back in ten minutes, or there are sausages, leftover cottage
pie. Is this what they do all day? Fabricate food problems and
discuss hypothetical solutions like a Women's Institute version of
Survivor. They know I'm trying to tell them about the post-
mortem.

Finally, we revert to my plan to battle it out for the steak and I win
(I always do, he's always rock, always panics on three). He has a
chicken Kiev and we swap plates when we are halfway through.

They're watching TV now, some medical thing, waiting for me to
leave. I'm in the kitchen, writing this, pretending to wash up – she
won't let me put the steak pan in the dishwasher. I could leave a note
on the side, slip out. Or wait until tomorrow. If they hear it now or

then, what does it change? What is there to hear anyway. You were perfectly healthy.

To: LRS_17@outlook.com
Wed 12/4, 18:39
SUBJECT: *Good news*

That's what she called it, when she finally listened. Good news.

When I went back into the lounge, someone on the TV was giving CPR to a motorbike rider on the hard shoulder.

'Hang on, Pebble,' says my mother. 'He's a father of two, another due any day.'

'Irresponsible to ride a motorbike in his position, if you ask me,' says my father.

'Honestly, Phil. No one plans to have a disaster.'

'I'm going now,' I say.

'Sit down a minute, Pebble. I'll be with you once they've got him breathing,' my mother says.

'What if they don't?' I ask.

'Shush,' she says. 'They're concentrating.'

When he's in the ambulance, I ask, 'Can I go now?'

'Do you want me to find you some pudding?' she says.

My father clears his throat, turns up the sound, leans towards the TV.

'Still full,' I say over the voice of the motorbiker's attractive girlfriend. 'I'll see you later in the week.'

I'm in the car when she calls from the front door. 'What about yesterday?'

I go back. 'You didn't seem to want to know.'

'I didn't want to ask in front of Dad,' she glances over her shoulder, 'in case it's lady problems.'

'It's not anything. Wasn't anything. They said he was perfectly healthy.'

'That sounds like good news.'

To: LRS_17@outlook.com
Thu 13/4, 01:44
SUBJECT: *Pointless*

This joke keeps going round in my head. Or it sounds like a joke.
    What do you call maternity leave without maternity?
    Seriously, what am I supposed to call it? What's the point of me?

To: LRS_17@outlook.com
Thu 13/4, 02:06
SUBJECT: *Eternity leave?*

I'll never be let back in. I'll always be 'Did you hear what happened to Rachel?'

To: LRS_17@outlook.com
Thu 13/4, 18:36
SUBJECT: *Outlaws*

He knows. I feel better, or angrier, or both. We did something outrageous in the park and I said it.

We had four dogs (Francis, Biscuit, Bug the Puggle and Jolene, a Vizsla). The park gives them more room to run than the cemetery. When we got there, white trucks were parked along one edge, film crews – but we didn't spot anyone famous. Just a man in a Land Rover. He pulled up on a path in the park (pretending it's allowed), opened the boot and a Dalmatian jumped out. It looked like an ITV drama and he was a well-spoken serial killer.

We hung back and watched them do the car bit three times, every time the same.

'Ever fancy doing that?' I ask Ben. 'Animal trainer for TV, bet the money's good.'

'Seriously? Can't imagine anything worse. Bet the dogs hate it too, being round TV types all day.' He pretends to do air kisses and does a cheeky smile that reminds me of the day he met Josephine. 'Want to see something cool?' he asks.

We walk behind the people with clipboards and walkie-talkies (so many of them, so inefficient) and he stops by a tree to tie the dogs' leads to the fence, puts Bug further along, out of their reach.

'Leave Francis, too, come with me,' he says.

We walk uphill to the furthest truck, where there's a mini marquee and a long table covered with food. As we get closer, Ben whispers, 'I've done this before. Walk past, help yourself.' He pulls a woolly hat from his pocket, puts it on so low it covers his eyebrows. 'My TV look,' he says.

'Oh God, what if someone sees us?' I ask.

'They're all busy and they don't know who's part of the crew and who isn't. And look how much they've got.'

He's right, it's like a spoilt kid's birthday party. It's only half-ten but there's pizza, garlic bread, sausage rolls, marshmallows, lollipops, muffins, cookies, several types of cereal.

'Want me to grab you a cookie, Sophie?' Ben's doing a posh accent, louder than he needs to. 'Nab me a Diet Coke while you're over there, will you, darling?'

I take two cans. A woman in a purple tracksuit appears on the steps of the truck, she's heard him. 'If I was you, I'd put that down.' It's fake East End, the scariest she can manage. 'That's crew only.'

'Err, excuse me, we are crew,' says Ben, still posh.

'How come I've never seen you before?'

He turns away from her. 'Usually bring our own food.'

'Why haven't you got badges?' She comes closer.

Ben checks his back pockets. 'Oh God, must have left them on set. Soph, you have yours, don't you?'

'Hang on—' I can't think of a name for Ben. I put the cans down, look in my bag. I can't do this. Jolene's howling to us from the bottom of the hill. 'Hang on—' I say. Ben's gone.

'You need to put it back and fuck off,' the woman says to me. She swipes her phone screen, ready to take a picture.

Thank God it's downhill. She's shouting something about calling security. Ben's ahead, he slips behind a tree. I fall to the ground next to him. The dogs greet us like we're heroes.

'We didn't forget you, my babies,' says Ben, and takes four sausage rolls from his pocket. He hands me a cookie, bites into another one himself.

'You were amazing,' I say. 'Scarily amazing.'

'And you were terrible. Scarily terrible.'

'Didn't mean you could just abandon me.'

'It was better for us both,' he says. 'Abort, abort!'

I'm still getting my breath back. Ben leans over me to look up the hill. 'Looks like se-cure-i-eee aren't coming,' he says, hands on his hips like tracksuit girl.

'If they did, I could totally handle it,' I say. 'I have it all worked out now. You're Rufus from sound—'

'Sound? Seriously? I'm Wilf from legal.'

'You could be anything and you pick legal?'

'Best paid. And you're Sophie, my over-eager assistant.'

'Cheeky git!' I shove him.

The dogs are stretching, they want to get going, and the bum on my jeans is wet. We walk along the edge of the park, out of view of the film crew, to a bench. Ben pulls another cookie from his pocket, breaks it in half.

'Do you believe everything happens for a reason?' I ask.

'Are we back to fortune cookies?'

'What?'

'You find that in a fortune cookie?' he asks.

'Similar. It was in this leaflet, about God, someone shoved it in my hand by Brixton Tube. Do you believe it, that everything happens for a reason?'

'I didn't know you were into that,' he says, leans away like I'm contagious.

'I'm not but sometimes you get these crazy coincidences. Like you and me. I didn't recognise you at first. But then—'

'It's not ... I just look like him. It's not me.'

'What? But it is you. From Oval,' I say.

'Oval?'

'When I got there with Francis and you opened the door, you looked familiar but I couldn't place you. A dad from Josephine's school? A friend of a friend, or from the gym? Then it hit me. God, sorry. But what are the chances? That we'd ever see each other again? It's me.'

He's pulled Bug onto his lap and he's kissing him behind the ears.

'I stopped you. At Oval. It was me,' I say. 'They shoved me out the way. I didn't stop thinking about you. If you'd try again. And then there you were, all thanks to Francis. And now we're here, stealing cookies from the rich together, starting a business, because maybe everything happens for a reason.'

His face is hidden in Bug's fur, he whispers, 'What am I supposed to say?'

'Maybe start with thank you?' I say. 'Oh God, I'm joking. Sorry!' I lean against his arm, stop myself reaching for his hand. 'You don't have to say anything. I just wanted you to know. But I didn't know how to tell you. And I get that you didn't recognise me, it was all so fast. And I had make-up on. Different hair, maybe.'

'Stop talking!' Bug flinches, jumps off his lap. Ben is up, putting their leads on. 'Bloody hell, Rachel. I don't know where to start. You act normal for a week and then this.'

I run after him. 'I get that you're embarrassed. That's why I didn't say anything when we met, I didn't want to make you feel uncomfortable. But you shouldn't be embarrassed.'

'About what?' he asks.

'About me being the one who saved you.'

'Seriously, you do hear how you sound, don't you? Saved? That must have been some leaflet. Should have known you were a lunatic religion freak.'

'You had the same coat,' I say. 'Oh God, I shouldn't have told you. I'll shut up. But it would be weirder pretending it wasn't me, wouldn't it? And I wanted to say I'm so glad you're better, out of it.'

'You saw someone in a coat at Oval last year, and this year, you meet me, same coat, possibly even the same person. Wow. London woman meets London man she once saw on Tube platform. Wow. What are the bloody chances? Yes, it's a small world. Yes, I was destined to meet Francis, my soul dog, wow! Wow, wow, wow.'

I'm laughing, can't stop.

'What?' he says.

I try to cup my hands round my mouth, have to fold over.

'For fuck's sake, Rachel.'

'Wow, wow, wow,' I manage through my hands, up to the sky. 'Is that your impression of Francis?'

A smile. 'He's not really a wow. More row, row, row.'

'Like us, then.' Our arms touch. I don't say any more. He'll need time to take it in, us finding each other. Did you notice how he said 'last year'?

He said he needed to get Jolene home, so I walked there with him. We talked about what they might be filming – he reckoned it was about a dog walker and his 'quest for peace', but what would he know, he said, he hated TV (which, I should explain, is commendable but also odd, and probably untrue).

When we said goodbye, I hugged him and he didn't pull away.

'It's just...' he started.

'I know. Nothing makes sense.'

When I got home I texted him that it will be OK, the business would make it all OK.

To: LRS_17@outlook.com
Thu 13/4, 20:32
SUBJECT: *Jump*

How long would you leave it to ask him why? Charlotte will know what to do.

To: LRS_17@outlook.com
Fri 14/4, 11:18
SUBJECT: *Winner*

I know I go on about this, but Gumtree is revolutionary. You can buy anything, exchange anything, find anyone. And so cheap. One man is offering tattoos for free, to 'expand his portfolio', and then there are the untold stories like the never-been-worn wedding dresses. I found a never-been-used Moses basket. I won't tell you what I found for Josephine's birthday tomorrow, it's a surprise.

Gill in Onboarding told me about her daughter's class – you remember, as soon as my bump (your bump?) showed they all unleashed their parenting advice. Competitive gifting, Gill called it. For her daughter's seventh birthday, one kid (or more likely their mum or dad) put a fifty-pound note in the card. Someone else gave her a talking pony robot.

'And you have the Pinterest mums who outdo everyone by making the gift,' said Gill. 'You know, the thing only time can create, because if there's one thing more important than money, it's time, and how much you pour into the little poppets. This one mum gave Annamaria a hand-knitted mermaid tail, her name stitched on in sequins, nine letters. Yeah, thanks so much.'

Gill later found out the mum has a knitting machine. 'Changes everything,' she said. 'Threw money at it after all.'

'She'd have had to do the sequins by hand,' I said.

'Your turn will come,' said Gill. Guess she doesn't know everything.

Hang on, a text. Phone's in the kitchen. And another one. Must be E, king of the afterthought. Back in a sec.

Not E. I know you think Ben needs space but sometimes it's better to keep the momentum up. Plus, it would be cruel to throw the Oval revelation in front of him and disappear, dangerous even.

Both messages from Ben:

Could do 12, Nunhead.

And:

If you promise not to start up again ;-)

He means the cemetery, Nunhead Cemetery. The punctuation is a winking face on its side; he's conceding that I'm right. There's no way I can collect Francis in time. And I need to buy new eyes for Josephine's birthday cake (E ate the last bag – white chocolate buttons). I'll write when I can.

To: LRS_17@outlook.com
Fri 14/4, 23:22
SUBJECT: Start up again

Dog food, Brexit, Afghanistan, business. Anything but Oval. On the way to Nunhead I made a list of four suitable topics in my head. I was driving so had to chant it to myself. Dog food, Brexit, Afghanistan, business. Anything but Oval. But all I could hear when I saw him was 'Don't start up again, don't start up again.' I read about 'don't' in one of your parenting books. Don't doesn't work. If I tell you 'don't think about flamingos', what do you see? Flamingos. (If you knew what they were – top-heavy pink birds, standing on one leg. You'd love them.) Or 'don't think about milk'. You're thinking about milk. Don't drop that ice-cream … there it goes, sorry.

I was desperate to start up again.

'Sorry about yesterday,' I said.

He pretended not to hear. 'Where's Francis?'

'Oh, I had to leave him with my mum. Funny tummy.'

'What did you feed him?' he asks.

'Nothing. The usual.'

'Did he pick something up in the garden? Snail?'

'Must have. You know dogs, he'll be better by teatime.'

It's a holiday today, called Good Friday (you'd know that, probably big there, but not a 'holiday'. Be brilliant if you could write back). E wanted to go to a spa for the day, but I said I didn't feel like it, and I reminded him he'd promised his mother they'd go to this big National Trust house while its tulips are still in bloom. Anyway, because of the holiday, Ben only had Biscuit, his other dogs were with their families, probably at other National Trust houses.

'Did you read about Afghanistan? The Mother of all Bombs?' I asked Ben as we walked.

'Try not to let that kind of stuff get to me,' he says.

'Oh God, you're one of those Trump supporters, the nicer ones who think the world needs some upset, clear out the elite, make way for the new, a voice for metalworkers.'

'No. Just the bomb was in Afghanistan and I'm in Peckham.'

In my head I'm willing Biscuit to get on with his business so that one of us has something to do. The planes above get louder as we walk, maybe one will take pity on us and drop the daughter of all bombs. I spot a poster on a tree and hang back to read it. It's advertising an Easter fair. He waits for me.

'Did you ever believe in the Easter Bunny?' I ask.

'Do you know how many dogs are killed by Easter egg hunts every year?' he says.

'What?'

'The chocolate.'

'What about it?' I ask.

'It's poisonous, isn't it?'

'Oh God, yes. I thought you meant they were doing the hunting, you know, climbing and falling out of trees and things.'

'It's not funny,' he says.

'I wasn't joking.'

He's more irritable than usual. 'Fancy an early lunch?' I try.

'Haven't got any money,' he says.

'I have cash. Or we could try the film buffet.'

We're the only people on the outside tables at a cheap café but I have my duffel coat and he has his Oval coat. I could be in a sauna or a hotel bar. Instead I'm eating an under-filled bacon sandwich in silence – aside from the rattling of cutlery whenever one of us knocks the table. I fold my napkin and wedge it under a table leg while Biscuit licks my face.

'Can we talk about the business?' I ask.

'Like what?'

'Like what we need to do, how we get going, whether you are even on board.'

'Of course I am. I found a guy with a van,' he says.

'You need to tell me stuff like that.'

'Because you're the boss?' He does the face I hate: big eyes and little headshake.

'Well sort of. I'm the only one who does stuff,' I say.

'I found a van. I just told you.'

'You're not being very nice.' I'm my mother again. 'If we're going to do this, we need to be able to talk to each other, nicely.'

'Then maybe we shouldn't.'

'We have to. That's why—' I stop myself. He knows we were brought together for a reason. I don't have to keep saying it. 'You know it's a genius idea. And it was your idea. Do it for your mum. And for the pets. All those pets you will rehome, save.'

'There's charities for that,' he says. He's being what Josephine's teacher calls a pelicant.

'We'd do it better.'

He rubs his beard, misses the ketchup. 'It doesn't sound like a full-time job.'

'Then you'll feel at home,' I say and go inside to pay.

Pelicants need time to see the opportunities life is hurling at them.

On the upside, BOB the dog cake is finished, despite E's attempts at sabotage.

He came in from a run, went straight for the replacement chocolate buttons.

'Oi! Those are my eyes,' I say, slapping his hand away.

'Make him a blind dog.' He laughs at his joke. (He means the Labradors that accompany blind people, 'dogs *for* the blind'. Yes, it's offensive.)

'Aren't you going to ask who he's for?' I say as he leaves, TV-bound. His indifference is convenient, but it's also hurtful.

'Who's he for?' he calls back.

'My friend's little girl. She's called Josephine. She likes palindromes, and dogs, I called him Bob.' He turns the TV up louder as I speak. 'The party's in the afternoon tomorrow but I'm going early to set up. They live in Brixton. She works at Oval. I met them...'

An American voice shouts 'you're kidding me', people laugh.

To: LRS_17@outlook.com
Sat 15/4, 18:26
SUBJECT: *m ,   b , Kanye and Kim*

Josephine loved her gift. Lola did not. It came with all the accessories a seven-year-old girl should need. I added the names to the outside with foam stickers. Turns out Yoruba is full of palindromes. I cut the dots out from leftover letters – given I had to buy four lots of the alphabet to get all the O's together, there was no shortage. What kind of sticker-maker doesn't put double vowels in the pack? Another thing we'd be discovering together if you were here. And right now, you'd have enough to write four Lukes.

You'd also have two gerbils. They're in your room. The party stress must have got to Lola, I've never seen her be unreasonable before. Even when that old bath addict upstairs flooded her kitchen three nights in a row she mopped it up, laughed like it was a running gag and declined my offer to go up and talk to him.

'Rats?' she shouted, as I pulled away the tablecloth to reveal my surprise.

'Gerbils,' I corrected. 'With a wheel and three tunnels. Multi-storey for extra burrowing capacity. And a water bottle, a food bowl. I have two more bags of bedding in the car, and food. And a book.'

'They're rats,' she says. 'Why you want to put rats in my house?'

There are squeals of laughter from the aunties – what Josephine calls her mother's many sisters and cousins lined up along the sofa and armchairs. Lola snaps at them and they laugh more.

'They're gerbils,' I say to Josephine, leaving the grown-ups to sing-song opinions back and forth. 'The lighter one is Ọbọ, "Monkey", and the grey one is Ọmọ, "Baby". Yoruba names.'

'They're sooooo cute,' she squeals, mimicking the way they tuck their front legs under their chins. 'Can I get them out?'

'No!' shouts Lola.

'Can I get them out when my friends get here. Cuddle them?' Josephine tries.

'No! They stay in that box and that box gets out of my house.'

Josephine stares at her mother for a few seconds and runs out, howling.

'My God, Lola,' I say.

'Don't God me, Rachel. What were you thinking – that this is a zoo? You'll get me thrown out. Building's no pets.'

'No one will—'

'You never think, Rachel. You live in the clouds. You—'

One of the aunties shushes her – Sola, the one who takes Josephine after school. 'The gerbils could live at Rachel's house,' she says. 'And JoJo can visit them after school.'

A negotiation ensues in Yoruba, I need Josephine here to help me. 'I'll check on her,' I say, but no one's listening. I take the gerbil cage with me.

Josephine's on her bedroom floor talking to a fluorescent squirrel with large eyes. I join her and her nose runs onto my black jumper, leaving slug trails.

'Mummy hates me,' she says.

'No, Mummy hates gerbils.'

'That's worse.' More wailing. I wonder how it sounds to Ọmọ and Ọbọ.

We cuddle and there's more snot. 'How about this?' I say. 'I'll keep them at my house, and when I collect you from school you can come and hang out with them.'

'I'll never see them,' she says.

'I promise you will. I could sort some regular days with Mummy.'

'What's regular days?' she asks. It's hard to gauge what she does and doesn't understand. Is 'regular' a difficult word?

'You know, like every Monday,' I say but she still looks lost. 'Or every Wednesday, or every Friday.'

'Like afterschool club?'

'That's it,' I say.

'So I come to you Monday, Wednesday and Friday?'

'Sort of.'

She runs out. I can tell Ọmọ and Ọbọ are laughing at me. It's talk-about-Rachel-in-your-own-language day.

'Mummy said yes!' Josephine skids back into the room. 'Monday, Wednesday, Friday.'

And then she says it. 'I love you more than a scientist can count.'

'I love you, too, JoJo, so, so much.'

The gerbils are the hit of the party. Lola eventually agrees we can open the cage if we keep it in Josephine's bedroom with the door closed. Josephine reads out the page on proper handling to her friends in a tone inspired by Miss Jones, her teacher.

'Be gentle,' she says. 'Gerbils are hunted in the wild and are nat-u-rall-y nervous.'

So far, I am the only one to have grasped the Lester problem.

After her little friends have been dispatched with party bags full of Bob cake, pencils, balloons and love hearts, Josephine and I hang back in her bedroom and leave the aunties to talk and laugh at things on their phones. More adults arrive and with each one we hear shouts of '*ba wo ni*' ('how are you?', explains Josephine) and the sounds of more food being dished up in the kitchen.

We watch the gerbils sleeping, curled up together, twitching as they dream – or relive the trauma of the party. Josephine picks at the foam letters on the tank.

'Hey, it took me ages to get those straight,' I say.

'They're not called that,' she says. 'They're Kanye and Kim.'

'Don't you want nice Yoruba names? And you can't have Kanye, they're both girls.'

'The grey one's a boy, Zara saw his thing.'

God, I hope she's wrong. I only flicked through the book but one thing stood out: 'Be sure of your gerbils' gender or you will soon be welcoming babies.'

They were words ripe for phrasal retention and have been circling my mind all week. Welcoming babies. I should ask a vet to check the grey one, or Kanye as she/he is currently known. I've texted pictures to Ben.

To: LRS_17@outlook.com
Sat 15/4, 21:13
SUBJECT: Fwd: Tomorrow???

Here's something to be grateful for – you escaped life with your grandmother, the other one.

> Begin forwarded message:
> From: Susan Summers
> Subject: Tomorrow???
>
> Rachel,
>
> Flo tells me you haven't replied.
>
> I know Eddie and you are struggling but a quick yay or nay on the shower and everyone knows where they stand. And between you and me, I think Maggie's quite hurt. And anyhoo, have told Flo, anyone calls me Grandma tomorrow I'll slit them through with a cake slice – you don't want to miss that, do you?! It'll be that one with the fat twins and a boy's name. Bobbie, Billie, Harry??
>
> Seriously, I do understand your pain and anger. After Roger, I let things slide too for a while – remember that time you all turned up at Rosehill expecting Sunday roast? But I honestly think tomorrow would do you good. Grief is about driving at hurdles head on, not locking yourself in the trunk. I love how you and I have always been able to speak so openly. Ergo it falls to me to tell you this. It's not just Maggie who's feeling hurt, Eddie needs you back. You'll get over this, Rachel. We all know you can.
>
> All Best
> S

P.S. A thought: If you really can't face tomorrow, you, Maggie and I could do our own little get-together, an after-shower (!) Come over at five and we'll send the boys to the pub. I'll make your roulade.

To: LRS_17@outlook.com
Sat 15/4, 21:37
SUBJECT: *Unfair*

I shouldn't have said that, about escaping. But do you see what it's like here? Your chart says at ten weeks you have all sorts of ways of making yourself understood. Squirming, arching your back and kicking are all signs of exasperation. I'll join you.

To: LRS_17@outlook.com
Sat 15/4, 21:42
SUBJECT: *Language*

'Trunk' – it's an affectation. She's been here forty-one years. And it's Harry, and she's the only one of Maggie's friends who still has her original nails, nose and voice. And the only one who ever remembers me.

To: LRS_17@outlook.com
Sat 15/4, 21:46
SUBJECT: *Over this*

You'll get over this, Rachel. We all know you can.
You'll get over this, Rachel. We all know you can.
You'll get over this, Rachel. We all know you can.

To: LRS_17@outlook.com
Sat 15/4, 21:59
SUBJECT: Names

Here's something I want you to remember. If someone uses your name, don't ever perceive it as politeness, it's aggression.

You'll get over this, Rachel.

Or Graham and Emma: Will we see you next week, Rachel?

The bereavement midwife: This is going to take time and hard work, Rachel.

Your baby's heart has stopped, Rachel.

See what they're doing? Locking me in a cage with their words. As the sentence starts, you glance around, hope it's meant for someone else, they can do the hard work or feel obliged to go to prayer night, and then comes the 'Rachel'. It's like those army-recruitment posters, a pointing man with a big moustache, YOU! Yes, I mean YOU, Rachel Summers.

Know the only other time we use names over and over? To order dogs around. I say 'Francis' fifty times a walk. Ben told me not to. 'You'll make him hate his name,' he said.

To: LRS_17@outlook.com
Sat 15/4, 22:53
SUBJECT: Refuge

I'm in your room. Lester returned from his evening rounds, smelled Kim and Kanye from the garden and crashed through his cat flap like a drunk who's found an open kebab shop. He jumped on top of the cage and scratched me when I tried to shove him off. The gerbils played dead, or I hoped that's what it was. The book said something about cats, stress and weak hearts. (Of course I read the whole book. You knew I did.)

Lester is one of those serial killers who befriends his victims. He settled on top of the cage to purr at Kim and Kanye through his front paws. My scratched hand still stinging, I tried to poke him with a wooden spoon but he growled a warning before I could touch him. I waved a napkin in his face, he didn't look up. I remembered the spray bottle Anca had for the ironing. That repelled him long enough to carry the gerbils to safety. Not sure what Anca put in the bottle, smelled like scented Christmas candles. Lester's friends will have some questions tonight. (Did I tell you he's a cat racist? Only ever see him with other Burmese.)

It took a while, but I could actually see their little hearts slow back to normal. I've put their cage on your changing table. I hope Charlotte won't mind sharing with them.

E came in late – cinema with someone, free work tickets, superheroes – and got himself some food before coming up to find us in here. The caveman diet continues to affect his vocabulary.

'What the fuck is that?' he asks.

'Gerbils, called Ọmọ and Ọbọ. Or possibly Kim and Kanye.'

'You do see how weird this is?'

'Kim and Kanye weren't my idea,' I say.

'The gerbils. In here. That's weird. And the names.'

'They're just gerbils. And don't worry, they only live about two years.' (Sorry, I was going to tell you.)

'Why would you even know that?' he says.

'Research. Did you know that fathers are central in gerbil families? The pups open their eyes sooner if the father is around.'

'Pups?' As he looked into their cage, it struck me how much he and Lester are alike. Same grey, tall, both athletic but not the sexy kind, more the I'll-force-you-to-run-in-the-mornings kind. I used to call it charm and confidence, now I see it's just that there's more of him – more height, more volume, more opinions.

'Why did you get two?' he asks, flicking their drinking bottle so it drips onto the new bedding.

'Better company.'

It's late. Too late to explain about Josephine, Lola's outburst, the Monday-Wednesday-Friday plan.

'Your mum emailed,' I say. 'I upset Maggie again.'

'I know. She told me.'

'Who? Maggie or your mum?'

'Both,' he says and walks out.

'Shut the door ... Quietly, they're sleeping.'

To: LRS_17@outlook.com
Sun 16/4, 02:52
SUBJECT: *Buttons*

Here's a new one: buttons in the oven. Button biscuits. I got a button press free with a magazine last year, remembered it at one in the morning. Even remembered Flo's email rant about no pink and blue. Yellow icing's ready to go. Nothing says 'over this' like a batch of personalised biscuits. (You know it's pretend. Over this is impossible. You were ripped out of me and the edges are so jagged, no one can patch me up.)

They need a couple more minutes. It was this or an intimate 'after-shower' – which sounds like a word for the lump of hair and slime you find when you clean out the shower drain.

To: LRS_17@outlook.com
Sun 16/4, 04:37
SUBJECT: *For sale*

I've composed my first Gumtree listing:

Mature blue Burmese, full of character, looking for his new forever home. Fully vaccinated, chipped, neutered. Heartbroken but change of circumstances leaves us no choice. No time-wasters.

I know he's in a malicious axis of powers with the rest of E's family. He is Mussolini to Susan's Hirohito.

To: LRS_17@outlook.com
Sun 16/4, 07:46
SUBJECT: Snuggly

I was forced to lie in my text to Josephine (via Lola):

> *[For JoJo, pls] Kim and Kanye all snuggly after good first night, can't wait to see you. R xxx*

Lola replied an hour later:

> *She's asleep. L*

To: LRS_17@outlook.com
Sun 16/4, 13:07
SUBJECT: Borrowed

I'm parked around the corner from Maggie's, can't be first. I was almost late. After the biscuits and Lester's night-time offensives (wailing and non-stop scratching at your door, then ours), I slept through the morning. E was oblivious, or out running. Anyway, I ran out of time, and I'm sorry, I know it's probably wrong, but you have so much – some still in its wrapping. I was going to unpack it all bit by bit. But there's far too much and it all taunts me from the shelves, I can't even open the wardrobe.

It's just a blanket. From Gill, funnily enough, the competitive-gifting one. So at least it'll be good enough for the Axis. I can replace it if you're annoyed.

To: LRS_17@outlook.com
Sun 16/4, 15:46
SUBJECT: *Blue*

Stupid, stupid, stupid. Stupid blue stitches. Can't write properly, in an Uber. Oh God. Shouldn't write, and Uber sick.

To: LRS_17@outlook.com
Sun 16/4, 16:52
SUBJECT: *No one knew*

We've never talked about this. Pictured it though, for when you were fourteen, maybe twelve these days with the Internet. I drank something called alcohol, you won't know it, and I avoided it even after you were ... whatever we're supposed to fucking call it. Sorry, that's the alcohol, makes people rude. It was supposed to be a party. But I'm having coffees now and a meatball sandwich, and that will make everything normal again. I'm in a place by Ben's park. Families coming in and out on their Easter Sunday walks. Hot chocolate with little marshmallows. They've got Frisbees, kites and footballs to prove they do things together. Ben won't be long. Get there when I can, he said.

You want to know what the cake said, Maggie's boy/girl cake? It was pink. Your cousin's a girl, thank God. Susan did a shit job at pretending not to be euphoric. My theory: none of that lot ever want any more boys because no one will ever be as perfect as E. Imagine growing up with Susan, every other sentence starting, 'When you run the country—'

His dad would cut in, 'The WORLD, you mean, darling, the WORLD.'

And Maggie goes along with it, even though she's ten times more successful than King Spudhead and a million times more useful.

Do you know what a horror story is? Like a bedtime story except it's never safe to sleep again. That's what today was.

Harry opens the door.

'Rachel! Thank God.' She leans to kiss me, whispers, 'I was worried I was on my own with this lot.' She gets louder as she leans back out. 'Didn't know if you'd make it, with the baby and everything.'

No one's put it like that before. I shrug.

'Who's got him?' she asks.

Give me ten, twenty years and I'll manage something witty to that. Something like, 'Depends on your belief system.' But in that moment, it feels like someone's let me glimpse a different world. I didn't nap, you didn't stop kicking, you are with my mother, our first time apart, I can't stay long, you need a feed at four.

Harry's waiting for a reply. 'Where is he?' she asks. 'Oh God, I mean "she". She, right?'

I feel sick for her, not me. How do I...? Her smile's gone. She knows. She's had twins, she's not like the rest of them, she knows about the risks, she knows.

'Didn't you hear?' I ask.

'Oh no. Please don't...'

'Did no one tell you?' I look over her shoulder for Maggie, for Susan.

'Oh, Rachel.' Harry falls onto me.

'I'm sorry. I'm so sorry,' I say.

'I don't understand why no one told me,' she says.

'I know.' I stroke her hair – it's tight curls, like those metal sponges for scouring saucepans.

'Rachel. You came!' Maggie, perfect bump in the perfect purple dress. I'm in my new mauve dress and look like I've tried to copy my cooler sister-in-law and failed.

Flo appears behind her in a cream skirt and jacket with a purple scarf. There's some sort of pattern on the scarf, storks carrying babies. Somewhere in China a small village will live for a year off the proceeds of this baby shower. Each of us received the same scarf in our party bag.

'You look amazing. Everything looks amazing,' I say. Tissue-paper pompoms hang along the hall, wall stickers read 'cute as a button' and a feathery purple garland is draped around the banister of Maggie's self-important staircase. I find the tin of biscuits in my bag. 'I made these.'

Flo doesn't take them, instead nods towards the kitchen. 'Drop them in there, will you?' (Ask around where you are, I bet they don't let in a single person who ends commands with 'will you?')

In the kitchen a woman in unnecessary chef's whites takes my tin, puts it on top of the fridge. I hang back to see if she wants some help. 'Bet you followed that Texan wedding cake disaster,' I say.

'I don't do weddings,' she says, Polish accent.

I nod to my tin on the fridge, 'The biscuits are part of the theme, buttons. And I swapped cardamom for vanilla. I mean I swapped it in. As in, I used cardamom, but the recipe said vanilla. Shall I find a plate for them?'

She's pulling something out of the oven, doesn't hear me over the fan, a tray of mini soufflés in purple ramekins.

In the lounge there's that party hum of twenty started conversations with no space for me. They all look the same: thin, wavy hair, wedge heels, even Maggie, whose ankles have yet to puff up. She's showing a group of them something on her phone – Button's future school, or its share portfolio. Susan sees me come in but continues repositioning a giant poster for 'pin the dummy on the baby' with Flo's supervision. Oh God, the baby on the poster is E, I recognise the photo, their green carpet. He's naked but Susan's stuck the laminated cartoon dummy picture over his thingy (we never agreed what we'd call it with you). All these women will be touching my husband's ... I can't say it. I suppose using Maggie's picture would have been worse.

I add my gift to the others and sit on the edge of the last chair, with my phone for company. The chair will be wide enough to share with Harry when she returns from the upstairs bathroom.

Maggie looks over as my text appears on her phone. Her friends' eyes follow.

Who else doesn't know?

She goes back to her phone, swipes me and my message away, more portfolios and ponies.

Harry reappears, asks me about you, and I give her the medium-length version – I start the day before, end with no heartbeat. She cries, I don't. When a waitress appears with a tray of champagne, I feel better about having handed over the last of my cash to Flo on the way in. Most of the others are on elderflower cordial and fizzy water. 'I call it fampers,' says Flo. 'Fake champers.'

'I thought it was for fizzy champers,' says Maggie, and it's the funniest thing they've ever heard. Even before she was pregnant she did the ditzy doctor act. Consultant at thirty-two, can't work the washing machine.

Harry and I have two or three glasses of real champagne each but are still unable to face pin the dummy, name the teddy and pass the sodding parcel – which comes as a relief to Flo, who didn't know whether to plan a layer for me.

Susan is the only guest in jeans (with a silk blouse that she's failed to button to the top). She manages a 'so glad you decided you could come' and spends the rest of the time in and out the kitchen or whispering to Flo. Harry and I watch as she untangles an earring from her hair. 'Know the one upside?' I say to Harry. 'I dodge a Glam-ma invasion. She was threatening to move in after the birth … It's OK, you can laugh.'

The compulsory pre-lunch singing is as bad as it sounds. Harry and I stand at the back and mumble along with the chorus. (I respect how Flo mimicked the bad rhyme of fame and train.)

They need loadsa money, but get no fame,
No chance to sleep or use their brains,
It's long and exhausting and it's smelly sometimes,
And without them there's no life.
That's the Power of Mums.
That's the Power of Mums.

The food is good, better than good, there is more champagne and the speeches are more numerous but shorter than feared – they go round the room, each starting, 'My top baby tip is...'

'My top baby tip is ... only have one at a time,' says Harry and they laugh because that's all she is to them, the woman with twins.

When it's my turn, I say, 'Work out who you can rely on.'

Then it's the bit when I want to evaporate.

It's Flo's fault. Her shower's fizzling out but she won't have it. We've worked through the scheduled fun and there's still an hour of the party to go. She totters from person to person, topping up their fampers, asking if they know any more 'parlour games', showing them three ways to tie a scarf. She's like Eleanor the Chihuahua: short legs, panicky gait, over-groomed. Then she has an idea.

'Ladies,' she shouts over everyone. 'Let's open the presents.'

Maggie takes the middle seat on a sofa and Flo brings the gifts over one by one. There's cooing at the pretty wrapping paper, the ribbons, something called gift charms (yet more good fortune for the good people of Guangdong Province).

Aha, text from Ben, wants to meet in the park, he has Biscuit.

My present follows a microwaveable hedgehog with silicon feet for teething and a mirror on its tummy. My biggest worry is how much even Maggie and Flo can find to say about a blanket. And Gill used plain silver wrapping paper. The hedgehog was swaddled in a rainbow muslin, inside a velvet pouch, in a purple gift box.

'A blanket!' says Maggie and mouths 'thank you' at me while doing yoga prayer hands. I now see that was God giving me a sign to leave because instead of moving on to the next gift, she seems to think she has to unfurl my blanket first. And there it is, sewn on in giant blue letters:

WELCOME TO THE WORLD
BABY SUMMERS!

I know what you're thinking. No, she took Damian's name. There is only one Baby Summers. You. (Or were you thinking about the missing comma?)

The others don't get it or they think it's a simple mistake, a mix-up when I ordered. But Susan, Flo and Maggie know what I've done. Harry knows it too. She leans away from me. 'I was in a rush,' I whisper to her. My cheeks are burning and the champagne is making me sick.

Flo thrusts a parcel shaped like a Moses basket onto Maggie's lap. 'This one's from me.' There's a collective wince for the bump.

'Back in a minute,' I say and disappear into the kitchen. I retrieve my unopened biscuit tin from the top of the fridge and grab a party bag from the hall. No one bothers to follow me. In the car, I turn the radio on loud and order an Uber, from the passenger seat to be safe – all that champagne. And now I'm here, in a café, without working toilets. And still no Ben.

Text from E. Back in a minute.

To: LRS_17@outlook.com
Sun 16/4, 17:03
SUBJECT: Wanted

E's not happy. Look at this:

Where are you? Maggie called, said you did something so weird she couldn't talk about it. Then my mother. Said you seemed unwell. And you left the car with the keys in.

I texted back:

My car, shit, sorry. First drink in a year, weird reaction. Getting fresh air. Battery going. See you later. X

And again:

P.S. Shower lovely. Niece! Bet you're chuffed x

And again:

Is your mum coming on Wednesday?

Finally. Ben called, says he's almost here. Now my battery really is going.

To: LRS_17@outlook.com
Mon 17/4, 00:23
SUBJECT: Ben knows

I told Ben. He knows everything, most of it. More tomorrow. Had to tell you.

To: LRS_17@outlook.com
Mon 17/4, 07:26
SUBJECT: Bank Holiday

Do you know where we're supposed to be? The Cotswolds – there's a hotel with bottle warmers and cots, everyone at work's been there.

You're supposed to sleep in on Bank Holidays but E woke me. He has a triathlon or something with tricycles in Battersea Park, and lunch with his mother. He always runs to Mommy and Maggie when there's trouble. We've conducted every discussion and every fight of our five years together under their supervision. They wanted you to be a September baby.

He couldn't find his sunglasses.

'In the drawer under the microwave,' I say.

'Where did you go?' he asks. 'You can't just bugger off like that.'

'I can.' My brain's swelling, my shoulders are knotted, my throat's raw. I need another ten hours' sleep.

'No one knew where you were,' says E. 'We called all your friends. Flo wanted to put your picture out on Twitter.'

'Because I went for a drink with a friend?' I ask.

'And got blind drunk, ran out of the baby shower, abandoned your car,' he says.

'That's not really—'

'Maggie says post-natal depression can happen suddenly, even without, you know ... that you get chemical imbalances. She wanted to go out looking for you, nine months pregnant, walking the streets and checking pubs because you couldn't be bothered to answer your phone.'

'My battery was going and I didn't want to be rude to my friend,' I say.

'Friend?'

'Jolene. From the baby-loss group,' I say. 'Wasn't the kind of drink where I could get out my phone and chat to you.'

'You have a friend called Jolene? What baby-loss group?' he says.

'What baby-loss group? It's a bit shit you have to ask, isn't it? The others go as couples. A group of strangers who all give more of a fuck than you.'

He's gone now. Water and more sleep.

To: LRS_17@outlook.com
Mon 17/4, 11:17
SUBJECT: *Fleas*

Ben has fleas. Slept more and ready to tell you everything. I couldn't stay, he said, he had fleas in his bed. Not like that. I drifted off, the sleep deprivation, the drinks, too much food. He woke me and ordered me an Uber – wouldn't work on my phone. Ben says they give you stars for good behaviour and drivers choose who they'll take. He had a clean record – guess they don't know about the fleas.

It's a four-digestive morning, plain ones. Five. Diet Coke is helping. Must have been something at the baby shower. Will put that in the *Life's Little Rule Book* that I'm writing for you. Never eat mass-catered seafood. Better still, BeVaE: Be Vegetarian at Events. A proper vegetarian, not a fish-eater like Ben.

Know what else Ben said? He hates buttons. We were sharing my biscuits in the park, after he found me.

'Always hated them,' he says. 'These are good.' He's on his third. 'But real buttons, hard and little, sticking out, waiting to catch on fences.'

'Deadly,' I say.

'Seriously, it's a thing.' He looks down for support from Biscuit (the beagle, not actual biscuit).

'I know, super serious,' I say. 'Pomp-pomp-phobia.'

'Koumpounophobia,' he says. 'My mum had it too.'

'I bet she was—'

He interrupts me. 'This is awkward, but I need the money for the van, the guy asked if we still want it.'

'Why's it awkward? I told you, we are supposed to talk about these things. How much?'

'Hang on.' He runs after Biscuit, who's befriending two nervous cockapoos. The owners have matching jackets, the same dark brown as the dogs. They've got to be from the catalogue my mother passes on to me, *Forest Fashions*. Tagline: 'From Field to Fireside'. 'Oldies love F-words,' E says whenever he sees it. We do this thing where I circle what I'm threatening to order him and leave it open on his pillow. The best one was a hollow walking stick that you can fill with whisky. It doubled as a stool.

Mr and Mrs Casual Suede want to know if Ben's a dog walker, last time Portia played with dog-walker dogs she caught kennel cough.

'Flattered you think I'm a professional,' says Ben. 'But he's all mine. Daddy's little boy scout.' (To be fair, Biscuit is wearing some sort of neck scarf.) 'Portia's a gorgeous name.' He says it 'pawww-shah' and 'gawww-jusssss', a talking-to-rich-people voice. 'What's your other baby called?'

'She's Carole with an "e"', says the husband. 'They're half-sisters.'

'This one's Biscuit,' says Ben, bending down to put his lead on. 'Short for Garibaldi Biscuit, sometimes he's just Gary.' Biscuit plays along, tail wagging, licking Ben's beard, he's found crumbs. I say nothing, I'm still tipsy and the cockapoo people remind me of my parents.

'Wish I could lie like you,' I say when we're further away. 'You and Garibaldi. He's even more devious than you.'

'He's as good as mine. Easter Sunday, and who's got him?'

They've gone to her parents. I wonder what Oliver had for his first Easter. Waitrose are doing bibs with egg puns.

'Anyway, I resent the word "devious"', says Ben, doing the voice.

'Apologies, Sir Benjamin. Or is it Sir Benedict?' The voice doesn't work when I do it. 'Just saying it's a skill, lying. Must be handy. One day a film crew, next day Portia.'

'Not lying, assimilating,' he says.

'Why didn't you do that voice for me?' I ask. 'When we met.'

'What voice?'

'The assimilated voice,' I say. 'Actually, that's not fair. You did have a voice for me. A fuck-off-back-to-Clapham voice. Which was weird given what—'

I stop myself because I know I'm doing it, what I always do. I talk and the more I talk, the more I say, and saying things is like the truth, there are layers you should leave alone. 'Stop halfway,' my mother used to say. 'Halfway's plenty.' She applied it to everything, and I hear it everywhere: most meals, cinema popcorn, daytime TV shows. 'Halfway's plenty.'

It's not like Ben's way is any better. He walks off. Clue's in the job title, he's a walker. Or is it all men? E has his phone, Ben has Biscuit. I always knew you'd be different. We'd have chats on the way home from school, stop for hot chocolate, collect Francis, go for walks in the woods. Paul the vicar said not to do this, when I met him to talk about Wednesday. Don't imagine what we'd be doing, he said, 'It makes the process longer.' Like grieving's a chemical reaction.

I run after Ben (in my baby shower sandals). 'I shouldn't have said that, about Oval. I know you don't want to talk about it. But I just don't get it, the whole coincidence thing, me and you.' He's sorry too, puts his hands over his face while I talk. 'And I don't … I mean we can't not talk about it. I don't get why you pretended, the other day, pretended nothing happened. My friend works as a psychologist and she says if you don't talk about these things, they come back.' He's still covering his face, I've made him cry.

No, not crying. He lets out a kind of roar. A woman pushing a buggy speeds up, Biscuit whimpers. Ben shouts, 'Why are you telling all your friends about me?'

'What?'

'It's all for your entertainment, isn't it? You've got nothing else to talk about. Bet you can't wait for me to try again.' He's making fists, straining to hold them back. 'Want me to go back to Oval?' he shouts. 'Call you first so you can be a hero? Fuck it all up again?'

'That's not … Oval fucked up my life too, you know.'

'Traumatic, was it? That what you're telling yourself? Sprinkle some shit in your perfect little world?'

'Perfect? You don't know anything,' I say.

'Course I do. You're all the same. You take the piss out of Biscuit's mum but look at you, flouncy dresses, champagne and baking. You're her without the baby.'

Don't worry, it didn't hurt as much as you'd think. He'd set himself up and it was delicious.

He kept going, it's the most I've ever heard him say. Why didn't I work? How could my husband stand me? Where was the money coming from? I stopped listening and ran through ways to tell him. He got faster, angrier, I caught words: '...ruined ... jumped ... hate marzipan ... Instagram ... Francis ... listening.' He yanked Biscuit's lead as he walked off.

I let him go, focussed on my delivery. I'd use 'died during childbirth', tell him you were due, slap him if he said miscarriage. A title came into my head, like for a poem: 'The Mortification of Ben Palmer'.

OK, I actually thought of that ages ago. Because that's what we'd wanted, wasn't it. To make him mortified for what he did to us. Then we found him and didn't tell him and then Luke's Touch happened. Because it had to.

'Want to know why I'm not at work?' I say when I catch up with him. 'Something happened.'

'For—'

'After Oval, after I saved you. I had a son, Luke. He died.'

He looks like he's not heard me at first. That happens.

'What?'

'I was pregnant when I saved you, and then when he was due, I was in labour and he died, during the birth. He's called Luke.'

He looks at me like I'm making it up. That happens too. 'Fuck,' he says at last. 'What happened?'

'No one knows. The post-mortem said he was perfectly healthy. His heart just stopped.'

'Babies don't just die, do they? That's, that's...' He doesn't know what to call it.

'I know.'

I want to tell you that we hugged and cried. But we didn't. He leaned to hug me, but from the side, and ended up with one arm round my shoulders like I'm his drinking mate or in a rugby scrum.

When he squeezes harder all I can think about is mud and fat men. We don't know how long to hold it. I twist towards him to make it a real hug, but he loses his balance, stumbles back, taking me with him. The smell makes me gag. That's why he was one-armed, the poo bag in his other hand. It's taken the brunt of the fall, split open, smeared on his coat.

It stinks. A smell you can taste. Oh God, whenever Ben smells dog poo, will he think about you? Will I?

Biscuit barks with joy. He climbs over Ben, nuzzling the poo patch, licking it off. He moves onto me, it's on my dress.

'Shit,' says Ben.

'Yes.'

Proof again there's no point planning anything. Know what I can hear? My mother's voice saying, 'Who's mortified now?'

I had alcohol gel in my bag but no tissues. We went to a pub, taking it in turns in the disabled toilet to clean it off.

While Ben's gone, I order us a bottle of wine and three bags of crisps.

'Is that for us?' he says. I take his coat, refold it to hide the mark. It reeks, or the smell is stuck in my nostrils. I squirt the last of the alcohol gel onto the wet patch on my dress. 'What's with the wine?' he asks.

'Biscuit's idea.'

'I don't drink red,' he says.

Should have known.

'But I'll have a vodka and lemonade.'

Again, you are new to drinking, and you won't know that vodka and lemonade is a drink teenage girls ask older men to buy for them, nor that Malbec is a very good wine that costs twice as much in a pub as in Tesco.

By the time I'd finished the wine, Ben had drunk four vodka and lemonades (the equivalent of thirty-six teaspoons of sugar) and it was eleven o'clock. And he'd talked.

He talked about the dogs and their owners, how one man never clears the dog poo from his back garden, offered Ben twenty quid to do it in one go. 'Three months' worth, you're looking at four a day, it's a big dog, Lab cross, hundreds of them, covered the lawn and the patio,' said Ben. 'I told him I'd do it a for a hundred, he said "leave it".' He talked about his dog-training plan, how he'll do one-on-one sessions, special deals for rescue dogs, save the money, buy a place, do it up, sell it, do another one.

'You've thought it all through,' I said.

'Had the plan for ages, was going to do it back home.'

'What happened?'

'Mum, and Dad, and then it got a bit messy with the person I was supposed to do it with.'

'Your partner?' I said.

'Yeah, if you like, I guess.' He scratched his head so both hands covered his face.

And I told him about you. What we were going to do together, how you'd have loved Francis. I finally told him we're calling the business 'Luke's Touch'.

'Used to walk a border terrier called Luke,' he said. 'Ferocious but so clever.'

He told me about his mother, Jackie, and about her funeral. There was a mix-up and they had to wait with the coffin outside the church for an hour in the rain – the hearse was booked for another family, emptied her out after ten minutes. 'We didn't have enough umbrellas. Whole service, all I could hear was water dripping off the coffin,' said Ben. 'Made a puddle.'

I'll call your undertakers in a minute and confirm timings. Forecast for Wednesday is light rain, moderate breeze.

What else?

- He went to university (subject and institution unspecified).
- His mother had six sausage dogs in total – not concurrently.
- His father designed houses, but Ben didn't call him an architect.
- His sister has a son about Josephine's age who's scared of dogs.

After the pub closed, we went to his flat and had more vodka and leftover vegetable curry. He said he'd made it, but the sauce was from a jar.

All night he kept saying the same thing about you and me. 'I can't believe how OK you are. It only just happened.' And he told me how his sister had a friend who caught something from their cat's litter tray and the baby died halfway through the pregnancy. 'You have a cat, don't you?' he said.

'It's called toxoplasmosis. We know it wasn't that.'

'I can't believe how OK you are,' he said again.

'I'm not OK. It's the worst thing I can imagine and it happened. Why do you think I couldn't tell you about it till now?'

'But you're so busy and out and doing stuff and the business.'

'What should I be doing? Sitting at home staring at his basket? Hiding?'

'Thank God you have Francis.'

And you know about the fleas. Because Biscuit sleeps in his bed, he said. You'd think a family like Biscuit's would treat for fleas. Guess Ben's right about them.

To: LRS_17@outlook.com
Mon 17/4, 11:19
SUBJECT: Loft

I can't stare at your basket. E put it in the loft before we came home from the hospital.

To: LRS_17@outlook.com
Mon 17/4, 11:46
SUBJECT: *Bad parent*

Two days in and I forgot them. Thank God for Josephine. She texted.

This is J. Can u send pics?

I replied with two selfies – tongue out, and tongue in. Both look like I've been in a fight.

LOL. Not u. K n K

Their food bowl was empty. Much like their human namesakes, they were excitable in front of the camera. They circled round their tank and came out as beige blurs with red eyes. Josephine was oblivious.

Awwwwww. Their smiling!

I'll make some *THERE, THEY'RE, THEIR* flashcards before Friday pick-up. I've reminded Lola I can't do this Wednesday. She said she wanted to come to your funeral but godless Vernon won't give her the time off. Relief really, what would I have said to E?
I've cleared the bed in your room for Charlotte. Found her some hotel slippers, she always goes on about how draughty London houses are – like it's tropical in Boston. I looked around the house for safe places to move Kim and Kanye, but decided Charlotte will find them quite fun. Maybe she'll get some for Zoe. And they barely make a sound, just the odd bit of digging. She lands tomorrow morning, goes straight to the office and will be here around six. I'm making fish pie, it was her comfort food in exam term, and chocolate fondants. Shame she's not around long enough to meet Josephine.

To: LRS_17@outlook.com
Mon 17/4, 13:52
SUBJECT: *Wake up*

When she called, Charlotte asked if I had pictures of you. I've printed some out, cropped and filtered. Shouldn't they be easier to look at now, after ten weeks? They make me want to shake you, squeeze you, put you in cold water until you wake, wash the blood off your lips. I missed you by minutes. What if I'd noticed you slowing, gone to hospital, they'd cut you out? I asked the consultant at the post-mortem. 'Nothing to say he wouldn't have died the next day,' she said. Would that have been better?

I printed two copies of the best picture, put one in my bag. Ben will want to see what you look like. That van he found, he just texted, the man wants four thousand pounds. Today. How do I tell Ben to slow down but keep going? I've asked him to look into rentals.

To: LRS_17@outlook.com
Tues 18/4, 12:10
SUBJECT: *Fwd: So sorry*

I'm an idiot. Thought she was in the air. Even thought about surprising her at Heathrow.

But here's the truth: She was never coming. People make promises they never intend to keep. How do I know this? Timing. If you're flying abroad you check in two hours before a flight, leave for the airport another hour before that. At the latest, she knew at nine our time last night, twelve hours before I made the fish pie, fifteen hours before she sent this.

Begin forwarded message:
From: Charlotte Southcott
Tues 18/4, 12:06
SUBJECT: So sorry

Rach,
Feel awful but had to cancel trip. Zoe's been sick for two days and getting worse not better. I know you'll understand I can't leave her – wish my evil-queen boss would too!

You know I'd do anything and everything to be there tomorrow when you say goodbye. Sending flowers.

I'll let you know how Zoe is.
We'll do it next time
C xxx

To: LRS_17@outlook.com
Tues 18/4, 13:20
SUBJECT: *Friends*

I emailed back and said no flowers. I was sorry to hear about Zoe, sounds awful, must have been a real blow when she'd finally got back into the swing of work, hope her boss isn't one of those Americans who holds a grudge. Of course, there's always next time, don't know what I'll be up to by then, but sure we can make it work if we try.

She'll understand. But for your sake, here's a translation:

I don't want your flowers. Kids get ill, at least you have one. By American standards, this has to be a shameful display of weakness from a woman who already took longer-than-average maternity leave. Doubtless your boss will put you top of the next redundancy round. I know you feel you have to mention a next time but my son's only having one funeral and you haven't 'done anything and everything' to come to that, so why make more promises?

To: LRS_17@outlook.com
Tues 18/4, 14:04
SUBJECT: *Those were her stupid words*

No one is saying goodbye to anyone.

To: LRS_17@outlook.com
Tues 18/4, 15:11
SUBJECT: *S.W.U.R.T.-Day*

It's International Monuments Day today. In Japan, it's Invention Day (did you know it was International Pooper Scooper Week earlier this month? Texted Ben). I want an international say-what-you-really-think day. That's what it's like in southern Europe, insults shouted across kitchens, in town squares, from rooftops. And people think it's the olive oil that makes them live to a hundred.

To: LRS_17@outlook.com
Tues 18/4, 16:52
SUBJECT: *Mess*

Can you see us? I've tried on six dresses, two trouser suits, two skirts and seven tops. Charlotte had said she'd help me 'pick something out' (been there less than two years and that's how she speaks). I'll need a coat. Forecast is still for rain. My mother's wearing the light-blue suit she bought for your christening. 'I didn't think you'd want us all in black,' she said.

She's being kind with 'all'. There will be five of us, including Paul the vicar, and my father, if he turns up. Maggie 'can't risk it' and Susan said it would be too much.

To: LRS_17@outlook.com
Wed 19/4, 08:35
SUBJECT: *Today*

How do I do this? You should be here, having milk in front of crap TV. Except this morning it's worse than crap, it's boring. They've called an election so there's none of the usual dieting and dementia.

To: LRS_17@outlook.com
Wed 19/4, 09:47
SUBJECT: *Warm*

Do you remember what he said, E, at the hospital? They'd dressed you in a plain white babygro, a bonnet that didn't suit you and they'd brought you back to us.

'You might want to take some pictures,' said the midwife – a new one, the day shift. 'Or maybe you have relatives who want to come.' She sounded Australian, she was young, passing through, she'll be home by now. Do you think she tells people about us?

I'd called my mother earlier, 'Mum, I have some sad news,' and before I could finish she knew, and afterwards that made me angry, like she thought it happened all the time. I asked E to call her back, to tell her not to come. The midwife watched it all. Looked at me for an explanation.

'She won't cope with this,' I said.

'Sometimes you just need your mum,' said the midwife.

I don't know how long I had you. Your weight dug into my arms, if I held you long enough, you would imprint yourself, never leave. I lay you next to me, fell asleep with my hand on you, they put the sides up on the bed so you wouldn't fall. I drifted and woke to the truth, drifted and woke. The body knows its limits, when to shut down. I didn't cry, you were sleeping.

E woke me. 'They have to take him back,' he said.

'They can't.'

'They have to,' he said.

'Why?'

'I think it's too warm.'

I kissed you, the midwife said we could see you again, 'as much as you need', she said, but I knew she didn't mean it, couldn't.

The next time I woke I felt for you in the bed, looked for a cot, an incubator.

'Where is he?' I asked E.

He yawned himself awake. 'Who?'

'Baby. Where's our baby?'

E looked around for help, pressed a button, held my hand. 'Don't you remember? He ... he didn't ... he...'

'Oh God. Sorry. I just thought...'

I never wanted to sleep again. Good dreams are worse than nightmares.

To: LRS_17@outlook.com
Wed 19/4, 10:16
SUBJECT: *Ache*

E's gone to buy more paracetamol. I tried the Calpol from your room but it tastes like warm orange juice with Campari and it's not doing anything. My mother's coming over with spare black tights ('I'll bring a couple of sizes'). I went with a dress, and the long black coat I bought last autumn, wraparound, to get more use out of it. Sodding hubris. I didn't dare ask her for paracetamol, she'll start up with 'what kind of household...?' Even today.

To: LRS_17@outlook.com
Wed 19/4, 10:35
SUBJECT: *The things you loved*

When I met him last week, Paul the vicar asked if I wanted to say something today.

We were at his long kitchen table drinking rooibos tea from mugs without handles. He looked like a vicar: mousey hair, the uniform, comfortable shoes. But he was a vicar squatting in someone else's house, a Scandinavian architect's house.

'Say something?' I asked.

'A few words, after my address,' he said, pen poised over his diary. That's where he made the notes for you, squeezed onto three lines under 'Wednesday 19th'.

'What would I say? What do other people do?'

'Most people say what the person was like, what they loved. I'm sorry.' He looked at his polished concrete floor.

I should show him. He wouldn't believe how well I know you. You love trains and driving, your first big kick was on the way to IKEA. You crave chocolate and mangoes and orange juice. You hate Britpop and the blender, but you love acoustic covers and the landline (remember when we tested it?). You tolerate Classic FM. You know Francis's bark, and most of the morning newsreaders. You're terrified of cinema car chases, unsure about swimming and open-minded about spicy food. You like to lie on your side, you fall asleep when your dad sings. You have a perfect nose, his ears, my feet.

It fills two index cards.

'Where would this be?' I asked Paul.

'Where would what be?'

'Where I speak.'

'In the church,' he said.

'What will it look like?'

'It's Victorian, quite plain.'

'I mean where will people be, and Luke, and where do I stand?'

He draws a diagram on Thursday 20th to show me. They are putting you in the middle, on a small table. I'd have to walk past you and back again. What if I knock into you? Hurt you again?

'I think I'll wait,' I said to Paul. 'Write something instead. Later.'

To: LRS_17@outlook.com

Wed 19/4, 15:23

SUBJECT: *He came*

This should be about you. But you'll want to know he came.

He didn't stay. No one stayed.

I bought food in for your wake, or whatever I'm supposed to call it. Made bruschetta, bought the cheesecakes, people would understand. I've eaten one. The fridge is full of pasta salad, olives, cheeses, antipasti, white wine, because how do you know what people will feel like? How would Maggie's Flo cater a funeral? Would there be grey bunting? Games?

When he delivered it, the Ocado man said, 'Having a party?'

'Depends who turns up,' I replied.

And there are the things I made for Charlotte.

I've only been to one other funeral, my grandmother's. She had about as many guests (mourners?) as she was years old, eighty-six. I counted them while her Mother's Union friends were reading out a poem they'd written. My mother was at the other end of our pew and scowled at me for twisting round. She made eyes-forward gestures with her hands and tried to pass a message along the line to me. Grandma Dunn had one guest per year. Your five was a strong turnout.

They put your tiny coffin on the back seat of a car like a box of books. 'A hearse wouldn't be right,' the funeral director had said. The world's not set up for your kind of death.

I couldn't see if they'd strapped you in. We were in the car behind. There were speed bumps on the road to the cemetery, nasty, high ones. I asked our driver, tapped on the glass to get his attention.

'It'll be secure,' is all he said.

My parents are so practised at pretending they are together, they can no longer work out if they are or aren't. I don't bother to ask. They held hands to walk from the car to the grave, my mother in her pale-blue outfit and matching clutch bag, my father in a dark suit and purple socks, you'd think it was a wedding. E and I were behind them, not holding hands, not knowing what to do or how we ended up here.

At the graveside, my mother pulled a comb from her bag, offered it to me, I stuffed my hands in my pockets, nodded towards my father. He let her comb his fringe.

Paul the vicar used a voice that he must have thought sounded full of contrition – like he acknowledged it was all his fault, his God had done this. But it was all pretend. The voice was what he thought I wanted to hear. He reminded me of American hotel desk staff – 'of course we can move you to a room away from the fracking site' and 'anything else we can do for you?' Two minutes later they're in the back office buying a ski chalet with your credit card.

As Paul says the dust-to-dust words, the funeral people struggle with your coffin (you'd think they'd practise). The difficulty is fitting two straps under it to lower it down, with one it topples, a tiny, disproportioned seesaw. My father tries to help by holding one end of the coffin, he kneels in the mud to reach into the grave. I picture him laying you down to nap in your basket after he's rocked you to sleep. This is all he can do for you, all any of us can do for you.

'What the hell is that doing here?'

Paul stops, either on account of E's language or the barking.

A dog, puggish, bouncing towards us, to me. I recognise the turquoise bowtie, it's Bug the Puggle. At the edge of the cemetery, Ben's half hidden by a tree. He has Biscuit on a lead, it looks like Biscuit, they're too far away to see.

'He must have got off the lead,' I say to E.

'He shouldn't be here, on or off a lead.' E looks to Paul for support.

'You can actually walk dogs in cemeteries,' I say.

'Not this one,' says Paul.

'It's disgusting,' says my mother. 'I wouldn't be seen dead with Francis in a graveyard.'

She doesn't hear what she's said, she never does. My father's still on his knees with your coffin, I mustn't meet his eye or we'll both be sniggering. Bug is jumping up at me. 'It's these shoes, bet he can smell Francis,' I say. I stroke behind Bug's ears and he stops barking. I go to pick him up but stop myself, it's overfamiliar. They've all spotted Ben. 'I'll take him back,' I say.

'Let him come and get him,' says E.

'Don't be like that. You can tell he's mortified,' I say.

Paul gives me a hopeful look. His Bible's open, he was cut off mid-dust and wants to move on.

'Come on, poppet, let's get you back to your daddy.' I tug on Bug's collar but he leans back, digs into the mud, shakes loose. He's sniffing the ground, working his way towards the grave, the coffin will be next. I grab him. He's heavier than Francis. I need Ben to meet me halfway. Bug's struggling, scratching at my neck. Ben steps out from his hiding place, looks over to E.

'Is this your dog?' I say too loud.

'I'm so sorry, came off the lead,' he says. Also too loud.

E is shouting. Something like, '...shouldn't be here ... cemetery'.

'I have fish pie for you,' I whisper. 'Are you in later?'

His face says yes, and that he's sorry, but he had to come. 'So sorry again. So, so sorry,' he says out loud, and then he whispers, 'Who has Francis? I could have had him. For free.'

'He's at home waiting for me. Thanks though, and thanks for this.' I want to tell him I feel better when I see him and that you'd be happy he came and brought Biscuit and Bug. But E is gesturing.

As Paul the vicar picks up, I look around, hoping for more interruptions, a last-minute pardon. Ben and the dogs have gone. Two squirrels are chasing each other up and down a tree. I look anywhere but at the coffin going down. It's not you.

On the walk back to the cars, my mother feels she has to apologise to Paul. Has he ever seen anything like it before? Bet he's seen all sorts, she says as she brushes imaginary dandruff off my shoulders. Bet some people bring their own dogs to funerals. Is it only dogs, or have there been cats? She wants him to know she has a sausage dog, and that she's one of his lot, says 'at my church' and 'we meet in Elephant and Castle'. Paul leaves her to talk until she's drowning.

'Mum's church is thriving,' I join in. 'New members every week, aren't there, Mum? All ages. What are your numbers like, Paul?'

E is on his phone before we reach the car park. It feels wrong to leave, I should go back, spend time with you alone. My father is asking Paul about practicalities, when can we get a stone, where would he suggest we order it. We need to talk to the funeral director for that, Paul says.

The funeral director is over by his car and having the same dilemma as me. When is it OK to leave? He shuffles from foot to foot, like Josephine when she needs the toilet. His junior is around the other side of the car, he lights a cigarette. Smoking at your funeral, a baby's funeral. The boss comes over to me, 'Do you need us for anything else?'

What am I supposed to answer? 'Not until the next one'? I glare in the direction of the smoking junior.

'Are you going past the station?' my mother asks the boss. Then to me, 'Try and do something nice for the rest of the day, Pebble. Keep busy.'

My father hugs me. 'I'll make sure the stone's all taken care of. I'll go in and see them and you can tell me which one you like.'

E drove us home. He tried to distract me, told me about a new American graduate who wore a hat in the office and called everything 'just awesome', 'sweet' and 'deranged'.

'Young people,' I say.

'Don't say that, it's giving in, like signing up to meals on wheels. And last thing I heard, you were into citizen filmmaking on YouTube.'

'What?' I ask.

'*Knees* or *Feet* or something.'

'There was this thing about feet on *The One Show*,' I say. 'Did you know a quarter of all your bones are in your feet. And they had a thing about meals on wheels actually, the push for vegan options.'

We put the radio on.

At the front door, he says, 'Is it awful if I go into the office?'

'When?'

'It's just the election. Bridget's called a meeting for four o'clock. And I don't know what else to do. It's all so strange. But if you need me, I can stay. Get someone to conference me in from here.'

You wouldn't want us to fight. 'I understand,' I say. 'I should sleep anyway. Catch up now it's over.'

'I love you,' he says, kisses the top of my head.

To: LRS_17@outlook.com
Wed 19/4, 16:09
SUBJECT: *Phrasebank entry no. 272*

Charlotte's flowers arrived. I should take them to your grave. Can I describe them for you instead? White, purple and late. Card says: 'My heart breaks for you.' I don't know which of us she means. And they should take away her passport.

Off to take Ben the pie, and some antipasti and white wine.

To: LRS_17@outlook.com
Wed 19/4, 17:43
SUBJECT: *Night in*

Ben didn't ask me in.

'Are you OK with prawns?' I say.

'Sorry. About today.'

'Don't. I wanted you there. It made it easier.'

'I shouldn't have brought the dogs,' he says.

'Stop apologising. I said it's OK. And it's research, for Luke's Touch.' I try to laugh.

'Guess so.' He scrunches his face up.

'What? You are OK with that name, aren't you?'

'No, I mean yes, I'm just ... I'm about to sneeze. Sorry.' He does a half-sneeze. 'I looked at van rental, by the way. Works out cheaper to buy one.'

'Can we talk about it next week?' I ask.

'Sure. Sorry. Just you brought it up, the business.'

I do need to talk to him properly, find out what went wrong with his last business partner, if that's what he or she was.

E had texted when I was on the way to Ben's. His meeting finished early, he was picking up basil for my pasta sauce, we should watch some comedy together. It'll get easier, he said. I wrote back, don't buy basil, we have the pasta salad.

I'm making our popcorn, with toffee and salted almonds. This is why humans have the most varied diet of all the species – to give us things to do and to talk about when we're together. If we were content, we'd all eat cereal every day.

To: LRS_17@outlook.com
Thu 20/4, 16:23
SUBJECT: *Fox and robin*

Would you like me to keep going there, a regular day? Every Thursday, because you were born on a Thursday? But you died on the Wednesday, or so they say.

It's warmer today, the ground was dry, dry enough to lie on. I took a picture of your little mound of earth – I'll send it to Charlotte, if she asks how the funeral was. Is that something people ask?

Should I come back tomorrow, bring Josephine? I'm still working out what to do with her. There's a new play area with a sandpit down the road, but maybe it's too young for her. And I'm worried foxes might be pooing in it, and if they're foxes who've eaten discarded Snickers bars, what would that do to her? Or we could take a bus ride, sit at the front on the top deck and look for palindromic shop names. But traffic will be bad on a Friday night. I don't know what I'm doing. That's what I said to the fox lying by your grave. 'Do you eat nuts?' I asked him. His footprints were in the mud around your little plot, the mound was flattened on one side where he'd been sleeping. A robin watched me from your neighbour's stone. 'It's rude to stare,' I said. No reply. I'll bring some birdseed next time.

You're next to Joyce Percival, 12th August 1923 – 22nd December 2016. She missed last Christmas but had ninety-two others. Facing you, there's a hedgerow with a cherry tree dropping its pink blossom. In the other direction there are more graves. You can hear planes overhead but no traffic from the roads. There's birdsong and the sound of a woodpecker working at a faraway tree. On your other side it's empty, I wonder who we'll get. It's wrong to wish for someone young.

Your flowers still look fresh. When I tugged out a rose to give to Joyce (I checked no one was watching), I noticed a card from E.

Luke,
We longed for you and cherished you,
always will.
Daddy and Mummy

To: LRS_17@outlook.com
Fri 21/4, 10:20
SUBJECT: *Cardboard city*

I got the idea from the palindromic shop names plan. What if you could be in charge of all shop names, of everything, mayor of your own town, ruler of your own empire? Maybe you are.

We'll build Kim and Kanye a city, Silopolis. (Pronounced 'si' like 'sit', not 'silo', because that's an ugly word about being stuck.) My mother hoards cardboard tubes and boxes 'in case Francis redevelops a taste for them'. The eternal puppy, never allowed to grow up. I rang her and said I was volunteering at a school, the outreach team organised it, I needed cardboard for a project. (It's half true: I pick Josephine up at school and Lola doesn't pay me.) I'm collecting them in a minute and I'll grab Francis at the same time, take him out with Ben for an hour. I've given myself this week off from the business planning, but I'll remind Ben that we need to get back on it on Monday. We'll start with death notices in the local papers, if we can find local papers.

To: LRS_17@outlook.com
Fri 21/4, 14:37
SUBJECT: *Holiday*

E texted earlier, said he thinks we should go away, I should choose somewhere and that May is good.

I asked Ben, 'If you could go anywhere in the world, where would you choose?'

'Borneo. To meet orang-utans,' he said.

Do you 'meet' orang-utans? Do they open a bottle of wine, put out pistachios?

'Why don't you just go then?' I asked.

'Jesus, Rachel,' he said. I didn't probe.

To: LRS_17@outlook.com
Sat 22/4, 10:35
SUBJECT: *Town planning*

Silopolis (or LondonodnoL, if Josephine prevails) is magnificent. Or it will be when it's built. We spent most of the evening planning on sheets of A3 but managed to make a school out of a shoebox (orthopaedic, my mother's), two toilet rolls and a Toblerone box (purchased especially – I ate it alone, realising almost too late about the nuts). I suggested we start with the most essential buildings and, unprompted, Josephine picked a school. We called it Luke's School spelled LOOKSKOOL – you can see why. Among the supplies I bought in was a pack of twenty-four Sharpies, lots of colours. When Josephine saw them she hugged me. 'You're a B E BFF,' she said.

'B E BFF?'

'Best-ever BFF,' she says, stabbing at the plastic pack with kitchen scissors.

I prise away the scissors – Friday night is peak time in A&E departments, I tell her. (It's actually not, Monday daytime is worst, I just checked. I'll let her know next time.)

'Here you go.' I hand her the opened pack. 'B E BFF: Best-ever Bright Felt-tips Furnisher?'

She presses her lips together, grins, shakes her head. She wants me to guess again.

'Big Fat Ferret? Fish? Farmer? Burpy Fish Farmer?'

Her eyes are watering and she's squeezing her lips tighter and tighter together, she bounces from side to side, crosses her legs.

'Go to the loo before you have a Big Fat Fail,' I say.

She leaves the door open, makes a long aaaah sound and shouts, 'Big Female Friend.'

'That's not a thing,' I shout back.

'Kayla told me.' She flushes, reappears.

'Go back and wash your hands, you big fat germ-spreader.'

'That doesn't work because it's not—'

'Go and wash your hands! We have a whole city to build.'

'And colour in,' she calls from the bathroom.

'Use soap.'

'To colour in?' she shouts back. I don't know if she's quick-witted or very literal.

Josephine made the sign for your school while I assembled the building. She wanted to colour the letters 'rainbow order and then rainbow order back the other way'. I told her how to remember the order with what they call a mnemonic. It goes 'Richard of York gave battle in vain', meaning: red, orange, yellow, green, blue, indigo, violet. That prompted new questions and I had to concede I knew neither about Richard nor his battles. We invented an alternative: 'Rachel of Yellowtown goes blue in vacuums'. Josephine wrote it out and drew a picture of a blue me with yellow hair inside a giant hoover. Silopolis is already a case study in how construction projects fall behind schedule.

We're building it in your room. As Josephine coloured in, she asked about you. I told her about how we drank orange juice and ate mangoes, your favourite music, how you were tall, looked like a fast runner. I showed her your picture.

'He's sleeping,' she says. 'Did he want to come out?'

'He was ready. There was lots he wanted to do. He would have loved to play with you.'

'He can't have Sharpies,' she says. 'Maya's baby Sharpied all over their sofa and Maya's school shirt and her mum put her Sharpies in the bin. Mummy says it's Maya's mummy's fault for having Sharpies and a baby.' She puts her hands on her hips, does her Lola accent, '"That woman, still a child."'

'Not everything is someone's fault,' I say.

'The baby took them out the bin and sucked on them and his lips went green forever.'

'That wouldn't happen,' I say.

'It's too hard to explain.' (She says that a lot. To me, at least.)

I've told E I'm having a friend's daughter after school some nights, that it gives me something to do. I was ready with more, how the bereavement midwife suggested it, how it would make me eat properly, that it was fun. But he didn't ask, said he'd be back and forth to New York for the next couple of months anyway. 'What's her name?' he said later. 'The little girl you've got. Is it the one with the birthday cake?'

'Wow, yes! Josephine, or JoJo for short. She loves dogs, and palindromes. She's brilliant. She's funny, but polite and so clever. I met her mum through the baby loss group, she's called Lola.'

I did find Lola because of you.

To: LRS_17@outlook.com
Sun 23/4, 09:55
SUBJECT: 80 – eighty – LXXX

You are eighty days old today. LXXX in Roman numerals, a different way of writing numbers, L for fifty, X for each of the tens. Josephine is learning about them at school. I'm making her a poster and we're going to your cemetery to find some on old graves. We used them on your school in Silopolis, 'Established MMXVII'. I know you can see what I'm doing, your chart says you understand cause and effect now. Of course I need to prove I'd have been good at this.

Back to work tomorrow. Ben wasn't in the right frame of mind to talk about the business on Friday. He asked if the funeral 'helped', said he was glad it didn't rain much, that he imagined E differently.

'Different how?' I asked.

'Not tall. Maybe with a beard.'

'Like you then?' I said.

One day I'll ask Ben if he thought about his own funeral. Did he leave instructions? Or was Oval a sudden decision? I make up suicide notes for him. But I lack imagination, they're all borrowed from one film or another: 'I can't live with what I've done'; 'living without you isn't worth it' (the 'you' varies – sometimes it's a dog, sometimes a woman, sometimes a man, the 'partner', his mother).

To: LRS_17@outlook.com
Mon 24/4, 14:16
SUBJECT: First employee

I start paying Ben on 1st May. Can't use our joint account, so I'm looking for a business loan, or I could use money from the savings account or ask my mother. But that would mean telling her and she won't understand. She stamps on things. Like school ski trips, the bike E gave me, my plan to bake our wedding cake. I have many more examples. When you were growing, I used to wonder what your list would look like by the time you reached my age. I told myself you would have nothing to put on it, I'd support you whatever, give you the best life anyone could imagine. 'Epic fail,' Josephine would say.

Off to collect her. I found a big piece of cardboard from E's cross trainer box in the loft to use as our base, she can draw roads onto it, or paths, Silopolis should be car-free. We have yet to discuss when and how Kim and Kanye will be allowed to roam it. Maybe Perspex sides or an electric fence, or enhanced gerbil obedience training. There'll be advice on YouTube.

To: LRS_17@outlook.com
Mon 24/4, 14:21
SUBJECT: *Misunderstanding*

Sorry, 'E's cross trainer' is a confusing term. It's not an angry sports coach, nor is it something that trains you to be cross. Picture attached. It's for physical exercise. E does seem cross when he uses it. I'm late.

To: LRS_17@outlook.com
Wed 26/4, 22:17
SUBJECT: *Accused*

More trouble at the school gate – a confrontation with Maya's mother, who is indeed still a child. A few inches left to grow, bleached hair in a messy ponytail, one of those tops with the shoulders cut out to show her tattoos.

'Was it you called my girl a liar?' she says as we wait for the children to emerge.

'Sorry?'

'You're Josephine's nanny.'

I've given up correcting them.

'You called my Maya a liar.' It's only now that the rhyme strikes me. Can't be a coincidence. From what I hear, Maya spends half the week in detention – recently renamed 'TT', or 'Thinking Time'. I've told Josephine it's important to accept everyone for who they are but that other children are a better fit for her than Maya.

'I can honestly say, I have never called your daughter a liar,' I reply.

'So you're saying she's lying about that too?'

'I'm saying I never called her a liar.'

'So when she says you called her a liar, you're saying she's lying?'

'I'm not saying that, you are,' I say.

This must be what having a younger sibling is like. It's fun, she's easy to confuse. We're cut off by Miss Jones calling over to Maya's mum, she needs her to 'come in for a chat'. It's like she's declaring me the winner, it feels amazing.

When Josephine emerges, I grab her bag and artworks before she can drop them on my feet. 'Quick, we're in a rush today,' I say.

It took a while to unravel the accusations against me, but in short, Josephine appears to have told Maya: 'My friend Rachel says you're a liar and I'm not allowed to play with you.'

'Why would you do that?' I ask. 'I didn't call her a liar.'

'You did, about her saying her baby's lips went green. You said that wouldn't happen.'

'You're right, I did. We should both be more careful what we say.'

For the rest of the way, Josephine sang and I replayed the row with Maya's mum in my head. This is how I need to be all the time. No more apologising.

I tried to tell E about it when he came in but I got myself tangled up in the details of the Sharpie and the green-lipped baby, and he'd stopped listening by the time I asked him if he was surprised, proud of me.

'Why do you care what these people think?' he says.

'I don't. That's what I'm trying to tell you. I don't care anymore.'

'I need to pack,' he says. 'And I can't get into that taxi booking account.'

'Usual password,' I say.

'You need to stop doing that.'

'It's a double-bluff. No one expects you to use the same password,' I say.

He's going to New York in the morning. Just two days but gives me time to focus on the business. I'm looking for PIMs (people in mourning) on Facebook and in the papers, working on a letter to them.

To: LRS_17@outlook.com
Thu 27/4, 10:27
SUBJECT: TYD

Been thinking about the school gate. It's thanks to you, this new state of calm, not caring. There's a newish saying that you'll find offensive. It's YOLO, stands for You Only Live Once, as in, 'yes, jump off that bridge with an elastic band tied to your feet' or 'have a seventh tequila/tenth Creme Egg because you only live once'. I have a new one, TYD: Then You Die. What's the point of any of it? TYD.

To: LRS_17@outlook.com
Thu 27/4, 13:55
SUBJECT: Handsome

He said you were handsome.

I'd asked if he wanted to see a picture of you.

'Not here,' says Ben. We were having a working lunch in the cheap café.

'It's just a picture.'

'Sorry, yeah. Of course.'

I slide your photo across the table like a TV detective showing the suspect his victim.

'Handsome,' he says, slides you back.

I wanted to show him your feet, tell him that's the picture we'll use on our website. But I can't tell him. We need a website but he can't know about it. The web's on my banned topics list for him, along with animal welfare and Oval. It's his tiny blue dressing gown, his bus past the hospital.

To: LRS_17@outlook.com
Thu 27/4, 15:15
SUBJECT: *Drafting*

How do you write to new PIMs – people in mourning who are freshly bereaved? I know what not to say. How would you want someone to write to you? Because I do recognise you are just as bereaved as me, you lost me, we're trapped in different worlds, you more than me. I don't like the word 'bereaved', it covers up what this is. I'll avoid it in the letter, and they'll know I understand. The thesaurus (a book of synonyms [a word that means almost the same]) isn't any help. It lumps everything under versions of 'lose' and 'lost'. 'We were sorry to hear you misplaced your loved one...'; 'it's so hard when a parent slips through your fingers...'; 'deepest sympathies on learning your wife was consigned to oblivion. Will you be downsizing? We can help...'

Next week, I'm visiting undertakers to talk about possible partnerships, it's a stuffy world but I'll find one who's open-minded. The undertakers were Ben's idea – go to the source, he said (he also suggested hospitals but that seemed invasive). Do you think he knows he owes us this?

On the pay thing, I'm taking the money from the savings account (previously your education fund). Lenders want to see a business plan, and what we're doing doesn't translate into columns and numbers. They wouldn't understand how I'm revolutionising a whole service (I don't like 'industry'). And it isn't that much – ten pounds an hour for twenty-five hours a week, works out about a thousand a month. More if we get any big jobs. And he still has his dog-walking money. The extra income could pay off his debts to his landlord, take him beyond porridge, stop the mood swings.

He's being stubborn, demanding it in cash. I feel queasy about the tax issue, of course. Going to the bank to take out a few months in one go.

To: LRS_17@outlook.com
Fri 28/4, 11:23
SUBJECT: *Prisoner*

I'm in the downstairs loo, looking up panic attacks. If you lead a
stressful life, they recur, and then you have panic disorder, where you
panic about having panic attacks. I'm breathing through my nose.

I want to kill him. Kill him and bury him without a funeral.

I should explain. I should tell you not to worry, that I'm OK. But
I can't.

It started with our bins in the road, the way people block space
for a moving van. Seemed Mr Slater had used our bins by mistake
(my number 7 stickers clearly not big enough). Perhaps he was
awaiting a bumper delivery of garden gnomes or a new dryer that
doesn't thump against our lounge wall. As long as he returns the bins.

It's so horrific, I may never leave this room. Lucky that two of my
basic needs are covered (don't worry, not while emailing). There is
no natural light, but that's the point.

What kind of person does this? I come out of the shower to it, the
sound everyone dreads. Metal pole bashing against metal pole as the
neighbour's house is clad in scaffolding. This means months of
occupation – vans, skips and shouting men with fizzy drinks, their
crisp packets in my garden waste.

I was in my towel in the bedroom, pulled up the blind to see if
they're doing Mr Slater's, or Jim and Vic's (they don't have the
money). There he is, level with me, one floor up, T-shirt and jeans,
no official uniform. My window. One hand on a rung, the other
holds a pole, there are more of them on the ground passing it up. If
I open the window, he'll fall and crush them all.

'What?' I mouth. And out loud, 'What are you doing?'

He lets go of the rung, waves like the queen: 'Morning.' His T-
shirt says

EAT,
PIZZA,
REPEAT

I wave back, elbows tight against the towel.

I need to go out to them, tell them it's the wrong house. I need pants, the rest of my clothes, from the chest of drawers under the window.

'Sorry,' I mouth as I lower the blind on him. He sings, the way they do, words of one song, tune of another. What are they trying to prove? *Manual labour makes me happy. Got it all worked out. Stay locked in your Victorian tower of failure...*

He's getting louder, or closer to the window. Can he see round the edges of the blind? Bet they make periscopes for scaffold perverts. I take an armful of clothes, flee to your room. There they are again. Scaffolding all up your side of the house. How long was I in the shower? A fat man in overalls is painting your window frame. Why didn't they check before they opened the can? Shouldn't they be sanding first? 'Wrong house!' I mouth to him.

A jungle scene unfurls as I lower your blind, a happy monkey family laughing at me. I crouch behind your cot, pull on my pants and the rest, and creep down here.

I forgot socks and there's no underfloor heating in this room. E said it was a waste of money in a loo. 'You don't need warm feet to pee,' he'd said.

'I can lift mine off the ground,' I'd answered. 'It's you I'm worried about. I suppose you levitate.' We discussed a rug, but it's unhygienic. I've put my jumper on the floor for now.

When I sneak out to look through the spyhole in the front door, whistling travels along the side passage. How? My dad promised he'd fix the garden gate. They've forced the lock. Oh God, they're not scaffolders, they're burglars. Scaffolders would knock, demand tea. Clever disguise. They thought I'd be out. I crouch behind an armchair. He's on the back terrace, his plank of wood knocks my herb pot. I need photos of their faces, video. No balaclavas, no tights over their heads. Totally brazen.

'You have to come home!' I whisper onto E's voicemail. It's night-time in New York. 'Call the police and get to the airport, we're ... I'm under attack.'

Of course it occurred to me that I could be wrong. But think about it: even if they're not burglars, they're trespassers. I don't know what you'd call scaffolding someone's house without prior agreement. Malicious prowling, false imprisonment, erectile stalking?

Finally, the landline rings. I run for the receiver and back to the bathroom.

'I've been trying your mobile for twenty minutes,' says E. 'Who were you calling?'

'There are men,' I say. 'In the garden. At the windows. Scaffolding. They broke the side door.'

'They had a key,' he says.

'They thought we were out. They have a van ready, like when they did Izzy's place.'

'They had a key,' he says. 'I gave them a key.'

'What?'

'They're doing the paintwork. Mike used them, his agent says it adds at least ten K to the house.'

'What?'

'They did me a great price. I left you a note,' he says.

'You didn't.' He didn't.

'In the diary. Got to go – call with London.'

'They're everywhere, I don't trust them,' I say. He's gone.

It's shock therapy, his way of driving me back to work. Work-work, not the business.

By diary he means the one on our phones. Made sense when it started, we did joint things: badminton, dinners, scans. Under today it says, *Dave doing windows*. I bet Dave's the one with the T-shirt where pizza and eating are separate things.

I message E:

How can you think this is normal behaviour?

I don't.

I think we should do our own laundry

**It'll be fine. Sure they're nice guys, just go and say hi.
See you tomorrow. xxx**

'See you tomorrow' is something dog people say to each other in the park. The ones who don't know each other's names.

Here's something else you should know. Ben offered to come. He picked up. He was ready to come. He stayed on the phone, made me breathe in through my nose and count, out through my mouth.

I'll wait for them to stop for lunch and sneak out. What if they have keys to the inside? They'll find Ben's cash. I could take it to his place. Then I'll go to school, take Josephine to McDonald's and they'll be gone when we come home. Tomorrow is Saturday, E will be home and can ask them how long they'll be. How long does it take to paint a house? Google says five days. Five days of Dave and his men (sorry, people) watching me. Five days of them listening for how long I use the toilet, judging my apparent economic inactivity (doubtless linking the two things). I could move to my mother's. We'll have to put Silopolis on hold, I can't have Dave and his people staring at Josephine. Or we could use the time to go shopping for supplies, we need a gerbil ladder to go up one side of our mini Shard. We'll eat picnics. Renovation refugees roaming the parks of South London until Dave's home time. Oh God, one website says two weeks if they do window frames and gutters. What's repointing?

To: LRS_17@outlook.com
Fri 28/4, 12:56
SUBJECT: *Safer*

I emptied out your talcum powder, rolled up Ben's cash, put it in the
bottle, hid it at the back of your vests drawer. Halfway to Ben's, I
turned back. An empty bottle was too obvious. I went back upstairs,
lowered the blinds, spooned the powder out of the bin and into the
bottle to cover the money.

To: LRS_17@outlook.com
Sun 30/4, 19:10
SUBJECT: *Reprieve*

Wonderful news. Tomorrow is a bank holiday (I'm told losing track
is normal in these early days). Dave and his people will not be back
until Tuesday.

E has booked lunch at a country pub, wants to stop at a car dealership
on the way. He says we need to talk about the scaffolding, which means
he's going to apologise but in return he'll want me to say I over-reacted
to a break-in by a group of men with ladders and heavy machinery.

I've told Ben we'll meet on Tuesday.

To: LRS_17@outlook.com
Sun 30/4, 23:02
SUBJECT: *Happening*

Maggie is in labour. Susan texted E, then called our landline (she
thinks it's cheaper). 'Thank God he's back from New York,' she says
to me. I hand E the phone. I haven't spoken to Susan or Maggie since
the baby shower.

E says things like 'I'll drive you' and 'no, not the private wing' and 'of course she'll get her own room' and 'no, not once she's born' and 'that was different.'

'It's been twelve weeks,' I say when he's off the phone. 'What makes her think we can cope with this?'

'She doesn't know how to act around us,' he says. 'Would you rather she leaves us out?'

'Than this? Yes.'

To: LRS_17@outlook.com
Mon 1/5, 12:56
SUBJECT: Mayday

This isn't what I wanted. But things happen for a reason. And this, with two hours of hindsight, was bound to happen. People prod and push and twist and sneer, and then you snap. We all have a snapping point – if you were here, you'd be testing out mine right now.

In E's case, this moment has been thirty-seven years in the making. And yet, it surprised me. I didn't expect it to happen like this, today.

There's too much to cover in one go but in brief: we both slept badly after the Maggie news and were woken early by Lester, who has been using the scaffolding to reach the bedroom window. He miaows until one of us lets him in. E was first to yield on Saturday evening and twice more in the early hours of Sunday. (Did I tell you Lester was named after the Godfather of direct marketing? He grew into his name, a master manipulator by the age of two.)

E felt bad about cancelling the pub lunch (I hid my relief), and so he suggested breakfast at the place down the road with eggs Benedict. We left our phones in a kitchen drawer, his idea.

Neither of us mentioned Maggie, and instead we managed to get through breakfast by talking about ham versus salmon and Donald

Trump versus Barack Obama. E seemed impressed that I'd been following the news. 'What did you think I do all day?' I asked.

'Walk Francis, look for cardboard tubes, bake?'

It wasn't the moment to tell him about the business.

'And I read,' I said. 'After what you said about how much is going on in the world. You were right.' (The three most harmful words you can say to a partner.)

We order a piece of cheesecake to share but he eats most of it, like a caveman tasting processed sugar for the first time. On the walk home, I say it first. 'Do you think she's had her yet?'

He stops, hugs me.

'It's OK,' I say. 'It's going to happen. There'll be others too. We're that age. I'll get used to them. I'll have to.'

He kisses the top of my head the way he used to when one of us came in from work. He kisses the top of my head and I can feel you there between us, half him, half me. You'd be in a sling against my chest and I'd say, 'Careful, don't squash him,' and I'd pass the kiss down to you, on to the top of your head. It would be our secret waterfall greeting, from him, to me, to you, year after year, until you grew taller than me and we'd swap places. 'I just want him,' I say.

Back at the house, he fumbles with the keys, drops them. We both know what's waiting for us on the other side of the door, like Maggie's baby herself is on our lounge rug, kicking away, full of life.

She might as well have been.

I've replayed the message three times. Babies do this to people, nothing else matters. Susan sounds beyond rescue.

The first time, E and I listen together. 'Ready?' he says, presses play.

'Where are you two? She's here. Baby Button! Maggie and Baby are doing great, as they say. Eight pounds, four ounces, all without any drama. Only spoke to Maggie for a minute, but Damian says it was seven hours, no epidural, first feed right away. Call me back. Damian's emailed a picture, you should have it, I'll forward it. She's perfect. How is it you're still sleeping? Call me. Visiting's from noon.'

I drop onto the sofa, curl up. If I cover my ears and my eyes, and hold my breath, I can leave this world. I should be telling E that I'm happy for him, congratulations, he's an uncle. And thank God they're OK, which he must be thinking too. But I curl up tighter. And it's not fair to do this to him, to this moment.

'I'm sorry,' I say.

'Don't.' He has both arms around me, squeezes me, kisses the back of my neck. 'My fucking mother.'

'I let you all down,' I say. 'I'm letting you down again. I want to be happy for you all. But I want both. I want Maggie to have hers and we get Luke. Why can't we have him?'

'You haven't let anyone down.' He's stroking my hair, too fast. I stop him, hold his hand.

'Without any drama,' I say.

'Draaah-maaah,' he says, the long, low aaah of Susan's wealthy American. 'Eight pounds, two ounces without any draaah-maaah.'

'Four,' I say. 'It was eight pounds four ounces. Same as Luke.'

The phone rings. 'We don't have to see her,' he says.

I hide my head. It's called a foetal position. Supposed to make you feel safer. We're wrong about everything.

He lets the answer machine pick up and her voice squawks out the tiny speaker.

'You're still sleeping? You've gone out? This makes no sense, you knew she was in labour. How could you not—'

E picks up the handset. 'We're here, Mum.'

I hear noises from her side, can't make out the words. He takes the phone into the hall but he's loud enough for me to hear most of it. 'Of course we're happy for her' and 'did it ever occur to you how hard this is for Rachel? For us?' and 'but it is about us. Our baby just died. Less than three months ago. Our baby, my son. Of course it's about us, and you'd see that if he was here. Do you even understand what we lost? He was your first grandchild. He still is. If he was here you'd be all joint photos and cousins and "don't they look similar" and "I'm grandmother of the fucking year, rushed off my fucking feet". You couldn't even be arsed to come to his funeral.'

There must be more from Susan, then E starts again. 'Fine, tell her to call me. She can rub it in, get her live baby to cry down the phone at me. Just like she made my wife go to her fucking baby shower.'

I find him at the bottom of the stairs, sobbing. 'I'm sorry,' he says. 'I'm sorry.'

It's all we ever say.

To: LRS_17@outlook.com
Mon 1/5, 15:24
SUBJECT: *Annabel-Susan*

That's what they're calling her. Susan emailed with a picture, subject line: 'Your niece'. She has dark-blue eyes, or so Susan says, I didn't look at the picture.

'I can't believe they gave her Mum's name,' says E. He's been slamming doors, shouting at the printer and swearing about the scaffolders all day (turns out they fixed poles across the cat flap).

'We gave Luke your dad's name,' I say.

'That's different. It was as a middle name, he wasn't Luke hyphen Roger and it was a way to remember Dad...' He's about to cry again.

'Shall I make you a sandwich? A wrap?' I try. It doesn't work. He stares straight ahead from the sofa, back flat against the cushions, arms tight against his sides, like someone's shot him. One eye makes more tears than the other.

'I know you think I wanted a girl, but I didn't. Well, I didn't mind. I just wanted a baby, made of us,' he says.

I wouldn't say this to E, but do you worry it was the name? Luke Roger. There's the hubris of picking it before you were here. And then taking the middle part from someone who is, you know, also not here.

Oh God. I don't know what makes me more angry: the phrase itself, my mother for saying it or its power over me.

This is what they'll write on my gravestone:

HERE LIES
RACHEL IRIS SUMMERS
BORN ON 3rd JUNE 1982
DIED ON XX XXX XXXX*
AFTER A LONG AND EXCRUTIATING
QUEST TO DISCOVER IF
EVERYTHING HAPPENS FOR A REASON

And, if you think it works:

REUNITED WITH LUKE

*I would fill this in for you if I could.

To: LRS_17@outlook.com
Mon 1/5, 17:16
SUBJECT: Questions

What colour are your eyes? Is it true all babies have blue eyes? What if Josephine asks me?

I asked E if it was in the post-mortem.

'We'd have noticed,' he says. He's watching tennis with the sound off, drinking red wine and eating crisps, one of those sharing bags but he's not sharing.

'They should list it,' I say. 'We should tell them to list it, for other parents. Something useful.'

To: LRS_17@outlook.com
Tues 2/5, 15:46
SUBJECT: *Fresh manure*

E's coming home early. He called three times from the office, 'checking in', he says. Are the scaffolding lot behaving? Did I manage to go out with Francis? Should he pick up a couple of ready-meals on the way home? He's texted Maggie that he has a cold and will wait until the weekend to visit Annabel-Susan. I'll be out dropping Josephine home when he comes in, I said. She's working on a bandstand for Silopolis town square – we had to find an old-fashioned box of Turkish delight, hexagonal. I've come downstairs to make her a sandwich.

In the graveyard this morning, I told Ben about Annabel-Susan. He's always been weird about Maggie, hates doctors, 'love themselves, help no one'. I did Susan's accent for him, her no-dramas message.

'People are shit,' he says.

'That's why the good ones need us,' I say. 'Luke's Touch. I'm almost grateful to Susan. Makes me more excited about what we can do, how we can support people.' He's looking away, about to go after Biscuit, I grab his arm. 'We're griefbusters, remember!'

'Seriously? Don't say that to any clients.'

'But that was your idea, and we are griefbusters,' I say. 'You do get what we're doing here? Our mission?'

'Mission? Seriously?' He runs off. Biscuit's rolling in a flowerbed while Francis looks on.

I call after Ben. 'You do remember I'm paying you now?'

'Fresh manure,' he shouts back.

I have failed to glean any more about the 'partner' but I am definitely on his or her side.

To: LRS_17@outlook.com
Wed 3/5, 20:43
SUBJECT: *How to handle this*

In the park after school, Josephine says to me, 'Do you know what I love most about Francis?'

He was licking an ice-cream patch on the path, his whole bottom wiggling from side to side.

'His pointy tail?' I tried.

'His shadow,' she says.

'It is a cute shadow. What do you love most about me?'

'Your hair. It's like a Dis-er-ney princess's hair. Long down your back and yellow. I want hair like yours.' She twirls a strand of my hair in her fingers.

'But I want your hair,' I say. 'It's perfect. I wish I had beads in my hair.'

'I hate them. I told Mummy I hate them.'

'Why would you hate them?' I ask.

'It's too hard to explain.' She tugs at one of the beads.

'Ouch! You'll hurt yourself.'

'It doesn't hurt.' She tugs again.

'Stop that!' I hold both her hands. 'Anyway, this isn't fair. Francis is having ice-cream without us. Run and get in the queue.'

I wish she'd asked me what I love most about her. I'll write her a card, something she can keep.

To: LRS_17@outlook.com
Thu 4/5, 10:26
SUBJECT: *Retreat*

I need to stay away for a while. Susan is filling our inboxes with updates and pictures of 'Anna-Su'. Under different circumstances, I would find it amusing that they have turned her into a country-music star. When I picture her, it's in cowboy boots, lipstick and a Stetson. I still haven't looked at the photos. Not even tempted.

Am I turning into Ben? Terrified of the 'worldwide weapon'. He said this thing the other day. 'Digital communication will be the death of decency, democracy and ultimately civilisation.' He'd read it somewhere. Probably on the web.

E is going to talk to Susan when he sees them on Saturday. I'll be back soon, and I am never really gone, never will be.

To: LRS_17@outlook.com
Sat 6/5, 21:52
SUBJECT: *The visit*

We bought the biggest available bouquets for both Susan and Maggie, a £45-bottle of whisky for Damian and balloons for Anna-Su. It was out of guilt, I suppose, or to buy us some more distance. It's something grown-ups do. There's what you call an inverse relationship between how much you spend on a gift for someone and how often you want to see them. For example, I regularly take Josephine chocolate buttons at 45p a bag, but when we were invited to E's boss's house, we took champagne, a White Company scented candle and wireless headphones for each of her daughters. It worked, we've never been invited back.

One of Anna-Su's balloons was the cowgirl from *Toy Story*, but Maggie didn't get the reference, E said.

'How was it?' I ask when he comes in. 'Were they OK about me not going?'

'I said you had my cold. Didn't want to risk it. Mum said it was thoughtful of you.'

'Thoughtful? She said "thoughtful"?'

'Something like that. Or careful, caring ... something.' He takes the white wine from the fridge.

'They're not the same thing. Was it thoughtful or careful?'

'Careful, I think it was careful,' he says.

'Couldn't help herself.'

'What?'

'Had to make a dig about me not being careful. On the day they're flaunting Maggie's baby at you.'

'She said you *were* being careful.' He pours himself a glass. 'There wasn't much flaunting. She was asleep the whole time.'

I reach down a second glass, put it by his bottle. 'Did you take any pictures?'

'Was I supposed to?' he asks.

'It's polite.'

He said Maggie was not the new mum he'd expected. She was complaining about the nights, how Anna-Su fusses when she's trying to feed, needs rocking to sleep. His mother made it worse, said to Maggie, 'It's little girls, you were like that, shock after Eddie, he knew what he was doing the minute he was born.'

The NHS website says colds last two weeks at most but I plan for mine to turn into pneumonia.

To: LRS_17@outlook.com
Sat 6/5, 23:39
SUBJECT: Considerate

Susan was right about him, he's always been a good sleeper. He'd drifted off in front of the TV. He just came up, stripped down to his pants, now he's fast asleep again.

'Considerate,' he said as he lay down and threaded his arm under me. '"Always so considerate of everyone." That's what she said you were. No one thinks it's your fault. Except you.'

To: LRS_17@outlook.com
Wed 10/5, 21:07
SUBJECT: *Take-off*

We have our first PIM! A man named Ross in Bromley. I don't want to get too excited, but this is us doing it, stepping in when people need us (Stepping In would also have been a good name). I run my own business. That's what I'll say when people ask what I do.

Ben found him – with an unsanctioned Gumtree advert, but a gig's a gig, as tradespeople say. We're meeting on Friday. It's close enough to get back for Josephine – and far enough to miss a whole day of Dave and his people, who now have access to the kitchen to make tea (they are what you'd call chain drinkers). When they are not in the kitchen, they are using machines to sand off old paint. I've put three of your fleece blankets over Kim and Kanye's house.

We need to work on Ben's telephone skills. All he got from this man was a first name and an address.

'Did you get any sense of his religion?' I asked.

'He's called Ross, so you can take a guess.'

'At what?'

'Well he's not gonna be a Muslim or a Hindu, is he?'

'Could be short for something,' I said.

'He didn't have an accent.'

'Whoa, non-Londoner alert! Little bit racist, don't you think?'

'For fuck's sake, Rachel. You're the one asking about his religion. And your non-London bollocks is just as prej ... prejis ... just as shit.'

'You're right. Sorry. I'm shutting up.'

On Google Street View it looks like a block of flats. Ross seems to be someone of medium income. The name sounds a bit Scottish, aged between forty and sixty, I'm guessing his wife died of cancer, or a car accident, but there's nothing obvious when you search for fatal crashes in the last year. He needs to move to somewhere fresh, where he can meet someone new (men tend to move on faster), but he's still grieving and needs professional help processing his possessions, and his feelings. It doesn't have to be a wife, of course. But I shouldn't have to guess at any of this. I've sent Ben a checklist (pasting below) for the next time a PIM calls him – and yes, there is the question of why he's giving out his number and not mine. He shouldn't be taking any calls until he understands what we're doing.

[ ] First AND surname of PIM (person in mourning, see email 27/4)
[ ] Address and phone number
[ ] House clearance, house move or memory-keeping work? (Mention full range, please, including scrapbooks AND video options)
[ ] If obtainable, name of deceased
[ ] Relationship to deceased
[ ] Age – guess if they don't tell you. We need to tailor!!
[And not to go on any forms, but if you can glean anything on nationality and ethnicity, pass it on to me verbally. The more we know, the better we prepare. The more we prepare, the more we help. KPI: Knowledge, Prep, Impact]

I'm thinking acronyms should work on him – he likes brevity. Seeing our work in practice with Ross will change everything.

I've never had to manage someone like Ben before. Typically you pick your staff based on ability, experience, likeability. Ben was picked for me, by the universe, or whoever's in charge of EHFAR. As Dog Collar Graham would say, some things are beyond our earthly understanding. But when something's hard work, you're doing your best work – we're giving Ben purpose, less than a year after Oval. You know I would still undo it if I could, given him an extra shove if it would have changed things for us.

To: LRS_17@outlook.com
Wed 10/5, 22:47
SUBJECT: *Story*

Ben and I will need to come up with something before Friday, in case
Ross asks how we met. He sounds like the kind of person who probes,
I sense he's university-educated. And he's grieving, he'll want to deflect.

I'm not saying suicide is taboo, but it's not great for business. Or
maybe it is. Picture the magazine profile. The journalist will ask how
we met. I'll say, 'It's a weird story,' and let Ben tell them about Oval
and how ten months later I turned up on his doorstep looking for a
dog walker. I already know the things I'll say about you and our
misunderstood grief. To Ross, I mean. But we would make a good
magazine read. People love a story where something is meant to
happen. And this is what I'm supposed to be doing. Until now I've
always been part of someone else's something, never anything I
started myself. Every job (three in total), every relationship (also
three, serious ones), every club (from badminton to that two-week
stint in a band). Even families – it was E's house we moved into, he
asked me. Worse with my parents. When I came along, they'd started
without me, they already had all their favourite meals, holidays and
TV shows. But Luke's Touch is mine from the start, my creation, and
a little bit Ben's.

To: LRS_17@outlook.com
Thu 11/5, 09:26
SUBJECT: *Yellow*

Anna-Su is in hospital. It's nothing. She's jaundiced, which means
she's gone yellow. All of them are visiting, there's a rota to sit and
hold Maggie's hand. E's going after work. 'Given you're in London,
for once,' said his mother.

If the scaffolders are here much longer, I'll even sign myself up. They are now topless thanks to a spell of sunshine and their lack of inhibition. More than two weeks of their shouting and I still can't tune in to their actual words. But I've observed subtle shifts between two main tones: physical-fight imminent and watch-out-serious-head-injury imminent. If Luke's Touch doesn't work out (it will), I'll start the Mindful Decorating Company.

To: LRS_17@outlook.com
Thu 11/5, 16:56
SUBJECT: Groundwork

Do you know what's worse than having Ben as a business partner? Having Francis and Biscuit as colleagues. I can't go back on it because I promised Ben he could combine the two.

People start businesses in garages and bedrooms all the time, but I checked and not one successful business has been founded in a graveyard. When the dogs are not rolling in stuff, they're eating it or humping it. Ben knows I'm annoyed, he says over and over, 'Dogs are dogs.'

'Then let them be dogs,' I say today. 'Stop going after them.'

Even as I'm saying it, he's running away. 'I'm paying you. You have to listen,' I shout. A woman with a poodle looks over. She'll think I'm a loner who's hired Ben for the day. I call after him again. 'You're supposed to be the operations manager. We can't keep having these meetings here. I've been looking at the schedule and...' I roll my eyes, mouth 'hopeless' to her.

To: LRS_17@outlook.com
Fri 12/5, 20:47
SUBJECT: *This is why we have a checklist*

If you were here, perhaps a little older, at nursery and having
playdates, I would explain to you that sometimes things don't go how
you would wish. It's trite, but a person is a complicated thing, put
two people together and you get an ugly tangle of nastiness. Think
of it like two jigsaw puzzles, advanced ones with small pieces and
busy pictures. Now imagine some deviant has mixed the pieces of
these two separate puzzles in one box. You feel like you'll never work
out what goes where. Or imagine you're one of the puzzles and you
have to put your own pieces in the right place, stepping around the
other puzzle while it does the same. It starts off polite: 'whoops!
That's your corner' and 'here you go, found one of your edge pieces
– swap you for my green bit!'. Then the hostility creeps in: 'sorry to
ask again, but you're sitting on part of my blue hat' and 'gosh, it's so
hard to see in here, but I think that's my top left corner' and 'I find it
works better if you turn them all face up'. Then the shouting: 'oh my
God, it's there, right under your browny-grey bit, my missing piece
of window frame, how can you not see it? Why do I have to ask
everything forty-two times? Why does it take you forever to do
anything? I'm not shouting, I'm just tired, and it's a mess in here, no
one can work like this. Where are your socks? You never have your
socks on.'

I've dropped her home now. I'll tidy your room in the morning.
She seemed OK. Enough other people speak to her like that.
Sometimes, you get into a jumbled puzzle mess. She'd fallen out with
Kayla and Maya, and I'd had the day I'd had. It was silly of me to
expect our first client to be deserving, or civil, or even a proper client.
I see why Lola snaps, it's so much easier to be with Josephine when
you haven't had to work with other people all day, when you're not
carrying their idiocy into your evening. I thought Josephine would

be an antidote. She was an irritant. Came out without her book bag, begged for doughnuts at the chicken place, didn't eat them, shredded toilet paper to make 'snow' for Silopolis' new winter sports district. Then the manipulation. 'You're not joining in. You're always on your phone.'

'You're not the only one who needs me. I have grown-up things to sort out.' One of your baby books advises walking out the room. I sat in the bathroom, with the door locked.

It wasn't all her fault, or mine. My day had started weird and got weirder.

'You never wear that new dress we bought, the purple one,' said E.

We were up together, and I was pulling on my black jeans and a long peach shirt. Skinny jeans, biker boots and pastel tops are the uniform of my new life. The jeans don't pick up mud, and the boots are flat but young. The pastels are multifunctional: They suit me, I blur into the background, but they also say, 'Look, I'm wearing colours, I'm OK.' (Don't worry, I'm not OK.)

'You like this top,' I say to E. 'And it's not like I have anything to wear a dress to. Walking Francis, collecting Josephine.'

His words must be swirling round my head when I get to Ben's, because when he opens the door, I say, 'Why don't you ever wear shirts? Ross sounds like the kind of client who expects a shirt.'

'No iron,' says Ben. He's dressed like a mugger: dark hoodie over a faded green T-shirt and baggy jeans.

'Throw cushions but no iron?'

'I don't have anything to be smart for,' he says.

'But your bed does? If you'd told me, I could have ironed you a shirt. Or brought you one of Ed's.'

'We're not the same size.' I can't tell if his tone's envious or disdainful. E is broader, but they're both quite bulky round the upper arms and slim round the waist. It's easier for men to stay slim.

I make him change into a smarter T-shirt, dark blue, and he bats me away as I smooth down the creases. 'I'll get you an iron for Christmas,' I say. 'Or, when's your birthday?'

'June. T-shirts don't need ironing if you fold them well.'

Oval was in June.

'Mine's June,' I say. 'The third. When's yours?'

'Fourteenth.'

Oval was the twenty-first.

'A month till you're twenty-eight,' I say. Then, because I've learnt to do this thing where I let people know I understand their world ('my father-in-law was in a wheelchair'; 'my mother had breast cancer'; 'I look after a little girl with terrible allergies'), I say something idiotic. 'Then you won't have to worry about the whole twenty-seven thing anymore.' He's waiting for more. 'There's that Twenty-Seven Club isn't there? All those people who died – Jim Morrison, Amy Winehouse. Hard age.'

'It's James Morrison,' he says opening the door.

'For God's sake, leave the hoodie.'

Ross is waiting in the car park outside his block. He gives us a nervous wave. 'Oh God,' I say to Ben, 'Poor guy can't even face being inside the place alone.'

Ben has ignored my pleas and hasn't made a follow-up call, so we still know nothing about who died and how big their property is. Ross looks early fifties, so it could be a partner or parent. He's at that stage of grief where clothes mean nothing, and it's clear he hasn't shaved for days. He's wearing a rugby shirt that's tight over his belly, joggers and Crocs. (I know you have lovely blue Crocs, but grown-ups shouldn't wear them, not even PIMs.)

'Thought we could go in together,' he says when we reach him.

'I understand,' I say.

He opens the main door, and we follow him up the stairs to the fourth floor. The building stinks of dogs, cigarettes and bleach.

'This is the problem,' he says as we're on the last flight.

'The memories.'

'All these stairs.'

He's not ready to talk about it.

Instead of opening the door with his keys, he presses the doorbell. It plays the first line of 'Jingle Bells'. He turns to us, shrugs, tries to laugh. She must have died at Christmas.

A voice shouts from inside, an old man. 'That you, Ross?'

Another shrug. 'No, it's Tina Turner.'

Hiding behind humour.

A man in a shirt, tie and brown jumper opens the door. The tie is over the jumper.

'This is my dad, Arthur,' says Ross. 'Dad, these are the movers.'

'Today?' says Arthur. 'Did you say it's today?'

'It's OK,' I say. 'Today we've just come to meet you. Have a chat, see how we can help you. I'm Rachel and this is Ben.'

'You're the carers,' says Arthur. 'They keep changing them. They have keys.'

Ben cuts in. 'No, we're the movers. Just need a quick look around, work out how much there is to pack.'

I tug on the back of Ben's T-shirt and then have to do that thing they do in legal dramas. 'Excuse me, I need a quick word with my colleague,' I say to Ross and Arthur.

I go down one flight and wait for Ben to follow.

'You can talk out here,' calls Ross. 'I'll go and put the kettle on.'

Despite my gestures for him to come down the stairs to me, Ben stays put – never has he looked more like Francis. 'Thanks,' he says to Ross. 'We'll be there in a minute.'

It's hard to convey my anger in a whisper, but I tell Ben I can't believe he called us movers, he's misunderstood what we're doing, and I point out that Arthur is wearing a tie.

'So?' says Ben.

'So your T-shirt is inappropriate. And we're grief services. Not a man in a van, or people in a van.'

'Whose fault is that? And they are grieving. The mum died,' says Ben.

'Why didn't you tell me that? Or put it on the checklist?'

'What checklist?'

'Very funny.'

Inside, Ross explains his father has to be out by the end of the month, they've found a ground-floor flat for him down the road. The new place is smaller, he can only take about half the stuff with him.

Arthur sits as far up one end of the sofa as he can. The TV remote is in his hand but the TV is off. He lets go of it to take sips of tea, picks it up again.

Ross shows us Arthur's bedroom, where there is a double bed with one pillow, a chest of drawers and a framed photo – a couple and a little boy standing by an airport luggage trolley. The spare room is full of boxes and suitcases. In the kitchen, Ross opens the cupboards. 'All that can go,' he says. 'Meals being delivered in the new place.'

One cupboard is full of cupcake trays, spring-form tins, loaf tins.

'Looks like she was a keen baker, your mum,' I say.

'God knows why he's still got those. You can have them if you like, love.'

'We're not here to take advantage.'

'Up to you. Chuck them or take them.'

We agree to come back next Thursday to divide everything into categories: move, keep and pass on.

As we're leaving, I say, 'So hard to lose someone at Christmas.'

'What?' says Ross.

'Your mother?'

Ross looks hurt. I need Ben to say something about his mother, how it gets easier, that she had sausage dogs, anything.

'I'm sorry, Ross. I should have known it's too soon,' I say.

'Soon?'

'Too recent.'

Ross calls to his father. 'How many years is it, Dad? Since Mum?' No reply. 'Hang on, it was March 2010, so what's that? Seven years.'

In the car I ask Ben what he told Ross when they first spoke.

'He asked if we do moves as well as clearance. Said he needed a bit of both,' he says.

'Did he say anything else? Did he like our advert, the tagline, our name?'

'He asked me for a price, I told him five hundred if we can keep and sell what he doesn't want,' says Ben.

'What's wrong with you?' I can't drive and do this, I need to stop, there's nowhere to pull over. 'Why can't you take this seriously? Understand what it means to me, to us?'

'Us? I found us a job. Which is more than you, sitting there with highlighters and notepads all day. I got us started,' he says.

Red light. 'A job? We don't do jobs. We're a service. We help people, PIMs. Create afterlives, collate lifetimes.'

'You can call it that if you like, Rachel, but it'll sound like a load of bollocks to normal people.'

'Normal people? What the hell would you know about normal? You're scared of shirt buttons.'

'That's not true,' he says.

'We don't want to do it the normal way. That's the whole point, and you're not getting it. We're changing things, so people don't suffer.'

'We? When did I ever say I wanted to do all that crap?' he says.

'Oh my God, it was your idea. You started it all. For your mum. And for Luke. What's wrong with you?' A cyclist shouts at me. I slow to catch the next red light.

'I never said I wanted all your bollocks about changing things, bringing back the dead like we're fucking exorcists.'

'That's not what exorcists do. And you're such a child, sitting there waiting for everything to happen for you. It already has, spot the sodding obvious. We found each other and now we need to do this, help people.'

'People don't want to be helped. And they don't want you asking about their afterlives. You're a fucking disaster about to blow up. Asking strangers what religion they are, talking about coffins and their shitty childhoods. You're the one who doesn't get it. People are waiting to go psycho on you.'

'Please don't say psycho.'

'Mental,' he says.

'People need help. Did you even read the stuff I sent you about that mum, whose baby died, then her mum?'

'Maybe. Was it in the ten thousand emails and texts you send me every day?'

I turn into a side road, there's a space.

'What are you doing?' he asks.

'You should get out.'

'For fuck's sake, Rachel. Do you want jobs or not?'

My legs are shaking. 'Stop saying jobs. They're not jobs. Please get out.' I undo his seatbelt for him.

He clicks it back in. 'Seriously. No one else thinks like you. No one wants your help-the-world bollocks.'

'You of all people—'

'God, you fucking love yourself, don't you? Only thing you love more than yourself is a lost cause. Thank God for Rachel, feeding off the losers, Rachel scavenger Summers.'

'Get out!'

He stiffens, superglued to the seat. I hold both hands down on the horn, shout, 'Get out, get out, get out,' over the noise.

People are looking in. Ben shoves my hands off the horn. I wrestle them free, hold down the horn again.

A man knocks on the window, wants to know if I'm OK. I nod and gesture that I can handle things. But I must look terrified, because he keeps knocking, shouts through the glass. 'Shall I call the police?'

Ben opens the door. 'It's alright, I'm going. She's mad. Totally lost it.'

The man shouts after him, 'Sicko!' He leans in to me, 'You sure you're OK?'

'Thank you, thanks for stopping him.'

'Do you want me to go after him?' he asks. It's tempting. He's twice Ben's size.

'It's OK. He wouldn't touch me really. We just got in a mess. But thanks.'

I wait for the shaking to stop. The radio doesn't help, I can still hear him shouting, hating me, wishing I'd let him jump. Scavenger. I should have let him jump. I'll tell him that.

My phone rings. It's him. I ignore it. It rings again.

'What?' I say.

'I'm sorry. I should have let you talk. Are you still there?'

'Where?' I ask.

'In that road.'

'Why?'

'I don't have any money for the bus,' he says.

'Get an Uber.'

'It's not working.' He appears in my rearview mirror, childish smile and a shrug.

I open the window and offer him the five-pound note I'd put in my pocket for Josephine's Friday treat. 'For the bus.'

'Can't you just drop me off?' he asks.

'I can't work with you, I can't be near you. You don't understand any of this, you and me, Luke. He died and you didn't. Do you even get that? Died. Does anyone get that?'

I close the window, lock the doors. He leans on the car, his bum squashed against the window. I hold down the horn. He goes, shaking his head and swearing.

The money was a mistake. I should have left him to walk home, thinking time. At Josephine's school they talk about making good choices and bad choices. They get points for good choices. She's top of the leaderboard. 'I don't understand,' she said the other day. 'Some people always pick bad choices.' That would make a good mural, on the side of Oval station.

I can help people. I'm always helping people.

To: LRS_17@outlook.com
Fri 12/5, 22:58
SUBJECT: *Outside world*

What I wanted to say was you are one hundred days old today. Under Chinese tradition, this would be the first day you are allowed out of your family home – Ling in Development told me about it when you were growing. She said she'd take us for lunch in Chinatown to celebrate, but it was the way people say they'll do something and you both know they never will.

Our plans were different. I meant every one. I put you on the waiting lists for three different music groups. I'm ignoring their emails.

To: LRS_17@outlook.com
Sat 13/5, 11:13
SUBJECT: *Top bottom*

I forgot to tell you the good news. Dave and his people (though I think 'men' is OK as I haven't seen a single woman) have dismantled their scaffolding. A note through the door said, *Top done. Back next week do bottom. £450 so far. Get cash from you Monday. D*

'That doesn't sound right,' E said, when he saw the note. 'You'll have to talk to them on Monday. Don't give them the money till they tell you a finish date and a final price. Whole thing was supposed to be six hundred.'

'I can't. And you booked them. Their relationship's with you,' I say. 'I'm flying on Monday.'

'I don't think you understand how difficult this has been for me,' I say. 'Having them here, now. And there's something wrong about them. I just … can't.' And I tell him how the whole Maggie thing has knocked me back, how hurt I am by his mother, how I'm trying to get an appointment with the GP, hoping they can give me something, or refer me somewhere.

'You seemed to be doing better. Making plans, getting out,' he says. 'But you're right, I hired Dave. I'll call him.'

To: LRS_17@outlook.com
Sat 13/5, 15:47
SUBJECT: *Aftermath*

Nothing from Lola after last night's Josephine tension, so either:

- A – Josephine hasn't told her;
- B – Josephine told her and Lola is embarrassed her daughter pushed me that far; or
- C – Josephine told her and Lola has nothing to say because to her it sounds like an average evening with Josephine.

My guess would be C, my hope is B.

To: LRS_17@outlook.com
Mon 15/5, 09:17
SUBJECT: *Carrying on*

Ben has not apologised (one sorry to get five pounds off me doesn't count). I have nothing to apologise for. Without reference to the car fight, we arranged to meet at the graveyard with Biscuit and Francis to plan Arthur's move. I called him. On reflection, I see why we've been brought into Arthur's life. He's brave to leave the home he shared with his wife.

To: LRS_17@outlook.com
Mon 15/5, 21:34
SUBJECT: Blind

Josephine hugged me longer and tighter today when she came out of school.

'Can I show you something?' she says.

I bend forward and she hangs her book bag round my neck. I breathe in her hair smell.

'Come on!' Her sticky hand tugs me along the pavement. We dodge bikes, pushchairs, scooters, dogs.

'What's the rush? Is it going to disappear?'

'Silly!' She turns back to do her big eyes at me. We stop at our usual crossing. 'This is it,' she says, pressing the button. 'Put your fingers here, on the sticky-out bit.' She guides my hand to a little knob underneath the box with the button. 'Now wait.' A little magician poised to unveil a floating rabbit.

We wait. The traffic stops, the green person (as we call him) lights up and the most amazing thing happens. The knob turns and its tiny ridges rub against my fingertips. I mouth 'wow' at Josephine.

'For blind people,' she whispers.

'Do they all have those?' I ask.

'Most of them. It was in my reading book. Non-fiction.'

We stayed and felt it spin twice more. People stared at us for not crossing and it made our secret even better. We went on a hunt for others and found five.

'I can't believe they've been there the whole time and I didn't know,' I say. 'What else was in your non-fiction book?'

To: LRS_17@outlook.com
Tues 16/5, 16:46
SUBJECT: *Ambush*

Francis is dead.

He went behind his favourite tomb (Timothy Shellcote, 1856–1906) and didn't come back. Biscuit found him under a holly bush. I don't know if he was still with us then or already gone.

'Come on, young sausage, up we get,' I said.

Ben put a hand on his chest. 'Call ahead to your vet, let them know you're coming.' He held Francis like a baby, walked and then jogged towards the gate.

'Watch his neck, support his head,' I say.

'Call your vet! And grab Biscuit.'

I grapple with Biscuit's lead, whisper to him, 'What do we do?' I call to Ben, 'I don't have my phone.'

'You had it just now. You texted me on your way over.'

'Oh God, yes, must have left it in the car,' I shout back.

'Again? Run ahead, call them. They'll want to know if it could be poison, tell them anything he's eaten, anything you've seen him sniffing at.'

If I run fast enough, I can get round the corner, call my mother before he catches up, she'll give me the vet's number. She put it at the top of her notes but they're in the kitchen drawer. It's something with Park. Or I can Google it. Something with Paws? Paws Park? Partridge Paws?

I text my mother.

Who's your vet again?

She calls as I'm reaching the car.

'It's Parkhouse Paws in Penge. Everything OK?'

'Penge? That's miles away.'

'It's near his breeder. Made sense to stay with his first vet. Why are you out of breath? Is everything OK?'

'All fine. It's for my friend. Do they have parking?' I ask. I pace by the car. Ben will think I'm speaking to the vet.

'It's hit and miss,' she says. 'Your friend getting a puppy? What breed?'

'A cat. Have to go.'

Ben's gesturing at me to unlock the car. I put Biscuit in the back, Ben keeps Francis in his arms. 'What did they say?' He's struggling to fasten his seatbelt, I do it for him.

'I couldn't get through,' I say. 'Left a voicemail. Told them everything you said to say.'

'What are you doing now?' he asks.

'Looking up their postcode for the satnav. Never remember how to get there.'

'Where is it?' he asks.

'Penge.'

'Penge? Why would you have a vet in Penge? Forget that. There's one on the main road. Next right.'

Ben whispers to Francis as we drive. When we stop at a red light he turns to me. 'There's no heartbeat.' Same words as the doctor.

My foot slips.

'Jesus!' says Ben.

It's a minicab, Prius, they'll be rushing to the next job and it was just a touch, no damage. The car behind beeps, the light's turned green. The minicab door opens, it's a woman, short hair, older. She's rubbing her neck.

'Oh God, we're so, so sorry,' Ben says before I can speak. 'We're trying to get to an emergency vet. He started fitting, knocked into my wife.'

She stares at Francis then notices Biscuit in the back – he's gone to sleep, self-preservation mode.

'How old is he?' asks the minicab driver. People behind us are beeping more, someone drives round us, shouts out his window.

'Only seven,' says Ben.

'Could be poisoning,' she says.

Ben looks at me, 'That's what I said, didn't I?'

'Or epilepsy,' I say.

'He'd have fitted before,' she says. (You won't know this, but dog people talk as if they have been to vet school for seven years and dog training for ten.) 'Looks like he's come out of it,' she says.

'Hope so,' says Ben. 'But he went like this before, thought he'd stopped and he started up again in the car.'

More horns behind us. 'Better get out their way,' I say. 'Get Francis some help.'

'Good luck,' she says. 'Mine lived to sixteen.' (Another thing they all do. I stop myself from saying Francis is really fourteen.)

Before she gets back into her car, she turns round, takes a picture of my number plate.

'What?' I say to Ben.

'She'll be onto your insurance about whiplash,' he says.

'How's he doing?' I ask.

'I told you. I can't feel his heart. I think—'

'He can't be. He was fine, you saw him, he was running around. He ate all his breakfast, whined for more.'

'He's old. Really old for a sausage dog. It happens.'

The vet didn't charge us. He went through the usual clichés. Nothing they could do, he'd had a good innings, probably his heart.

They kept the body and will move him to the Penge vet tomorrow. I dropped Ben and Biscuit home. I leaned across to hug him before he got out. 'I'm so sorry, Ben.'

'No, I'm sorry,' he said.

'I know how much you loved him. And how much he loved you.'

'He was your first baby,' Ben said.

It was a competition to prove who was worst hit. E and I should have done it with you, or at least done something.

How do I tell my mother? Do I call my father first, ask him to go over? It will comfort her to know Francis is with you. It helps me. Do you like him? Is he how you pictured him? Watch your ankles.

To: LRS_17@outlook.com
Tues 16/5, 22:52
SUBJECT: Calamity

I went with Ben's idea, told her in person. I was lying on your monkey rug thinking about what to say when he texted.

How are you now?

So so. Putting off calling my mum. She was so fond of him.

Better to tell her in person? Do you good to see her.

You're right. Ed's in New York, house feels empty.
What you up to?

Nothing back. I texted again.

Thanks for today. So grateful you were there.

Bet he's run out of credit on his phone.

Also told E. He'd texted to ask *How are things?* (He has that saved on his phone as a one-key shortcut.)

Should I come home early? he asked when I told him. And, *You OK alone?*

I have Lester, I texted back.

I drove to my mother's, let myself in.

'Stop!' she shouts from the kitchen. 'Don't put him down. I've had a calamity. It's everywhere.'

'Are you OK?'

'Olive oil. Your father's fault. Left it on the edge.'

She's on the floor picking broken glass out of a puddle of oil.

'What was he doing with olive oil?'

'Massage. He's gone to squash with Glen,' she says, not looking up. 'Get me a Tupperware to put these big bits in.'

'Massage?' (This email excepted, lubricants are top of the list of things never to discuss between parent and child.)

'My bad shoulder,' she says. 'What have you done with Francis? Oil and glass everywhere. Why can't your father put things where they belong?'

'God, Mum. Try this.' I pass her some kitchen roll, take more for me. Shards of glass scrape on the tiles as I mop. 'I have to tell you something. Francis died.'

'Pass me the roll,' she says and puts three pieces together, lays them in the middle of the puddle. 'We need another roll, top cupboard.'

'Mum, I'm trying to tell you something. Francis died.'

She tugs on the neck of her cardigan. 'What? When?'

'Just now. We were walking him. It was such a nice afternoon, thought we'd take him for a quick run around the park before I brought him back. He lay down, couldn't get up, stopped breathing. It was so quick.' The olive oil is seeping into her cream trousers, it's stained her cardigan. 'I went straight to the nearest vet, there was nothing they could do. They've kept him there. I'm so sorry, Mum.'

'My baby,' she says.

'Let's get you up out of this mess. I'll clear up the rest.'

'I thought Ed was in New York.'

'He is.'

'You said "we", "we were walking him". Who's we?'

'A dog friend. He's a dog walker really. Francis loves him. I know it's hard to understand. So sudden. But he was old, Mum. He'd had a great life. He had you as a mum.' It comes out of nowhere, I'm crying. 'Best mum any dog could wish for. I'll pour you a brandy.'

'I don't want brandy.' She pulls at her wet knees. 'Ruined.'

My little finger's bleeding. I wrap tissue around it but the blood comes through.

'For goodness sake, Rachel,' she shouts. 'What are you doing? Get a plaster. You can't even look after yourself. And you take my dog and walk him with a stranger. Dog walkers always over-exert them, big packs, all running wild.'

'He's not a stranger. And this is your fault, it's not my smashed bottle of massage oil.'

'Not a stranger? You meet him in a park, take a couple of walks and he's your best friend, or worse? Pass me the phone, I want to speak to the vet.'

'They'll be closed now.' I pick from the many sizes of plaster she has in her three first-aid boxes and go back to mopping. 'God, do you have to do that now?' She's emptying the dishwasher, stepping around me with a pile of plates.

She comes back for more plates, I shuffle out of her path, there's something sharp under my other hand. 'You should have gone sooner, to the vet,' she says.

'It wouldn't have made any difference. At least he had a lovely walk.' I go to get the hoover from under the stairs.

'At least he had a walk? A walk with strangers. He died thinking, *Where's my mummy?*'

'For God's sake, Mum. Do you think before you say anything?' The hoover's jammed behind her supplies of sparkling water. I bang my head on the stairs trying to free it. 'Shi—, sugar, ow.'

'What on earth's wrong with you?' she shouts from the kitchen.

'You! "Where's my mummy?" He had fourteen years with his mummy. And you had fourteen years with your precious baby boy.'

She slams the dishwasher shut. 'Right. So even on the day he dies, you're jealous of Francis.'

'I'm jealous of you. You and your fourteen years with Francis. I didn't get a minute.'

'You had him all the time,' she says.

'With Luke, you stupid woman. Not with Francis. With Luke.'

I sat in my car for twenty minutes, maybe longer. She didn't come out to me, and that's OK. Even if she is how she is, it was wrong to call her that. It's wrong to call anyone that. But she makes me say things I shouldn't, feel things I shouldn't. When I was six, I called the police and asked them to come and arrest her. We laughed about it when I was a teenager, but I remember the social-worker visits right after it happened. Or maybe that was someone else, in a film. You won't understand, but memories get reinvented.

When I went back into the house, she'd changed into clean clothes (black) and was on the phone. I caught 'what to believe', her free hand gesticulating as she spoke, something about a funeral and, 'She's here. I'll call you back.'

'Your father.' She nods at the phone. 'Left him a message. I couldn't say it.'

'I know. Telling people makes it real.'

'Is he the one from the funeral?' she asks.

'What?'

'The man at the funeral. With the little dog off the lead. That was your dog-walker friend.'

I pause too long and she knows she's right.

'I met him with Francis. We walk together sometimes. I told him about Luke. He's sweet but he's awkward. He wanted to come but didn't know how. And he had two dogs booked.'

'He doesn't seem your type,' she says.

'What's that supposed to mean?'

'You know what it means, just like you know why you didn't tell the rest of us about him,' she says.

'Why should I?'

'Because you stopped to talk to him, at the funeral, for far too long. I had to tell Ed you'd be asking the dog's names, being polite. That you felt sorry for the man, wanted to make him feel better.'

'What did Ed say?'

'It was awful,' she says. 'Heartbreaking.'

'What?'

'He said the dog walker was lucky it was you who went over. Then he said something like, "Of all the people for this to happen to, it shouldn't have been Rachel," and he looked right at Paul the vicar, who didn't know what to say. I didn't get a good feeling about that vicar, all wrong for the occasion.'

The things E says to other people.

I let my mother babble on about Paul the vicar, how Graham and Emma would have done your funeral, how they're ready for me to come back to their Tuesday nights, how they held a little girl's funeral last year, Graham wrote a song, Emma released butterflies. ('Hundred pounds for ten in a box. But the little girl loved all things nature.')

'He's called Ben,' I say. 'My friend.'

'Was that his dog?'

'They were dogs he sits, both of them. The puggle's called Bug, or Ben really, but that's Ben's name so we call the puggle Bug and the beagle's called Biscuit.'

'Are they related?'

'Who?'

'The beagle and the puggle? Father and son?'

'God no. The beagle's actually really nasty to Bug, nips at him, growls. That's why Bug's off the lead.'

'We all have our place. Which one's older?'

'It's OK to ask about Ben,' I say. 'Just like it's OK to talk about Luke.'

'OK then. What are you doing with him? You have friends.'

'I don't. I don't have a single friend who understands me. Want to know about my friends? One of them sent me a spa voucher last week, with a note saying *to cheer you up*. As if I want anyone looking at this, prodding at this.'

'Everyone looks a bit bigger after pregnancy,' she says.

'They have something to show for it.' I'm shouting.

She waits, asks again, 'What are you doing with him?'

'It's because of what you said. That everything happens for a reason. I went and found him. He's the man from Oval.'

'The car dealer?'

'The Tube station. The man I stopped from jumping. It was the same day I found out I was pregnant with Luke. And then Luke died and you said, "Everything happens for a reason." And what other reason could there be? Save a life, lose a life.'

She's fiddling with the corkscrew, like she's not listening. It helps, I keep going. I tell her about Lola, how we looked everywhere, found Ben on Gumtree, and he was a dog walker and she'd told me to get out in the fresh air, borrow Francis. How it started to make sense.

'And when I met him, he was a mess, he's living off a few pounds a day, eats porridge made with water, behind on his rent. I was worried he'd try again, I still am, and then it would all be for nothing. Luke would have died for nothing, just because I saved Ben.'

She's listening now, the wine's open. 'He sounds...'

'What? He sounds what?'

'A bit dangerous. Or like he needs help. Help from someone else.'

'I thought you'd understand.' I take the bottle from her frozen hand, pour us two glasses. 'He's better now. He was having a bad time, his mum died. And he's helping me. We're helping each other. Isn't that what proper Christians want? You're the one who started it.'

'Started what? The beginning of the end of your marriage?'

'Seriously?' I hear Ben's voice as I say it. 'No. The beginning of my new business.'

She leans back into the sofa. 'Business?'

So I tell her almost everything. How we came up with it, because of his mum, the lost sudokus, all the women online and how we'll help people, make scrapbooks for them, sort their things, donate lots to charity. She sips as she listens, like she's stopping herself from interrupting. 'We're calling it Luke's Touch,' I say. 'And we met our first client last week. His wife died.'

She tops up her glass. 'What about your job? You'll be going back. You were doing so well.'

'We'll see. I get a year's leave anyway. This is my chance. If you knew Ben, you'd see it. It's changed him, he's motivated.'

'Do you know why he did it? What he was running away from?'

'God, Mum. Running away? That's not what suicide is. Suicide is everyone else running away, not understanding someone, abandoning them. No wonder there's so much of it.'

'And you understand him?' Her cheeks are red, she's emptied her glass.

'I've bothered to try. Like I bothered to save him, when everyone else looked away.'

'When you knew you were pregnant?'

'What's your point?' I ask.

'There isn't...'

'No, what's your point?' I know but I'm forcing her to say it.

'That I don't know which of you is more selfish, you or your friend.'

'You think I did this on purpose? To my baby? You think your stupid reasons-God warned me He'd take him, expected me to stand back and watch Ben throw himself in front of a train?'

'That's not ... It's just all this for a stranger. What does Ed think about it?'

'Everyone's a stranger when you first meet them. Tell me what it was then, what was the reason? Perfectly healthy, they said, taken on the last day.' I follow her eyes to Francis's food bowl. It's his dinner-time. 'I'm sorry, Mum, I'm sorry about Francis. He was an amazing dog, so, so clever. But he was old. The vet said there was nothing anyone could have done. Call them tomorrow, they'll tell you.'

We finished the wine in front of the TV. I made us scrambled eggs on toast.

Before I left, I put Francis's bed and his bowls in the garage. Like when E moved your basket. In time, she'll see the difference.

I feel relief. Lola won't talk about anything to do with Ben – she seems awkward about how she helped me find him. E never has time to listen. But my mother understood. In between the wine and the Francis shock, she saw what we need to do.

I'll tell her about Josephine another time.

To: LRS_17@outlook.com
Wed 17/5, 11:42
SUBJECT: Slippery web

'That's what I've woven,' she says, our thoughts still drenched in olive oil.

I went to collect my car from outside her house and she ran out to me. She was still in black but seemed better and was rattling off ideas about the business. She said it came to her in the night, how Jean had to empty her parents' house last year, a 'hoodlum' offered to eBay their cut glass, kept the money, disappeared.

'Like losing them twice over,' she says.

She says that I was right, that Luke's Touch will change lives, she wants to help. And I don't know how or why, but I agree to let her join us.

When I'm home, I call her.

'I'm worried about you meeting Ben,' I say.

'Because of Francis?'

'He feels awful about it. As the professional, he felt he should have done something. Resuscitate him. Or see it coming. I suppose we all feel that, don't we?'

'It'll be fine. I'll tell him I understand,' she says.

'Mum, this is a man who tried to jump in front of a train. It's not safe. He's tricky. You never know what might make him ... you know.'

'What would you like me to do all day? I've lost my dog, and your father. My friends are all off looking after grandchildren.'

I hang up. She calls back. 'We got cut off. I was trying to say you can't start a business alone,' she says. 'Not in your state. Let me help. I won't cost you anything, I'll be the work-experience girl.'

'It's called an intern,' I say. 'And you haven't lost Dad. He's there all the time. If I let you join, you can't say anything to Ben. Not about Francis, not about God, not about Oval, not even about how I know him. Just pretend that I told you he's a dog friend I met in the park.'

'Is that what he thinks you are?'

How is she stupid and clever?

'It's too complicated to explain now,' I say.

'It's a slippery web. That's what it is. From where I see it, you've woven yourself into a slippery web.'

'And from where I see it, you're the latest woman to have an affair with your husband,' I say – after I've hung up.

To: LRS_17@outlook.com
Wed 17/5, 20:48
SUBJECT: DOG-GOD

You'd think I'd be an expert, but E suggested I Google it before collecting her. He called when he was eating breakfast, my lunchtime, always does now.

'What will you say to Josephine?' he asked.

'How do you know her name?'

'You told me. And you said she loved Francis. You should work out how you're going to tell her.' It's like living with the NSA, you never know when he's listening.

I followed his advice. The general message online is: be truthful, be literal, answer all questions and if you can't answer, be honest about it.

I'd planned to wait until we were home, in Silopolis. But she asked me where he was when she came out of school.

'I don't have him today,' I said. (Truthful.)

'Where is he?'

'Not here,' I said. (Literal.)

'Where then?'

'I don't know.' (Honest.)

'You're being weird,' she said.

'Let's get to the bus stop.'

When I've perched her on the bus stop bench with her apple slices, she asks again. 'Where is he?'

'He died. Yesterday,' I say.

Her face doesn't move, her eyes are waiting for more, or something else. There's an older lady next to her on the bench, listening in.

'Sausage dogs get old, then they die,' I say.

'He wasn't old. He was younger than you,' says Josephine.

I look for a smile on the lady's face.

'He was old in dog years. Really old, and tired. He just fell asleep.'

'I don't want to ever be old,' she says.

As we climb onto the bus, Josephine grips my hand so tight I have to shake it loose. Our spot – upstairs, front right – is free, save for someone's used tissue. She sits on it.

'Where is he now?' She forces a crying sound, it's what she thinks she should do, not what she feels.

'His body is at the vet's. But he's not in it,' I say.

'Where did he go?' she asks.

'Some people would say heaven. To play with the other dogs.'

She's quiet for two stops, looks ahead but glances up every minute to check my reaction.

I stroke her hair. 'It's OK to be angry, or sad, or to feel nothing.'

After a while she says, 'Do you think he's bossy there too?'

'He's already in charge.'

'Dog God,' she says after a while.

'What do you mean?'

'He's become Dog God.' She says it with such certainty, like she was told by someone who knows. I've read about this. Children sense things, they have something that we've lost.

'Can he see us?' I ask.

'Everything. He can hear us too.' She whispers, 'I hope they have your cheese, Francis.'

Francis is with you and he's keeping you warm, she said. (That came from her, I didn't mention you.) He's watching us too, she said, 'managing' us. It's what she needs to believe. And who am I to say what's true?

To: LRS_17@outlook.com
Thu 18/5, 20:35
SUBJECT: Interning

On her insistence, I took my mother with me to Arthur's.

'I've told everyone I'm interning and they want to know what I do,' she said on the phone last night.

'Everyone? I'm not ready for people to know about this. What if work find out?'

'Do you think there's much crossover between my squash club and the powdered-drinks industry?' she asks.

'I'm in spreadables now. Have been for three years.'

Arthur answered the door in striped pyjama trousers. On his top half, he was wearing his shirt, jumper and tie ensemble.

We took away three shoeboxes of photos and another full of papers, including the invitation to Ross's wedding. She was called Lisa and it was May (no year given) at a register office followed by an Italian restaurant. (Lapsed Catholics?)

Tomorrow, we'll arrange the pictures chronologically or by theme or face. I've had a quick look and around a third of them are of aeroplanes – passenger jets, from far away.

To: LRS_17@outlook.com
Fri 19/5, 19:56
SUBJECT: *Teeth*

The new intern is finally showing promise. She made two albums labelled 'planes' and one labelled 'family', all before cooking us macaroni cheese for lunch.

'This was his favourite,' she said as we ate. 'Do you think they give dogs cheese in heaven?'

'You're the expert. But yes, I hear they do.'

While we ate, I looked through the albums she'd made for Arthur. She wasn't happy about them being near the macaroni cheese but it's my business.

'Why have you used the ones where they're behind clouds?' I asked.

'To see them emerge on the next page.'

I go back to the beginning and she's right, the planes hide, peek out and appear like in a flick book. Between them, Arthur and my mother have unwittingly created the kind of book that sells for £45.99 in the Tate Modern gift shop.

It was time for me to collect Josephine, so I sent my mother out scouring stationery shops for a sensitive way to collate Arthur's sentimental papers – a mix of letters, orders of services (mainly funerals), newspaper cuttings (all local) and birthday cards (*Love you Pet xxx* it says in Arthur's eightieth card. She was called Ann). We also found a bag of children's teeth, presumably Ross's, unwanted by the tooth fairy.

E's back in the morning. I should bake something. We're taking you flowers.

To: LRS_17@outlook.com
Fri 19/5, 22:07
SUBJECT: Babe

Guess who messaged – first contact since your funeral. Screen-grabbed our exchange – you'll like what I did.

> **Charlotte (mobile)**
> **Hi Babe, I'm in London Tues to Fri, can we have dinner? Xx**

> > *Next week not great.*
> > *Have things every night.*

> **Shame!! Can you move any? I really want to know how you're doing.**
> **How are you doing?**

> > *It's too hard to explain.*

To: LRS_17@outlook.com
Mon 22/5, 20:07
SUBJECT: Unprepared

'Will you get another baby?' Josephine asked on the bus today. Thankfully, all surrounding witnesses were wearing headphones. You notice how many people wear headphones when you're with Josephine.

'What makes you ask that?'

'Mrs Wood is having a baby. We said goodbye in assembly. Her class made a card, and the other teachers gave her a cake and nappies. Kayla says you get loads of presents when you have a baby.'

'You don't do it for the presents,' I say.

'Did you get presents?'

'You've seen them, the things in Luke's room. And after there were flowers, they made the house smell funny.'

'Funny?'

'Wrong. Anyway, we need to talk about half-term. We have the whole day on Monday. We could take a train somewhere, the beach or a museum.'

She's quiet for a minute, closes her eyes, opens them and says, 'Francis says beach.'

To: LRS_17@outlook.com

Tues 23/5, 09:37

SUBJECT: *Someone*

E woke me up on his way out. He'd heard Charlotte's in town.

'You two should try and have dinner,' he says.

'I can't face her.'

'It might help. Someone to talk to,' he says.

'I have someone to talk to.'

'I mean someone other than me.'

To: LRS_17@outlook.com

Wed 24/5, 13:56

SUBJECT: *Still not here*

You're starting to babble now, so you'll understand how hard it is to use new words.

Like this morning, at my doctor's appointment. Nothing serious, what my mother calls a 'delicate infection'. I imagine you're relevant (not blaming you), so I tell her I was expecting you but stop halfway, wordless. She just thinks I'm inarticulate, or depressed. I wait for her to look at my notes, she'll see you in there soon enough.

I don't mean I can't tell people, I'm getting better at that. The problem is finding the correct words. Like when you can't work out the past tense of something. Is it, 'I dived into a quagmire' or 'I dove'?

Is it, 'I had a stillbirth' or 'my baby was stillborn'? And if you're writing it, is it one word or two? Still born or stillborn? Because my spellchecker doesn't like newborn, but it's happy with stillborn. None of us know what we're doing. On the forums they use acronyms, GTS, Gone Too Soon. My mother once said you'd 'moved over'.

'You mean moved on?' I said.

'No. Over. Over there.'

Like it's America and I can visit, or apply for a visa and watch you grow up.

The doctor gave me antibiotics and a leaflet. 'It's one of our better ones,' she said.

'Nice font,' I replied.

On the way home, I caught myself telling Francis about it in the car, like he was still there on the back seat.

To: LRS_17@outlook.com
Fri 26/5, 21:56
SUBJECT: *Skip skipped*

Every new business has a phase like this, it's called 'teething problems', something you're also facing right now. It will pass.

And I'm learning all the time.

For example, when you call skip-hire people, it's like buying coffee, you need to know what you want in advance.

'Small, medium or large?' says the woman.

'How do I know?'

'How much are you skipping?' (I'm learning new verbs, too.)

'Half a flat's worth. He lives alone but used to have a family. He's bereaved, we won't want to skip too much.'

'Medium is like a Mini, the old ones. Large is a Land Rover,' she says.

'The boot of a Land Rover?'

'Small is like the boot. Large is the whole car. If you took out the engine, seats and steering wheel and turned it upside down.'

'Is the Mini also upside down?' I realise I'm tipping my head.

'If you don't know, better to go large, only fifty quid more,' she says. 'They fill up like the Blackwall Tunnel at rush hour.'

Maybe I was distracted by her dedication to car similes, or maybe she's lying, but she now claims she also checked with me if the skip would be on a private drive or if I'd need a permit. In short, a neighbour called the council, the council fined the skip company, the skip company took away the skip before we'd filled it and emailed me a bill that exceeds what Arthur is paying us.

The upside of the skip fiasco was that my mother spent the day driving back and forth to her rubbish dump, keeping her away from Ben and Josephine. EHFAR.

For their short time together both Ben and my mother kept to their instructions. I told Ben not to mention Francis in front of my mother ('she's terrible with loss').

'What about, you know, Luke?' he asked.

'Even worse. I would never normally say this, but pretend it didn't happen. She's just not able to talk about it.' Sorry, but it's true.

In turn, I reminded my mother that Ben was the Luke's Touch co-founder and anything else was irrelevant. ('He's awkward about the dog walking, he's only doing it while money's tight.')

'And please don't touch him,' I said to her.

'Touch him? Why would I touch him?' she asks.

'It's what you do. And sometimes he has a loose bit of food in his beard. If he does, ignore it.'

Josephine spent the afternoon talking about Monday's trip to

Brighton. Will the sea have sharks? (I should ask Lola if Josephine can swim.) Is the train all night? Miss Jones went on a train with beds. Can we take Kayla?

'Only if we can leave her there,' I say. 'Sorry, mean joke ... Oh God, please don't tell it to anyone at school.'

I've set aside the weekend to plan trains, read reviews of child-friendly sights and to make her a factsheet about the Pavilion. To be polite, I accepted Lola's offer to pay for the train tickets.

To: LRS_17@outlook.com
Sun 28/5, 19:23
SUBJECT: *Impossible*

How can we run a business together? Not a rhetorical question. We have to find a way. For you.

Ten minutes after I'd bought the Brighton tickets, Ben texted to ask where we're meeting 'in the morning'.

'You mean Tuesday,' I reply.

'No. Tomorrow.'

I call him.

'You knew,' he says. 'We promised Ross we'd have Arthur in his new place by tomorrow night. Move Monday, empty old place by Wednesday.'

He's forcing me to pick between Arthur and Josephine.

To: LRS_17@outlook.com
Mon 29/5, 21:40
SUBJECT: *Moved*

It's done. Josephine was less upset than I expected. Less upset than I was. We'll go on Wednesday. Arthur needs stability more than she does.

I haven't told Ben about the skip fine, but somehow he's worked out we're in the red and that there'll be no extra cash from this job. How else to explain his approach? He left halfway through the morning to walk Biscuit and was gone for two hours. Josephine begged him to take her with him but he refused. We're getting close to the anniversary of Oval, do you think that's it?

Much like for my mother – whom I dispatched to IKEA for the day to find storage boxes and sheets for Arthur's move to a single bed – I created various tasks to include and occupy Josephine. She used her Sharpies (always in her rucksack) to make labels for the boxes and a *Welcome to Your New Home* poster. She stayed in Arthur's kitchen while I made four trips to his new flat, meeting my mother there on one of them. Her slippery web phrase is on repeat in my head. I'll have to tell her about Josephine soon.

We had drive-thru for lunch and the biscuits that Lola had given us for the train to Brighton. We made Josephine a work station in the new flat while Ben and I unpacked.

This is irritating: Josephine's started singing 'Happy Birthday' whenever she washes her hands. She sings it to Francis, because where he is 'it's always birthday day'.

Like most people singing 'Happy Birthday', she gets higher as she goes and is squeaking by the time she reaches 'Happy Birthday, Dear Dog God'. Then she sings it a second time, in a different key.

'Does it have to be twice?' I ask.

'It kills all the germs,' she says.

'Does it have to be "Happy Birthday"?'

'Has to be twenty.' She means seconds. It would take 'Bohemian Rhapsody' to remove all the Sharpie splodges.

I've promised to come up with alternatives to 'Happy Birthday'. In the meantime I've suggested she counts to one hundred in fives.

When he brought Arthur over at teatime, Ross commented on the vase of tulips and the lemon drizzle I'd made in one of Ann's loaf tins ('Haven't they done it nice, Dad?') but I expected more. When

Ben was out the room, I asked Ross if he'll write a review for our website.

'Like what?' he said.

'How happy you are. That we've been sensitive to your father's needs. Or I could write something and you tell me if you're OK with it.'

Arthur sat in his armchair. I'd placed the TV remote ready for him. I pointed out the luggage-trolley picture, in a new frame that doesn't topple over. 'Jersey,' he said.

We're going back to the old place tomorrow. There was a loft we didn't know about. It contains six boxes, three camp beds, ten bin bags and a wasps' nest. As I said to Ben, nothing's rewarding all the time.

E's just come in. He thought I was in Brighton for the day. Oh God, there's someone with him. Sounds like Maggie's Damian. I'm lying on your bed. He'll see I'm in no state to come down.

To: LRS_17@outlook.com
Mon 29/5, 22:17
SUBJECT: A talk

Damian didn't stay.

Did I mention Lola was odd when I dropped Josephine back? She was quieter and insisted on giving me another box of biscuits. (She seems to have a stockpile in her cupboard, like my mother keeps emergency greetings cards. I worry your sympathy card was one of them.)

The first thing Josephine told Lola when we came in was how we'd shared the whole tin of Brighton biscuits because 'we worked so hard'.

'Not that hard,' I said. 'We had fun too.'

But Lola seemed angry, said something in Yoruba to Josephine and fetched the new box.

God knows what else Josephine has told her about today (Ben did snap at her about McDonald's). And now Lola's texted:

When can we have a talk?

> *Sorry about today. I promised her we'll go*
> *on Wednesday instead*

I need to talk with you

> *Call me. Now's good*

I need to see you. Talk properly

We've agreed on Wednesday morning, before Brighton. I'll explain about the business, she'll see that she's over-reacting, realise that it's good experience for Josephine. I'll tell her I'll make up for today, give her the train-ticket money back. I just don't want any more of her Ben questions – seems she will only ever think of him as the man from her platform. I could call her. This is silly.

To: LRS_17@outlook.com
Mon 29/5, 23:12
SUBJECT: Waiting up

Will give Lola a bit longer to reply before I go to bed. I sent her another message at eleven:

> *Wednesday tricky with early train. Can we just chat now, pls? BTW,*
> *did JoJo tell you about the hand hygiene thing we came up with –*
> *counting in fives? She's soooo clever. I'll be up late, call me when suits*
> *xxx*

Also messaged Ben:

I need you to apologise to Josephine. You really upset her and now her
mum's cross with me. I know you didn't mean it, but she's only seven.

To: LRS_17@outlook.com
Tues 30/5, 07:40
SUBJECT: No replies

She must have gone to bed before my texts, Ben too. I can't think
about it now. We need to clear that loft and the rest of the kitchen
by tonight, or no Brighton tomorrow. Ben is in charge of finding a
pest controller – animals are his area. My mother is on dump duty –
she's borrowed the Audi from my father. I heard her on the phone
to him: 'He's very young ... They'll work out what they're doing in
the end ... They could do with Ed.'

To: LRS_17@outlook.com
Tues 30/5, 16:13
SUBJECT: In pursuit of After-Barry

I am at Arthur's waiting for Gary himself from Gary Gets It Done
(tagline: 'Bromley's Pest Kept Secret'). He was due between two and
four. Ben had to walk Biscuit and, for Biscuit's sake, I gave in. The
flat is empty, except for the nest. I'm sitting on the carpet wishing
we'd hoovered.

We cleared the loft, armed with two cans of wasp spray. I can still
taste it. Don't worry, I've worked out I weigh 6,666 times more than
the total pile of wasps we killed. Any harm (to me) will be temporary.

Does every founder feel this? The loneliness before the world
knows it needs you. Remember After-Barry, our first imaginary

client? I tried to explain the After-Barry concept to Ross, said we could send birthday messages from his mother, mark other special dates, asked if she was the type to write to local papers, but he didn't have time to listen ('Just checking you know where to leave the keys') and Arthur couldn't even cope with the photo albums ('Are they for Ross?' he asked). An After-Ann wouldn't work for him, he's not on email and the gap's too big – we'd be rousing her from seven years of silence.

I'm taking Ben for dinner tonight, a Thai place near his, partly debrief, partly to make up for there being no extra money.

To: LRS_17@outlook.com
Tues 30/5, 17:46
SUBJECT: *Mick Jagger*

Gary-Gets-It-Done got it done only partially.

'They're dead already or will be by bedtime,' he said. (Grown-ups don't normally use 'bedtime' among themselves.)

'But is the nest removed? The buyers wanted the nest removed,' I say.

'Then they're morons. Wasps are Mick Jaggers, never return to the same nest twice. It'll rot away in time.'

I don't know the buyers of Arthur's flat but they deserve the full story. I squeezed a message onto the white space on Gary's card and left it on the kitchen counter: 'Wasps dead. No point removing nest, will rot. Call to discuss.'

And I checked, Mick Jagger had eight children with five women. He made at least three return visits.

To: LRS_17@outlook.com
Tues 30/5, 22:47
SUBJECT: *Growing*

Do you remember this time last year? You were growing and we
didn't know it yet. The Thai food made me think about it. We had
Thai takeaway on that bank-holiday weekend and I felt sick all night,
blamed the prawns. Or maybe I'm mixing that up, imagining it.
Everyone becomes a liar when they become a parent. Lie to their kids,
lie to everyone else about their kids, lie to each other.

Ben had three beers, but I didn't drink. Brighton in the morning
and the Lola 'talk'. Whatever it was, she will have calmed down by
now.

Dinner went OK. As I've said before, he's not your average recruit.

We agreed Arthur wasn't a proper PIM, and that he'd taught us
what we don't want to be. Ben says he'll take down the Gumtree ad
until we agree on the right wording. He's found a way round the cash
problem too. There are these new shared bank accounts where I can
top up the balance and we each have a card.

To: LRS_17@outlook.com
Wed 31/5, 09:17
SUBJECT: *Lagos*

We're on the train. Josephine is drawing the blue whale she believes
we will see at the aquarium. Given the ticket price, I expect to see
whales and more – Elton John performing 'I'm Still Standing' on
water skis or Madonna being eaten by a giant squid (Josephine's had
us listening to 'oldies' on Spotify, one ear bud each).

She has a doughnut. I'm having a coffee and wondering how to
tell her to use a different pencil. It says 'Jesus Loves You' and the man
opposite keeps staring. They gave them out at her Sunday school.

I don't know why I expected the Lola 'talk' to be something bad. My guilt problem, I suppose, but don't blame yourself, that's the whole point, we can blame me.

Lola is going home, to Lagos. And she wanted to meet face to face because she wants me to have Josephine. I was first choice. It's a short trip, something's come up, could be a big opportunity for her and Josephine. I didn't understand what the opportunity was, something with a cousin and property, or land or a factory. Any questions I thought of sounded like scepticism in my head, and maybe it's not really about a business opportunity, that's OK.

'Josephine begged me to ask you,' Lola said. 'But my sisters will take her if it's too much.'

Josephine looked up from the TV with her biggest grin. She was in her shoes and unnecessary coat, rucksack on her lap. I should probably have asked E first. But he'll be stuck in the office for the election and then away, again.

'Will you see your sister, Grace?' I asked, trying not to look at the picture next to us of Lola's smiling niece, Grace's dead child. Lola looked down, I'd insulted her. 'Of course you will. My stupid questions. She'll be so happy to see you. And she'll be doing better, you'll see for yourself and you'll see your nephew.'

'Thank you,' she said.

Her trip's not for a couple of weeks or so. 'I'll let you know when I have the dates from my cousin,' she said.

'Not like I'm busy. The business is being a bit slow to get going. We had—'

'I'm so grateful, Rachel.' She looks at the time on her phone. 'I'll leave you two to lock up. Be good in Brighton.'

'We'll bring you a present.'

To: LRS_17@outlook.com
Wed 31/5, 22:39
SUBJECT: *Tooken*

Remember that time Josephine told me what she loved most about me (yellow hair) and about Francis (his shadow). I've started a list on my phone for when she asks what I love about her. Her hair is on it, and not because I think she needs to hear that, but because I love the way her beads shake when she moves, the sound they make. It's a pitter patter and I can almost feel it in my palms, a memory of plunging my hand into bowls of beads in a shop by the sea. I need to take her to a bead shop.

She laughs so much. She has fits where she folds over, her eyes water and just when you think she's finished she starts again. It happened in the fish-and-chip place (we'd promised ourselves seaside fish but not in the aquarium café, because it's wrong to simultaneously visit and eat your food group).

'Someone's tooken our vinegar,' Josephine said as we sat down.

'Tooken?' (Her Josephinisms are also on the list.)

'They've tooken our vinegar. That table has two.'

I type into my phone, hold up the photo. 'Tooken like this? Or some people pronounce it toucan.'

'Does it like bananas?' she asks.

'Why?'

'Its beak is shaped like a banana.' She traces her finger over the picture.

'Your mouth's not shaped like an apple,' I say.

'Weird.' She means me. Then she gets it and the giggling starts.

I make it worse, and surprise myself, by leaning over to the next table and saying, 'Excuse me, I think you've toucan our vinegar.' They didn't speak English, but I added gestures.

I'll have to go. I'm falling asleep. You'd love Brighton. Bright lights, brazen seagulls, pebbles (most of them now in Josephine's rucksack).

To: LRS_17@outlook.com
Thu 1/6, 09:19
SUBJECT: *June*

I'm stronger and ditching phrases every day. Today's: 'Don't set yourself unrealistic deadlines.' It was one of the early ones, in a leaflet about 'baby loss'. (I won't start. But as if I'd misplaced you...) 'Don't set yourself unrealistic deadlines.' I heard it whenever I thought about when I might sleep again, or go on Facebook or look at a baby.

I love deadlines, they make you do things. June is the month it all happens. It's obvious. My birthday, Ben's, the Oval anniversary, a year since I first saw you. By the end of June we will have the perfect PIM and our first After-Barry, or After-Barbara, or After-Bogdan. Someone who's about to die any day now.

Mesh from work has emailed back. He finishes early tomorrow, says he'll set me up with a new site before the weekend. I'll keep Peckhamexperts for when Ben admits he needs a site for the dog walking. Mesh immediately understood Luke's Touch, called it 'brave'. I didn't mention Ben.

'We've just suffered our own loss,' Mesh wrote. 'Kel had a miscarriage.'

Maybe he could be our tech head, when we're a bit bigger. He could run the digital afterlives.

Next on the to-do list:

- Open bank account
- Compile list of funeral directors (FDs)
- Research hashtags (Josephine started me off on the train home last night #loveher #brighteststar #webadvisor)
- Luke's Touch Twitter and Instagram accounts
- Find jobs for the intern (Market research among friends? Role play FD meetings? Earmark future PIMs?)

To: LRS_17@outlook.com
Thu 1/6, 09:33
SUBJECT: *Snuggle watch*

Forgot to say, June is also when Kim and Kanye reach three months, meaning they're old enough to breed. The book says female gerbils hide that they're pregnant. There's something to admire. I need to find advice on separating mating gerbils. Kanye's bitten me twice since we got him/her. That would make a good gravestone: *Savaged by a frustrated gerbil.*

They're pregnant for twenty-five days and can get pregnant again within hours of giving birth. And they're not picky about who they snuggle with. The siblings would start up too. Exponential gerbil growth, a dynasty within months. They'll out-Kardashian the Kardashians.

To: LRS_17@outlook.com
Fri 2/6, 16:25
SUBJECT: *Launching*

Mesh left a minute ago. We can't make him tech head. There's this thing I can't forget. It was before Kelly (she's in Human Performance on the sixth floor, they met at Friday Spinning). He didn't like my engagement ring. The first time I wore it to the office, he said, 'It's not what I imagined for you.' I took it off before he arrived today, stop him getting distracted.

I let him hug me when he arrived, because that's how people seem to say hello now. They do it at the school gate even though they've seen each other six hours earlier. Ben never goes in for a hug, and I never have to fear he will. Our history of hugging is not something we'd want to build on (Oval; the dog-poo day; 'I've got fleas').

Mesh held me too long but everyone does since you – like I'm a soggy sponge they can squeeze out.

'Come from the office?' I asked. He was in trainers, shorts and a tight shirt.

'Casual Friday.'

'How is Kelly doing? I'm so sorry about the ... I mean for both of you. How are you both doing?'

'Up and down. You know what it's like.'

I led him to the dining table.

'I've set up a little home office in here,' I said. 'Means Ed can help me in the evenings. He's back early today.'

'Nice. So I think I've found the best starter package for you.' He'd brought his own laptop and showed me how to change the words on the website, add pictures, change fonts. It's easier than you'd think. My goal for this weekend is the 'About Us' section.

When I asked Mesh how much I owed him for his time, I knew what he'd answer. If I do take him out for a drink, I'll bring my mother.

Need to go. Josephine texted on Lola's phone to say there is something she 'urgently' needs to give me. I asked if it can wait. 'Don't be silly,' she said.

To: LRS_17@outlook.com
Fri 2/6, 20:48
SUBJECT: Brace, brace

My mother calls when I'm watching a film about a plane crash. I pick up on her third attempt.

'Catch you in the act?' she says.

'In the—'

'In the ladies? You didn't answer.'

'The "ladies", in my own house? With a hand dryer and a sanitary bin? I was trying to watch a film.'

'Where's Ed?' she asks.

'The office. I told you. He's there all weekend, for the election.'

She's chosen to forget. From her perspective, E's helping the wrong side.

'You haven't come back to us about tomorrow,' she says.

I pause the film, they're in the brace position, except for one man who's in the aisle, trying to reach his daughter six rows back. 'I'm not feeling great and I have some work to get done,' I say.

'No one should work on their birthday.'

'You say one thing, you vote another,' I say.

'Pardon?'

'We'll do something later in the month,' I say.

'We're away later in the month. A cruise. Round the Canaries,' she says.

'What? We?'

'Your father,' she says.

'Were you going to tell me? I thought you wanted to help me.'

'It was your father's idea. Now that I don't have any ties, after Francis.' She pauses after his name. I don't feel bad, he was old. 'Hang on, how about you come with us. A well-earned rest after all our manual labour. We'll get you a cabin, or upgrade ours to a bigger one.'

How did we get here? 'That's OK. Ed's also been talking about going away, once the election's over. Mauritius or the Seychelles. Somewhere quiet, with land.'

To: LRS_17@outlook.com
Sat 3/6, 10:45
SUBJECT: *Pebble*

The mystery of Josephine's padded envelope (the urgent package) is over. A pebble, with a face, mine, drawn in Sharpie. I have oversized blue eyes, a tiny mouth, pink circles on my cheeks and yellow hair. On the back is a heart with a bird inside, possibly a toucan. The card says:

To Pebble/Rachel,
Happy Birthday! (Sing it twice!!!!)
I hope you like your Pebble/Rachel.
Love, Josephine Adeyemi xxxxxxxxx
P.S. Kisses from Kim and Kanye Adeyemi-Summers

In a separate card, Lola wrote: *God Bless You, Rachel.* (He owes me at least that.)

I video-called to thank them and to show Josephine how much my Pebble looked like me. 'You didn't have to use one of your Brighton pebbles on me,' I say.

'I wanted to get you guinea pigs, but Mummy said no.'

Lola shouts in the background, 'Two wrongs don't make a right.'

'Very clever,' I say.

'They were going to be Beyoncé and Jay-Z,' says Josephine. 'And I was making them their own house and swimming pool in Silopolis.'

'Maybe next year. I love my pebble. It's the best present I've ever had.'

I've put Pebble in Silopolis town square, by the water feature (yoghurt pot).

I didn't expect Ben to remember. I'll text him, tell him the bank account's set up.

E brought flowers home last night, told me to keep next Saturday free.

To: LRS_17@outlook.com
Sun 4/6, 09:27
SUBJECT: *Selfish*

Still nothing from Ben. Something happened last night but he's not picking up. I texted when I woke up at five: *Please tell me you weren't at London Bridge.* People are missing, they say they fell in the river, or jumped.

We had just minutes on our own, you and I. Ninety minutes for the two of us. That's how long it was between the pink lines and Oval. Ninety minutes when we didn't have to wonder where he was, what he'd become, when he'd try again.

To: LRS_17@outlook.com
Sun 4/6, 19:56
SUBJECT: *Wolves and porridge*

What do the best-selling food brands have in common? A story. Founded by Quaker immigrants ... invented in the trenches ... a happy accident in the kitchen. Go on any big-brand website and there's a 'how we got here' story. Because if you want people to pay attention, you tell a story. You want them to learn something, you tell a story. It's been going on for centuries. Goldilocks and the dangers of trespassing. The three little pigs and the consequences of corner-cutting. The gingerbread man and the threat of urban foxes.

I'm nearly there with our story. I've gone with 'bereaved' instead of 'PIMs'. It was after something E said about the election, how every party was making voters feel 'misunderstood'.

'I'll tell you what people hate most,' he said.

'Being told what they hate?' I said.

'Being turned into an acronym. Imagine someone called you a JAM, told you you're Just about Managing. You'd feel condemned.'

Person in Mourning is a statement of fact. But I see his point and PIMs are generally sensitive, so I've made bereaved work.

Photos are more of a problem. I can't let work know about the business yet. That rules out pictures of me and my full name (but first-names-only seems to be how it's done at start-ups). I have a couple of nice ones of Ben moving Arthur's boxes – Josephine made him see how many he could lift in one go. They're smiley but is that the tone we want? They'll do for now.

Finally, he's texted back:

Busy with a new rescue, needs lots of training.

My reply:

Know how you feel

To: LRS_17@outlook.com
Mon 5/6, 10:27
SUBJECT: *Hampshire*

The website's live, the 'About Us' story's up and I've found a solution to the pictures problem that simultaneously solves the Ben problem. It may even open up a new branch of services for us. It's a bit far but we'll turn it into an offsite. I found a great photographer in Hampshire and she's near a spa hotel (if I can get separate rooms) as well as a natural burial ground in a wood – pets and humans. We'll get shots of both of us and add mine to the site once I've cleared it with work.

Brighton reminded me what it's like to escape London. If I can take Ben away from dogs and noise, we can talk. About the business, about why we need a website, about him, how he's doing, why he did it.

I would choose me as the person I tell.

To: LRS_17@outlook.com
Mon 5/6, 10:39
SUBJECT: *Bitten*

Ben picked up but couldn't talk. Said he was at the vet's, with Biscuit.

'Why aren't the owners taking him?' I ask.

'Because it happened on the walk.' He's whispering, they must be in the waiting room. 'Bug bit him.'

'Bug? Little puggle Bug? Ben Bug?'

'Have to go.'

To: LRS_17@outlook.com
Mon 5/6, 12:46
SUBJECT: *Putting things right*

It was our Bug. They've finished at the vet's. Biscuit needed sedation, stitches and antibiotics.

Ben said Biscuit 'was asking for it', not a phrase you should use.

'Biscuit kept pinning Bug down, way he always does. I pulled him off and Bug went for him, got his ear.'

'What will you tell the owners?' I ask.

'I didn't tell Bug's owners anything. Biscuit's will understand, he's always been scrappy. Hope they'll be OK about the vet bill, emergency rate.'

'But it was your fault,' I say.

'It was Biscuit's fault. He's been bullying Bug for months, pushing and pushing. Bug was putting things right.'

'You think violence is how to put things right?' I ask.

'I'm talking about dogs. Why do you always make them out to be people?'

'I do that? "Bullying", "putting things—"' I stop because he'll hang up. Instead I ask him if he's free at the weekend, and I tell him about the offsite plan. He says he has two dogs booked in, would need to find cover.

I've reserved two rooms for Saturday night and can cancel up to the day before. It will force me to tell E about Luke's Touch. I'll explain that I was waiting to have it clearer in my mind first. He'll understand the importance of finding the right photographer – he went through seven before the wedding. And he'll be exhausted after the election anyway.

To: LRS_17@outlook.com
Mon 5/6, 20:35
SUBJECT: *The 'Happy Birthday' resistance project*

We're working on a new handwashing song. We trawled Spotify for twenty-second options but few choruses fit the bill. We've changed the parameters to twenty seconds minimum. And we're writing new lyrics. The shortlist:

- 'Washing Me, Killing You' (by what Josephine calls the palindrome people (ABBA).)
- 'You Won't Survive' (Needs work. 'I have all this soap and foam, And the patience of a gnome.' Those fishing gnomes do look patient.)
- 'Killing You Softly' (Germs bring out a ferocious side in Josephine)

To: LRS_17@outlook.com
Tues 6/6, 11:03
SUBJECT: *Insta-baby*

Anna-Su looks like E – the blue eyes, round face, hamster cheeks (those of an attractive hamster). I'm supposed to be researching Instagram and hashtags, because as 'live' as the website might be, it's actually pretty much dead (sorry). No one has clicked on it. We need social media and I need to come up with hashtags. Instead I'm looking at pictures of Maggie, Damian and Anna-Su. And of E, when he visited them at home, and at the hospital. He has his arm round Maggie, she's captioned it 'King Eddie Hugs' and used the hashtags #family #stayingpositive. Susan's on there too, with #dontcallhergranny.

I've never liked mass communication, similar to Ben I guess.

At the hospital, the thought of it made me panicky. 'How will we tell people?' I asked E. You were with us, in my bed.

'Quickest would be Facebook,' he said.

'Not on Facebook. I don't want him on Facebook. I don't want them writing about him on Facebook.'

He wrote individual emails, with some copying and pasting, lots of 'we're so sorry'. Some people he called. He relayed bits of the conversations to me, read out replies. We talked about the two who didn't reply, a colleague of his, my cousin.

We'll add that to the list of Luke's Touch services: Notification. They hand us a list of names, we do the rest. No more having to say it over and over, no more apologising and paring the story back until it sounds like your loved one had a little fall and slipped into the afterlife.

To: LRS_17@outlook.com
Wed 7/6, 11:36
SUBJECT: Badlands

Today is Twitter day. The Instagram is launched – I used a screengrab of the website, a link and these hashtags:

#grief
#recovery
#afterlife
#newwayforward
#disruptors

I'll use the same on Twitter and do more when we have the new photos and that review I asked Ross for. The tone on Twitter is nastier. What if someone says something about you, blames me? There must be other ways to get the traffic we need. If we were proper disruptors we wouldn't do it the same way as everyone else. I still like undertakers and death notices – precision PIM hunting. I'll send one or two tweets and move back on to that.

Planning something like this (they're so strict about length, probably good for me):

We were sickened by way bizworld treats grievers so found a better way w/ full AFTERLIFE SERVICES. Read our story: [LINK] [hashtags]

Grieve at ur pace with our bespoke clearance and memory-keeping. Why we created Luke's Touch: [LINK] [hashtags]

To: LRS_17@outlook.com
Wed 7/6, 19:27
SUBJECT: *#lasttoknow*

Lola's leaving on Friday. She told me when I dropped Josephine home. How long had she known? People flying off everywhere, no one tells me. She said her cousin called, had booked her on a flight leaving Friday lunchtime.

'I thought you said a couple of weeks,' I said.

'Is it a problem now?' Lola asked.

'It's all good. We'll have a brilliant time.'

There's not enough time. I'd started a letter for her to give her sister Grace in Lagos. I'm telling her I feel like I know her, how I'm glad she has Lola as a sister, how Abi must have been wonderful, that she's with you, you're friends.

What do I do about Hampshire? I could leave Josephine with one of Lola's sisters. Or I'll cancel. Or we'll take Josephine with us, the hotel has a pool and stables. Except Lola hinted she doesn't want Josephine around Ben. OK, not hinted, it was almost a row.

'You've found him and it's not what we thought. You know he's OK, now leave him,' she said.

I tried explaining again, what we need to do, how we'll help so many people, I showed her Mia's mum's post on the forum.

'Do it alone. You'll be better alone. No more complaining about him and his dogs. Or do it with your husband,' she said.

'Why can't you just let me prove we can do this?'

'Because I don't want that man around Josephine. I'm trying to trust you with my daughter.'

'Then why are you asking me, if you don't trust me?' I said.

'I do, because I know that really you understand what you need to do, that he's no good.'

So Ben only during school hours, that's easy enough.

The tweets have had a few retweets – that's people passing them on to their followers, implying they are something worth reading. The website's had twenty-two visitors. No one has been in touch directly. I should be more targeted, use #grieving, #heartbroken and #RIP. I'll send out the same tweets with new hashtags in the morning. I got a good picture of Josephine's daisy chain in the park for Instagram, #rebirth #healing #eternity. And you'll be reassured to know I popped into your account while I was working, cleared out your spam folder, all the things you shouldn't see, emails beginning 'Hello Dearest...' How dare they?

To: LRS_17@outlook.com
Thu 8/6, 21:39
SUBJECT: *Election night*

Soon they will count the votes and the contenders will know. It's like you and me, but with less to lose. For months you work and hope; the day comes, followed by a sleepless night and it ends with everything or nothing.

I'm supposed to be applying for a trademark and working out what we need to do tax-wise but I stopped to check pregnancy/election ratios. #procrastination

PREGNANCY
280 days of gestation for an average lifespan of 29,200 days
104 days of life per day of gestation

ELECTION
36 campaign days for a potential 1,825 days in power
51 days of power per day of campaigning

In other words, when pregnancy works out, it's better value. But take our case and imagine I have another forty-five years left:

280 days of gestation for 16,425 days of emptiness
58 days of emptiness per day of gestation
– so a better correlation with elections

16,425 days of emptiness for one day I took the wrong train

I should go to bed or fill in some forms.
This is weird, Twitter notifications. Lots of them. Loads of them.

To: LRS_17@outlook.com
Fri 9/6, 02:15
SUBJECT: *What I did*

Sorry, I tried to sleep. Pretend it isn't happening. I should have told
you straight away. I don't know how. The shaking won't stop and
there's that burning too, I need to be sick but I can't. Like when they
told me to sleep and I lay there, flat on my back, eyes closed, counting
backwards from ten thousand and maybe I'd wake and it would be a
different world. I made it all the way down to zero and I was still
empty. How could he hide all that? How could I swap you for this?
Sorry, I'll try again later.

To: LRS_17@outlook.com
Fri 9/6, 02:34
SUBJECT: *Is it real?*

Is there someone in charge there? Someone on EHFAR watch?

Why is this one way? WRITE BACK. Tell them to write back, to
explain. Tell them I said please.

Stopping to make coffee, find biscuits. (After being sick, because
that's what I am, someone who makes a bad problem a million times
worse.)

We're out of biscuits.

I went along with it because of his eyes, how he talked to Francis,
and he was a little bit like you, and because he needed me, and we
needed each other and everyone needs Luke's Touch. It's bollocks.

To: LRS_17@outlook.com
Fri 9/6, 02:46
SUBJECT: *So utterly fucking awful*

I hide nothing from you. Here it is: Ben isn't Ben. Ben Palmer is Mark Westmore and Mark Westmore is a racist. Ben is an undercover racist.

To: LRS_17@outlook.com
Fri 9/6, 04:17
SUBJECT: *Snowman*

Explosive reaction to the coffee. E slept through it. He'd come in at three and given up on a conclusive outcome. 'It's a mess,' he said. 'Tomorrow's going to be one big shitshow of a post-mortem ... Sorry.'

I laughed to make him feel better. 'Know what you mean. A fucking mess. I'm staying up a bit longer.' I took the laptop downstairs.

I'm trying to convince myself it's a weird hoax, that I was chosen as the butt of a sick online joke.

I'll be as clear as I can.

It started with the Twitter notifications, more than three hundred. Two hundred people had 'mentioned' my tweet in their tweet, others had retweeted me, some had messaged me in a way that the whole world can see. Things like:

Why u doin this?

Scumbag hoar, sick exploiting dead

Reported you for offensive content

My first thought? Luke's Touch had been misunderstood. Twitter was the worst place to talk about death. Everyone is waiting to be offended. Oh God, I've turned into Ben.

I read more of them:

Why you helping him?

Shoulda let him do it.

They all had the same hashtag: #snowman

Some had screen-grabbed the 'our story' from our website and Ben's picture at Arthur's house. The one with all the boxes. The smiley one.

Look who's resurfaced in a grisly new role, said one tweet, and he'd linked to his blog where there was a whole section on #snowman. *Remember #snowman aka #britainsbiggestbigot?* said the newest post. *Now he's preying on grieving families.*

No. Why are they saying this? We're stopping the preying.

The blogger's had more than four hundred retweets. They all have the same two pictures. Ben from our website and next to him, Ben without a beard. It looks like he's in a TV studio and he's wearing a badge. It says 'Mark'.

The blog has everything. Video clips, pictures, his whole life, all him.

Short version: in 2016, Ben was on a TV quiz show, some Saturday teatime thing before the lottery numbers are drawn. It's on YouTube. He made it to the final, stood to win some money, in the thousands, but not that much. He was Mark. Mark from Bedford, the presenter said.

And what did he do in Bedford?

'I like to go for long walks with my mum and her sausage dogs.' He looks over to the audience, acknowledges the big ahhhh. The picture cuts to his mum in the front row, she has his eyes and she's skinny, the cancer's already spread.

'Is that a full-time job nowadays?' says the presenter, and he gets a laugh.

'Ha!' says Ben (he's better on camera than you'd expect, warm and relaxed). 'I'm an estate agent.' Apologetic smile to the audience as they boo. Estate agent. The cushions. The way he jangles his keys. He called Biscuit's garden 'south facing'. Estate agent!

The bit everyone uses as a clip comes in the final. Ben's up against a woman called Sufia from Tipton. She's wearing a turban instead of a hijab. I don't know if you're allowed to say it suits her, but it does. It's bright blue with yellow patterns and matches her tunic. Her topic's geography, they want a capital city in West Africa beginning with B, she goes with Bissau, it's right. (I'd have said Bamako, also right, not important.)

Ben gets current affairs, he winces. His question is this:

'What did several schools ban this winter on health-and-safety grounds?'

'Muslims.' There's no pause. Ben's smiling, like he's certain it's right. Banned Muslims. Sufia covers her mouth – you can watch it normal speed or in slow motion, but it's impossible to tell if she's hiding a laugh, shock or hurt.

There's a wrong-answer noise, too short for the presenter's brain to start up.

'Wow,' he says. 'Wow. Never had an answer like that before. Sorry, Mark, the correct answer was snowball fights. Err, not Muslims.' He looks to the audience for a laugh, they know better – most of them.

I need to sleep, it's too late to recount everything that came next. Articles, blogs, people collating his previous tweets and Facebook posts. If you type 'Mark Westmore racist' into Google you get twenty-eight thousand results. These are the kind of headlines:

'Britain's Biggest Bigot? Ten Tweets That Reveal the Real Mark Westmore'.

'TV Producers Slammed For Missing Contestant's EDL Past'. (There's a picture where they've circled someone who could be Ben doing a Hitler salute at an English Defence League rally.)

'Race Hate? Police Probe "Repulsive" Quiz Show Answer'.

'Never Been So Afraid – psychologist reveals what co-contestant's body language is really saying'.

Since Oval, I've been keeping a list of reasons on my phone. It's grown since I found him.

- Debt
- Depression
- His mother's death
- His father's dementia
- A woman, possibly a man
- His own cancer
- Post-traumatic stress disorder from a secret past as a soldier in Iraq or dog handler with the police

No, I didn't think to include 'Racist outburst on TV, national humiliation'.

I'm an idiot, a dangerous idiot.

To: LRS_17@outlook.com
Fri 9/6, 04:43
SUBJECT: Helper

I've been trawling my sent emails, everything I've told you. Have I been enabling him, nodding along at his casual fascism? Vonny in Diversity ran a workshop on unconscious bias last year, how we pick people like ourselves for jobs, for promotion, as lunch partners in the canteen. 'Harmful blinkers,' she said. 'Pushing everyone else out.'

To: LRS_17@outlook.com
Fri 9/6, 06:55
SUBJECT: *Who?*

Ben's phone is off. Or Mark's. I texted and said I was sorry, that I had no idea, that the website was a mistake, that I should have checked with him. No reply. Then I texted again: *Actually, why should I be sorry?* And again: *You should have told me.*

I'm in the car outside Lola's house, we've arranged to drop Josephine to school together, before Lola goes to the airport. That way we can explain to Miss Jones, and I'll pick up a key to Lola's flat, the EpiPen and Josephine's things for the next week or so.

I'm early. But it's safer in the car, away from the laptop. I've taken Twitter and Instagram off my phone. It took a while, but I also closed our website. People will move on and I'll start again, on my own. It will have to be under a different name. I'm sorry.

Language is a big thing for you right now. You're eighteen weeks, or do we move on to months? I'm not ready to round up and down. It's been 3,049 hours (there are upsides to the Internet). Your chart says you recognise sounds, how people communicate. But that can't be right. No one understands anything about how anyone communicates. We can't believe each other, we refuse to believe each other. Every aspect of being human has been warped by the web. God, I AM him.

Maybe those headlines twisted his life, made him something he wasn't. He did say 'Muslims' but that doesn't mean he thinks they should have been banned from schools, he thought it was the answer to the question, that schools had banned Muslims. You're cross that I'm defending him. I'm not. I'm trying to do what no one else did, to calm down and look at it for what it is. I need to read more.

I'll close my eyes for a while before I go up to Lola's. Josephine mustn't detect any of this.

I need painkillers. I have iPhone-user shoulder: shooting pains down my arm and a head stuffed with Britain's collective outrage. Where was I when this happened the first time? It must have been during the milk and fats deal.

To: LRS_17@outlook.com
Fri 9/6, 07:15
SUBJECT: Wrong

The wrong train. The wrong train. The wrong train. Sometimes people just take the wrong train. I've texted Dog Collar Graham, asked if we can talk. He'll tell me it's not my fault.

There are so many things I pretended not to see. Things I hate. The unread messages on his phone – like he's too busy to read what anyone else is telling him. His deodorant wears off by the end of a walk. He never listens. He'd do anything for a dog. He picks his back teeth with the one long nail on his little finger. He sniffs. He never asks about you.

Friday morning. We should be at Monkey Music. Monkey Music then coffee in the park and a feed, a walk, lunch at my mother's and dinner in front of Netflix with E. Tomorrow E would take you to your swimming class while I slept. They called last week to ask if we still wanted the place.

To: LRS_17@outlook.com
Fri 9/6, 07:22
SUBJECT: Depraved

He clipped his nails in front of me. We'd hardly met. In his kitchen. Finger and toenails.

I'm not blaming you, but this only caring about the big stuff has muffled my senses. I've stepped so far back, everything looks tiny.

To: LRS_17@outlook.com
Fri 9/6, 07:46
SUBJECT: *Not a lasagne*

It's like the time with the lasagne. One of the ones E had made. He'd
stocked the freezer before you were due, because when he'd asked
her, the antenatal teacher told him that was how he could be useful.
It was one week on, the first Wednesday without you. My mother
was coming round, I'd told her not to, that I was fine, she'd insisted
and so to prove I was fine, I was going to serve lasagne. But it was like
Ben, it wouldn't defrost. I tried an hour in the oven, then another
half hour, blasted it for ten minutes in the microwave, still frozen in
the middle, the knife wouldn't go in.

She's there, setting the table, demanding real napkins, picking cat
hairs off the dining chairs. And I'm in the kitchen stabbing and
blasting, stabbing and blasting. It's gone nine when it's finally soft in
the middle, and do you know what? Turns out it's a moussaka. My
mother hates moussaka. I hate moussaka. Ben is a moussaka.

To: LRS_17@outlook.com
Fri 9/6, 14:23
SUBJECT: *Waiting is dangerous*

Have to go soon to collect Josephine. I tried to nap, but there is
always one more thing to click on. I have my mother's voice in my
head: 'Everything can wait until tomorrow, Pebble, even you.' (She
loves a phrase that starts with 'Everything'.)

Ben's phone is still off. He's not at his flat. Another thing I hate:
he leaves his blinds down all day.

I did two loops of the graveyard, parked near Biscuit's house for
an hour or so. She left with the baby and Biscuit.

Lola's goodbye wasn't ideal. I fell asleep in the car outside their building. They waited for me, called (phone on silent), gave up and set off to school. That's when they saw me parked outside and Lola banged on the window.

'Are you sure you're OK to take her?' she says as we run back up to the flat for Josephine's suitcase.

'Absolutely. Just nodded off. Migraine last night. So wonderful when it clears, isn't it? Must have been the relief sent me to sleep. I was early, thought I'd close my eyes.'

Josephine tugs on my arm. 'Look, Rachel.' Her mouth's open wide, she wobbles a front tooth.

'Yuck,' I say. 'I mean, wow!'

'My sister can have her, I just spoke to her,' says Lola.

'It's all fine. JoJo's room is ready. Homemade burgers for dinner, and jelly. Look at this, I've set alarms on my phone for school pick-ups, teatime, bedtime, getting-up time, leave-the-house time.'

'It'll be ringing all day,' says Lola. 'And your husband's in New York?'

'Just us girls,' I say, because he's almost in New York, will be next week.

Josephine was tearful at the school gate, but Miss Jones and Lola explained it was only for a week or so. We said we'd do a video call with Lola as soon as we could, that she'd bring presents back for both of us and that we'd watch *Moana* tonight.

Lola texted on her way to the airport:

Thank you, Rachel. And thank you for listening about Ben. You already helped him more than he knows. Get some rest.

I replied:

Thank you for trusting me.

She's sent me a whole address book of emergency contacts. I should have made one for you.

Back home, I watched the quiz-show moment again. Ben looks over to her turban before he says it. I'm not saying it's not racist, but what if it was the first thing that came into his head?

Some columnists at the time said he looked like he regretted it, that he tried to change his answer, explain it, but the edit cut him off. He couldn't look at Sufia, they said, and they were right about that. Others made him their crusader. 'Mark Westmore was vilified for saying what everyone's thinking. Our schools need to change,' wrote one columnist. Liberals seemed to want to simultaneously pity Ben and profit from him. One writer asked, 'Who hasn't said something as bad as Mark Westmore?' She ends her column with 'Another Five Things Mark Westmore Must Wish He Never Said':

1. 'Is it me or are Bedford buses like souks on wheels? Woman next to me's got a dead rabbit, man behind eating a kebab ... at 8 in the morning #carinshop #garlicoverload #greatbritishpublic :-(' (Facebook, March 2014)
2. 'Jus chillin' with my bitches' (Caption for a selfie on a picnic mat with his mum and two sausage dogs, Instagram, May 2015)
3. 'Sis calls, says she's sick of getting paid less than men at her work, finally confronted her (female) boss about it, got same excuses. Me: did you try speaking to a man? LMFAO' (Facebook, November 2011)
4. 'Showed couple round a two-bed. They wanna put in his n his bike racks, sinks and ... TOILETS! #synchronisedshitting LOL' (Facebook, February 2015)
5. 'Which of you chubsters nicked my pasta from the fridge? Try salad.' (Work email shared by anonymous colleague, April 2015)

Do you think they're made up? Or maybe he's changed.

I'm not clicking on new posts and I'm staying off Twitter, too many mention you and me. I've gone back, it was the #RIP ones, someone called desertdog2000 recognised Ben's picture, then this blogger joins in and it spreads. I'm really not saying it wasn't racist, but why do they care so much? If you were here, we wouldn't have time for this. Work can't have found out yet.

I missed the deadline to cancel the hotel. I'll take Josephine instead. We'll be safer there and give E some space.

To: LRS_17@outlook.com
Fri 9/6, 23:42
SUBJECT: Drip

Josephine's asleep in her bed and I'm the other side of her wall reading about a racist, our racist. We're at Lola's – I'll explain later. In short, big row with E, in whispers, Josephine was there.

I need to sleep. Long drive tomorrow. I'm in Lola's bed, on top of the sheets. I should move to the sofa but the ceiling leak is back, I'm catching it in a saucepan and the noise is unrelenting. I pushed a note under the neighbour's door.

I thought I envied Ben's living day-to-day thing. He isn't anything, he isn't becoming anything. He's hiding.

One tabloid wrote an 'inside the sheltered life of' thing. Said he 'was one of the brighter kids' at school, left at eighteen, became an estate agent, lived down the road from his parents in an 'upmarket apartment building'.

He told me he went to university. He said, 'when I was in halls'. He was telling me about a girl who cooked fish fingers in a toaster.

They'd spoken to people at his local pub who knew him from the weekly quiz.

'He was shy but friendly after a drink or two. Good general knowledge,' said a barman, who refused to be named.

A woman, also unnamed, said, 'He used to have a dog with him, little sausage dog. Sometimes a girl too.'

The partner?

To: LRS_17@outlook.com
Sat 10/6, 00:12
SUBJECT: *Search*

I'm trying every word I can think of, and using speech marks. 'Mark Westmore apologises', 'Mark Westmore speaks', 'Mark Westmore sorry'.

To: LRS_17@outlook.com
Sat 10/6, 00:53
SUBJECT: *Attempt*

Found it. It was in April 2016, two months after the quiz. An account set up to send that one tweet, deleted a day later. No one seems to question if it was him.

> Mark Westmore
> @iamMarkWestmore
> Statement:
> I am sorry if I upset people. In the pressure of the moment I panicked and that answer came into my head. That's all it was, an answer. A wrong answer. Not an opinion.

Some people took his side, congratulated him for 'owning his mistake'; some berated him for 'surrendering to the snowflakes'; lots of 'Snowflakes 1, Snowman Nil'. For most people, he'd made it worse. He was putting the blame on the victim – the oldest and worst kind of racism. He'd said the people who were offended were the ones with a problem.

To: LRS_17@outlook.com
Sat 10/6, 04:35
SUBJECT: *Fwd: Your upcoming booking at The Chiltern Firehouse*

This is what he thinks I want. Champagne and celebrity watching. How do I go back?

> Begin forwarded message:
> From: ERSum
> Sat 10/6, 01:23
> Subject: Fwd: Your upcoming booking at The Chiltern Firehouse
>
> You said you'd keep Saturday free. I can't believe you. I'm your husband, not some housemate. When were you going to tell me about running off to a hotel with someone else's child?? Going to New York early.
>
> Sent from my iPhone
>
> > Begin forwarded message:
> > From: no-reply@bookxyz.com
> > Date: 8 June 2017
> >
> > To: ERSum@rello.com
> > Subject: Your upcoming booking at the Chiltern Firehouse
> >
> > We are looking forward to seeing you for our champagne cocktail and tasting menu package.
> > Table for two at 7pm on Saturday 10th June 2017
> > Name: Edward Summers
> > Menu ••• Directions ••• Cancel

To: LRS_17@outlook.com
Sat 10/6, 05:45
SUBJECT: *Spinning juggling balls*

We forgot Kim and Kanye, and we don't know how much water they
have left. I can't ask E. I know I should have told him sooner about
Josephine and the hotel, but he's been home a total of three hours
this week, and he wouldn't want me to waste the booking. We'll go
back for the gerbils, smuggle them into Lola's under a blanket, set off
later to the hotel. Hampshire's not far but everything takes longer
with Josephine.

    Spinning juggling balls. Now I see them.

To: LRS_17@outlook.com
Sat 10/6, 14:37
SUBJECT: *Zip wire*

We made it: back to collect the gerbils – E was gone, guess he meant
it about going to New York early, he'll be comfort shopping – then
to Lola's, where we put the cage in Josephine's room, then the drive
to the hotel. Now the adventure playground. There are two
playgrounds, hotel stables and an indoor play area. You'd love it here,
now that you're trying to get on the move. Early developers roll at
four months. I did a loop of the high-wire course with Josephine to
get her settled in. Everyone else can wait, E, Ben/Mark, the
Twitterers. Can you believe he's emptied the bank account, Ben, the
joint business one? The card wouldn't work when I gave it to them
at the hotel check-in. That can wait too. We've left it all in London.

    The playground's high-tech. You wear a harness hooked onto a
cable and follow a trail in the trees. It's not that high, but something's
changed in me since having you, I felt sick whenever I looked down,
my legs were shaking. The cable system meant no one could overtake

me and I created a bottleneck of seven-year-olds shouting encouragement and advice – it's that sort of clientele.

'You'll be super proud when you finish,' said one girl with two French plaits. I was rewarded with a zip wire at the end and screamed the whole way to make Josephine laugh. My landing was a mess but the hotel has a laundry.

Josephine has made new friends, they've all compared wobbly teeth. She's going round again with them. I'm on a bench in the sun, a waiter's bringing me a coffee. A waiter in the kids' playground.

Do you know what Josephine said when she saw our room? 'We should move here!' They brought her a mini white dressing gown, slippers and a chocolate duck.

She's mentioned Lola a few times, so I'm taking an approach that's always struck me as naïve but effective in others: saying things so they become true, or so everyone believes they could become true. Like the Australian personal trainer I booked with those vouchers from E. 'I can tell we're going to have a lot of fun together.' (She was wrong, but it made me book a second session to find out.) Or my mother's watercolours teacher: 'Jean-Pierre said he knew I'd be a natural.' She'd dropped in after her first lesson, brandishing a mucky snow scene. 'He knew from looking at my clothes that I have a gift for colours. He's a very famous artist.'

'If he was, you wouldn't have to say that.'

I tried the positive projecting in the car. Josephine was staring out the window, arms crossed tight, not even singing along to the palindrome people.

'It's going to be amazing,' I say over 'Super Trouper'. 'I know we're going to have the best time ever. We'll be outside all weekend. On Sunday there's a zoo near the hotel, with toucans. And next week we'll go to the park every day after school. We'll finish Silopolis.'

'Mummy lets me sit in the front. I'm not sick in the front,' she says.

'It's not safe in the front. You'll be happier in the back, you can spread out.'

'You let me go in the front before.'

'That's when I first met you. Plus this is the motorway. Did you know five people die every day in traffic accidents?' I don't reveal there are ten times more fatal accidents on rural roads than motorways.

'Mummy brings a bag for me to be sick into,' she says.

I didn't have any bags, so we stopped and she moved to the front, promising to look tall and old if a police car should pass us.

When we arrived at the hotel, I'd had four missed calls from the photographer. I texted her to say I'd had a family emergency.

I'll have to charge you 50% for no-show, she texted back.

After a death?! I replied. (Ben Palmer has technically died.)

We've only heard once from Lola, a WhatsApp message last night saying she'd landed in Lagos and was on her way to her cousin's to borrow a car to drive out to the other cousin in the morning, the one with the business plan. Don't forget the EpiPen, she said, and don't give JoJo breakfast right before the drive. I wrote back saying to have fun and not to worry and that Josephine missed her. That's what Lola would want to hear.

Josephine's waving at me to come and do another loop on the high wire. She's shouting, 'You'll be better this time.'

To: LRS_17@outlook.com
Sat 10/6, 16:20
SUBJECT: Last

What was the last thing you heard here? Did we watch the one o'clock news?

The drive made me think about it. I felt my eyes closing and I realised, if we crashed, 'Fernando' would be the last thing I heard. Is the last thing you hear what you hear forever? If so, there should be a function on Spotify where you tailor your music quality to the riskiness of your driving terrain.

Was it my voice? Was I talking to you? I'll never stop talking to you.

To: LRS_17@outlook.com
Sat 10/6, 22:42
SUBJECT: *Black eyes*

I need to call E. He'll know what to do. Ben's phone is still off.

To: LRS_17@outlook.com
Sat 10/6, 23:10
SUBJECT: *Accident*

E's not answering. I can't leave a message. It's too much at once.

A voicemail from Lola's sister, Kiki. I picked it up when we got back to the room, we'd stopped at the kids' disco. I thought it was about money. I know that sounds awful but Lola had me on standby in case things didn't work out with her bank in Nigeria.

'I need to speak to you. Urgently,' says Kiki. 'Call me.' No please, no thank you.

But I can't reach her, it's engaged and I've promised Josephine we'll watch a film. I text Kiki to say I've been trying her. She calls at half-ten.

'Is Josephine with you?' she asks.

'Where else would she be? Hang on.' I put us on speakerphone so Kiki can hear Josephine snoring next to me in our double bed. She's flat on her back, arms splayed out. She made it twenty minutes into *Minions*.

'Something happened,' says Kiki. I switch off speakerphone, and *Minions*. 'Lola was in an accident.'

'Oh God. Is she OK?' I say.

Josephine rolls onto her side.

'They don't know what happened,' says Kiki.

'Is she OK?' I step towards the bathroom but something's pulling me back towards Josephine.

'They're checking her now,' says Kiki.

'Who? Who's checking? Is she in hospital? What did she hurt? When? Is she alive?'

'What? Yes! I only had our cousin a few minutes on the phone. She found Lola on the bathroom floor, in the morning, eyes puffed, black eyes, sleeping.'

'Did someone attack her?' I ask.

'Why would you say that? It was in her house.' Kiki's voice is angry.

'The black eyes. How would she get black eyes in a bathroom? Why did no one tell me before? We'll come. We'll come to Lagos. We could have been there by now.'

'You can't go. My cousin's there. She'll keep us informed.'

'But Josephine needs to see her mum,' I say. She's stirring. Do I wake her?

'You keep Josephine. I have more calls,' says Kiki.

'You have to let me know what they're saying, the name of the hospital, the ward, what we can do. I don't understand...' She's gone.

Is Lola conscious or unconscious? Attack or fall? Is she alone? It's like when you wake up after a busy dream, all you can see are the missing pieces. I try to video call Kiki, I need to see her face. She doesn't pick up. Lola's phone is dead.

I'll tell Josephine in the morning, I'll know more then. I'll get us a flight to Lagos. I checked, we can go via Istanbul, be there early hours of Monday. I've texted Kiki for the name of the hospital, the ward, the doctors. E can help me find a hotel. It's still early for him, teatime in New York. His travel people will book it. The doctors can speak to Maggie, she'll find out what's going on, doctor to doctor, they do that.

To: LRS_17@outlook.com
Sun 11/6, 0:13
SUBJECT: *Promises*

I am crap at this. Josephine woke up, she needed the toilet and wanted to finish *Minions*.

'Go back to sleep. We'll watch the rest in the morning.'

'Pinkie promise?' she says.

'I can't promise.'

'Why?' she asks.

'Because we might need to go somewhere.'

'Go where?'

'It's too hard to explain,' I say.

'How come? Is it a surprise? Is it the toucans?'

'Yes. Go back to sleep.'

Nothing more from Kiki. In the morning, we'll go back to the playground and I'll call round Lagos hospitals while Josephine plays. Not your position to answer this, but what do I tell E?

To: LRS_17@outlook.com
Sun 11/6, 02:27
SUBJECT: *Deserve*

I forgot to tell you, Dog Collar Graham called. Yesterday afternoon. Said he was excited to get my text, that they have a new service on Sundays, I should come, we'd talk afterwards.

'I'm away at the moment,' I said.

'What about next week?'

'I can't wait that long. Remember that man I saved, at Oval? What if I told you he was a racist, and a liar?'

'Well ... everyone deserves to live, a chance to become what they should,' says Graham.

'Where does that leave Luke?'

'I'm sorry. I mean—' He stops.

'You're right. Everyone deserves to live.'

To: LRS_17@outlook.com

Sun 11/6, 06:20

SUBJECT: *Lucky*

Kiki texted, to everyone:

> *Spoke to doctor, said she was so lucky, praise God. Cracked skull but no bleeding on brain. Thank you for prayers. KIKI xx*

Everything happens for a reason: Francis was my dry run for this, I know what to do. When Josephine wakes, I'll tell her what I know, that it's OK, that Lola will be home soon.

To: LRS_17@outlook.com

Sun 11/6, 15:30

SUBJECT: *X shapes*

All Josephine wants to know is how. 'How was Mummy hit in the eyes? Who hit her? How did she crack her head? What on? Kayla's brother cracked his head on the roundabout.'

'The baby was on a roundabout?' I ask.

'Another one.'

'How many are there?'

She made a get-well card with a picture of Lola wearing a head bandage, black X shapes over her eyes, we took a photo and WhatsApped it to Lola's phone.

Every five minutes, Josephine asks, 'Has she seen it yet? What did she say?' Our message is unread.

Josephine's in the zoo playground. The toucans were a good distraction, they put them in with the sloths. I've promised we'll go to the shop and drive home from here. E's not replying, must be napping. I'm having to make lists for everything. We will stop at Lola's on the way to ours.

- Collect Kim and Kanye
- Change saucepan
- Call Kiki, and cousins, find Lola address book
- Email Miss Jones
- Josephine packed lunch??
- Ben/Mark – where??
- Twitter – close? Block? How? E??

To: LRS_17@outlook.com
Sun 11/6, 22:39
SUBJECT: *Count and breathe*

I should learn to break promises. I thought there'd be time to make biscuits when we got home. That it would help. But after we'd changed saucepans at Lola's, left a new note for the neighbour, found the many parts of Josephine's PE kit and gone back for her book bag, it was seven o'clock. She says bedtime is eight on a school night.

Flour everywhere. The island's too high for her, so she reaches into the air, tips in too much, spoons it back out, flour goes into the sugar bag, sugar into the baking powder.

The whole ordeal is accompanied by 'Happy Birthday' handwashing. On her third trip to the sink, I snap, 'It's only us eating them, stop washing your hands.'

'What about Ben?' she asks.

'He's away.'

'Where?'

'None of your business.' It's too harsh, she's crying. 'Only joking. He's gone to visit his dad,' I say. She's still crying.

The biscuits (oat crispies with maple syrup) came out the oven at nine-thirty, she was asleep at ten. She's wearing the dressing gown from the hotel over her nightie.

To: LRS_17@outlook.com
Sun 11/6, 23:24
SUBJECT: Popcorn and wine

Crises have upsides. You are allowed to eat what you want. No one says it, but everyone revels in it – go to any hospital café if you want proof, plates piled up with pastries, chips and sausages to offset the loved one dying down the corridor. And you can watch more TV. I'm eating toffee popcorn with golden syrup on top while catching up on my recordings of *The One Show* and shopping for toys online.

To: LRS_17@outlook.com
Mon 12/6, 10:04
SUBJECT: Slipped

She slipped, they think, hit the back of her head. Shook it so hard she got the black eyes. She's dizzy, can't get up without falling over, they're doing more scans, need to check her inner ears. Kiki says they don't know what to expect

'When can she come home?' I ask. 'Or move to a hospital here?'
'If it's her ears, she can't fly,' says Kiki.
'Is there any way we can call her, for Josephine to talk to her?'
'I'll ask,' says Kiki and she's gone again.

To: LRS_17@outlook.com
Mon 12/6, 11:36
SUBJECT: *Hard for me*

Message from E:

> *I do know it's hard, so much to deal with. This is the worst part, they said it would be. Won't always be like this. We'll talk when I'm back. Or call me, tomorrow's better. Josephine's a lucky girl having you to herself. Love you x*

I should call, tell him. He'll help. Or tell him some of it. Did they say this was the worst part? The bereavement midwife told us to expect 'phases but no timetable'. 'Let things happen,' she said.

To: LRS_17@outlook.com
Mon 12/6, 13:48
SUBJECT: *Unwitting meddler*

The blogger with a whole section about Ben/Mark is called Terrence Dunbarr, his blog's called Ferreting Files (a ferret is a stretched rat, known for going down trouser legs). He's the one who collated the video clips and links, he used the photos from your site. I don't know whether to tell you this, he called us 'creepily named Luke's Touch'. And I'm an 'unwitting meddler'.

This post's from May last year (it doesn't let you copy and paste, but I'm learning from my enemies, I screengrabbed it):

We all face justice in the end
Mark Westmore could have done the decent thing and gone quietly. But the Bedford-based yuppie estate agent was (surprise, surprise) too arrogant for that and presumed he

could carry on as normal. Now his employers have pulled the plug, one anonymous colleague exclusively telling me, 'no one wants to be shown round a house by a C-list racist'.

Deluded Westmore was marched out last week. 'The boss waited for him to realise we couldn't keep him on, what would it say about the business? We got tired of waiting,' the colleague wrote in an email to this blog.

Westmore is deep in debt and behind on his rent. His neighbours want to know how they can get him out … Mark NoMore!

I'll say it for them: Mark, do us all a favour and disappear.

To: LRS_17@outlook.com
Mon 12/6, 14:52
SUBJECT: *Day over*

I wanted to go back through my emails to you. Did he say anything about Muslims? He only ever talks about dogs. But there's no time. Back from dropping her half-nine, out again at three, and I can't do anything when she's here. Last week they had an assembly about screens. She reported back at length (an hour and a half to relay a ten-minute talk). 'Smartphones ruin your brain,' she said. 'And your manners.'

To: LRS_17@outlook.com
Tues 13/6, 14:56
SUBJECT: *Guardian angel*

I was in Peckham anyway because there's the big Morrisons and I'd promised Josephine I would buy her a different breakfast cereal, meatballs for dinner, more apples, a surprise for pick-up.

I tried his flat first. Then Biscuit's mum, Jessica. She answered the door with Oliver in her arms. He's bigger than you'd expect for eighteen weeks. She'd put him in white leggings and a blue vest.

'I'm a friend of Ben's,' I say. 'Rachel, he might have mentioned me. I can't get hold of him and my dog's booked in all week.'

Biscuit runs to the door. He knows my voice.

Jessica tries to pull him back. 'Biscuit, just stop it. Down!' She's clutching Oliver to her shoulder with the other arm, he's about to get bitten or dropped or both.

'It's alright,' I say, crouching down to Biscuit, stroking his neck. Part of his ear is shaven and there's a scar. 'Isn't he gorgeous? I love beagles. And what a great name.'

'He likes you,' she says. She has a new fringe that's not on the pictures. It makes her look younger. 'He's been going nuts. He needs to go out. Ben didn't show up, same yesterday. There was this stupid thing last week with another dog and Biscuit's ear. Now Ben's gone all awkward, disappeared. I'll have to take him myself, but I've spent three hours trying to get Oliver changed and into his buggy. He's overtired, he's not feeding, his tummy's bunged up.'

'It'll get easier,' I say, but don't know why. Maybe we'll become friends.

She's about to cry, Oliver's arching his back and then comes something I've never seen before, or heard. A long wet fart, really long, old-man long. A yellow patch appears on the vest and spreads up his back. It seeps out the sides and onto the leggings.

Biscuit can smell it. He pulls away from me and jumps up at Jessica, bouncing on his back legs like she's a tree and Oliver's a squirrel.

Again, I say something and don't know why. 'How about I take Biscuit out for you? Get rid of all that energy?'

I shouldn't have said it, she looks shocked. I could be a dog thief. She's thinking up polite ways to decline. Biscuit jumps up, rams into the bursting nappy. 'Oh God, you mean it? You're my guardian angel,' she says.

'It's nothing. I have to walk mine anyway,' I say. She looks at my feet. 'He's in the car. Windows open.'

It felt good to be with Biscuit. I wonder if he knows where Francis is. I told him about Josephine's Dog God theory and that Ben had let us down. I asked him if he knew about Mark, if Ben was racist when they were on their own. Had Ben said anything about Josephine? About me?

I asked everyone we met if they'd seen him. Most of them knew who I meant, having Biscuit helped, but no sightings in the last week. Time to collect Josephine.

To: LRS_17@outlook.com
Tues 13/6, 22:39
SUBJECT: *Not happening*

Lola wouldn't want this. Until ten minutes ago, I barely knew there was a father. Not one that anyone knew how to contact.

To: LRS_17@outlook.com
Tues 13/6, 23:27
SUBJECT: *Take her*

They're saying Lola may never be well enough. One slip in a bathroom.

'She'll need to go to her father's,' Kiki said. 'Can you take her?'

'But she's fine with me. I love having her, she can stay as long as is needed.'

'They have no idea how long it will be. Or if they can get her well enough,' says Kiki.

'To travel?'

'To look after a child. The dizziness isn't going away. They need more tests. I called the father, he's expecting her.' Her voice is rushed, there's always another call waiting.

'You could have asked me first? Is this what Lola wants? Can I talk to Lola?'

'They're not telling Lola, the stress would make her worse. She needs rest. She's confused. I'll text you everything. If you can't drop her, I'll ask Isaac,' says Kiki.

'Who's Isaac?'

'My husband!'

'She has her own room here,' I say. 'Books, toys, we're building a cardboard city.'

'I'll text you.'

This is all wrong. Lola wanted him out of her life, out of Josephine's, that's all I know about him. The only thing she ever said about him: 'Better this way.' I've waited and waited for Josephine to bring him up but she never has, even when we talked about you and E, or about my father. ('The dentist in assembly gave us red tablets,' she said.) It's like she doesn't know about him. Or she's been told not to mention him and she's actually kept to it – unlike with you. ('Mummy says I'm not allowed to talk about babies when you're there,' she said the night we started Silopolis.)

Kiki was going to text by now. I've sent her pictures of Silopolis, Josephine's bed, the bookshelf.

To: LRS_17@outlook.com
Tues 13/6, 23:48
SUBJECT: *Wales*

He's in Wales, not Brixton. Wales is another country, sort of. What will we do about school? She can't just move. Kiki texted an address in Newport, said he's expecting her on Friday. He's called Jason Owens. Do you think Josephine is named after him – it's similar.

That would mean he meant to stick around. But he didn't and now he gets to have her.

To: LRS_17@outlook.com
Tues 13/6, 23:57
SUBJECT: Runaways

I've moved her to my bed. She's so light. When I hold her, I picture us running away from disaster, an attack on London or an earthquake, I'd carry her the whole way. After a few miles, we'd stop and make a sling for her like yours and tie her on.

She lies on her right side when she sleeps, facing me. She's beautiful. Do I find her beautiful because I've fallen in love with her? Or have I fallen in love with her because she's beautiful? Everyone sees it. She's one of those lucky people, everything in perfect proportion.

I should have called E when he said. I've been silent too long.

I need to speak to Lola. I'm not telling Josephine until I've spoken to Lola.

To: LRS_17@outlook.com
Wed 14/6, 00:02
SUBJECT: Birthday

It may be Ben's birthday today.

To: LRS_17@outlook.com
Wed 14/6, 09:35
SUBJECT: *Windows*

We woke up to it on the radio. It started in the night and the whole
building was on fire by sunrise. A tower block in West London,
twenty-seven floors, hundreds of people. I turned on the TV at
breakfast and Josephine saw it first, she made me keep it on. The
building was black and smoking, red flames inside. A headline
running along the screen: 'Parents threw children out of windows'.
It repeated over and over, enough times for her to read it.

'Why did they throw them?' she asked.

'What?'

'"Parents threw children", it says. Why did they throw them?'

She loops her arms around my waist, tears are going into my
mouth, my nose is dripping. It's too big to take in. The tower, the
children, the smoke, the floors too far from the ground. Josephine
shouldn't see it, she shouldn't know what can happen.

'Why did they throw them?' she asks again.

'To get them away from the fire. And there were firefighters
underneath with big mattresses and cushions to catch them. And
then the parents jumped, onto the mattresses.'

The screen says 'Six dead'. I switch off. They say it will rise. People
were trapped. Woke too late to escape.

There are no reasons.

To: LRS_17@outlook.com
Wed 14/6, 11:06
SUBJECT: *Is this him?*

I was online, trying to understand how it happened. Then Terrence
posted this:

Guess who

Is it OK to give racists a platform? Sure you'll all let me know in the comments ;-) An email last night, bona fide him, same address as before. Mark Westmore, head back over the parapet. After thinking it over and talking with some of you, I've decided to share carefully chosen parts of the Mark mail. Read on if you can bare the self-pity:

'...You wanted Mark to disappear and I made him disappear. Now you're digging him up again. What do you want? Why do you do this?'

'There's so much going on in the world. So much worse. What am I to you? What will it take for you to leave me alone? Seriously, what will it take?'

What will it take??!!!! Why do I do this??!!! What do I want??!!!

I WANT YOU TO SHOW YOU'RE SORRY, you whining, loathsome, racist scumbag. SHOW US YOU'RE SORRY.

!!! A plea to the journalists riding on my coat tails: Feel free to quote, even to copy, but credit/link to my blog. This is what I live off. !!!

It's bear (teddy) not bare (naked), but you have to register to write in the comments. This isn't me taking Ben's side, but he has a point: why does Terrence Dunbarr do this? And why would Ben engage with someone like that? Oh God, he's trying again, on his birthday. He was asking Terrence to tell him to try again and Terrence as good as ordered him to.

One of the neighbours will have a key.

To: LRS_17@outlook.com
Wed 14/6, 15:17
SUBJECT: *More secrets*

He wasn't there. If he tried again, it was somewhere else. I've checked, no disruption reported on the Northern Line.

All those people dead, bombs, stabbings, a fire while families slept, they're calling it an inferno and for once it's the right word. ('Can you see the smoke?' E asked, calling from a New York coffee shop.) All those people dead, and I'm chasing around London after him, Ben, Mark, whatever we're supposed to call him.

No one had a key. I asked the man in the flat opposite, I'd seen him a couple of times, he has long grey hair in two plaits. (I imagine that's the norm where you are, but it's not here.)

I knocked three times before he answered, he had music on at a show-off volume, classical.

'You don't have a key to number six, by any chance?' I ask.

'What for?'

'Oh gosh, silly me, should explain. I can't get hold of him and he's been sitting my dog. This is going to sound ridiculous, but I'm worried he's locked him in there, forgotten. I heard a whimper. He has a weak heart. I was about to call the police, get them to knock it down. God knows how long Francis has been in there on his own, if he has any water, in this heat. But then I thought, I bet you have a key, it's that kind of building. Like that tower. I mean, tight community. That's what they're saying.'

I'm getting good at this. It's like Francis is in there, head flopped over the rim of an empty water bowl.

'If there was a dog locked in there, I'd have heard it,' says plaits. 'And he's not supposed to keep them in there, I've reported him twice.'

'But I know he's in there.'

'I don't have a key.'

He shuts the door. My dog is dying of thirst a few metres across the landing and he shuts the door. Ben was right not to trust him with a key. I shout through the letterbox over Beethoven, 'The world is divided into people who let dogs die and people who break down doors.'

I had no choice but to call a locksmith – something I've become expert at since E had that latch thing installed. They never ask you to prove you live there, not me at least, I have that kind of face, and the voice. To be safe, I used a different company. Did I have my credit card on me, the woman asked. I paid over the phone and he came within an hour.

Plaits came out when the locksmith was working on it.

'Thought you were gonna get the police round. Locked her bloody dog in,' he said.

His phone rang and he shut the door. Ben said that plaits works from home as a broker. Not sure what he's brokering. Mortgages? Boats? Women?

The bed was made, cushions plumped and that was enough to reassure the locksmith it was my flat. I tipped him ten pounds before he could ask about the dog and he left.

I've done a little reading since Oval and since meeting Ben, but most of my suicide knowledge comes from films. Ben's flat was as empty as ever. No whisky bottles, no pill packets, no ropes or any other paraphernalia (lovely word in other circumstances).

You'd think if someone left a note they'd put it on a desk or the bed. But you know what Ben's like, a shy, deceitful bastard. He'd hide it in a drawer.

No note. But guess what instead? Scratchcards and lottery tickets. Hundreds of them, in neat piles in the kitchen drawers. I tried to work out if any were winners – it's trickier than you'd think, I packed them into a plastic bag to go through at home. You have to match symbols, line things up, check three different boxes. I shouldn't say this, but the required skill level doesn't fit their target audience.

There were bank statements too, for Mark Westmore, balance negative. There were bills, warnings about bills. Each one was addressed to Mark Westmore in Bedford, but someone with a woman's handwriting had packed them into larger envelopes addressed to Ben Palmer in the Peckham flat. On the back of one, she'd written, *Call, let us know how you are.* And there was a postcard of a sausage dog, a message in her writing:

I've changed phones, this is the new number. We'll be here when you're ready to call. Dad has a new carer, Beverly, she's a Godsend. Still waiting to see consultant. Take care, Carrie x (and Dad)

I tried his newsagent. The man knew him, said he buys scratchcards most days, but not this week. I bought one for me, to be polite. I'm saving it for Josephine. She'll be out in a minute.

Carrie must be the sister. I'll call her again later. It's been going through to voicemail. She'll be at work. Do you think she's a veterinary nurse? She could be a vet. Or a teacher.

To: LRS_17@outlook.com
Wed 14/6, 20:29
SUBJECT: Not lol

I told Josephine after dinner. Kiki wouldn't back down. We're taking the train to Newport, then a taxi.

Josephine did a face like I was playing a joke on her, almost laughing at me, or with me. She said the same thing over and over: 'Which Friday? This Friday? Which Friday? This Friday? Just Friday? Or the weekend? Just Friday and Saturday?'

I told her it was longer, it was Kiki's idea, and Jason's. 'Your dad can't wait to see you,' I said.

'I don't know him.'

'You're half him, so he must be amazing,' I try.

'Why can't we go after Maya's party? What about the Year Two play?'

'It's just until your mum is well enough to come home.'

'My tooth! Miss Jones says it'll be out by next week. The tooth fairy won't find me.'

'I'm sure he will.'

'He?'

'Could be a he,' I said.

'Why can't I stay with you?' She squeezes me as she says it.

'It'll be an adventure. They have different writing on the signs, did you know that? And it says *araf* on the roads instead of slow. I bet Welsh has awesome palindromes.' We looked it up. There's a Welsh word, '*lol*', it means nonsense.

The scratchcard also helped, she won four pounds and made a list of how she's going to spend it.

We waited for the clock to say 20:05 and said good night.

To: LRS_17@outlook.com
Wed 14/6, 21:46
SUBJECT: Carrie

I took a risk and told Carrie I was one of Mark's dog friends and I was trying to reach him for his birthday. It must be the only true thing he told me, because she said she'd been trying him too. She had his voice, a tough edge, London mixed with Essex.

'He called at the weekend, and he was all over the place,' she said. 'He told me he was moving. Then my friend saw the new stuff about him online. Wait a minute, you're that woman, aren't you?'

'Who stopped him, at Oval? Yes.'

'You put his picture all over the Internet, you told everyone he tried to kill himself, where he lives, his new name. What's wrong with you?'

'I didn't know,' I said.

'You've ruined his life. He was getting better and now we've lost him again because of your sick website.' She hung up.

I texted her: *He ruined my life first.*

To: LRS_17@outlook.com
Wed 14/6, 22:10
SUBJECT: *If I'd known this was our last week*

I found a toucan, paid £7.99 for express delivery.

Is a phone too much? I could send her the finished handwashing songs, pictures of Kim and Kanye in Silopolis, check he's packing her EpiPen in her school bag. Does she even have a school there? It's all so strange. Am I allowed to say that?

To: LRS_17@outlook.com
Thu 15/6, 10:52
SUBJECT: *Ample notice*

I emailed Miss Jones, copied in the head, Mrs Dougherty. The addresses were in Lola's emergency notes along with her GP, Josephine's two consultants, the allergy clinic, the dentist, an afterschool club, six aunties and the pharmacy. Jason Owens was not in there.

I gave the school Kiki's number in case they had any questions. Mrs Dougherty emailed back to say she would certainly follow up with Kiki and that in normal circumstances they would expect a parent to come in to discuss such 'life changes'. 'Furthermore, we strongly advise moves take place, at worst, at the end of a term, and at best, at the end of the school year, with ample notice,' she wrote.

I emailed back:

'I couldn't agree more. I feel uncomfortable saying this, and would never want to meddle, but I feel the whole situation is unusual. Kiki is under enormous strain and I am certain having a professional like yourself to consult can only help. I hope that together we can achieve the best outcome for Josephine.'

To: LRS_17@outlook.com
Thu 15/6, 14:12
SUBJECT: *Stepsisters*

I called Jason Owens on the landline number Kiki gave me. I didn't expect to reach him during the day. His voice was friendlier than I imagined, the Welsh accent does that. But he interrupted when I was explaining who I was, and when we'd be arriving.

'Kiki's filled me in,' he says.

'We can take a taxi from the station, if it helps,' I say.

'There's a bus.'

'Josephine has two bags.'

'She won't need much, my stepdaughter's the same age,' he says.

'Lovely. How many stepchildren do you have?'

'Two girls, and my son.'

'That'll be nice for Josephine. I bet you're all so excited.'

He laughs. Not in happiness, but like I'm an idiot. 'Yeah,' he says. I'll chase Mrs Dougherty.

To: LRS_17@outlook.com
Thu 15/6, 14:39
SUBJECT: *Smaller than the picture*

The toucan arrived. I'll take her with me to pick up. I'll catch Mrs Dougherty then. We're going for ice-cream at McDonald's then home to pack and make pizzas. Josephine sent me to Lola's for her purple rucksack, and I bought her a suitcase the same colour from Argos. They'll be enough. Lola will be home soon. Then I'll go back to Newport with the car, collect Josephine and we'll go to the airport, wait for Lola with flowers and a banner.

To: LRS_17@outlook.com
Thu 15/6, 23:32
SUBJECT: *Refreshing*

Josephine's using the toucan as a pillow. We've named her Tooken, or Miss Tooken to strangers. I took a selfie of us while she was sleeping. I draped my hair over hers. I'll print it out, post it to Jason's address tomorrow, she can open it before school on Monday.

I'm refreshing my emails, nothing from Mrs Dougherty.

When I tucked Josephine in, she asked if it was because of the burning tower. 'Kayla's mum says flats aren't safe. People have to leave till they stop the fires, that's why I have to go.'

'Mummy's flat is super safe. This is just until Mummy gets better. It's nothing to do with the fire. Don't think about that at bedtime.'

Lola would see what this is, what it's doing to me. She'd think about you.

Does Kiki even know about you?

To: LRS_17@outlook.com
Fri 16/6, 03:07
SUBJECT: *Cave*

Eight hours. Shorter than your labour. Three and a half hours there, an hour to settle her in, three and a half hours back. I'll be home by 4.30. Normal working day. Then no one will make me do anything again. I'll never leave the house, never meet anyone, never lose anyone. Disney films only, but not *Lion King*. E can pre-approve books.

To: LRS_17@outlook.com
Fri 16/6, 13:26
SUBJECT: Rucksack

No one stopped me. Not Mrs Dougherty, not Kiki, not Lola. I was calm, like I promised myself, didn't let her see how messed up it is. Even chatted to the taxi driver on the way back to the station. Then sodding 'Happy Birthday', trying to wash my hands in the toilets. Couldn't stop the tears. It was one of those taps that switches itself off before you can finish 'Happy Birthday', and it was too stiff to press with my arm so every time I used my hand, that was new germs on my hand. I went round and round, sang it six or seven times under my breath. A woman in a station uniform stared at me, didn't ask if I was alright. What if it's the same for Josephine, she'll try one of our new songs and forget the words and need me? Or what if she forgets to wash her hands? We've been on a train, in a taxi, she touched a cat.

She'll be OK, she's like Francis was, lives in the moment. When we got there, she went ahead while I was paying the driver, brave and grown-up as ever. She'd carried her own rucksack the whole journey and as she crossed the empty drive to their door, Tooken peeped out the top, her shiny blue eye fixed on me, saying, 'You! You need to do something!'

Their house is a semi-detached new build, I'm guessing four bedrooms – he didn't invite me in. The front lawn needed mowing, the flowerbeds were flowerless. There were scooters and half a bike propped against the wall. All good signs that they are focussing on the children rather than appearances.

Jason was tall and their hug was awkward. He patted Josephine's back while she squeezed him the way she squeezes everyone. He's blond and has Josephine's broad mouth, but it doesn't work on him. He was in shorts and flipflops. It looked like he was the only one home. He gave me a nod of thanks. I handed him the EpiPen bag, explained it on the doorstep.

'My wife knows what to do, she worked in a nursery.' At least he married this one.

'Everyone needs to know what to do,' I say.

I pick Josephine up to say goodbye. Over her shoulder, I spot a ginger cat on the stairs. 'Look who lives here! Go and say hello. I'll call you when I get in tonight.' I turn to Jason. 'She's had a small lunch, she'll need more.'

'That's Alfie,' he says to Josephine.

I bet she's still on the stairs with Alfie, tickling him behind the ears, telling him about Francis and Lester. I'm on a kerb outside the station with a coffee, a lemon muffin and a rocky road bar. I've tidied up my face, as my mother says. I put mascara on, so I won't start again. I keep checking the photos and videos on my phone, like something will appear. The only videos I have of her are the time-lapse kangaroo and her lying on the floor so Francis can lick her face, he blocks her smile and when he moves away the video stops, I should have kept filming, filmed her every day, filmed her sleeping, asked for some of her hair lotion. I'll buy some, and my own toucan.

Next train in twenty minutes. I'll be home by five, eat the rest of the pizzas, go to bed, see my parents in the morning before they leave for their cruise. I could still go with them. E will understand. Or I could fly to New York, surprise him. Go anywhere. I'm like my mother now, 'no ties'. There's a train goes from here to a place called Fishguard Harbour. From there you take a ferry to Ireland.

Jason's calling.

To: LRS_17@outlook.com
Fri 16/6, 13:43
SUBJECT: *Monster*

She had the gerbils with her. In the rucksack. He said he'd let them loose in the garden if I didn't come and get them.

'I had no idea,' I said.

He wouldn't believe me. Wouldn't let me talk to her.

To: LRS_17@outlook.com
Fri 16/6, 15:52
SUBJECT: *Unfit*

On a later train.

She'd put them in an empty ice-cream tub with toilet paper, even made holes in the lid. I told him he could buy a cage for them at any pet shop, said I'd send him the money. He shouted down the phone, 'Not having them in my house.'

'Calm down. Be nice.' Someone had to be the grown up. 'She's coping with so much. Mum in hospital in another country, you, all your kids. What if she can hear you?'

'They're just gerbils.'

'They're not. They're her gerbils. Don't touch them. I'm coming.'

Sorry, toilet emergency, back in a minute.

To: LRS_17@outlook.com
Fri 16/6, 16:17
SUBJECT: *Unfinished*

They're safe now. So's she.

You'll understand, everyone will. I'll explain.

After he called, I took a taxi back there, told the driver I'd be two minutes.

Jason was on the doorstep with the tub, he shoved it into my hands. 'Careful!' I wanted to stamp on his bare toes.

He looked over to my taxi, willing me away, me and my tub of gerbils.

'You're a heartless bastard,' I said. 'You don't deserve her. They shouldn't let you near any children.'

'They're fucking gerbils.'

'Where is she?' Her suitcase was still in their hallway, the open rucksack next to it.

'In the garden.'

'I need to see her, tell her I'll look after them.'

He shouts towards the back of the house. 'Jooooo.'

She's been crying, has Tooken tight to her chest. She runs at me, I lift the ice-cream tub just in time. Her smell, her tiny feet on top of mine, her fingers digging into my back. 'It's OK. It's OK.'

Jason sits on the stairs with the glare of someone who will never understand her.

'I need to talk to Josephine for a minute,' I say. 'Let's pop outside, precious.' I close the front door behind her.

He would have heard the taxi door. We gave him so much time. The driver was facing the wrong way, took ages to turn around.

I sat in the middle, kept my arms around her. She was upset about the rucksack and the Sharpies, but I've already ordered replacements, coming tomorrow. At the station, we bought a magazine and gel pens. No snacks, he has her EpiPen. Everything 'may contain' deadly nuts according to the wrappers. There's a spare EpiPen at Lola's. We went into the toilets and did our best at giving the gerbils a drink. The woman in the uniform was in there again.

It's been two hours. Jason knows where to look for us. We were at the station for an hour. Nothing on the news, nor Twitter (#missing).

I told Josephine that Jason will send the bags on, that we had to change plans, had no time to take things, there aren't many trains to London, we'd be stuck. 'Like a duck?' she said.

'Do ducks get stuck much? Suppose it's those wide feet.'

'They get lost, unless they're friends with pigeons,' she said.

I should put my phone away. She needs me.

To: LRS_17@outlook.com
Fri 16/6, 17:11
SUBJECT: Almost

Nothing online, nothing from Jason. Twenty-five minutes to Paddington. I can't call him, the train filled up at Reading.

To: LRS_17@outlook.com
Fri 16/6, 17:14
SUBJECT: Unworthy

His wife must be home by now. Wouldn't she do something? Tell him to call? I could be a mad woman, selling Josephine on Gumtree.

To: LRS_17@outlook.com
Fri 16/6, 17:23
SUBJECT: Lesson

She looked at my screen.

'Why are you writing my name?' she asks.

'Indoor voice on trains,' I whisper back.

'"Selling Josephine on Gumtree",' she reads out loud.

'Silly joke to myself.'

'Tell me, tell me, tell me. Tell me the joke.'

'Haven't finished it yet. It's a list of fun things to write. Like I made a note to write down all the best things you say, I call them Josephinisms. And this is a note to remember to write the perfect Gumtree advert for you.'

'How much am I?'

'At least fifty pounds. Maybe sixty. But they'd have to collect you, you don't fit in a box.'

'I do.' She curls up. I nudge her feet off the seat. 'What else is on there about me?' she asks.

I show her the list of things I love about her. She reads it over and over, out loud, people listen. 'My hair smell? Weird,' she says, and, 'I don't point my toes in.'

I tell her she has ten minutes to finish her colouring-in page before we reach London.

'Can you help me?' she asks.

'I'm busy, writing down all the other million brilliant things about you. Look, number 1,372, you always colour inside the lines, in silent concentration.'

To: LRS_17@outlook.com
Fri 16/6, 18:25
SUBJECT: *Missing*

Finally, a missed call from Jason. I texted that I can explain. Nothing back. I'll call him when we're home. We're at Lola's so Josephine can gather up some new clothes and teddies. I have the EpiPen and found sun cream, forecast's for the heat to get worse. #missing now brings up a spaniel named Clive from Truro.

While on there, saw I have a tweet from a journalist. Her profile says 'freelance and amateur pâtissier' (she means 'pâtissière' or is being modern). She's called Beth, wants me to follow her back so she can send me a private message.

To: LRS_17@outlook.com
Fri 16/6, 20:47
SUBJECT: *Instinct*

Remember the 'life rules' list I'm writing for you? Number one: if something seems wrong, it is.

She never belonged there. Jason didn't argue. I took his daughter – abducted her, if you want to exaggerate – and he didn't fight back.

I waited for her to fall asleep and I called him back.

'Thought I should let you know we're fine. Got back safely. She's fast asleep,' I start.

'It was me called you,' says Jason. There are children in the background, after eight.

'I should have knocked and explained, I know, I'm sorry, but Josephine was frantic. I thought you were going to come out and help me. She was sobbing and then she was screaming, that you tried to kill the gerbils. I couldn't get her to stop and your neighbour was staring so I ran to the taxi, didn't know what else to do. And I'd just got a text from Kiki that Lola's due back any day. Figured it was for the best. I wanted to call but my phone died. I bet you were trying to call, I can only imagine how worried you were. Then there was a problem with the train, someone on the line, they said.'

'So she's staying with you?'

'Until Lola comes home, yes. It's no trouble. I love having her and she's happy here, has all her things, her school, her friends. It's what she needs.'

'Will you tell Kiki?' he asks.

'Already done. We've been texting about Lola coming home.'

'OK.'

It's what people don't do that shows you what they are. No 'how's Lola?' For all he knows, she's in a wheelchair for life. No offer to send on the bags. No pretending he tried to find us. Just 'OK'.

We put the stowaways to bed first, the round trip to Wales

appeared to have little effect on them, but Josephine insisted they were more tired than her. Their ice-cream tub is now in Silopolis, in a soon-to-be-created caravan park. She went to bed in your room. Once she was asleep, I moved her to mine. One of your sleeping bags came with a free room thermometer. It says it's dangerously hot in here. No one is more tired than me.

To: LRS_17@outlook.com
Sat 17/6, 09:12
SUBJECT: Settled

Kiki understood. I explained Jason wasn't set up for it. And how I'd sensed Mrs Dougherty would involve social services if we didn't prove Josephine had a school place in Newport. I said I was desperate to help, at least to let Josephine finish her term here.

They now think Lola had food poisoning. ('Always had a weak stomach,' says Kiki.) Explains why they found her in the bathroom. She fainted and fell backwards, hit her head on the hard floor.

To: LRS_17@outlook.com
Sat 17/6, 10:41
SUBJECT: Miscarriage

This must be how Ben feels, everything warped.

I can't find a picture of Terrence Dunbarr, but I know what he looks like, in his pants and a hoodie in his mother's basement, squeezed into an armchair. He puts his keyboard on his lap, gets it sweaty. His biography says he's been a 'professional writer for more than a decade'. His writing's appeared in 'all the mainstream national newspapers', but anyone can say that if they write in the online comments or send letters to the editor. I sift out CV bullshit for a living.

Miscarriage. I'm emailing him. We can't let them keep calling it that. You were big, ready, perfectly healthy.

I'll let you read it for yourself. He posted it last night. That journalist, Beth Morris, tweeted me a link to it. 'Don't you want to tell your version?' she wrote. I've followed her back. Need to call Mesh, work out if our website's still out there.

Who's Rachel?

A few of you have asked what I know about 'Rachel', hapless Mark Westmore rescuer and co-founder of his new venture ransacking the homes of the dead and vulnerable.

Her sob story about how they met (on their now blocked website) suggests they became close after her miscarriage in February. She claims she found 'Ben' (MW's new fake name) by chance and recognised him as the stranger she saved on a Tube platform. A flavour: 'Brought together first by tragedy then by serendipity, we knew there was something deeper there, a shared purpose. We felt an instant need to collaborate and help others.'

She's on a break from a 'senior-level corporate role' and like every middle-class white woman, assumes her experience in the business world makes her the ideal person to launch a start-up/dabble in counselling/sell antiques.

Can't say much for her instincts. My early findings suggest she had no idea about Mark's real identity.

What else do we know about Rachel?

I have it on good authority that Rachel's her real name, but I won't reveal her surname publicly. She's early thirties, married. One source told me 'Ben' is more than just a business partner.

She's rarely active on social media, more a lurker. She set the website up from Clapham, South London, the pictures were taken in Bromley, Kent.

Chasing a few leads and when I know more, so will you.
If you know Racist Rescuer Rachel, follow the 'contact
me' link below to get in touch anonymously.

Want to donate to Ferreting Files? Click **here**.

To: LRS_17@outlook.com
Sat 17/6, 13:12
SUBJECT: *Made up*

Mesh called back while we were in the park. If Terrence knew my
surname, he'd have used it, he said. The Clapham thing was his fault,
we could have hidden that, but he didn't think we'd ever need to. The
pictures were my fault, settings on my phone. Then he got angry.

'Why didn't you tell me you were doing Luke's Touch with the
same guy? The dog walker?' he said.

'I thought I did, didn't I?'

'You made it sound like it was just you and your mum,' he said.

'What?'

'God, Rachel. If I'd known it was him, I'd have stopped you. I told
you before, that guy's a mess. Why are you helping him?'

'Because I have to, for Luke.'

To: LRS_17@outlook.com
Sat 17/6, 22:32
SUBJECT: *Away*

Just heard a woman's voice outside. 'He's away a lot,' she said. 'Big
job.'

I was too slow, they'd gone. What if Terrence sent paparazzi? Ben
gave him my address. Or it's the Beth the journalist.

We have to get out of London. The heat's killing us here. There's a pollution alert. Southend's supposed to be good for fairground rides. Or somewhere with air conditioning: IKEA, an airport. She'd like an airport.

To: LRS_17@outlook.com
Sat 17/6, 23:16
SUBJECT: *Knowing what I know*

I messaged Beth. 'It's time to put my side,' I said.

'Brilliant. When?' she replied.

I said I could talk on Monday, after the school run. I need to talk to E first, he's good at this stuff, he's supposed to be back tomorrow. I gave her my number. Two minutes later she texted:

Or we could talk now if you like? B x

Before I can reply, she calls.

'Where are you?' I ask, looking round the blinds.

'At home,' she says.

'Where's home?'

'Islington. Where are you? I can come and meet you, if you like,' she says.

'Don't worry.'

Do I feel bullied, she asks. Exploited? Is there anything I'd like to say to Terrence Dunbarr?

'It wasn't a miscarriage,' I say. 'You get over a miscarriage. My baby died.'

'And Mark. Would you save him again, knowing what you know now?' she asks.

'What?'

'Would you save him again, knowing what you know now?'

'Actually, I can't … My daughter's woken up, she's been sick.'
'Wait. I need your surname, for my notes,' she says.
'We can talk on Monday.'

To: LRS_17@outlook.com
Sun 18/6, 08:33
SUBJECT: *That voice*

Lola called. I'd messaged her pictures from the park yesterday, said we were desperate to talk to her, know she's OK. Then this morning she called. She has a new phone, she'll call every day, she said. We put her on speakerphone and she said things to Josephine in Yoruba. It sounded like she was checking Josephine was being good, so I told her she was an angel. Josephine kept kissing the phone. 'I want to see you, I want to see you!'

Lola said she felt dizzy and weak, but the doctors were 'astounded' she wasn't brain-damaged. She said, 'praise God' after most things, more than usual.

She didn't know when she could come home.

'Next week?' asked Josephine. 'Before the summer holidays?'

'In the summer holidays,' said Lola. 'Not long.'

We told her about the heatwave, and how the pavements were sticky and how there were gorillas on the news with giant ice lollies. And that we were going to the beach today but taking a big umbrella and bottles of water from the freezer. That we'd send pictures, bring her more rock.

No one mentioned Newport.

To: LRS_17@outlook.com
Sun 18/6, 15:27
SUBJECT: *No air*

The heat is killing us here too. Josephine's having one last paddle and we're driving back. No word from E.

I shouldn't look but people keep posting under the blog that I'm as bad as Ben/Mark. One said I was worse, because I knew what I was doing. Someone said they knew me, that I'd always loved a lost cause. 'Patronising cow' they called me.

I've texted Mesh: *Why would you say that? Can't we just talk?*
What are you talking about? he replied.
I tried Ben too.

To: LRS_17@outlook.com
Mon 19/6, 01:16
SUBJECT: *Same*

He's back. He was waiting for us, heard the car, came to the front door. 'Wait here a minute,' I said to Josephine and gave her my phone.

I wanted to tell him he'd abandoned me, that he'd waited too long, but I knew he'd win, tell me he'd been texting, calling, trying to check on me. And he smelled the same as before, before everything, and when I leaned against him he felt the same, strong and solid, mine. Nothing else is the same as before, and I shouldn't say this to you but before was good. He's my only way back there. And he's my other half of you, your dad.

His face pressed onto the top of my head, his arms squeezed tighter as he breathed in. 'I've missed you,' he said.

We went for dinner. Millie from three doors down babysat – E asked her. Josephine loved her. She was wearing a Mickey Mouse top and had a sketchbook in a handbag. She showed Josephine how to draw gerbils and they did a still life of Josephine's tooth, which had broken free on our car journey home.

E said it was his fault, for leaving me so often, so soon, for not talking, for forgetting our promise. We'd made it on the babymoon, said we'd always keep one night a week for us. We could catch up, he said. We sat in the beer garden at the pub on the corner, shared pizzas and drank beer. He said New York had cooled down but they still had the air conditioning on full blast in his office, and his hotel. He'd had to buy a jumper. Blue. I hope you got his eyes.

I told him bits about Luke's Touch, my plans. I expected him to be all costs, permits and risks. But he said he could see a place for it and that my mother was an 'interesting choice' as business partner. I told him about Josephine, about Lola's accident. It felt good to tell him about Newport, how I realised my mistake, went back for her, that Jason wouldn't have coped. I told him about Silopolis and he listened. He asked if I had a piece of paper and a pen in my bag. He wrote something, placed it in the middle of the table and said, 'Show her this in the morning.'

dip
dollop
SWIMS
suns

'Dip, dollop, swims, suns? I don't get it,' I say.

He rotates the paper.

'That's amazing. You're amazing,' I say.

'Ambigrams. Heard them on the radio.'

He's started a digital detox programme. Decided at 2.00 am one night in New York when he caught himself reading 'Ten Ways Your Pizza Topping Reveals Your Darkest Secrets'.

'What's your darkest secret?' I ask.

'That I hate pepperoni. What's yours?'

'That I hate sharing, so I order pepperoni.'

He pretend punches my arm, I catch his hand, hold it there. 'Anyway, phone for work only, then it goes away from 6.00 pm to 7.00 am,' he says. We could have a no-phone-box by the front door, it would be good for me, he says. And for Josephine. And then he says what he really came home to say. He's been offered a job in New York.

To: LRS_17@outlook.com
Mon 19/6, 09:23
SUBJECT: *SmollowS*

She loved the ambigrams. We thought up our own. Silopolis now has a wood named SmollowS.

I'd emailed the school ahead, easier to fudge things in an email, told them about the change of plan, that Josephine's back, the family decided this was for the best.

I have four missed calls from Beth, the journalist.

The tooth fairy left a two-pound coin.

To: LRS_17@outlook.com
Mon 19/6, 10:21
SUBJECT: *New post*

Look at this.

Bombshell

Well, well. Goes away for a year, creeps out his hiding place then asks for a fight.

Mark Westmore wants 'a meeting'. Let's 'talk this out face to face', he says. If that doesn't sound like a man getting taxpayer-funded 'therapy' on the NHS...

Mark, AKA Britain's biggest bigot, emailed this morning saying he's 'finalising plans', has an easy meeting place and 'no excuses that way'. Typical thug, says it's 'time to put things right.' Then, the killer line, he says to **ME**, 'Time to stop hiding.'

Looks like he wants an audience for his great redressing of the injustices we've done against him. So check in for updates on the time and place. Or better still, set up alerts for every new post **here**.

Good for him. Ben, I mean.

To: LRS_17@outlook.com
Mon 19/6, 10:42
SUBJECT: Block

The journalist keeps calling. I'm blocking her. E's right, we need to detox, and I need to think.

To: LRS_17@outlook.com
Mon 19/6, 21:17
SUBJECT: Lies

Tears at bedtime. Maya called her a liar in the playground, said she'd made the moving to Wales thing up, other kids joined in. I found out what I could about what she'd told them. There were no teachers around.

'Sometimes things upset some people,' I say, tucking her sheet under both her shoulders the way she likes. 'Some of your friends don't have a daddy and a mummy so they probably felt left out. You got a special day off school to visit your daddy because Mummy is in hospital. But it's our special trip. Best not to talk about it at school.'

'But I thought I was supposed to stay there,' she says.

'We went to look but then it wasn't right for Kim and Kanye with the cat so we came home. And you like it here best, don't you?'

No answer. She turns away, hides her face in Tooken. 'I want to go home to Mummy. I want Mummy back.'

'I know. So do I.'

To: LRS_17@outlook.com
Tues 20/6, 09:54
SUBJECT: *Gaps*

Lola called just now. I asked her what she remembered from the night it happened.

'I woke in the night, felt so bad, went to the bathroom,' she said. 'I was sick, and sick again and again. So sick I fell asleep there and woke on the floor.'

'But you hit your head, had black eyes,' I said. 'And a massive skull fracture and—' I stop myself, remembering what Kiki said, that they weren't telling Lola everything, not to shock her.

'That's what they keep saying. The doctor said I have to accept it, that I fell. I told him, I'd know if I fell, that I just went to sleep. He said that's what my brain says, it made up a story to fill the gap. Brains don't like gaps.'

I'm watching Terrence's blog, waiting for something new on the Ben meeting.

To: LRS_17@outlook.com
Tues 20/6, 23:36
SUBJECT: *Train*

Oh God, he's doing it again. I know I've said that before but this time he is. New Terrence post. They're meeting tomorrow, the 21st. ON A TRAIN PLATFORM. He wants Terrence to watch. Tomorrow. Blackfriars Station.

To: LRS_17@outlook.com
Cc: ERSum
Tues 20/6, 23:58
SUBJECT: *Fwd: Help*

I've emailed Terrence. Told him things I don't mean but had to say. Used a new account, first name only.

> Begin forwarded message:
> To: TDFerrets@ff.xyz
> Tues 20/6, 23:51
> SUBJECT: Help

Dear Terrence,

 I need your help. You can't meet Mark tomorrow. I understand you're angry, that you hate him, you hate me. But there's so much going on you can't see.

 Mark can't be anywhere near a station tomorrow. I don't expect you to know this but 21st June is the anniversary of his last attempt, when I stopped him. And now he's asking you to meet on a train platform, ONE YEAR TO THE DAY. Then it will all be for nothing.

 God knows how it got to this, that you're the only one he listens to. You have to talk him down. Tell him to call me. Tell him there are so many people who want him back. He's not who you think he is. He's a real person. He has a sister, Carrie, a dad who's really ill, friends. Don't let him go there, tell him to call me. Tell him I'm sorry. I didn't know.

Rachel

P.S. I can tell you're a good person behind that blog.

To: LRS_17@outlook.com
Wed 21/6, 00:55
SUBJECT: *What's human*

I woke E. Not on purpose. All the rolling over to check my phone, trips to the bathroom, the kitchen, to Josephine's room – she's sleeping flat on her back, just as I left her at bedtime.

'What's up?' E said.

'Too hot.'

'There's water in the fridge. Filled it up before I came to bed,' he says.

'Thanks. It's a year tomorrow.'

'Brexit? That's Friday. The twenty-third.'

'Since we found out, about Luke, the pregnancy test. The twenty-first,' I say. 'And a year since I saved that guy, at Oval, remember? Do you ever wonder what happened to him?'

'Honestly? No.' He sits up, holds me. 'But you did what you could for him.'

'I should have put Luke first. Would you have stopped him? If you saw someone like that, near the edge? Or would you worry he'd drag you down with him?'

'I guess it's something you do on instinct, don't think about it,' he says and reaches for his phone.

'Who knows?' I've lost him to his screen. 'Shall I bring you up a glass?'

'Did you ... I mean, what?' he says.
'Water. Do you want some water?'
'Sure. Thanks.'

To: LRS_17@outlook.com
Wed 21/6, 01:47
SUBJECT: *This is good*

Terrence has put my whole email in his blog. Called the post 'Panic Stations', like it's a time for jokes. It's OK. He's helping me, Ben will see it.

My insomnia's contagious. E said he couldn't get back to sleep, he's gone downstairs to the laptop. 'Might as well get that pitch done,' he said. 'So bloody hot.' Says he's working but he'll be looking for air-conditioning quotes again, it's the American in him.

To: LRS_17@outlook.com
Wed 21/6, 11:22
SUBJECT: *Nearly there*

Waiting for a train to Blackfriars, gets in 11.39, they're meeting at two. Knowing Ben, it's the one time he'll be early, trick us all.

Or maybe he'll be late. Make us wait. Change his mind, then change it again.

E was already gone when I woke up. I've texted to ask if he'll be on standby to collect Josephine, said I had to go somewhere, might get stuck. No reply.

To: LRS_17@outlook.com
Wed 21/6, 11:28
SUBJECT: *Stay*

What do I say when I see him? I should make notes, reasons to stay: dogs, Carrie, cookies, scratchcards, the business, me, you. I should have borrowed a puppy.

To: LRS_17@outlook.com
Wed 21/6, 12:04
SUBJECT: *Dumb*

No Ben yet. I've found a bench near where he'll come in. Blackfriars Station is on a bridge, you'd love it, in other circumstances. Entrances either side of the river.

Carrie keeps texting. She's cross that I put her in my email and that Terrence put it in his blog.

'You need to stop him,' I replied, and, 'Why does it always have to be me?'

To: LRS_17@outlook.com
Wed 21/6, 12:18
SUBJECT: *Re: Stop*

What? WHAT IS THIS?

> On 21 June 2017, at 12:14, LRS_17@outlook.com wrote:
>
> Mummy,
> Ben was never the reason. Stop this, forget Ben, let him go, let it all go. Luke x

To: LRS_17@outlook.com
Wed 21/6, 12:26
SUBJECT: Re: Re: Stop

Whoever you are, you don't understand. You're sick. I'm not saying it's not you. But how? Why would you say that?

You wouldn't say that. Why are you saying that? You know I can't let him do this to you.

HE KILLED YOU. WE KILLED YOU. HE'S NOT ALLOWED

> On 21 June 2017, at 12:18, RIS_82@outlook.com wrote:
>
> What? WHAT IS THIS?
>
> > On 21 June 2017, at 12:14, LRS_17@outlook.com wrote:
> >
> > Mummy,
> > Ben was never the reason. Stop this, forget Ben, let him go, let it all go. Luke x

To: LRS_17@outlook.com
Wed 21/6, 12:38
SUBJECT: Bad

You wouldn't tell me that. Not now, not then, it's not who we are.

Ben?

So stupid, so, so, so stupid.

You saw me writing them. Found a way in. You're sick. Oh God, suicide note. Your suicide note. Let you go.

Why did you sign it 'Luke'? Call me that? I'm not your mummy.

To: LRS_17@outlook.com
Wed 21/6, 12:52
SUBJECT: Read

I went into the account. They're all read. 277 emails in the inbox, all from me, all marked read, even the last one. One sent email. Today 12:14. How? Tell me how? Ben, we can stop now. I know what happened, I know Terrence is a bully. You should have told me. I'll help you. Let me help you. Don't come to the station. I want you to stay where you are. Where are you?

To: LRS_17@outlook.com
Wed 21/6, 13:06
SUBJECT: Costa

You have to stop. Need to meet somewhere safer, no platforms. Costa, north entrance, after the barriers, pic attached. I'll be outside. I'll buy cookies, you love cookies. I'll fix everything. I'll talk to Terrence. Remember our stolen cookies. That's what life is.

To: LRS_17@outlook.com
Wed 21/6, 13:39
SUBJECT: Money

If it's about the money from the account, keep it. I want you to have it. You think you're nothing. But not to me, not to Luke. Do you need more?

To: LRS_17@outlook.com
Wed 21/6, 13:48
SUBJECT: *Me*

I get it. 'Let it all go.' You're asking me to jump instead. Or jump together. Is that you on the platform? Stay on the platform, I'm coming.

To: LRS_17@outlook.com
Wed 21/6, 23:19
SUBJECT: *The longest day*

The heat's keeping me awake. The heat, what they did to me, what I've done to myself.

The others are asleep. We watched *Shrek* in bed. When it ended, E carried Josephine to her bed, little legs dangling. Five minutes later he was asleep too, Lester stretched over his feet. It was barely dark. The sun waited for 21.21 to go down, because today's the twenty-first, the longest day – or the day when it's light for longest.

It was Ben, there on the platform, the end where the trains come in. He was early, ten to two, alone on a bench, wearing the same squeaky trainers and his smartest T-shirt, the dark-blue one. I watched him from the other end of the platform, picking away at his teeth, in a trance and ready to startle at anything.

I looked for Terrence. Someone waddling, long hairs poking out his collar – a man-ferret.

His blogpost had failed, no one had come to watch. No vigilantes, no freedom-of-speech crusaders. No police either. They'd promised me they'd send someone.

The next trains were 13:56 and 14:02. He'd wait for the 14:02. I had time. No sudden movements.

I tuck myself behind a post.

Two more minutes go by and a man with a rucksack sits on Ben's bench. A tourist wandering into a hurricane. He reaches his hand out. Not a tourist, Terrence. He's the opposite of fat, his short-sleeved shirt baggy and pale against his bony arms. Ben says something.

13.58. I move closer. Ben and Terrence are hunched over something. A laptop. Ben's talking, dictating his last words. Terrence doesn't fight him – just keeps his head down, dutiful and resigned, a prison chaplain on death row. Over the speakers, the voice says, 'The next train will not stop here. Please stand back from...' That's the one, fast, instant. Time to move.

'Don't!'

'Rachel, God!' He's standing.

I push him back. He's too strong.

'Ben. No! I can fix it.' I hold him as the train speeds through. Safe for now.

'Ben? She calls you Ben?' Terrence is Irish. 'Does she even know?'

'Of course I know, you've told the whole bloody world,' I say.

'You told the world first,' says Terrence. Not Irish, Scottish. 'You and your sick website.'

'My website's sick?' I slam his laptop shut.

'Don't touch that.' His face is old, too old to blog. He points his phone at me, he's filming.

'God, just stop it, stop it, stop it!' I say, hands over my eyes.

'You're making things a billion times worse,' says Ben.

We're loud, people are watching.

'He's right, sweetheart,' says Terrence. 'You're interrupting. Your Ben wanted to show me something.'

'You're sick, the world's sick. The police are coming,' I shout. My spit hits his forehead but Terrence just laughs. It's all so funny: me, Ben, how brilliant his video is. He pushes his phone towards my face, his grip is loose. I shove it out his hand and it skids across the platform, over the edge.

'You fucking maniac!' Terrence shouts. 'Anyone get that? You, you get that?'

The staring strangers say nothing. Terrence reaches down to the tracks, on his knees, arms dangling. A girl films him. He shouts and shouts and the girl keeps filming. 'You fucking maniac. Do you know what was on there? That's my fucking life and death.'

He's left his laptop on the bench. But now the girl is filming me, and laptops are more expensive than phones, and heavier.

'God, Rachel, why do you make everything worse?' Ben hides his face from the girl's camera.

I stand between her and Ben, say, 'Please. This is private...'

She turns away, her train's here.

We watch Terrence, still on his knees, twisting to look under the carriage.

'Why didn't you tell me?' I say to Ben. 'I could have helped you.'

'You don't get to know everything.'

A whistle blows, a guard shouts. Terrence tries to move back and topples over. No one helps him. When he's up, he glares at me and jogs to a guard, who looks like Lola's boss, godless Vernon. He's not going to help.

'What about Luke's Touch? It's going to be amazing,' I say to Ben. 'I just want you to picture it in one year's time – if you don't do this, where we'll be, what your life will be like.'

'What my life will be like? Do you even get what you've done?' says Ben.

'This is how you feel now, but you'll get better. We have to do this, we're brilliant at it, we're meant to—'

'Reported you.' Terrence is back and out of breath. 'All on CCTV.' He sits the other side of me, a mix of sweat and aftershave, and leans over to Ben. 'What was it? What you wanted to show me?'

'You know what he wants to show you!' I say. 'I told you in—'

Ben talks over me. 'I need to take you somewhere. Bedford.'

'Alright,' says Terrence. 'I'll come to Bedford.'

'Now you're live-blogging his suicide road trip?' I say.

'She needs to give me money for a new mobile first,' says Terrence.

'I don't have any money,' I say. 'Ask him, he owes me hundreds.'

'Next train,' says Ben.

'With him?' I say. 'You're just going to jump on a train with him? Like best mates going to the match? Stop at the pub, better still, off-licence, get some scratchcards before you go? You should both fucking ju—' It's not what I want. It is. I don't say things like that. The train's coming, I grab Ben's arm. 'Don't. Or take me with you.'

'Seriously?' says Ben. 'Just go.'

'I don't abandon people,' I say. Terrence types as I speak and I turn to him. 'Write this down, you freak, you ruined everything.'

'And now he's going to fix it,' says Ben.

'He's toxic. He can't fix anything.' I let Ben's arm go as the train leaves. 'I'm fixing it. Whatever you need me to do.'

'I need you to fuck off. I was getting better. Had stuff, people were forgetting.'

'They'll forget again,' I say.

'You don't get it. You'll never get it. No one hates you.'

'We'll track down Sufia,' I say. 'The quiz-show people will help. We'll ask her to forgive you.'

'Forgive me? I didn't do anything,' he says.

'But you did. It was racist. I know you didn't mean it, but you need to say sorry.'

'Everyone gets to tell me what I am, don't they?' he says.

'You hurt people. You hurt me. You hurt Luke.'

Terrence looks up. 'Luke is?'

'Her baby,' says Ben.

'You know who Luke is,' I say. 'Luke's Touch, that's our business. Service. Helping people.' Terrence is grinning, he knew who you were. 'What do you do for people?' I say. 'You're a life ruiner. A big fat giant, squishing everyone into the mud with your laptop. Stop typing. Look at me. I'm talking to you.'

'I'm not fat.'

'I wish you were.' I hide my face in my hands. Terrence holds up his laptop to take a picture. He'll call his next post 'Cry Baby'.

'Stop laughing. You're complicit, you and your blog,' I say.

'In what?' asks Terrence.

'Murder. Manslaughter. You killed my baby.'

(That's the headline. 'You Killed My Baby'. He posted it tonight.)

I feel around in my bag, empty it out on the ground, find your picture. 'Look what you did. And you,' I say to Ben. 'Look at him. He's not handsome. He's dead. Because of you.'

'You know that's bollocks,' says Ben.

I say nothing.

'Come on, no one believes your cosmic-destiny crap,' says Ben. 'I know what you did. I know Josephine's mum works at Oval, she told me.'

The emails, he knows everything.

'And I know what you did,' I say.

'So what? Everyone does.' Ben looks at the departures board. 'Next train. Just me and him.'

More teeth picking, his other hand plays with his hair, his feet fidget up and down in those squeaky trainers, those stupid squeaky trainers.

'You've never thanked me,' I say. 'You've lied, stolen from me, hacked into all my secrets, but you've never thanked me.'

'Thanked you? For this?'

'You have so much hate,' I say. 'And all I ever did is try to see past it. This whole time, I could have gone for revenge. But I tried to make something from it, help you, help people.'

'Oh, you've always bloody loved that, haven't you? Bet you wait there on your bench for them – messed up, starving shitbags like me. Sick way to pick your friends, Rachel.'

'If I hadn't been there—'

'But you were because you're a snooty, interfering bitch, too scared to look at your own fucked-up life.'

Brakes screech, the train stops further along the platform, Ben and Terrence run after it. As they leap on, a voice comes over the speakers. A phrase just for me, a good one: 'Please keep all your belongings with you at all times.'

So I pick up your photo, your lock of hair and our pink stripes, pack it all back into my bag, and I let Ben go.

I should have left right away. It was late, time to go for Josephine. But I stayed and watched the trains. His voice was in my head, calling me that, blaming me. I watched the trains and pictured what could have been, blood and brain splattering the windscreen, the driver's face frozen as he asks 'was that a man?' and knows it was. For the rest of us, on the platform, there'd be nothing more to see. The train would cover him. I'd think about him for a week or so, and probably whenever I stopped at Oval, but he'd be gone, and you'd be here. Anything for you to be here.

I didn't notice him sit down, just heard his breathing, knew his smell. E.

'Shall we get you home?'

'You're here ... how?' I fall into him and he kisses my head.

It's warm as he talks into my hair. 'It's OK. This was always going to be a rubbish day. All the anniversaries will be. But it will get better. We'll get better.'

'You followed...'

'I'm here now.'

He orders us a taxi to Josephine's school, and I lean against him in the back. His eyes are closing the way they always do on journeys.

'My mum told you, didn't she?' I say, and the driver twitches, he's been waiting all day for someone like me to entertain him. I squeeze E's thigh and whisper, 'She told you about Ben. Whatever she said was wrong. He's not even called Ben. He was lying to me.'

'It's all worked out,' says E.

I want to tell him he's good at following, that he's amazing, that he's been paying attention this whole time and I hadn't noticed. But it sounds silly in my head.

I go right up to his ear, 'Don't you want to know what I was doing?'

'Sure you'll tell me everything soon enough,' he says, forgetting to whisper. He slumps back, pulls out his phone. 'Couple of things I need to reply to.'

Josephine squeals when she sees us both waiting for her. The mums stare at E, and it's obvious he's enjoying it. I am too. We stop at the ice-cream van and Josephine talks him through every option until he asks her to pick for him. We take another taxi home. 'I like it when you pick me up,' she says to him.

When we're home, she spreads her Sharpies across the kitchen table, sorts them into colours. E gives her some extra-large paper from his desk.

I've stopped myself checking my phone until now. He won't have said sorry, nor anything else. But there it is, another email:

'No one killed me, not you, not Ben, not Mark. Sometimes babies just die.'

From your account. Hours earlier.

I need to show E, but where to start?

Josephine tugs my arm. 'Look! I used my metallic ones. You can do the seaweed.' Fish swim across her page in a line: silver, gold, silver, gold, silver. I run my finger over them and my own pattern forms.

LUKE

MUMMY&LUKE • JUMPING BEN • MUMMY • BEN JUMPING • LUKE&MUMMY

BEN

My perfect palindrome of people, maybe I'd found some logic after all. Except I hadn't.

Ben didn't jump. I was right before, they went to the pub, in Bedford. And his sister's house, met his dad. Terrence called it 'meeting the real Mark'. It was Ben's ear-biting moment, putting things right.

Ben is deluded, of course. Just as Biscuit will now bully Bug twice as much, Terrence's attacks on Ben will resume with new vigour (and new material) and put him back in his corner of shame. Terrence will soon run out of things to say about me (where do you go from the caption 'Stalker Claims Quiz Show Mark Killed Her Baby in a Freak Body Swap'?) He can say whatever he likes. I won't look. We choose what we're complicit in.

To: LRS_17@outlook.com
Wed 21/6, 23:52
SUBJECT: *Not Ben*

How did I not see it? So obvious – bet you saw it. He didn't follow us. He knew. I checked the laptop. I left your account logged in. He's read them all. Except the last one and now this one. Should I say hello?

Hello, Ed. I have told you everything.

To: LRS_17@outlook.com
Wed 21/6, 23:59
SUBJECT: *Watched*

Why am I not more angry?

You were right, Ben was never the reason.

To: LRS_17@outlook.com
Thu 22/6, 05:23
SUBJECT: *Entangled*

'What else could I do?'

That's what he said. What else could he do?

I'd waited until 4.00 am, woken him with coffee and biscuits.

'You wanted me to read them,' he said.

'Luke. I wanted Luke to read them,' I said.

'And me. You copied me in. An email about a strange Terrence. What was I supposed to think?'

He's right. I checked. Clumsy fingers, late at night, we put his address in. Tuesday, this one:

'I've emailed Terrence. Told him things I don't mean but had to say...'

'But how did you—' I start.

'I panicked about ... you know, Terrence.'

'You looked at my phone,' I say.

'Only for a second. To check you weren't...'

'With someone called Terrence?' I shove him, he smiles.

'And when I tried the laptop, you'd left it all there for me. You wanted to tell me but you didn't know how. And I've been gone so much, and I guess, well, I've been crap at this, and you have this whole life, you and Luke. I stayed up and read and read.'

'But Luke's message – how?' I say.

'From my phone.'

'With our password,' I say.

'Always the same. And I didn't know what else to do, what you'd do. I thought it would stop you.'

'It did. I let him go.'

E's crying, holding me too tight. 'You talked about jumping.'

'No, no, no. Never. I was asking. Asking what he meant.' I won't say Ben's name. 'I thought I was asking him.'

We sit on the edge of the bed, his fingers lost in my hair, my face pressed into his neck. My breathing slows to match his. We fall back, still holding on.

He's asleep now. 'Why didn't you tell me you hate moussaka?' he said as he drifted off.

To: LRS_17@outlook.com
Thu 22/6, 05:37
SUBJECT: *Privacy*

Should I change the password?

Stratford-12812. We use it for everything, we shouldn't. 12812, the night we met, Olympics closing ceremony, corporate box. He was that person everyone talks to. The one you wish would turn to you, notice everything about you and love it all. He did and he's mine.

I'll leave it for now.

Hi, Ed. I was cross when I wrote that about moussaka, cross when I wrote most of it. We've both been crap at this.

To: LRS_17@outlook.com
Thu 22/6, 05:41
SUBJECT: *Firm*

I do hate it a bit. The potato slices. Maybe if you made them thinner. Sleep now.

To: LRS_17@outlook.com
Mon 21/8, 22:36
SUBJECT: *Who to keep*

Lola comes home tomorrow. Josephine's made a banner. I convinced her to throw away the first one – *THANK YOU FOR COMING BACK*. We've gone with *WELCOME HOME, MUMMY*.

She's baked biscuits like smiley emojis and wrapped twenty presents in tissue paper. Half of them are shells from Brittany. We left the day school broke up, took the overnight ferry (with travel-sickness tablets). Ed barbecued every night for dinner, I made picnics for lunch and Josephine put herself in charge of breakfast – which mainly involved waking one of us to walk her to the bakery, where she ordered in French and was rewarded each day with a free mini pastry. Ed soon became her favourite because he carried her there on his shoulders and let her take Tooken (I have a rule that Tooken stays at home, where she's safer). We called Lola every bedtime and she made up funny stories for Josephine about Tooken and her friend Puff Puff. When Josephine was in bed, Ed and I stayed up on the terrace, drank and said the things we should have said before. We're not going to New York.

We've been warned Lola will be tired, and dizzy some days. Kiki is moving into her place to look after her. I'll collect Josephine most mornings, drop her back in the evenings. Silopolis needs more work, and we have a list of London sights to visit: deer in Richmond Park, pelicans in St James's Park, pigs at a city farm. You can spot the pattern. Twenty-eight weeks, you listen intently now, and you love repetition. You don't like it when I'm not there, it's called separation anxiety, but it will pass, you'll learn I always come back.

You need to know I'm not OK. By now you should see that I never will be. There will always be an emptiness. Maybe it will shrink and the edges will soften. I'm not ready for that. Every little boy I see, every advert for baby shampoo, a voice screams, 'I just want him.' It will never make sense.

It's six months today since EHFAR came to stay. At dinner, I asked Ed, 'Do you think everything happens for a reason?'

'I don't get it,' says Josephine.

'As in, everything that happens, there's a special reason for it,' I say. 'Like I met your mum, and now I know you and we have an amazing time.' Ed looks at me like I'm an idiot. He's always ahead.

'Like Mummy falling?' asks Josephine.

'Oh God, no. I'm not saying it's even true. Not for everything. That was an example. Of what other people think. Sometimes.'

'Your mum fell because the floor was slippery, that's all,' says Ed. 'But the doctors have fixed her and this time tomorrow, she'll be here.' He reaches across the table and squeezes her hand the way he does to me in restaurants.

'But it's funny the way people say it,' I say. 'So many people...'

'Because they want it to be true,' says Ed. 'It's reverse engineering. If you look for it, a reason happens for everything.'

'But how things bring people together, you and me at work ... Josephine?'

'No one brings anyone together. You meet people and you decide who to keep.'

Among the pile of post that came while we were in France was a postcard of a sausage dog. He was in Bedford, walking dogs, doing some work for an old colleague, and 'seeing someone'. I think he meant a therapist. It would explain the last line. 'I should have thanked you.' He signed it neither Ben nor Mark.

To: LRS_17@outlook.com
Fri 2/2, 10:01
SUBJECT: *Happy Birthday, my love*

This is what I'll mark. Your birthday.

The daffodils we planted are coming up. Your gravestone will be ready next week, light-grey slate, rounded top, no sharp corners. We talked about spelling out the absurdity:

Born 2nd February 2017
Died 1st February 2017

Instead, we chose:

Luke Summers
2nd February 2017
A lifetime in our secret world

We're going together when they fit it. Your grandma's made a fruitcake for afterwards. Without nuts, with fussing. 'It's the nuts that lift it,' she said. Nuts are heavy.

I'm off to collect Josephine in a minute. We're baking biscuits shaped like groundhogs (small American animal, predicts the weather). It's our last week of the old Monday-Wednesday-Friday routine. When I go back, I'm doing half-days on Fridays, I'll go straight to school, bring her back here. It won't be long before I'm off again, they'll understand. Then she wants me to pick her up every day. I didn't say no.

'Rachel Summers, you live in the clouds,' said Lola.

'And Silopolis.'

ACKNOWLEDGEMENTS

My first thanks go to you for reading this. By that, I mean you picked up a book with the death of a baby at its heart and you let Rachel tell her story. If you read this because you have suffered your own loss, I am so sorry. I hope you know that you are not alone, as lonely as grieving can feel.

As Rachel says, in a world full of baby showers, it can feel like there's no place for this story. But Karen Sullivan at Orenda Books knew better. Karen, you and your wonderful team have given Rachel a voice and given baby Luke a place to live. I will be forever grateful. I am also indebted to West Camel for his careful editing, sensitivity and suggestions.

One of Rachel's earliest allies was the writer Clare Allan, my Masters tutor. Clare, thank you for your friendship, your amazing teaching and for stamping on my self-doubt in the kindest possible way. And thank you to Meg, auburn-haired paragon of resilience.

Thank you to my agent, Caroline Hardman, for believing in Rachel's story, for astute editing and for taking this out into the world.

It's a tough test for a friendship (and marriage) when one of you says to the other, 'Here's this thing I've been working on for years, the fruit of heartbreak and sleepless nights, will you read it and tell me what you think?' Several brave (or silly) people said yes to this. Thank you. Naomi Hilton, thanks for decades of friendship, wisdom and for championing this book. Thank you, Simone, for reading, dog-walk pep-talks and daft gifts. Thank you to Modupe Banks for love, encouragement and Yoruba. Thank you to Fiona Walsh for friendship, straight talking and kindness. Thank you to those who listened to me plot and replot: Ralf, Laura Homer, Elsa Humbert, Alex Pitt, Louise Harland and all my MA class. For asking 'how's the book going?', thank you to my neighbours, old colleagues, school-run companions and park friends.

While some of Rachel's experience mirrors my own, I am relieved to say I had far superior friends and in-laws. Thank you to you all. Thank you to King's College Hospital and our community midwives for outstanding care in Finn's pregnancy and the one that followed. I am grateful to the support of friends made through Sands, the stillbirth & neonatal death charity.

Thank you to those who helped my characters come alive: Francesca Catling at Hotel du Hound; all the children and staff at Crawford Primary School; my brother Nick, for making us go on a quiz show, and Isobel Wilson for exhaustive revision sheets. Inspiration for Ben's story came from Jon Ronson's *So You've Been Publicly Shamed*. Inspiration for ambigrams came from Tony Hawks on BBC Radio 4's *The Unbelievable Truth*. Proof that a story can be told as one-way letters (or emails) came from Michael Frayn's brilliant book, *The Trick of It*. 'Tooken' was tooken from my daughter, Ella. Silopolis was inspired by the cardboard creations of my son, Alex.

My biggest thanks and undying love go to my family: Ralf, Alex, Ella and our baby, Finn. And finally, to Monkey and Miko – you are excellent and gluttonous colleagues.

NEED HELP?

If you have been affected by, or need support for, any of the issues in this book, I am deeply sorry for what you are going through. I can only speak from my own experience, but talking to others after our son died eased my sense of isolation and helped make many days that little bit better. I would certainly advise against taking Rachel as a role model – as much as I love sausage dogs, borrowed or otherwise.

I have brought together some organisations here that may be able to help. I think it's worth remembering that strangers can sometimes be easier to talk to than those close to you. I wish you gentle days and easier times ahead.

While based in the UK, all of the following charities also offer international support. If you'd like something a little closer to home, visit the International Stillbirth Alliance, which has details of all member organisations around the world: https://www.stillbirthalliance.org/member-organizations/.

Stillbirth and neonatal death charity **Sands** provides support for anyone who has been affected by the death of a baby. Its services include a free and confidential helpline, a mobile app, an online community and a wide network of regional support groups. The helpline team also responds to emails from outside the UK.
W: https://www.sands.org.uk
T: 0808 164 3332
E: helpline@sands.org.uk

The charity **Tommy's** provides information and support for anyone who has experienced the loss of a baby, whether through miscarriage, stillbirth, neonatal death, or termination for medical reasons. Its website provides articles with information on baby loss, blogposts that share experiences and a list of online support communities.
W: https://www.tommys.org

Saying Goodbye is the primary division of the Mariposa Trust, a UK-based charity supporting anyone who has suffered the loss of a baby at any stage of pregnancy, at birth or in infancy. The charity also supports anyone who is grieving the fact that they have not been able to have children, for whatever reason that may be.
W: https://www.sayinggoodbye.org
T: 0845 293 8027
E: support@sayinggoodbye.org

The Good Grief Trust aims to bring all UK bereavement services under one umbrella. It provides an extensive list of helplines, some available twenty-four hours, and a directory to help people find local support. It also provides a coronavirus bereavement advice, including information on where to find support after a sudden bereavement.
W: https://www.thegoodgrieftrust.org

Samaritans is available twenty-four hours a day for anyone who is struggling to cope, and who needs someone to listen without judgement or pressure. The organisation also provides guidance to anyone supporting someone with suicidal thoughts.
W: https://www.samaritans.org
T: 116 123
E: jo@samaritans.org